2/7/94

# BLACK CALIFORNIA

## The History of African-Americans in the Golden State

*B. Gordon Wheeler*

HIPPOCRENE BOOKS
*New York*

For information, address:
HIPPOCRENE BOOKS, INC.
171 Madison Avenue
New York, NY 10016

ISBN 0-7818-0074-9

*Library of Congress Cataloging-in-Publication Data*

Wheeler, B. Gordon.
    Black California : the history of African-Americans in the
    Golden State / B. Gordon Wheeler.
        p.   cm.
    Includes bibliographical references.
    ISBN 0-7818-0074-9 :
        1. Afro-Americans—California—History.   2. California—
History.
    I. Title.
    E185.93.C2W47   1992
979.4'00496073—dc20                                                92-35382
                                                                              CIP

Printed in the United States of America.

# Dedication

Why God should take from this world a beautiful little girl is beyond explanation. But take her He did. It is that little girl, whose skin was the color of brown sugar, to whom this book is dedicated. Shortly before her death, while lying in a hospital bed in Las Vegas, Nevada, she asked if black people were a part of history. When I answered yes, she asked if I would write a story about them. I promised I would.

I've never kept many promises in my life—but this was one promise I couldn't do anything but keep.

This, Princess, is your story. It is my way of saying Hail, and farewell—and I miss you.

Bobby

# Contents

# Acknowledgments

*Black California: The History of African-Americans in the Golden State* could not have been written without the assistance of a great number of people, including Sibylle Zemitis, reference librarian at the California State Library, Stanleigh Bry, library director for the Society of California Pioneers, Michael Harvey, chief librarian for the California Historical Society, Brian Young, reference services supervisor for the British Columbia, Canada, Archives and Records Service, Jayne Sinegal, chief librarian for the California Afro-American Museum, and a number of people in Central California who chose to have faith in my ability to complete the project.

Also, this book could not have been written without the unselfish assistance of Antonio Smith, Tonie Brock, and Caryl Prunty.

I am in debt to all of you.

# Foreword

Pio Pico was the last governor of Mexican California. William Alexander Leidesdorff was the Robert Fulton of San Francisco Bay. James P. Beckwourth built the first house in the Sierra Valley. William Pollack opened the first catering service in Placerville. It is not widely known, but these California pioneers shared a common bond: African ancestry.

★  ★  ★

The African-American helped make California what it was and what it is. Since the founding of Mission San Diego de Alcala on July 16, 1769, men and women of color have been an important factor in many of the major issues in the state's history. Generally speaking, however, the role of black people in the making of the Golden State is neither well known, nor correctly known. Most books on California history are silent on black people, except for a description of some problem they presented. In describing the role of other racial groups, historians have tended to stress those traits held by Californians in common; but in treating black people the approach has all too often been one of "deviation from the norm." As a result, it is not surprising that many people have come to feel that although black men and women have been among Californians, they have not been one of them.

When books on California history do not mention black people, significant omissions result. When black people are mentioned solely with reference to problem areas, an incomplete, distorted picture emerges. In either case, a more balanced focus is desirable.

Such a proper perspective on African-American history in the

13

Golden State would be of value to those uninformed persons who believe black people have an unworthy past, and thus have no strong claim to all the rights of other Californians; indeed, other Americans. Books which seek to present an accurate picture of the African-American's past are, in essence, bridges to intergroup harmony—black people would be more readily accepted into the full promise of California life if their role in the state's history were better known. Sociologist Kelly Miller once said, "We are so anxious to solve the race problem that we do not take the time to study it." Those who seek an insight into human relations require the dimension of historical perspective.

California's African-American history not only furnishes a preface to racial respect and understanding; it unfolds a dramatic story, if indeed not an epic one, studded with fascinating and arresting black personalities, male and female. This remarkable story will probably never be completely known, however, for these reasons:

*The subject of Spanish-speaking black people who were among the first settlers of California is familiar only to a few specialists.

*It presents an image of the African-American disturbing to those who wish to present simple generalizations about the place of black people in California history.

*Fear of publicizing the fact that appreciable amounts of African blood have seeped into the white population by means of old first families in California, Louisiana, Texas, Florida and elsewhere.

These explanations for the obscurity shrouding the full story of Spanish-speaking black people were put forth by Dr. Jack D. Forbes, an outstanding authority on minority group history and culture and former executive director of the Far West Laboratory for Educational Research and Development.

Forbes, whose research carried him into archives in Spain, Mexico and the United States, reported that after Columbus discovered the New World in 1492, countless men of African ancestry were recruited into the Spanish armed forces for conquest of the vast territory. He noted that these black men, along with other Spanish-black and Indian-black men from Haiti, Borinquen (Puerto Rico), Cuba and Jamaica, appeared in New Spain (present-day Mexico) in the very earliest days of the Spanish conquest, and that they remained loyal to and fought with distinction for the Spanish monarch.

Hundreds of these black men were full-fledged conquistadors, not slaves or servants, and they participated in many land and coastal expeditions. In fact, some of them led expeditions. In 1539, for instance, famed black conquistador Estavanico—scout, guide, and ambassador for Panfilo de Navaez and Cabeza de Vaca—led a party of three Spaniards and a group of Pima Indians in a search for the fabled Seven Cities of Cibola. Not only was this black man the first person actually to set eyes on the Seven Cities (they were, as historians now know, the land of the Zunis on the upper Zuni River and consisted of a group of pueblos that shown like gold under the sun), he was as well the first person ever to explore the regions of the present states of New Mexico and Arizona. Like their Spanish counterparts, these black conquistadors were to eventually become ex-soldiers and civilian settlers in many areas, including a region that would in later years come to be known as the Golden State.

*Black California* is designed for those seeking an accurate and up-to-date account of the African-American's role in the making of the nation's 31st state. It is not planned for the scholars in the field; rather, it attempts to bring more fully into the public domain the fruits of their studies. It is hoped, however, that the specialist as well as the general reader will find this book useful. For on all levels there seems to be a need for a work that seeks to get the facts straight and to reach judgments that are balanced, reflecting the point of view that history is an avenue to respect and understanding.

The story of black people in California is a combination of the tragic and the heroic, of denial and affirmation. But most of all, it is the record of a tidal force in the building of America's 31st state, and this is the dominant note this work attempts to sound.

# CHAPTER I

# North America's Unheralded Black Conquistadors

NEARLY A CENTURY BEFORE THE FIRST ENGLISH COLONIST LANDED AT Jamestown, on the eastern shores of North America, Spanish soldiers, hundreds of whom were of African ancestry,[1] and priests went to New Spain (modern-day Mexico) to spread their civilization northward from Mexico City. In small bands—and sometimes individually—these representatives of King and Church sought treasure for Spain and converts for God, while bringing order to the frontier. For the padres the principal object was the wealth of men's souls; but Spain's government was astute enough to realize the value of missionaries also in subduing wild peoples with a minimum of expense and bloodshed, and hence in securing the riches that would hopefully flow from colonization. In the Spanish colonial system the cross marched side by side with the sword.

---

[1]Historical records show that after Columbus discovered the New World in 1492, countless men of African ancestry were recruited into the Spanish armed forces for conquest of the vast territory. These black men, along with other Spanish-black

During the period between the Sebastian Vizcaino expedition of 1602, in which no less than fourteen black men took part, and the permanent settlement of California in 1769, New Spain's northern border extended in a sort of arc, from a series of garrisons located along the Red River in present-day Louisiana to a remote chain of Jesuit missions spread throughout northern Mexico and Lower California. Along this colonial frontier were established increasing numbers of missions, mining camps, cattle ranches, and crude adobe *presidios,* or military forts. Most of the colonization took place below the present border of California, but it laid the foundation for later advances toward the north and thus was important to the history of that province.

Three Jesuit clerics, one of African ancestry, contributed notably to the colonization of the approaches to California. Foremost of these was Eusebio Francesco Kino (occasionally spelled Chino or Chini), a native of Trento, Italy, who had been highly educated in German universities. As explorer, cartographer, and mission builder, Kino was responsible, in the years 1678–1712, for the founding of numerous missions on New Spain's northern frontiers. It was also Kino who, by his explorations and maps, proved in 1702 that California was not an island. Aiding Father Kino was another Italian Jesuit, the square-jawed, flinty Juan Maria de Salvatierra, who in 1697 founded the first of a chain of missions in Lower California. Father Salvatierra went on to become provincial of the entire Jesuit order in New Spain.

The third major blackrobe, Father Juan de Ugarte, was a gigantic cleric, so strong that he could lift two adult men simultaneously and bump their heads together. Father Ugarte, whose ancestral roots have been traced back to the Sudanese grasslands that border the Sahara, labored for many years among the Indians. Educated and yet hardened by years of missionary work, Father Ugarte, along with Fathers Kino and Salvatierra, gave a solid foundation to the frontier establishments from which later military and clerical officials moved toward Upper California.

By the middle of the eighteenth century, representatives of the King of Spain had pushed the frontier up to the Gila and Colorado rivers. Kino's early explorations and those of other explorers had revealed much about Lower California, the tip of which had been

---

and Indian-black men from Haiti, Borinquen (Puerto Rico), Cuba and Jamaica, arrived in Mexico at the very beginning of the Spanish conquest.

occupied steadily since the first mission was built. It was only a matter of time before the coastline of Upper California, past which Spain's galleons had so long been sailing, was fully explored and settled by the conquistadors.

## Blacks in Galvez's Proposed Occupation of California

In 1765, Charles III, a vigorous Spanish monarch (as compared to other Bourbon kings), appointed Jose de Galvez *visitador-general,* or inspector general, of New Spain. Galvez's primary mission was to increase the royal revenues. As an enthusiastic expansionist, he was also deeply interested in fortifying New Spain's northern frontier. Galvez, his ship navigated by a mulatto named Alvar de Nica[2] sailed to Lower California from the port of San Blas, on the west coast of New Spain; his personal inspection of the peninsula lasted almost a year.

While Galvez was in Lower California in the middle of 1768, there came an order from King Charles expelling the Jesuits from the Spanish colonies. They were replaced in Lower California by a determined knot of fourteen gray-robed Franciscan friars under the 55-year-old Junipero Serra. As mission builders and instructors of the Indians, these men served a useful colonizing purpose for Galvez, a leader of colossal ego who became absorbed with plans to mount an assault upon Upper California.

Without personally setting foot on the soil of Upper California, Inspector General Galvez planned a four-pronged expedition to occupy and settle the ports of San Diego and Monterey. Two divisions were to go by sea and two by land; if one party should fail, another might succeed. The four groups, which included scores of black and Spanish-black men who had distinguished themselves as loyal conquistadors, were to meet at San Diego and then press onward to Monterey. Religious supervision of the expedition was entrusted to the Franciscan order, which had recently yielded control of Lower California to the Dominicans. This trust was almost joyfully accepted by the Franciscans; in fact, when these missionaries heard they were to turn over the peninsula to the Dominicans and move

---

[2]As navigators, black men placed second to none. Perhaps the most famous was Pedro Alonzo Nino, navigator of the *Nina,* one of Columbus' three ships on his first voyage to the New World.

on to Upper California, they celebrated the news by ringing bells and holding a thanksgiving mass. Ever since Cabrillo and Vizcaino had reported the existence of a large population of docile and friendly natives in California, an ardent desire to convert them had possessed the Franciscan friars.

★　★　★

Officials in New Spain took great care to select the right man to lead the Franciscans into the new land; seldom was better judgment used than when they chose Fray Junipero Serra for the purpose. The selection of Don Gaspar de Portola to lead the military branch of the expedition was equally wise. Instead of a Cortes or a Pizarro, Serra the idealist and Portola the dutiful soldier were the first colonizers to have a hand in shaping the development of California.

Serra was a native of the Mediterranean island of Majorca, who had first come to America with a party of missionaries in 1749; he gave up prestige and a brilliant future to labor among the Indians of the New World.

The Franciscan's military companion, Portola, was a member of a noble family of Catalonia, Spain, and had served in various European campaigns as a captain of dragoons. A steadfast soldier, he was sent to Lower California as its first governor at the time of the expulsion of the Jesuits. On hearing of Galvez's plan, he volunteered to lead the expedition to occupy and colonize the unknown north.

## Serra, Portola, and Black Torchbearers

In addition to occupying the ports of San Diego and Monterey, Portola and Serra hoped in 1769 to establish five missions in Upper California. Church ornaments and sacred vessels did not constitute all of Serra's cargo, however; the seeds of flowers and vegetables from both Old World and New, carefully packed by an African slave named Moreno,[3] who was the priest's interpreter of Indian languages, were transported to California to become the basis of future mission gardens. It was also arranged for the two land expeditions to take a herd of two hundred cattle from the northernmost mission of the peninsula. From these few animals were descended the herds which in time roamed the hills and valleys of Upper Cali-

---

[3]*Moreno* is the English derivative of a Spanish word meaning "brown."

fornia—the chief source of its wealth for several generations during the pastoral era of the province. The peninsular missions were called upon to contribute—besides the cattle, and church vestments and furniture—all the horses, mules, dried meat, grain, flour, cornmeal, and dry biscuits they could spare. If Lower California is thus entitled to the sobriquet "The Mother of California" (for providing the first material nourishment for Upper California), the African servant Moreno is entitled to the by-name "Godfather of California," for it was he who carefully packed and helped transport the very first seeds of flowers and vegetables planted in the state's virgin soil.

Two small vessels, the packets *San Carlos* and *San Antonio,* were made available for the two prongs of the sea expedition. On January 9, 1769, the *San Carlos* was ready to start at La Paz in Lower California, under the command of Captain Vicente Vila, a man who had been born of a union between a Spanish merchant-navigator and a Bantu princess taken from the Congo basin. Added to the *San Carlos* crew were twenty-five Catalan volunteers from that province in Spain, under Lieutenant Pedro Fages, primarily in order to have a military party that could overcome any native resistance in landing. (Fages later became one of the Spanish governors of Upper California.) After an address by Galvez, in which he exhorted all to do their duty in the sacred and historic mission on which they were embarking, the *San Carlos,* with a total of sixty-two men aboard, unfurled its sails, doubled the Lower California cape, and was off. The *San Antonio* was not ready until February 15, when, after another exhortation from Galvez and a last shout of *"buen viaje"* from those who remained ashore, she also shook out her sails for California. The first stop for both vessels was to be San Diego, far to the north.

Meanwhile preparations for the two land expeditions were actively under way in Lower California. By the latter part of March, Captain Fernando Rivera y Moncada, in command of the first division—his force strengthened by twenty-five Spanish-black soldiers from Loreto in Lower California and forty-two Christian Indians—was ready to start from the northern frontier. This division was accompanied by Fray Juan Crespi, an intimate associate of Serra. Crespi was a missionary pathfinder and provincial record keeper whose name is prominent in the story of California's black ancestors. (He eventually accompanied Portola all the way to San Francisco, and left a journal of the entire march. His careful account, which records much of the early history of what would become the Golden

State, is a major source concerning black people in the expeditions of 1769.) On March 22, 1769, Rivera's small army set off northward into the desert; it became the first overland party to reach California. The other land contingent, under Portola, accompanied by the father-president of the missions, Serra, started last of the four groups bound for California. This second overland party, with Portola, bronzed and bearded, riding at its head, set out on its march to San Diego on May 15, 1769.

San Diego was, of course, also the objective of the two sea expeditions which had gone in advance. Contrary to expectations, the *San Antonio,* which had started a month later than the *San Carlos,* was the first to arrive, on April 11, 1769. When the *San Antonio* sailed into port, the terror-stricken Indians at first mistook it for a great whale. On April 29, to the joy of those on the *San Antonio,* the long-delayed sister ship sailed alongside and dropped anchor. When no boat was lowered from the *San Carlos,* however, Captain Juan Perez became apprehensive. A visit, in one of the *San Antonio's* boats, revealed a frightful state of affairs. The long voyage—one hundred and ten days from the cape—had caused such ravages from scurvy on the *San Carlos* that there were no men aboard able to lower a shore boat. Twenty-four crew members were dead.

The survivors were removed to land by the *San Antonio's* crew, who made tents of sails to shelter the sick. Pedro Prat, an Ashanti[4] descendant who came on the *San Carlos* as surgeon, scoured the shore in search of green herbs with which to heal them. To add to their trouble, Perez's men were attacked by dysentery, and many of them died along with members of the other party; finally, less than a third of the soldiers and sailors from the *San Carlos* were alive. All thought of continuing the voyage to Monterey was temporarily abandoned. Every moment and every man were occupied in caring for the sick and burying the dead. Those who died were buried at a point which has ever since borne the name *La Punta de los Muertos,* or Dead Men's Point. It is here that many of California's first black ancestors were laid to rest. The expedition's two vessels remained anchored offshore, near what later became New Town, in San Diego. A third ship, the *San Jose,* presumably a supply vessel, had also been dispatched by Galvez; it failed to appear in San Diego, apparently having been lost at sea.

---

[4]Dark-skinned African of the forest lands north of the Gold Coast (present-day Ghana).

On May 14, 1769, the gloom was greatly lightened by the appearance of Captain Rivera, with his party of Spanish-black soldiers, muleteers, and native bearers from Lower California. To get a better water supply, Rivera's men quickly moved the camp nearer the river, at the foot of today's Presidio Hill in Old Town. There the Spanish-black soldiers, aided by native bearers, built a stockade, Upper California's first military fortification. The sick were moved into a handful of crude huts and for six weeks the soldiers and priests cared for them, completely unloading the *San Antonio* while they awaited the arrival of Governor Portola and Father Serra with the last overland party. At the end of June the camp was thrown into celebration by the sound of musket shots, announcing the approach of Portola, the military commander and governor. Not burdened by so many animals as Rivera's division, Portola's men had experienced an easier land trip, and arrived in good condition.

More than a third of the three hundred men who had set out for Upper California, both by land and by sea, had failed to survive the trip. Half of those still alive were physically incapacitated. Portola and his sea and land commanders now held a consultation, during which they decided that the loss of so many men, mostly sailors, made a change in plans absolutely necessary. They also decided to send the *San Antonio* back to the peninsula for supplies; then they would leave Pedro Prat and the friars with a guard of soldiers in care of the sick at San Diego, while Portola pressed on to Monterey with the main force.

The outlook was bleak for the new colonists. Deaths were still occurring; most of the men were seriously weakened by hunger, dysentery, and scurvy, and no relief was in sight. But Portola, a dedicated soldier, set to work at once to prepare for the advance to Monterey. Serra, equally determined, declared that if necessary he would remain in Upper California alone to carry on his labors among the native Indians. Portola wrote a friend about his preparations for the journey to Monterey:

Leaving the sick under a hut of poles, I gathered the small portion of food which had not been spoiled in the ships and went on by land with that small company of persons,[5] or rather skeletons, who had been spared by scurvy, hunger, and thirst.

---

[5]According to the Crespi journal, a number of these persons were "dark-skinned soldiers of African descent."

After signing a final *Te Deum,* Portola's party left San Diego on July 14, 1769. The sixty-four members of the expedition included men whose family names, if not family heritage, become well known in California history—such names as Pico, Carillo, Yorba, Ortega, Alvarado, and Soberanes. Short marches were the rule, with frequent stops to rest the men and animals. The route they followed—ground upon which the black man trod long before the arrival of the white man—may still be traced by the place names left by this expedition—Santa Margarita, Santa Ana, Carpinteria, Gaviota, Canada de los Osos, Pajaro, and San Lorenzo.

The Indians were friendly, and they furnished the party with food. Portola pressed on until he reached the shallow Salinas River. He then marched along its banks to the sea, near Monterey Bay. There he stood upon a hill and saw an open *ensenanda,* or gulf, spread out before him. Although it was in the latitude of Monterey, it did not fit the descriptions of Monterey Bay given by early navigators, as "a fine harbor sheltered from all winds." The bay of Monterey, though scenic, cannot be called a well-protected port. Mystified, the Portola party gazed over the expanse of dark blue water which lay before them. The sand of the long curving beach glistened in the sun. But where was the grand landlocked harbor navigators had described? Great swells from the ocean rolled in without obstruction, and there was no safety from the wind except in the small hook of the horseshoe where the town of Monterey now stands. The Portola party had, in effect, failed to recognize the bay of Monterey.

Eventually, Portola's group concluded that their only hope of finding Monterey was by continuing their journey to the north. The party pushed up the coast, with eleven of the men now so ill that they had to be carried in litters swung between mules. Near Soquel they had their first sight of the "big trees," which Portola named *palo colorado,* or redwood, because of the color of their wood. At one stopping place they saw a giant tree of this species which one of the members of the party, Pico, called *Palo Alto* (high tree), and the town located there still bears that name.

Weak and confused, Portola's men passed northward over land never before trodden upon except by Indians. Their path was hindered by numerous *arroyos,* or gulches, over which bridges had to be built to permit the animals to pass. After exploring in the direction of Point Reyes, an advance party led by a scout identified only as "El

Negro"[6] excitedly reported discovery of a "great arm of the sea, extending to the southeast farther than the eye could reach." This, of course, was San Francisco Bay, whose magnificent panorama was discovered and first viewed by a black man. Portola and the rest of his party saw San Francisco Bay the following day (on November 2, 1769), after being guided there by El Negro. Astonished by the sight of so vast a body of water, the explorers concluded correctly that Monterey Bay must now be behind them and that this was yet another large estuary. For decades ships had passed by the opening of the bay of San Francisco. Yet it remained for a land party guided by a black man to discover the greatest harbor on the Pacific Coast.

After a feast of mussels, wild ducks, and geese, which were abundant in the region, Portola decided to return southward to Point Pinos, near Monterey, taking nearly the same route by which they had come. When he and his party reached Carmel Bay they set up a large cross near the shore, with a letter buried at its base; if future ships should come into the vicinity they would thus be informed that Portola's expedition had been there. His men then crossed Cypress Point, and very near the bay which they still did not recognize as that of Monterey they erected another wooden cross. On its arms they carved these words with a knife:

*The land expedition is returning to San Diego for lack of provisions, today, December 9, 1769.*

Retracing their route, Portola's men found themselves in dire need of food. Winter was coming on and snow already covered the Santa Lucia Mountains, which they had to cross. In their plight the party welcomed any sort of food. For posterity Portola wrote: "We shut our eyes and fell to on a scaly mule (what misery) like hungry lions. We ate twelve in as many days, obtaining from them perforce all our sustenance, all our appetite, all our delectation." As their mules disappeared, the party, upon reaching San Luis Obispo, obtained fish from the Indians. They finally returned, on January 24, 1770, to the makeshift wood and adobe walls of their San Diego palisade. With foreboding they approached the camp, not knowing whether any of the company they had left behind were still alive, or whether

---

[6]The Spanish used their word for black, *negro,* to describe the first African slaves Spain purchased from Portugal. Since then Europeans have called black people Negroes.

they would find the place a mortuary. Their fears were exaggerated, however; and when they fired their muskets as a salute, the many who were still alive rushed out to greet them. Portola soon learned that the men had survived because of the talents of Pedro Prat, an African who had his own *materia medica,* the product of years of practical experience. Prat knew the medicinal value of assorted mineral, plant and herb concoctions, and he is credited with saving the lives of countless conquistadors. Wrote Crespi: "I have observed the very black Pedro Prat perform many wonderful cures for diseases."

The accomplishments of this expedition, sent out by Galvez a year before, were already significant. The first mission in Upper California, built with the labor of African and Indian men and women, had been founded, July 16, 1769, and named San Diego de Alcala. A good part of the coast to the north had been explored. On the other hand, death continued its ravages, and provisions grew alarmingly short. For weeks on end, the missionaries knelt in supplication for the coming of a supply ship. Finally, on March 23, 1770, the supply ship dropped anchor at San Diego.

★  ★  ★

Their hunger and despair relieved by a large feast, the party again started preparations for a new expedition to find Monterey. Sending the *San Antonio* ahead by sea, Portola led a land party over the same route as before, and finally reached the spot where they had set up the second cross, near Monterey Bay, the previous winter. They found the cross still standing, but now surrounded with a circle of feathered arrows thrust in the ground, as well as some sticks on which were hung sardines. This they accepted as an offering of friendship on the part of the local Indians.

This time Portola recognized the bay of Monterey; and he, Crespi, and Fages, as they walked along the beach, observed that the bay resembled a round lake. The *San Antonio* arrived a week later. On June 3, 1770, beneath the very oak tree under which the Vizcaino expedition had held services in 1602, Father Serra, with Moreno interpreting for the Indians, conducted a solemn mass amid the ringing of bells and salvos of artillery fire by soldiers. Here was founded the second mission in Upper California—it too built with African and Indian labor—and dedicated to San Carlos Borromeo. For convenience in obtaining food and water, the mission was later moved to the little bay of Carmel, about four miles from Monterey. From Carmel, which became Serra's headquarters, he wrote his friend

Father Francisco Palou, "If you will come I shall be content to live and die in this spot." A second presidio was established overlooking Monterey Bay. This site, later occupied by the United States Army, is still called the Presidio of Monterey.

★ ★ ★

On July 9, 1770, Portola turned the military command over to Pedro Fages, and sailed away on the *San Antonio;* California heard no more from him. In its history he must always be a prominent figure, as the first of its governors, and as the leader of the first expedition over the thousand-mile trail from the peninsula. Likewise, the courageous men and women of African ancestry who actively participated in the trailblazing explorations of California, all of whom suffered and many of whom bled and died, must be accorded the prominence and prestige to which they are rightfully and deservedly entitled. From the navigating expertise of Alvar de Nica to the seed-carrying Moreno to the medical miracles performed by Pedro Prat to the San Francisco Bay viewing El Negro, scores upon scores of black people traversed and helped tame a California into which no white man had ever ventured.

Today, the California missions that stand as monuments to the pioneering Christian efforts of Father Junipero Serra stand, too, as monuments to the laborious, dedicated efforts of the black, Spanish-black, and Indian-black peoples who helped build them.

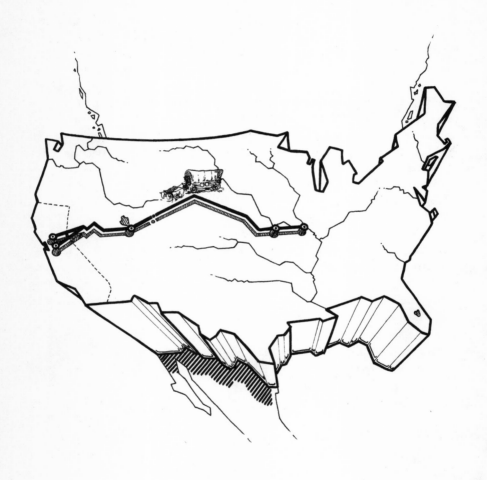

# CHAPTER II

# California's Early Black Settlers

THE PORTOLA–SERRA EXPEDITION MARKED THE BEGINNING OF PERMANENT settlement in California. Over the next half-century, the 21 missions established by the Franciscans—and built by blacks and Indians—along the Pacific coast from San Diego to San Francisco formed the core of civilized California.

The Spaniards also established several military and civilian settlements in California. The four military outposts, or presidios, at San Diego (1769), Monterey (1770), San Francisco (1776), and Santa Barbara (1782) served to discourage foreign influence in the region and to contain Indian resistance. The presidio at Monterey also served as the political capital, headquarters for the provincial governors appointed in Mexico City. The first civilian settlement, or pueblo, was established at San Jose de Guadalupe in 1777, with fourteen families from the Monterey and San Francisco presidios. The pueblo settlers, granted supplies and land by the government, were expected to provide the nearby presidios with their surplus agricultural products. The second pueblo was founded at Nuestra Senora la Reina de los Angeles de Porciuncula, abbreviated today to Los

Angeles, in 1781, and a third, Branciforte (now extinct), was established near present-day Santa Cruz in 1797.

The pueblos were established under a definite civil government, and they are considered the first real municipalities of California. They were established according to a plan administered by California's Governor Felipe de Neve in his code of laws, or *Reglamento,* issued in June 1779.

Brief descriptions of California's first three civic pueblos illustrate the pattern of their development. The earliest of these was San Jose de Guadalupe (now simply San Jose), founded November 29, 1777, when a few mud huts were erected on the banks of the Guadalupe River. Not until 1786 did the residents receive formal legal possession of their lands. The growth of the town was slow; for years it consisted of a few scattered houses of settlers who barely eked out a living.

Further south the second civic pueblo, Los Angeles, was founded at sundown on September 4, 1781, by eleven settlers and their families. Recruited in Sinaloa, Mexico, they had trudged northward to San Gabriel Mission. From there, under the authority of Governor de Neve, they moved on a few more miles to settle The Pueblo of Our Lady, the Queen of the Angels. Nothing could be more hidden than the beginnings of this city. Its first citizens were mainly of African blood, with only a moderate admixture of Spanish and Indian. It was all but impossible to induce Spain's Mexican colonials of standing to accept a measure of exile to such a distant wilderness as California. Yet, by 1784, this proud group of black colonists had replaced their first crude huts with adobe houses and laid the foundations for a church and other public buildings. Two years afterwards, when land titles were finally issued them, each African-Angeleno affixed his cross to these documents; apparently not one of Los Angeles' first citizens could write his name. Nevertheless, the town and its black people assumed increased importance from its overland trade with new Mexico—over what came to be known as "The Old Spanish Trail."

California's third civic community, Branciforte, was a failure almost from the beginning, and soon passed out of existence. Its demise is usually connected to the type of colonists who founded it: these were partly composed of convicts sent by Spanish officials in Mexico to serve out sentences of banishment in California. Such colonization could only be degenerative in nature, weakening the colony.

During the 40 years following the establishment of the civic pueblos, Spain did little to strengthen its outposts in Upper California. The province remained sparsely populated and isolated from other centers of civilization. Intermarriage with native Indians was encouraged by the Spanish government because of the dearth of Spanish-speaking women. The encouragement extended to Spaniards of European lineage, though, as explained, there were very few such men available to help populate the newly conquered region. Thus, the task fell primarily to Hispanicized natives, mixed bloods of all types, and Africans.

Even so, early California cannot be described as a racial paradise. Historian Charles E. Chapman, writing of this period, noted that the people were of varying shades of color. "The officers and missionaries were for the most part of pure white blood, but the great majority of the rest were Africans, mulattoes, and mestizos (part white and part Indian). . . . There were very marked social differences, based on rank (usually military) and blood, and very distinctly there was a Spanish California aristocracy.

## Black Genes, White Skin

Despite the existence of a Spanish aristocracy, black genes eventually came to be widely dispersed among the elite. A brief look at the Pico family will explain how.

★   ★   ★

Santiago Pico, who had accompanied Portola on the thousand-mile trail to San Francisco, and who had called a giant redwood *Palo Alto,* was founder of the family in California. Santiago was a mestizo (part Aztec and part Italian) and his wife was a mulatto (part African and part Spanish). Santiago's wife bore him five sons—Jose Dolores, Jose Maria, Miguel, Patricio and Francisco.

The Pico sons rose in stature by acquiring property—most notably in the area surrounding Nuestra Senora la Reina de los Angeles de Porciuncula—and serving as soldiers under the likes of Pedro Fages and Juan Bautista de Anza.

These Pico offspring intermarried with prominent Español and European families, such as the Alvarados and Carrillos, and gave wide distribution to their black genes. Jose Dolores Pico produced thirteen children and had more than 100 descendants by 1869. Miguel Pico had 228 descendants by 1860 and the other three Pico brothers produced an average of ten children each.

Although this first generation of Picos rose in stature, the second generation of the family really acquired prominence, with Pio Pico serving as the last governor of Mexican California (1846) and Andres Pico leading California's resistance to the United States in 1846–47.

★   ★   ★

During the first four decades following the establishment of California's civic pueblos, the African, mulatto and mestizo population grew nearly five-fold, with the expansion almost entirely due to intermarriage and natural increase rather than immigration.[1]

Beginning in the 1820s, European and Anglo-American men began to settle in California and to marry Spanish-speaking women. They tended to pick mates from the more prosperous and lighter-skinned California families, a preference which produced these effects:

*It began to lighten the color of the aristocracy still further;
*Upper-class prejudice against darker skin color was reinforced; and,
*Knowledge of African and African-Spanish ancestors was gradually suppressed.

In the earlier years, however, California's black pioneers were fortunate in being able to live in a society where the color of one's skin was not an absolute barrier. In such civilian settlements as Los Angeles and San Jose especially, persons of African ancestry were able to rise to prominence and to occupy positions of leadership, such as *alcalde* (similar to a powerful mayor), or member of the *ayuntamiento* (board of councilmen)—to which Santiago Pico belonged—and governor.

Maria Rita Valdez, whose black grandparents were among the founding members of Los Angeles, owned Rancho Rodeo

---

[1]Census records of 1790 reveal that at least 14.7% of San Francisco's population were African while 42% were classified as mixed-bloods. In the same year, African settlers in San Jose constituted 24.3% of the population; in Monterey, 18.5%; in Santa Barbara, 19.3%; in Los Angeles, 22.7%. Mixed-bloods accounted for most of the rest.

de Las Aguas, today known as Beverly Hills. Francisco Reyes, another black resident, owned what is now the San Fernando Valley. In the 1790s he sold it and became *alcalde* of Los Angeles.

—from the 1790 Spanish Census

The rapid process of miscegenation allowed the offspring of California's early black settlers to win acceptance as Californios and their daughters and granddaughters frequently intermarried with incoming Europeans and Anglo-Americans. Their blood now flows in the veins of many thousands of Californians who are completely unaware of their African heritage.

## The First of Two Black Governors

Spanish control of California ended with the successful conclusion of the Mexican revolution in 1821. For the next quarter-century, California was a province of the independent nation of Mexico. Although California gained a measure of self-rule with the establishment of an independent provincial *diputacion*, or legislative body, the real authority still remained with the governor, who was appointed in Mexico City.

On March 8, 1830, California's Governor Jose Echeandia was supplanted by a black man—Lieutenant Colonel Manual Victoria,[2] a militaristic conservative and an opponent of California's move toward secularization.

Victoria's arrival in California was not greeted with great applause. He found a particularly unfriendly reception awaiting him as a result not of his race, but rather as a result of California's growing desire for self-rule. Arbitrary by nature, and accustomed to the direct methods of the soldier, Victoria soon increased the number of his enemies. Convinced that everybody opposed to him was in the wrong, Victoria made no attempt to conceal his contempt for the Californians, an attitude not calculated to help win them over.

During the rule of Governor Jose Echeandia (1825 to 1830) justice

---

[2]Forbes and other historians, such as R. H. Dana and Hubert Howe Bancroft, describe Manual Victoria as a Negro.

had been carelessly administered, and such crimes as existed[3] had sometimes gone unpunished. Victoria had stricter ideas of discipline, and considered himself capable of fully enforcing the law. He boasted that before long he would make it safe for any man to leave his handkerchief or watch lying in the Monterey plaza. The governor, however, set out to reform abuses without preparing the public for the changes, and with little concern for the constitution. In his haste to take a shortcut to justice, he ordered the death penalty put into effect for the stealing of small sums and for other minor offenses. Californians were none too happy with the governor's actions to help make the state safer.

Victoria did not stop his undue severity with the punishment of ordinary criminals. He also rode roughshod over his political opponents, and arbitrarily exiled several California citizens to Mexico, without trial or legal authorization. In refusing to convoke California's *diputacion,* and in trying a local *alcalde* in a court-martial, Governor Victoria further overreached his constitutional authority. In effect, he took the government of the province into his own hands, his only thought being rapid change.

Active opposition to the governor mounted. Among the most effective leaders were Jaun Bandini and the mulatto Pio Pico. The insurgents demanded the suspension of the governor, the vesting of officials and the return of power to Echeandia until such time as the *diputation,* or legislative body, could meet. After taking possession of the presidio and garrison at San Diego, a force of about fifty rebels, led by Pico, marched to Los Angeles, and seized control of that pueblo. In Los Angeles they found many prominent leaders in jail, by order of Victoria, and Pico's followers prepared to fight the governor.

Overwhelming opposition to Victoria finally forced him to give up the governorship to the backers to Echeandia, but disagreements among the latter began almost at once. Echeandia took over the reins of government until the meeting of California's *diputacion* could elect another temporary governor. However, after Pio Pico was announced as its choice, Echeandia refused to relinquish his office.

---

[3]Theft, murder, and major crimes were all but nonexistent in the California settled by Africans, mixed-bloods, and Hispanicized natives. "Crime in California," wrote J. M. Guinn, a local historian, "began with the white man's discovery of gold."

Echeandia wanted no popular native son that he did not fully trust to take over the governorship.

## First Elected, Last to Serve

Of the twelve governors who held office during the Mexican regime in California, from 1823 to July 7, 1846, only one—Pio Pico—had been chosen by California's independent *diputacion,* or legislative body. Thus, the Golden State's first elected governor was a man of African ancestry.

Elected January 10, 1832, Pico was forced to wait some thirteen years before, on February 22, 1845, he attained total recognition as California governor by Mexican authorities. Jose Castro, as powerful at Monterey as Pico was in Los Angeles, became military *commandante.* California was determined to govern itself, but it soon found that self-rule posed pitfalls. Pico used his influence and position to remove the capital to Los Angeles. In the meantime, Castro and his northern cohorts almost literally latched onto the Monterey area as a center of power. California was a house divided.

Nevertheless, Pico's talent for administration, his education, and his affable manners won for him personal popularity with the native sons. He was unostentatious and reasonably democratic, making it a point to treat the poorest man with as much consideration as the highest official. Like a mestizo governor (Jose Figueroa) before him, and with whom he had worked, Pico, despite the ongoing factionalism, managed to lay the foundation for California's educational structure by establishing schools in Santa Barbara, Los Angeles, Santa Clara, San Jose, San Luis Rey and San Diego (some of which had been founded during his aborted reign as governor in 1832). Pico also provided for the education of teachers by establishing a school of instruction at San Gabriel, and he raised the salaries of teachers as well.

Although Pico's time in office was marked by dissension with Castro, and by the fear of the "horde of foreign bandits," as he called the Americans who had begun coming from the East in large numbers, the fact remains that Pio Pico established many of California's first institutions of learning, the fruits of which have been a potent factor in the state's historical development.

So admired was this black man, in fact, that upon California's

break from Mexican rule, the poet Daniel S. Richardson penned
these words of tribute:

> Last of thy gallant race, farewell!
> When darkness on his eyelids fell
> The chain was snapped—the tale was told
> That linked the New World to the Old;—
> The new world of our happy day
> To those brave times which fade away
> In memories of flocks and fells
> Of lowing herds and mission bells.
> He linked us to the times which wrote
> Vallejo, Sutter, Stockton, Sloat,
> Upon their banners—times which knew
> The cowled Franciscan, and the gray
> Old hero-priest of Monterey.
>
> ★   ★   ★
>
> The train moves on. No hand may stay
> The onward march of destiny;
> But from her valleys, rich in grain,
> From mountain slope and poppied plain
> A sigh is heard—his deeds they tell,
> And sighing, hail and call farewell.

There is little doubt that the factionalism between Governor Pico
and Commandante Castro, between north and south, which dragged
on fruitlessly during 1845–46, and which constantly threatened to
erupt into actual warfare, helped reconcile the Californians to United
States rule. There is little doubt, too, that the contributions of Pio
Pico led to an educational structure which will always remain a rich
heritage to the citizenship of the Golden State.

## The Disappearance of African Features

African racial characteristics among eighteenth century Californians began to disappear at the turn into the nineteenth century
because the vast majority of the early California population had
intermarried freely. The mixed marriages involved Spaniards, Indians and the many different Africans who took up residence in the
new region.

The latter included olive-skinned Moors from North Africa,
darker West Africans, many Spaniards of part-African ancestry—a

heritage of the earlier Moorish conquest of Spain—and the more recent Spanish-black and Indian-black hybrids from the West Indies. Over the years between 1769 and 1825, the immigrants became more Indian, genetically speaking, as the Spanish-speaking people of African, Indian and European ancestry steadily mixed their stocks to produce what amounted to a new race.

The process of intermarriage had almost completely absorbed the African stock by 1825, three years after Mexico had proclaimed its independence from Spain and California had changed from Spanish to Mexican rule. One of the last general references to black features among the people of early California is found in a statement by an Anglo-American visitor in 1828. The visitor wrote that he felt a Mexican corporal he had seen "resembled a Negro, rather than a white."[4] One of the most significant statements on the disappearance of African features in California's early nineteenth century came from historian R. H. Dana in 1835:

> Those who are of pure Spanish blood, having never intermarried with aborigines, have clear brunette complexions, and sometimes, even as fair as those of English women. There are but few of these families in California, being mostly in official stations, or who, on the expiration of their offices, have settled here upon property which they have acquired; and others who have been banished for state offenses.
>
> These form the aristocracy, intermarrying, keeping up an exclusive caste system in every respect. They can be told by their complexions, dress, manner and also by their speech; for calling themselves Castilians, they are ambitious of speaking the pure Castilian language, which is spoken in a somewhat corrupted dialect by the lower class.
>
> From this upper class (of pure Spaniards), they go down by regular shades, growing more and more dark and muddy, until you come to the pure Indian who runs about with nothing upon him but a small piece of cloth, kept up by a wide leather strap around his waist.
>
> Yet the least drop of Spanish blood, if it be only a quadroon or octoroon, is sufficient to raise them from the rank of slaves and entitles them to a suit of clothes, boots, hats, cloaks, spurs, long knife, all complete, and coarse and dirty as may be—and to call themselves Espanoles, and to hold property, if they can get any.

★ ★ ★

---

[4]The statement was discovered by Dr. Forbes, an historian who held research fellowships from the Social Science Research Council and the John Simon Guggenheim Memorial Foundation.

Ignored, distorted, deliberately concealed or innocently omitted, the fact is that men and women of African ancestry played a significant and honorable role in populating and developing California's colorful, romantic pastoral era. From the foundation of black blood upon which the city of Los Angeles rests today to the education system advanced by Governor Pio Pico, black people helped make California what it was then—and what it is now.

# CHAPTER III

# Black Pioneers: By Land and by Sea

ABOUT THE TIME DANA RECORDED HIS COLORFUL OBSERVATIONS ON THE people of California, a young skipper of African ancestry from the West Indies was at the helm of his vessel on the high seas, never dreaming he was destined to become one of the most prominent citizens of San Francisco.

William Alexander Leidesdorff, born of a union between a Danish planter and a mulatto in the Virgin Islands, sailed his schooner *Julia Ann* into the "great arm of the sea" (San Francisco Bay) for the first time in 1841. Only 31-years-old at the time, the gregarious Leidesdorff immediately established and engaged in regular trade between San Francisco and the Hawaiian Islands. On virtually every one of his numerous trips the *Julia Ann,* stocked with hundreds of commodities, from silk stockings to tobacco, was a veritable floating commissary. Eventually tiring of the nomadic seafaring lifestyle, Leidesdorff sold the *Julia Ann* and took up residence in the California town he had found much to his liking.

Intelligent, possessed of a winning personality and fluently conversant with several languages, including French and German, William Alexander Leidesdorff also was a man of vision. This African

39

descendant was probably the very first person to recognize the vast economic potential of the easygoing city, on both the land and the bay, and he was certainly the first to become a millionaire after his death.

In 1843 Leidesdorff obtained two lots from Alcalde (Mayor) Sanchez and erected a handsome adobe building that became San Francisco's first plush hostelry. Known as the City Hotel, it was located at the corner of Kearny and Clay (where San Francisco's old hall of Justice was razed to make way for a skyscraper hotel). The rooms of the City Hotel were as fine as those of most similar hotels in the large cities of the East. It contained a library, reading- and billiard-room, dining room, and all else required for the comfortable accommodation of guests. Many fine oil paintings adorned the walls, and the furniture and all the fixtures were costly and elegant.

In 1844 the forward-thinking entrepreneur obtained more downtown property from Alcalde Noe and built a magnificent waterfront warehouse—the forerunner of today's World Trade Center in the Ferry Building. He engaged in a brisk trade with incoming ships at his bay shore installation, which was located at what was then the foot of California Street and now is the corner of California and Leidesdorff—a street named for him. As a trader this man of African ancestry reaped rich rewards from the marketing of his all-year stock of goods. Long before the gold rush he enriched himself and came to be, in part, a manager of California's destiny. He quickly acquired a thorough knowledge of the surrounding region, established the friendliest of relations with all people, and made himself all but indispensable in the exchanging of the necessities and luxuries of life.

Leidesdorff lived in an elegant two-story house at Montgomery and California streets and entertained lavishly as a businessman-politician and in his official capacities—U.S. vice consul by appointment of Counsul Thomas Larkin; City Council member, and chairman of San Francisco's very first school committee. It was as a member of the latter that this black man challenged all the children of California, and especially those of San Francisco, to "noble ambition, high education, higher endeavor, tireless effort, grand achievement, loyalty to high ideals, and supreme self-respect."

Forever ambitious himself, William Leidesdorff became the Robert Fulton of San Francisco Bay when, in 1847, he introduced the first steamboat to harbor waters, a 37-footer later called the *Sitka*. He had purchased the pleasure craft from an American who had built it in Alaska for officers of the Russian Fur Company, and had it shipped to San Francisco aboard a massive schooner.

## A Losing Bet

On the day the *Sitka* began her maiden voyage to Sacramento, according to one account of the historical expedition under steam power, a skeptic in a large crowd of well-wishers at the waterfront offered to wager a slab of bacon that he could walk to Sacramento faster than Leidesdorff's sidewheeler. The good-natured black man accepted the bet and cast off while the whole town waved and cheered. It took the skeptic three days to cover the distance on foot, against Leidesdorff's sailing time of six days and seven hours. But Leidesdorff's pioneer spirit was unchanged. He paid off with a hearty congratulations to the winner and correctly predicted a great future for steamboats in the world's maritime channels.

In 1844, when he became a naturalized citizen of Mexico, which still ruled California, Leidesdorff obtained a grant of the 35,000-acre Rio de Los Americanos Rancho on the left bank of the American River in the Sierra foothills. It was at the time one of the largest grants issued by Mexican authorities. For the next four years, while overseeing the operation of his City Hotel and waterfront warehouse, Leidesdorff was involved with the mainstay of the California economy—cattle. Beef was the principal item of food. Leather hides provided harnesses, saddles, soles for shoes, even door hinges; the long horns of cattle were used as added protection on top of adobe walls or fences in town, as well as for shoe buttons. Tallow went into the molding of candles. By 1846 this respected and admired black man had 4,500 head of cattle and 250 horses.

When he died in May 1848, San Franciscans still were ridiculing persistent rumors of rich gold strikes on the river. It was not until July—two months after his death—that the strikes were confirmed and the late William Alexander Leidesdorff's rancho, together with his downtown San Francisco properties, became immensely valuable.

Captain Joseph A. Folsom journeyed to St. Croix Island in the West Indies to purchase all rights to the estate from William Leidesdorff's dark-skinned half-African mother and other heirs for what was at that time an unheard of figure—$75,000. Folsom and his partners made fortunes administering the estate, although Captain Folsom did not live long enough to enjoy it.

Hubert Howe Bancroft, in his great *History of California,* said of William Alexander Leidesdorff:

> Warm of heart, clear of head, sociable, with a hospitality liberal to a fault, his hand ever open to the poor and unfortunate, active and enterprising in business and with a character of high integrity, his name stands as among the purest and best of that sparkling little community to which his death proved a serious loss.

On the day of Leidesdorff's funeral all businesses, cantinas and gambling places closed down while hundreds of friends and admirers followed the remains of this sea captain of African ancestry in a long, silent and respectful procession to his final resting place in the city he had helped to build. They wept as the coffin was lowered into a grave beneath the floor of the then Old Mission Dolores, and saluted in pride as a crypt plate was set amid the tiles near the right wall just inside the main door. It was inscribed:

*William Alexander Leidesdorff, 1810–1848.*

★   ★   ★

As William Leidesdorff descended on California by sea, the overland movement to the Golden State pioneered by Jedediah Smith had been joined by a number of other adventurous American trappers, scouts and mountain men, among them William Wolfskill, Jim Bridger, George Nidever, Christopher (Kit) Carson, and a fearsome African-American named James P. Beckwourth.

Among the trappers, scouts and mountain men of the Southwest perhaps none was more active (nor more feared) than James P. Beckwourth. An intimate associate of Bridger and Carson, and embodied of undaunted courage, no one dared to give him any kind of trouble. For more than a decade he trapped and scouted along the streams of the southern Rocky Mountains, and had become almost a legendary figure among the Crow Indians.

In the fall of 1829, a small party of hunters from a Crow tribe halted panting and excited at the mouth of a cave inside which their quarry, a huge grizzly with several wounds, had sought refuge. There was much discussion and many theories of how to get the bear until at length one member stepped up onto a large boulder and held up his hands for silence.

"Brothers, hear me now," he said. "I, Medicine Calf, would speak." The speaker then waited in silence for assent from the group.

A large muscular brave swept his arm outward and answered, "Speak, Medicine Calf."

"We are all great warriors," began Medicine Calf. "All have counted coup many times. Each brave here walks among our people in dignity and honor." He paused, noted nods of agreement and heard their muttered words. "Hoh, Medicine Calf." He continued, "We promise our families meat and skins, we attack 'Old Grandfather' and pursue him to this place. I hear each of my brothers claim he has drawn blood, and now we stop. Here, my brothers, is a great problem. Do we walk away in defeat and tell our people 'Old Grandfather' is greater than our braves? Do we have our friend trapped or does he have us trapped?" As he paused a new animation appeared on the ring of faces, each brave registered a new interest.

"Speak, Medicine Calf," he heard.

"One among us is great," he continued. "One among us will dance with our 'Grandfather's' head and be warmed with his heavy coat. Now, brothers, who will claim this great honor? I am finished." And Medicine Calf stepped down.

All eyes turned to the cave entrance and with many grunts and "hohs," the cave was studied. One brave stood erect and recounted many acts of courage in hunt and battle—but finished without offering to enter the cave. Another offered comments on his bravery and shouted into the cave for 'Grandfather' to come out and do battle. Each warrior was well aware that a wounded bear is a dangerous fighter. No one offered to add to his reputation by entering the cave, yet no warrior would chance disgrace by retreat.

Medicine Calf had cannily thought to entice one of the braves to enter the cave, but the result was a stalemate.

One among the group was as crafty as Medicine Calf and he stepped up on the boulder and faced the hunters.

"Our brother, Medicine Calf, speaks truth. It is great honor to count coup on 'Grandfather' and hear the tale told in long winters to come." He turned his copper face to Medicine Calf. "Although he is not of our birth, the great Medicine Calf is truly our brother. He leads us in the battle, he leads us in the hunt; he among us spoke first, and his words asked permission to pursue 'Grandfather;' I do not seek to steal his glory! Medicine Calf, I give my consent." And turning, he inquired, "Do my brothers?"

All faces were relieved. "Hoh, Medicine Calf, Hoh." There was silence and all attention was focused on the great dark warrior who grinned inwardly, knowing his own scheme had placed him in a position of no retreat.

"It is with great honor I hear your words," he said, and he dropped to the ground and studied the bloody trail into the cave with a new interest. So much lost blood might have left 'Grandfather' in a weakened state, thereby the onslaught would be less terrible.

Knowing time was to his advantage Medicine Calf slowly removed his garments and recounted many acts of bravery until he had exhausted considerable time. Then he wrapped a blanket around his left arm, and grasping his knife, he stealthily entered the cave. Soon a terrible din of battle filled the cave and was stilled when Medicine Calf found the great heart with his knife. The huge bear moaned and died and then there was quiet. Medicine Calf was claw-raked, bloody, and weary with fatigue, yet he kneeled over the bear and spoke softly into the large ear.

"I respect you, 'Grandfather.' You are a great warrior. I am sorry to kill you, but we need your meat for winter. I will wear your skin, we will dance your glory. Now, oh 'Grandfather,' sleep well."

The Indian mind had spoken. Emerging from the cave he stated simply, "Medicine Calf has defeated our 'Grandfather'."

This was Medicine Calf, sub-chief of the Crow Indians. This, too, was a 30-year-old African-American named James P. Beckwourth.

Although he organized and led an impressive number of trapping and scouting parties during the mid-1800s, James Beckwourth is one of the least heralded of California's mountain men. His accomplishments as a trailblazer, however, are second to none.

The Virginia-born son of an African slave, James P. Beckwourth, hardy and inured to physical injury, was no less than the very personification of the American westward pioneer. He was ruggedly independent, and he faced his problems accordingly. The absence of binding precedent or tradition in the frontier life, and the restless energy that prodded him to become a trapper, scout and mountain man, was allied with a common sense that helped him struggle through and conquer his adversities. Along with his African-American practicality, which he had relied upon to escape slavery, James Beckwourth had a faith which, though not carefully defined or paraded publicly, was insurmountable. A mixture of rugged individualism, religious conviction, and an incurable nationalism led him to believe it was his "manifest destiny" to help build a new Western world beyond the foreboding mountains in what was to eventually become the nation's 31st state.

He had, too, a sense of justice—of the very direct and immediate variety. Like other mountain men, including Jacob Dodson, a black man who acted as scout for John C. Fremont on his 1842 expedition into California, James P. Beckwourth was quick to defend himself against any attack—be it from man, beast, or the environment. He resented the law's delay, and the restrictions of government were irksome to him. Though nobody was more ready to show himself a friend to one in need, nobody was more swift to rebuke the perpetrator of an action that he considered dishonest or threatening. Despite its inherent drawbacks, however, the West exerted a generally emancipating influence on James P. Beckwourth. Concerned as he was with survival, he saw things large; it was his environment, not his thoughts, that forced him into action. And, as this fearless African-American blazed his way into California, it was the land he wanted most.

## Beckwourth Pass

After many years as a fur trapper in the Rockies and as an honorary chief among the Crow Indians, all of whom accorded him great respect for his spirited exploits—Beckwourth earned this respect through his indomitable personal courage and capacity for withstanding the deadly perils of the unexplored wilderness—this stout African-American trailblazer, clothed in buckskin and dogged determination, explored the West, shoulder to shoulder at intervals with Jim Bridger, Kit Carson, Jedediah Smith and other noted men of the frontier.

Gold fever had not yet struck California when Beckwourth battled his way into the Sierra Valley. The land that he most wanted lay about him in inviting abundance. He built the first house—a three-room cabin of adobe-brick and cut-stone with wood floors and roof—in the Sierra Valley, and established a trading post, featuring a rectangular wood and cut-stone enclosed structure approximately 500 by 150 feet, where he conducted business with California Indians, such as the Hupa and the Pomo, and with immigrant travelers. As would be the case with William Leidesdorff's waterfront warehouse in San Francisco, Beckwourth's trading post featured a year-round supply of commodities, including suet, lard, furs, and jerked beef.

While Beckwourth had a fleeting interest in finding gold, his greatest love was for hunting and exploring. Up and down the Sierra Nevada he roved, exploring each stream and valley. He drifted south a hundred miles and crossed the mountains, roaming the lengths of the great California valleys. Eventually he found the mining community of Bidwells Bar.

At Bidwells Bar his keen sense of direction and geography told him he was immediately westward and below his Sierra Valley ranch. Upon returning to his trading post from a southern route Beckwourth explored the area to the west, and in so doing discovered a route he believed could be developed into a new, faster, and much less perilous pass through the Sierra Nevada—one which would save many miles and hazards for westbound wagon trains.

Beckwourth discussed the possibility of establishing a new route with an American Valley rancher, Mr. Turner, who encouraged him to do so.

Full of enthusiasm, James Beckwourth moved westward through the newly discovered pass and emerged at Bidwells Bar. This was in the spring of 1850, and excitement about the gold craze was at its peak.

Miners and citizens of the area applauded loudly when Beckwourth explained his plan for establishing a new route. In Marysville, also, Beckwourth's plan was met with enthusiasm, and rightfully so, for Marysville would benefit far more than any other if all westward traffic arrived in this city at the end of the road.

Marysville's mayor, Dr. S. M. Miles, and the city council met with Beckwourth and agreed verbally to pay for such a route if he would chart and help build it. An amount of $10,000 was offered.

Although hesitant to do so without a written contract, Beckwourth received added assurance from the mayor concerning reimbursement. So, using his own funds ($1,600) and $200 provided by Mr. Turner, Beckwourth charted and opened the pass. It was ready for travel in the spring of 1851, and Beckwourth traveled to Truckee to personally lead a wagon train northward to his Sierra Valley ranch, then westward through his pass. A wagon train of seventeen Conestogas followed the African–American pioneer down his pass and safely to Marysville.

Incorrectly called *Beckworth* Pass for several decades, the route through the Sierra Nevada was, at the insistence of the California Historical Society, officially renamed *Beckwourth* Pass in 1950 by the United States Board of Geographic Names. Beckwourth Pass is today's Sierra Valley route of the Pacific Railroad and U.S. Highway 70.

A new northern route had been established and Beckwourth had been assured of payment and reimbursement. Payment, however, was not to be. As a result of a fire that had nearly destroyed Marysville, the mayor and his council informed Beckwourth they could not pay. It is of record in the minutes of the counsel, September 1, 1851, May 9, 1853, and January 1856, that Beckwourth attempted to collect again and again by petition. Eventually he was informed, in 1856, that his business transaction and agreement of payment had been with members of the City Council and management of 1851, and that those persons were no longer in office.

James Beckwourth, it seems, was given a lesson in the ways of the white politician.

★   ★   ★

After establishing a trading post in the Sierra Valley, after charting and building a new, faster, and much less perilous route through the Sierra Nevada (in what is now Plumas and Lassen counties), James P. Beckwourth, his thirst for adventure far from quenched, moon-lighted as a pony express mail carrier, racing the letter-filled leather pouches between Monterey and southern California. Leaving his Sierra Valley enterprise in the care of Hupa and Pomo Indians, among whom he had earned much trust and admiration, this in-trepid African–American galloped his ponies through the very heart of California's bandit country, all but daring confrontation with the likes of Tiburcio Vasquez, Charles E. Bolton (Black Bart), and rov-ing bands of hostile Indians. His reputation, however, had preceded him. On not one trip was the bold and courageous James Beckwourth challenged by outlaws or renegade Indians. He did not miss a scheduled trip, he was never late, and he lost not one single piece of mail during his service with the pony express.

Beckwourth, who served as a scout for the Army between Missouri and California, was also a marrying man, known to have had eight wives during his life, some on the frontier and others in more civilized areas. He spoke often of two sons among the Crows, "Black Panther" and another he referred to as "Little Jim."

Ultimately, in the latter years of his life, Beckwourth returned to the New Mexico-Colorado region to rejoin his old friends and hunting companions—the Crows. His return brought great rejoicing and feasting, and it is at this point that legend takes over to complete the last chapter in the life of this great African-American scout, trapper, mountain man and Indian chief.

Beckwourth's death, in 1867, was due to poisoning. He was sixty-nine years old. It is believed by most people that the poison was administered by his Crow brothers. During earlier years, when Medicine Calf was a chief, the Crows had reigned victorius. After his departure troublesome times followed. Crow warriors decided—so the legend goes—that this time he would remain. He did. Medicine Calf, James P. Beckwourth, was buried in the soil of the primitive wilderness he had admired so much.

Beckwourth's influence upon the early history of the Golden State overshadows even his dramatic, colorful adventures. He was a pioneering pathfinder whose descriptions of the terrain he crossed constituted a unique and valuable contribution to the development of overland communications. As a direct result of his pioneering leadership, James P. Beckwourth, offspring of an African slave, is entitled to the credit for the opening of California's Sierra Valley. Unfortunately he left little in writing, and the complete record of Beckwourth's life can never be written;[1] but even the scraps that have been pieced together mark this African-American as one of the significant contributors in the overland movement to California. Without him, without his undaunted courage and dogged determination, northern California might have remained dormant and undeveloped behind the foreboding Sierra Nevada for perhaps another generation.

★   ★   ★

---

[1]Beckwourth's experiences were told "from his own dictation" by T. D. Bonner in a book entitled *Life and Adventures* (1856).

Beckwourth was but one of many African-American pioneers and trailblazers. Jacob Dodson, who had been born a slave in Virginia, was a scout for John Fremont on his first expedition into California in 1842. This black man's own tenacity, tempered with a sobriety unusual among mountain men, had earned him much respect among the early pioneers. The mulatto Salem Dean was a member of the Fremont party that trapped on the Gila River in 1826. Another visitor to California was Isaac Bridges, an Ashanti descendant who was noted for his outstanding horsemanship. Other African-American figures among the trappers, scouts and mountain men were Walker Crabb, James Rolle, Parker Hill and Richard Henry. Each in his own way helped expand American and African-American influence in the West. They earned the right to share the acclaim accorded to this country's great frontiersmen, and deserve to be applauded for their outstanding contributions.

CHAPTER IV

# The Gold Rush and African-Americans

EXCEPT FOR CALIFORNIA'S INTERLUDE OF *KNOW-NOTHINGISM*, THE
state's voting record has been Democratic since its admission to the
Union on September 9, 1850. In spite of the influence of the Southern Democrats, however, its constitutional convention had determined that California was to be a non-slave state.

> Antonio M. Pico, a tolerant, well-educated African descend-
> ant, was a member of the Constitutional Convention of 1849.
> He was a vocal force in helping to determine that California
> would enter the Union as a free state.

Even before the discovery of gold at Sutter's Fort, anti-slavery
leaders frequently claimed that local conditions made slavery in California unlikely to succeed as a social system. Relatively few African
slaves had been freighted to California from the South. There were,
however, countless Africans and persons of African ancestry in the
original California pueblos and, later, black pioneers and frontiersmen.

Then came the Gold Rush.

Hundreds of Southern slave owners, who, like thousands of other Americans and foreigners, were stricken with gold fever in 1848 brought their slaves with them in the helter-skelter rush to California's gold fields.

> Southern slave owners reintroduced "men and women of color" to the expanding California scene and by 1850 census takers who took their assignments seriously counted more than 1,000 new black residents in the Golden State, with most of them in the Sacramento and San Francisco areas.

In the spring of 1850 the *Daily Alta* of San Francisco stated that in their opinion most forty-niner Negroes had become free. The 1850 census supported this view, of course, since slavery was declared illegal in the 1849 state constitution and there was no provision for enumerating slaves on the census forms.

The fact, however, of a significant number of black people in a slave condition in a state that had excluded the barbaric practice provided the foundation for the beginning of what can rightfully be called African–American rights struggles in the Golden State.

> From the very beginning Anglo-Americans in California were intent upon preventing black people from entering the state and prohibiting black Californians from exercising their rights. At the 1849 constitutional convention in Monterey delegates spent more time debating whether to exclude black migrants from the state than on any other topic.

Had every black person who came to California with the promise of freedom been granted that freedom and had every slave who came to the state without freedom commitments not had any freedom thoughts of his or her own, there would not be any story. But slave owners did break their promises, and slaves did decide to strike for freedom in Gold Rush California.

★   ★   ★

The Southern slave owners who made the journey overland by wagon faced a number of incredible struggles, due largely in part to their own ineptness and lack of common sense. Bad luck and poor judgment plagued many of the parties, although some of the participants, such as a 32-year-old black woman named Biddy Mason, displayed incredible courage and endurance.

The Southerners came, too, by horse and by ship, all hoping to harvest fortunes in gold from rivers and hills through the forced labor of their slaves. These Southerners found it simply unthinkable that they should dig for gold themselves, believing that such efforts would reduce them to the status of white trash who worked for a living by their own two hands. En route to the Mother Lode and after they arrived, the African slaves were compelled to labor as servants, miners, cooks and barbers not only for their white owners but also for employers who bought their services from slave merchants.

In California, however, the newly arriving white migrants ran headlong into a different breed of black.

★   ★   ★

On a September day in 1848 a black man was walking near the San Francisco docks, when a white man who had just disembarked from a ship called to him to carry his luggage. The black man cast him an indignant glance and walked away. After he had gone a few steps, he turned around and, drawing a small bag from his pocket, he said, "Do you think I'll stoop to lugging trunks when I can get that much in one day?" The sack of gold dust that the black man displayed was estimated by the white man to be worth more than one hundred dollars.

By December 1848, this story had found its way into the newspapers of New York City and New Bedford, Massachusetts, where there were large, well-organized, and highly literate free black communities. It was read by black people to whom the notion of travel on the high seas and to far-away places was neither strange nor frightening, for many of them were seamen or had seafaring men in their families. The pull of the West for African-Americans was strong and could only have been intensified when, in January 1849, a New York newspaper reprinted a letter, written by an army officer stationed in California, in which he said, "The merest Negro could make more than our present governor."

Through reports like this the California gold fever spread throughout the nation and gripped black people as well as white. The fever was sustained through 1849 and 1850 by the continued enticing press reports that reached the free black communities of the North. Even the abolitionist press, normally negative about the

West, carried stories of lucky strikes by black people in the mines. Frederick Douglass reinforced the impression of black luck with gold when he reprinted in his *North Star* a letter written by a Southerner that stated, "The whole country . . . is filled with gold," and that "there are but three classes of individuals that can even work these mines, the Negro, Indian and Irish."

**The white miner's fear of the black man was heightened by a widely held belief that blacks had some mysterious power to detect gold.**

California became irresistible for many African-Americans when the anti-slavery press noted that groups of black men were already there in the early phases of the gold rush and to all appearances were surviving successfully. Early in 1850, the anti-slavery *Liberator* published a letter from San Francisco sent by thirty-seven black men in which they announced the organization of the Mutual Benefit and Relief Society. They noted that the mutual-aid society was not just for themselves, but also for newcomers. Their letter reported that they were earning from $100 to $300 a day. In the Eastern newspapers black people read glowing accounts of success in the Mother Lode and such hopeful remarks as, "There are no gentlemen here. Labor rules Capital. A darkey is just as good as a polished gentleman and can make more money."

New York African-Americans who were considering going to the Golden State might have been encouraged by the public notice that preparing to sail for the gold fields was an all-black mining company, whose members included several who were well known and politically prominent. Among them were Jonas H. Townsend, a journalist, and Newport Henry, a well-known employee of the business firm of the anti-slavery Tappan brothers. This group, which left New York in November 1849, was in turn undoubtedly encouraged by a story in the *New York Tribune* reporting the gold-hunting success of a black man, Reuben Ruby, a familiar name to them and to anti-slavery circles in general. Ruby, of Portland, Maine, a friend of white abolitionist William Lloyd Garrison and supporter of the first black newspaper, *Freedom's Journal,* raced from Maine to New York in time to catch a ship to Panama and arrive in California in 1849. By April, Ruby had acquired $1,600 from four weeks' digging of the Stanislaus River.

There is irony in the probability that more than a few Americans followed the American Dream because as ex-slaves they had to flee the slave hunter. New England and upper New York State had a considerable number of black residents who had fled slavery in the South and lived for many years in comparative security until the passage of the Fugitive Slave Law of 1850. Countless Northern blacks who now felt threatened went to Canada. Many, however, had second thoughts, and soon were on their way to the Golden State.

> Racial lines had been ignored before California became American territory, but customs changed rapidly once the United States assumed control.

The greatest resentment toward black people—slave or free—came from the mining districts. In fact, at the 1849 constitutional convention most of the petitions favoring black exclusion from the Golden State came from the mining regions. One delegate from a mining area claimed that whites would not dig alongside black men, claiming the white men "would leave this country first."

Delegate McCarver, who introduced the exclusion resolution at the convention, insisted "an evil so enormous" as migrating black people would see "idle, thriftless, free Negroes thrown into the state." Another delegate warned that "you will find the country flooded with a population of free Negroes—the greatest calamity that could befall California." And still another delegate prophesied "a black tide over the land—greater than the locusts of Egypt."

Before the delegates left Monterey, they decreed that black men could not testify in court, vote in elections, own property, use public facilities equally, serve in the militia, or exercise their voice in the education of their children—all of which laid the foundation for further discriminatory acts by the incoming white government.

> Black people were excluded from the Homestead Act, which entitled white settlers to 160 acres or more of public agricultural land after working it for five years. Further, if a white settler wanted the public agricultural land that a black settler had cultivated, all he had to do was to claim it. The black settler had no recourse for he was denied the right to bring suit or to testify in court.

The free black settler's right to remain in California after it became a state was even challenged by its first governor, Peter Burnett, in his first message at the first meeting of the legislature: "That this class Negroes is increasing in our State is very certain," said Burnett. "If increase is permitted to continue for some years to come, we may readily anticipate what will then be the state of things here, from what we see now occurring in some of the free states. We shall have our people divided and distracted."

Following the governor's message, a bill was introduced in the state senate which would prohibit free African-Americans from coming into California. The bill attempted to justify the exclusion of black people by claiming (1) they were an inferior race; (2) their labor would degrade legitimate work; (3) they would be exploited by monopolies and social inequalities; (4) they would constitute a vicious and disorderly element in the community; and (5) they would increase the tax burden. (These arguments have a familiar contemporary ring, for there is still a large school of thought that holds to these ignorant convictions and they work overtime in trying to convert others to their belief.)

★　★　★

For white Californians, particularly white miners, the slavery question was not an academic one. In 1850 Thomas Green and several other Texas slaveholders arrived in California with fifteen slaves. No sooner had they staked out claims at Rose's Bar than the white miners called a protest meeting. These bigoted whites resolved "no slave or negro should own claims or even work in the mines." A second protest meeting informed the Texans that unless the slaves left, they would be forcibly kicked out. The outnumbered Texans left. White prospectors, explained traveler Walter Colton, were not concerned with "slavery in the abstract or as it exists in other communities; they must themselves swing the pick, and they won't swing it by the side of negro slaves."

Despite this atmosphere of white hatred, threats, and discrimination, African-Americans, slave and free, continued their migration to the Golden State.

### Diary of a Black Forty-niner

I started from St. Louis, Missouri, on the 2nd of April in 1849. There was quite a crowd of neighbors who drove through the mud and rain to St. Joe to see us off. About the first of May we organized the train. There were twenty wagons in number and from three to five men to each wagon. . .

We got across the plains to Fort Larimie, the 16th of June and the ignorant driver broke down a good many oxen on the trains. There were a good many ahead of us, who had doubled up their trains and left tons upon tons of bacon and other provisions. . .

Starting to cross the desert to Black Rock at 4 o'clock in the evening, we traveled all night. The next day it was hot and sandy . . .

A great number of cattle perished before we got to Black Rock. . . I drove our oxen all the time and I knew about how much an ox could stand. Between nine and ten o'clock a breeze came up and the oxen threw up their heads and seemed to have a new life. At noon we drove into Black Rock. . .

We crossed the South Pass on the Fourth of July. The ice next morning was as thick as a dinner-plate. . .

On the morning of the 15th (of October) we went to dry-digging mining. We dug and dug to the first of November, at night it commenced raining, and rained and snowed pretty much all the winter. We had a tent but it barely kept us all dry. There were from eight to twelve in one camp. We cut down pine trees for stakes to make a cabin. It was a whole week before we had a cabin to keep us dry.

—Alvin Coffey

The plains took their toll of the many black men and women, free and slave, who came by the overland route into the Golden State. In 1849 the dread cholera from Europe competed with the gold rush for the attention of the migrants. In fact, the gold rush facilitated the spread of the disease. Slaves had no choice but to expose themselves to the disease when ordered by their owners to attend to cholera victims lying along the trail. As George Mifflin Harker wrote:

An emigrant who falls sick, unless he has some personal friends, receives scarcely any attention . . . otherwise, he is left to die, gazing on vacancy, after having swallowed a quart or so of medicine, received from the hands of some Negro servant."

The most common relationship of black man to white man, in the meandering stream of human beings headed west on the overland routes, was that of servant, laborer, or slave. There were, however, interesting and notable exceptions to this relationship. At least three men of African ancestry were guides for overland parties. In 1849, a Virginia company employed an African-American guide to cross the plains. Forty-niner Edmund Green from Michigan recalled that on his way to Fort Hall, after leaving the place of famed mountain

man Peg Leg Smith, his party encountered a black man hunting
horses who was thoroughly familiar with this part of the country
and could speak the Indian language. He accepted employment with
Green's company to take them as far as Fort Hall. For Ina Coolbrith,
who later became a San Francisco poet, it was a matter of safe guidance across the treacherous Sierras. James P. Beckwourth took the
company with which Miss Coolbrith's family traveled across the
mountains in 1851. She recalled, years later, that she sat with him
on his horse on this trek. In 1852 Beckwourth assisted a Virginian
and his group who were probing their way through the eastern slope
of the Sierra Nevada to the gold fields.

M. Durivage, gold rush correspondent for the *New Orleans Pica-
yune,* who ordinarily reported the presence of black people to his
newspaper only in a derogatory way, thought at one point on the
westward trail that he was dying of thirst. It was his own black
servant who brought him water at a crucial moment. In Durivage's
words, "A mile ahead was my black servant, Isaac, on horseback
rushing toward us at a headlong gallop. Spite his black hide he
looked like an angel."

Others were not so fortunate, despite the heroic intentions of
African-Americans. According to historian Bayard Taylor, a sick
white man was moving along so slowly on the trail that he was
arriving at the company camp a little later each day. Finally, three
days passed and he failed to appear in camp at all. But on that third
day, a black man traveling by himself came into camp to report to
the company that their ailing companion was unable to move. He
had begged the black man for water and asked him to bring help
from the company. The members of the company did not act. The
next morning a group of Mexicans came along and reported that
the man was dying. Still his companions made no move to assist
him. It was then that the black man

> retraced his steps forty miles and arrived just as the sufferer
> breathed his last. He lifted him in his arms; in the vain effort
> to speak, the man expired. The mule, tied to a cactus by his
> side, was already dead of hunger.

A picture commemorating such a scene, and the unselfishly heroic
humanity of the African-American, would better adorn a panel of
the Capitol, than any battle piece that was ever painted.

Another African-American, one with a daring spirit, is credited with saving the lives of many gold seekers stranded in the Humboldt Sink, which was the last area to be crossed before ascending the Sierra Nevada. During the summer of 1850, it became known that hundreds were immobilized, sick, and starving in the Sink. When Captain William Waldo, a Sacramento resident, issued a call for a volunteer party, only a very few responded. Among the few, however, was a fearless African-American named Ed Louis, an expert with horses. With Waldo and a handful of white men, Louis traveled about 250 miles through the mountains and desert to reach the Humboldt Sink. They were appalled at the distress they found. Captain Waldo calculated the emergency needs of the stranded travelers and it was Ed Louis who rode the 250 miles "express" to deliver the message to the people of Sacramento—and to return with the life-saving supplies.

★   ★   ★

As hundreds of black people were crossing the expanse of the United States toward California in the early years of the gold rush, as many and perhaps more were taking the water route to the same destination.

Among the first to go by water was an African-American named Jackson, who would later be well known in the San Francisco area for his culinary accomplishments. He served as a cook for the first company that went to California by way of Nicaragua. Late in November 1849, the *New York Tribune* observed that the first of the future black leadership of California was on its way. The notice read:

Some merchants of this city have formed an association of colored men for the purpose of mining in California. The company consists of ten men, and is composed of the most intelligent and respectable colored men of our city.

More of the future black leadership were on their way to California by the Panama route the next year. While in New York, Mifflin Wistar Gibbs, a Philadelphian, caught the California fever. He had just returned from a lecture tour with Frederick Douglass when he made his decision.

Fortune . . . may sometimes smile on the inert, but she seldom fails to surrender to pluck, tenacity and perseverance.
—Mifflin Wistar Gibbs

In his recollections, Gibbs noted that he managed the trip on the

*Golden Gate* from New York to Panama with "some friendly assist-ance." Gibbs' comment hints at the probability that some black men and women of limited means but unlimited courage came to Califor-nia with the informal assistance of black crewmen or anti-slavery members of ship management. In the same year that Gibbs departed, Daniel Seals and Edward Johnson, both of whom were destined to become active in state-wide black activities, left New York on the *Empire City* for California via Panama. And there were others that year. William M. Chapman, a white passenger on the ship *Ohio* leaving New York for Panama, noted several black passengers on board.

The family of Edward Booth, who was also to become an Afri-can-American leader in California, had its own special set of diffi-culties in joining the black migration to the West. The four brothers and two sisters, led by Edward, the eldest, left Baltimore, the city of their birth, where they had always been free persons. Their depar-ture was briefly delayed by the demand of the state authorities that the Booths prove they were free. They finally arrived in New York, where they took passage to Panama. After a difficult journey across the isthmus and a three-week wait for their ship in Panama City, they found that more tickets had been sold than there was ship space. But Edward Booth, who had been a West Indies businessman, discovered that the ship's captain was an old acquaintance of his, and passage was arranged for himself and his sisters. The three remaining Booths found passage on another ship arriving in San Francisco many weeks later. Edward had alerted all African-Americans who worked on the boats in San Francisco Bay to watch for his family, and they were eventually reunited in Sacramento.

Another who came to California by the Panama route was Abner H. Francis of Buffalo, New York, a black man with a long career as an anti-slavery activist. A series of articles that Francis wrote for *Frederick Douglass' Paper* described his impressions of this travel experience. He revealed mixed feelings about the people he observed in Central America: "I would not want to take up my abode among them for all that they possess, although it was gratifying to see colored men in authority." Still he reported no overt racist insults in the course of his journey. Others were not so fortunate.

For one black man the rigors of the trip were accentuated by a racist crew member. On board the *Oregon,* leaving Panama for San Francisco, a black man was sitting alone by the rail enjoying the sea air, when a white fireman, who had just come up from below, attempted to eject him from his seat. The black man refused to give up his place. The fireman then went below and brought up a shovel-ful of hot ashes and threw them into the black man's face, where-upon, to the delight of some onlookers, the black man proceeded to beat his aggressor soundly. When other firemen came up and at-tempted to assist the aggressor, a number of whites and blacks inter-ceded and told the firemen, "if they offered to do the Negro any more vengeance they would butcher the offender like a bullock."

Many African-Americans of humbler stations, whose lives in the Golden State would receive less notice, also came west by the Pan-ama route. Scores, perhaps hundreds, of white Southerners in the early years of the gold rush came to California with their slaves by this route.

The natural hazards of the Panama route were the same for blacks and whites, and many died on the way. For some black people, however, there was an additional human hazard. As the cash value of the American black slave became apparent to the natives, robber bands on the isthmus went into the business of kidnapping slaves to resell in South America.

## Freedom Papers

Many African-Americans, as slaves, headed for California with the promise of freedom echoing in their ears, having been told by their owners at the outset of the perilous journey westward that they would be set free if they dug enough gold. Although this promise was in most instances a ruse to elicit the slave's cooperation during the dangerous journey, there are some cases of slave owners who actually did allow their slaves to buy freedom in the Golden State, as attested by the records of Peter Green, Dennis Aviery, and Negro Bob.

State of California
County of Mariposa

Know all men to whom these presents shall come that I, Thomas Thorn, of the State and County aforesaid, being the rightful owner of the Negro man, Peter Green, and entitled to his services as a slave during his life, have this day released and do by these presents release him from any further services as a slave.

And I do by these presents for myself, my heirs, executors and administrators declare him, the said Peter Green, to be free to act for himself and no longer under bonds as a slave. Provided, however, that said Peter Green shall pay me the sum of one thousand dollars, good and lawful money or work for the service, from the present time until the first day of April, A.D. 1854.

In testimony whereof, I have hereunto affixed my hand and scroll for seal, at Quartzburg, this 5th day of February, A.D., one thousand eight hundred and fifty-three.

—Thomas Thorn

In the case of Dennis Aviery, the record is not so loquacious.

To All Whom It May Concern:

This is to certify that Dennis Aviery has been my slave in the State of Georgia for about the term of eight years, but by virtue of money to me in hand paid, he is free and liberated from all allegiance to my authority.

—E. H. Taylor

Coloma, El Dorado County, Calif.

February 8, 1851

In the case of Negro Bob, the record is repugnant.

Taylor Barton to Negro Bob:

Know all men to whom these presents shall come: I, Taylor Barton, lately a citizen of the State of Missouri, and owner of slaves, do here by this instrument, under my hand and seal, given this ninth day of October, in the year of our Lord eighteen hundred and fifty-one, set Free from Bondage to me and all men, my slave Bob, and do declare him forever hereafter his own man, wherever he may go. Nevertheless, I make this condition, that said Bob shall remain with me as my slave, faithful and obedient to me, until the twenty-fifth day of December next, commonly known as Christmas.

Witness my hand and seal on the day and date aforesaid.

—Taylor Barton

Since money was not mentioned in the repugnant Barton-Negro Bob transaction, it has been presumed that Barton gave Negro Bob his freedom as a Christmas present.

★  ★  ★

The promise of freedom, however, as discovered by Alvin Coffey, was all too often broken. Born a slave in Missouri, Coffey used the gold dust he mined in the High Sierra to purchase his freedom, as he had been promised, from his Southern master. He had to pay one thousand dollars for his own manumission and equal amounts to free several members of his family in the Show Me State. After accepting his hard earned money, Coffey's Missouri master took him back to St. Louis and sold him to a new owner. In 1854, Alvin Coffey, duped and re-enslaved, returned to the California gold mines; after several more years of hard back-breaking labor, he earned another seven thousand dollars, with which he bought freedom (again) for himself, his wife, and three children. By 1860 the Coffeys were prosperous and respected residents of Tehama County.

More than a few slaves decided not to pay for their freedom, choosing instead to just simply declare themselves free. They took this bold course after coming in contact with California's native African descendants, all of whom were quick to inform the newly arriving black people that California was a free state in which no man could hold another in bondage. As to be expected, however, a slave's declaration of freedom was seldom greeted with favor by the Southern slave masters.

In San Jose, for instance, in February 1850, a white man beating a black man with a club on a public street caused several people in a crowd of spectators to shout insults—at the white man. The town marshall took both parties into custody for a hearing before the *alcalde*. To the dismay of San Jose citizens, a great many of whom were African or of African ancestry, the *alcalde* ruled in favor of the white man, telling lawyers for both parties that the black man was a slave and that the white man was the rightful owner. One of the spectators, however, suggested to other local authorities that the slave be allowed to leave San Jose with him, reminding them that California was a free state. The authorities agreed, and as lawyers sympathetic to the slave prepared to have a writ served on the *alcalde*, the black man was spirited away from San Jose by the one man with whom authorities dared not disagree—a pony express mail carrier by the name of James P. Beckwourth.

In Sacramento a few months later a similar incident became a matter for court attention after a street brawl between a white man and a black man named Charles. Intervention by Beckwourth would not be needed. The judge in this fugitive slave case set the black man free. He told the presumed master that laws passed before as well as after the American conquest of California had made Charles a free man.

In March 1851, another slave master invoked the National Fugitive Slave Law to jail a black man named Frank in the city of San Francisco. The white man claimed that Frank had run away from him in the Sierra and said he had tracked his "property" to San Francisco because he wanted to take him back to Missouri. A lawyer, S. W. Holliday, heard about the case and submitted a writ demanding that Frank be set free. The judge in this case, Judge Morrison, deliberated the matter for a few days and finally ruled in favor of Frank. Judge Morrison held that the National Fugitive Slave Law was not applicable in Frank's case because he had come to California as a slave, not as a fugitive. The judge pointed out that Frank ran away within the boundaries of the state and held that his escape was not a violation of California law, although it would have been a jail offense (or worse) in Missouri.

Judge Morrison also had a sardonic sense of humor, for in his decision he poured a bit of salt on the wounded feelings of proslavery listeners. It seems that in the course of interrogation Frank had stated that he had been a slave in Missouri. The judge calmly rejected this bit of testimony "because the California state legislature had only the year before made African-American testimony illegal in civil and criminal cases. (This case was probably notable in another way. It appears as if the black community of San Francisco was noticeably involved in its outcome, which indicates it may have been the first stimulus to active organization.)

It soon became apparent that slave owners who were tarrying too long in California were in danger of losing their "property." If the word got around, Judge Morrison's court could have become quite busy.

In the first month of 1852 a champion for the slave owner emerged. He was Assemblyman Henry A. Crabb, a Southern aristocrat, who gained a tragic fame a few years later by losing his life in a Sonoran filibustering adventure. Crabb introduced a fugitive slave bill in January 1852 that gave white men arbitrary powers in returning blacks whom they claimed as slaves in Southern states. Assemblyman Ellis of San Francisco believed that a portion of this bill was written in such a way as to allow slavery to establish itself in California through the back door. Crabb's bill did not sharply define any limits on how long a slave owner might remain in California with his slaves. Ellis' amending proposals were rejected. When the unchanged bill reached the Senate, it faced formidable opposition. Here David Broderick voiced his apprehensions. He feared that the bill did nothing to protect African-Americans who came to California with the promise of freedom from a callously capricious former owner or from white men with the morals of a kidnapper. Through much of April 1852, the Senate debated the bill with Broderick gaining strong but not quite sufficient support. The bill was passed 14 to 9 with Broderick in the minority.

It was not too long before Broderick's fears were realized. In April of the following year the first publicly noted attempt to return a free black girl to slavery was reported in the *Daily Alta*. The attempt took place in Auburn, California, but a local lawyer was the custodian of the young woman's freedom papers and could produce them in court. The claimant was the son of the man who had freed the girl, and he professed not to know of his father's action.

> Of equal, if not greater, importance to white support was the sturdiness of African-American organizations and their determination to act. A German observer noted that wealthy California blacks had become "especially talented" in stealing slaves to freedom. He added that they "exhibit a great deal of energy and intelligence in saving their brothers."

It was inevitable, of course, that the constitutionality of Crabb's Fugitive Slave Act would be tested. The opportunity arose in what is called the *Perkins Case*. A Mississippian named Perkins claimed through agents that three African-Americans working in Placer County, two of them bearing the name Perkins, were his fugitive property. A justice of the peace and then a county judge gave the three black men to Perkins' agents, but a battery of legal talent managed to temporarily rescue the three African-Americans from a ship that was about to leave San Francisco. The case was brought directly to the California State Supreme Court. To the dismay of many Californians, the proslave court upheld the entire California Fugitive Slave Law. It even upheld the section of the law that corroded the genuinely free African-American's right to maintain his or her freedom. In essence, the California State Supreme Court ruled that blacks brought into California before the advent of statehood could be reclaimed and returned to slave states. In several instances, however, slaves brought into California before its ban against slavery became effective were given their freedom by Southern owners who wished to remain legally in the state.

As a result, a number of African-Americans succeeded in striking it rich during the Gold Rush.

CHAPTER V

# The Fight for Rights and Riches

MINING GOLD IN CALIFORNIA DID NOT HOLD THE SAME ATTRACTION FOR African-Americans that it did for whites. Black men saw this difficult, often deadly, venture as a chance to buy their freedom more swiftly than they might back home. Unknown numbers of these men were in the hordes that crossed the plains and thronged the routes across Central America. Some left wives and children behind as hostages and departed for the gold fields with the approval of their owners, from whom they hoped to purchase their liberty. Others who were already free hoped to buy freedom for their families. A white Ohio forty-niner wrote in his journal, as he was on his way across the plains, "I saw a colored man going to the land of gold prompted by the hope of redeeming his wife and seven children. Success to him. His name is James Taylor." When this Ohioan reached the mines at Ophir (present-day Oroville) he met more African-Americans in the same position. One of them, a Texan, hoped to buy his wife and children and move to New York or Massachusetts. Jessie Benton Fremont recalled that on her first trip to California to meet her husband, John C. Fremont, she met a free black man

67

en route who was hoping to attain the means of purchasing his family's freedom.

★  ★  ★

The precise status of the black miner in California is not clear to present-day historians. State and local authorities rarely interfered with the practice of slavery, although it was prohibited by state law and had been illegal under the laws of Spain and Mexico for nineteen years before California was admitted to statehood. In most mining camps the miners had laws of their own.

**Where law reached, it did so with the rope of the vigilante committees, separating "guilty" from "innocent" with little attention to evidence.**

Generally, miners refused to allow a man to hire or control another man's labor because the use of hired workers or slaves gave those who employed such tactics a distinct advantage over competitors who did not. And, men like James P. Beckwourth stood readily available to help enforce fairness. Some slave owners, however, skirted this prohibition by either congregating together in certain camps or by making it appear that their slaves were individual miners working their own claims.

Although early photographs and diaries indicate that individual black miners were welcome in some areas throughout the course of the mining period, the general tendency of white miners was to drive non-whites away—particularly from the desirable locations. Try as they did, however, white miners and claim jumpers failed in their attempts to drive Fritz Vosburg, Abraham Holland, Gabriel Simms, and several other black miners away from their Sweet Vengeance mine in Brown's Valley. One such attempt was described by African-American reporters Robert Purvis and William Wells Brown, writing for the *Libertor:*

> Shortly after our arrival, a perfectly deafening volley of shouts and yells elicited from Mr. Purvis the careless remark that "the Sabbath-day's fight is apparently more serious than usual!" Almost as he spoke there succeeded a death-like silence, broken in a minute by a deep groan, at the base of the long tom followed by the words, "My God, he stabbed me!" Mr. Gabriel Simms gave an excited account of what had happened. He said that in a melee between Fritz Vosburg and a gang of white claim jumpers, Vosburg—who is a tall, majestic-look-

ing Negro—had stabbed the leader of the claim jumpers and at the very moment, said Mr. Simms—with Abraham Holland at his side, and brandishing threateningly the long knife with which he had inflicted the wound upon the leader, was parading up and down the long tom unmolested. It seems that when the white leader fell, the other would-be claim jumpers, not prepared for such a staunch defense, were seized with a sudden panic and fled.

Despite continued attacks by would-be claim jumpers, the Sweet Vengeance mine remained in operation throughout the entire gold mining period (1848–1854), and reaped notable profits during 1852, when gold worth $81,294,700 was taken out of California's mines. A portion of the Vosburg-Holland-Simms journal indicates that the Sweet Vengeance was especially profitable during a three-week period in April–May 1852:

The week ending April 24. It is rich dirt.[1] We have taken $1200.

The week ending May 8. Take is $956.

The week ending May 15. The dirt again is rich. We have taken $1142.

★ ★ ★

Like Vosburg, Holland, and Simms, countless black men combined endurance and perseverance to achieve financial success in the Golden State. Reverend Barney Fletcher, for instance, gained his freedom in Maryland and then went to Sacramento, where he mined enough gold to purchase freedom for his wife and children. While in that city, he founded its first black Methodist church. James R. Starkey, for many years one of the most active leaders of San Francisco's African-American community, reached California in 1853, after buying his freedom in North Carolina. He worked the Cosumne diggings to buy his son and daughter. (Starkey did not immediately succeed. The white man who owned the children went bankrupt in Maryland, and sold the boy and girl to slave traders. Not until the Civil War was over did James Starkey finally track down and free his children, and that was accomplished through advertisements in the African-American press.)

---

[1] "Dirt" was the word universally used in California to signify the substance dug—earth, clay, gravel, loose slate, or whatever other name might be more appropriate. Black miners talked of rich dirt and poor dirt, and of "stripping off" so many feet of "top dirt" before getting to "pay dirt," the latter meaning dirt with so much gold in it that it would pay to dig it up and wash it.

A combination of events made Samuel Burris decide to head for the California gold mines. A free black and a native of the slave state of Delaware, he was actively involved in the work of the Underground Railroad there. After moving with his family to the Philadelphia area to take up farming, he remained active in underground work and occasionally returned to Delaware to aid escaping slaves. It was during one of these dangerous trips that Burris was caught by authorities. The Delaware court ordered him sold into slavery for seven years. The method of sale was the auction block in Dover. But Burris' long years of work with abolitionists, black and white, resulted in his own rescue. A Southerner who was known privately to be an abolitionist was solicited by the underground movement to bid for Burris at the auction with funds they supplied to him. In a tense bidding scene, the Southern abolitionist bought Burris. It was only then that Burris learned he had been "purchased" by friends. He quickly hurried off to his home near Philadelphia. While he was again a free man, the efforts of friends and family to raise the funds necessary for this project left Burris without his farm and penniless. Finding that he could not make a decent living any longer in the East and with the allure of gold still strong, Burris departed with his family for California in the hope of improving his economic condition. He settled in what is today the town of Strawberry and panned for gold along the Stanislaus River. Within a relatively short period of time, Burris earned enough money to relocate his family to San Francisco. (There is no evidence that Burris was involved in the civil rights activities of the 1850s, but his anti-slavery concern was again aroused during the Civil War, when he took the leadership in San Francisco of raising funds for the relief of the great numbers of runaway slaves who were flooding into Philadelphia.)

With black men came black women—and their accomplishments have for far too long been completely ignored.

★  ★  ★

In 1851 Biddy Mason, who was born a slave in Hancock County, Georgia, in 1818, crossed the plains on foot, driving a herd of sheep behind her owner's wagon. It was a westward journey of cruel conditions—particularly for Biddy, who crossed the deserts of present-day Nevada and Arizona without the benefit of a horse or wagon or mule. Herding the flock of sheep along the chalky banks of the Sevier River southward toward the Virgin River, continuing to the Colorado, and then to the desolate Mojave villages, this African-

American female proved herself capable of inconceivable endurance. In the midst of the blistering white heat of the desert by day and the chilling winds that blew by night, Biddy Mason, proud and determined, ventured across sandy alkali wastes, over part of the route today traversed by transcontinental railroads, following her owner's wagon toward the California coast.

At the age of thirty-two, and the mother of three daughters, Biddy Mason, the color of her skin approaching true black, walked, stumbled, and fell across the unforgiving Mojave Desert, surviving hunger and thirst and attacks by Indians and her owner, Robert Smith, a Georgia redneck who believed his ownership of Biddy entitled him to sexual favors, forced or not. Despite the perilous environment and criminal cruelty of her owner, Biddy Mason somehow endured the six-month journey. She was not, however, satisfied with mere survival.

Biddy's owner settled in San Bernardino and began raising cattle and sheep. Ultimately, Biddy learned that California had adopted a constitution outlawing slavery—and not long thereafter she learned that Smith was preparing to move to the slave state of Texas to avoid losing her and her daughters. While Smith was moving fast to get out of California, Biddy, with the aid of free blacks and a few sympathetic whites was moving even faster to stay. She challenged Smith in court and in 1856 was granted her freedom by Judge Benjamin Hays who declared: "All men should be left to their own pursuit of freedom and happiness." At the age of thirty-seven, Biddy Mason was a free woman. Judge Hays granted freedom to Biddy's daughters as well.

After obtaining their freedom papers, Biddy and her children moved to Los Angeles, the city built by Africans, where Biddy secured a job as a practical nurse at $2.50 a day. She worked hard, lived frugally and accumulated savings enough to buy two parcels of land (about 10 acres). She paid two hundred and fifty dollars for the land—and sold it five years later for two hundred thousand dollars. The land she had bought had become the center of the downtown business district of Los Angeles.

**Through clever investments and shrewd business transactions, Biddy Mason acquired many parcels of land. These she donated for schools, churches, and nursing homes.**

Long before she became wealthy, Biddy was a frequent visitor to the jail, reading the Bible to the prisoners, speaking a word of cheer and on occasions securing the release of certain ones. Her missionary work escalated throughout Los Angeles County and she found herself involved in securing jobs for many, feeding and clothing many who were destitute and supporting the charitable work of her church. As a most devout religious woman, Grandma Mason, as she was known in her later years, personally paid the taxes and expenses of her church.

**After a flood in the 1880s, Biddy Mason ordered a merchant to supply food to all homeless victims and to charge it to her account.**

Biddy Mason always remembered what it was like to be poor, what it was like to be oppressed, and she never forgot during her years of prosperity. On January 15, 1891, at the age of seventy-three she died, not as a slave nor as an African-American, but as the *Los Angeles Times* indicated "as a pioneer humanitarian who dedicated herself to forty years of good works."

★   ★   ★

Not all the Southerners who headed for California with their African and African-American slaves in the mid-1800s were thinking about gold in the beds and banks of the rivers and creeks, or in the flats and hollows high up in the mountains. Some, like Green Dennis, a slave trader from Mobile, Alabama, saw riches to be reaped in other ways.

Dennis set out for the Golden State with his slave, George Washington Dennis, in the summer of 1849. At New Orleans he joined a group of gamblers for the seafaring journey to San Francisco via Panama. Much to the slave trader's chagrin, he had to pay $850 for his slave's passage—a fare more than double the average. (Although New Orleans was mistress of the slave trade, many ship captains did not like to carry slaves as passengers because of the ever-present possibility of a slave mutiny.)

Dennis and his high rolling partners gambled throughout the entire journey. In one poker game Dennis put up George as a bet, and lost. The winner bet his new chattel in another game, and he too lost. In still another game Dennis won his slave back again. The party arrived in San Francisco on September 17, 1849—and it was in the city by the bay that George Washington Dennis, a man who had been born into the brutality of slavery, was to show he had more nerve and more business sense than any of the white men who had gambled with his life.

Not long after their arrival in San Francisco, Dennis and his group of gamblers established the Hotel El Dorado at Washington and Kearny streets (in the vicinity of Portsmouth Square). Elegantly decorated with plush furniture, a spacious bar, mirrors, and eight gaming tables, the El Dorado attracted the greatest crowds. George was forced to work as a porter in the gambling casino and as a manservant in the prostitution cribs maintained upstairs. George was, however, working toward a specific goal—freedom. Green Dennis, who, like the owners of Dennis Aviery and Peter Green and Negro Bob, had learned that slavery was an unpopular practice in northern California, and had offered George his freedom for $1,000—at that time the going price tag of a ticket out of slavery.

Like countless other black slaves, male and female, George Washington Dennis had accepted the offer eagerly.

In an incredibly short period of time, the enterprising Hotel El Dorado porter had saved the necessary $1,000, mostly in nickels and dimes he had swept up from the floor of the gambling casino while on the job. With the foresight of a William Leidesdorff, George saved an additional one thousand dollars and sent the money to Alabama with a white friend to buy his mother out of slavery and bring her to San Francisco.

Once his mother was free of the bonds of slavery, once they had been reunited in the city by the bay, George Washington Dennis descended upon the business world with a shrewdness equal to that of America's greatest entrepreneurs, then and now. He immediately rented a restaurant concession in the Hotel El Dorado for his mother, who inside of three weeks was averaging about two hundred dollars a day selling hot meals to the hotel guests and gamblers. George, meanwhile, accumulated $18,000 which he invested in a parcel of property on Montgomery Street. He sold this land six months later (in June 1851) for $32,000 and then bought the block bounded by Post, O'Farrell, Hyde and Larkin streets, an area today crowded with hotels and apartment buildings. Then, about the time Biddy Mason obtained the deed to more than 15,000 acres in what is present-day Pasadena, George Dennis purchased the block bounded by Post, Sutter, Scott and Divisadero streets, which is the present location of Mount Zion Hospital.

Less than two years after buying his way out of slavery, this Afri-

can–American owned appreciable amounts of choice San Francisco
property, and had established the city's very first livery stables (at
Sansome and Washington streets) and its first wood and coal yard
(on Broadway near Montgomery). George Dennis had established,
too, a "no nonsense, no deals" business reputation, which prompted
this complaint from Eastern journalist Bayard Taylor:

> You enter Mr. Dennis' place of establishment to buy something; he
> eyes you with perfect indifference, waiting for you to state what you
> want, his counter top sporting heaps of gold dust, kept in neat doeskin
> bags; if you object to the price, you are at your liberty to leave, for
> you need not expect to get it cheaper; he evidently knows you simply
> cannot buy it elsewhere.

In hindsight, slave trader Green Dennis (he gambled himself into
a debt from which he could not escape) must have realized he would
have been more prosperous if he would have come to California as
a slave owned by George Washington Dennis.

After he had attained a position of prominence in San Francisco's
business world, George Dennis married Margaret Ann Powell, a
free black girl who had traveled to San Francisco with her mother
and father from Baltimore, and together they moved into a two-
story home George built at 2507 Bush Street.

> **As was the case with virtually all other African-American
> females who journeyed to California from the East, Margaret
> Ann Powell endured terrifying ordeals and inconceivable hard-
> ship. Margaret's trek was documented by another traveler who,
> in a letter sent to the *North Star,* said he saw "the young Marga-
> ret Powell . . . tramping along through the heat and dust,
> carrying a cast iron bake stove on her head, with her provisions
> and a blanket piled on top—all she possessed in the world—
> pushing on for California."**

George and Margaret Dennis had ten children, the eldest of
whom, Edward, was to become San Francisco's very first African-
American police officer.

★   ★   ★

Not all of the slaves carted to California were willing to labor
towards freedom money. A few, like Negro Josh, allegedly sought
a quicker, albeit illegal, route to the road away from slavery. A letter

written by Mrs. Louisa Amelia Knapp Smith Clapp to her sister describes the Negro Josh incident:

August 4, 1852

We have lived through so much excitement for the last three weeks, dear M., that I almost shrink from relating the gloomy events which have marked their flight.

On Tuesday following the Sabbath, a man brought the news of the murder of a Mr. Bacon, a person well known on the river, who kept a ranch about twelve miles from Rich Bar. He was killed for his money by his servant, a negro, who not three months ago was our own cook. He was the last anybody would have suspected capable of such an act.

A party of men, appointed by the Vigilance Committee, left the Bar immediately in search of him. The miserable wretch was apprehended in Sacramento and part of the gold found on his person. On the following Sunday he was brought in chains to Rich Bar. After a trial by the miners, he was sentenced to be hung at four o'clock in the evening. All efforts to make him confess proved futile. He said, very truly, that whether innocent or guilty, they would hang him; and so he died "and made no sign," with a calm indifference.

Guilty or not, and he was denied the luxury of a trial by a jury of his peers, Negro Josh died worthy of a better cause.

★   ★   ★

California's African-American population doubled in the first three years of the Gold Rush. By 1852 two thousand new black men and women were residing in the Golden State. In spite of the apprehensions of the anti-slavery press, California had become a free state, though hardly possessed of significant, inalienable rights for black people. Nevertheless, its lure as a land of opportunity persisted. African-Americans could brush aside the reports of prejudice, hardship, and death when they heard stories such as that of William Henry Hall, a leader of New York's black community. A forty-niner, Hall returned in 1851 with so much gold that he was married in a wedding that was reported as having a "splendour" that was "without parallel in the history of coloured society in New York." New York's black community also came to hear Hall at a public meeting, where he gave an address entitled "Hopes and Prospects of Colored People in California," and his speech undoubtedly produced more California-bound black migrants from New York. Philadelphia's black citizens read in an anti-slavery paper that two African-American men returned to the East early in 1851 with thirty thousand dollars, accumulated in four months of gold mining.

Tales of business opportunities also abounded, and the hope of high wages helped attract even more black people to the Golden State.

**African-American cooks, in tremendous demand in California by 1849, were paid no less than $125 a month.**

Through 1852 and beyond the California fever persisted in many free black communities. In St. Genevieve City, Missouri, Mrs. Alley Brown, a black woman, received a letter early in 1852 from her husband, who was working the Cosumne diggings in the Golden State. He wrote, "This is the best place for black folks on the globe. All a man has to do is to work, and he will make money." Frederick Douglass noted in that year that returning black men were feeding this fever.

So strong is the excitement that it has become a question of who ought to go and who ought not to go. . . . Discretion and reasonable considerations seem to have been abandoned. Lovers hurried and married their sweethearts and left them. Young husbands have left young wives. . . . Some have returned much better off and some much worse.

—Frederick Douglass

Some who returned "better off" found the limited economic opportunities for African-Americans in the East no longer tolerable. A number of black men and women who felt this way returned to California in spite of its non-existent civil rights. These people, male and female, attained heartwarming triumphs in the Golden State, but, like Biddy Mason and George Washington Dennis, their victory over their oppressor never came easy. Their almost incredible experiences were recorded by Delilah L. Beasley in *The Negro Trail Blazers of California,* a little known book published in 1919.

Mrs. Beasley, a Zulu descendant who was fiercely proud of her race, spent nearly nine years writing her book. Among numerous carefully documented cases, she included:

**\* \* In September, 1852, Justice Shephard of San Francisco issued a warrant for the arrest of a young woman of African**

ancestry as a fugitive slave claimed by I. J. Smith of Missouri. Smith had brought the woman to the Golden State with several other slaves in 1850 and she had run away from him to marry a free black man who had been born and raised in San Jose. The slave owner swore out a warrant after he learned his missing "property" was aboard the *Flying Cloud,* a clipper ship about to sail for the Atlantic coast from San Francisco. The "fugitive" bride was arrested on the ship, turned over to Smith, and taken back into slavery.

* * An Alabamian who had brought a boy slave to California in 1849 planned to return to his native state and decided not to take the boy with him. The homesick slave owner advertised his "property" as the object of an auction sale and the boy was purchased on the block for one thousand dollars by Calib T. Fay, an ardent abolitionist, who gave the boy his freedom. (Place of sale was San Francisco.)

* * On May 23, 1850, an African-American woman named Margaret, who had been hired out to service by a white man named William Marr, was married to a free black man named Lawrence. Early the following morning, Marr, who claimed the woman as his slave, forced her at gunpoint to leave her husband and go with him. Then he placed an advertisement in the *Placer Times,* on May 27, 1850, offering to release her on payment of one thousand dollars. (Later that day, Marr, accompanied by James P. Beckwourth, returned Margaret to Lawrence. In lieu of payment of one thousand dollars, Beckwourth offered to allow Marr to leave California—alive.)

* * Slave Daniel Rogers was brought to California, via the overland route from Yell County, Arkansas, in 1849. During the day he labored in the gold mines in Sonora for his owner and then worked for himself at night, until he had earned $1,101 to buy his freedom. Soon afterward, his owner returned to Little Rock, taking Rogers with him. When Rogers expressed a desire to return to the Golden State on his own with his wife and family, the slave owner, who had not obtained formal freedom papers for Rogers, retaliated by putting him on the auction block. A group of sympathetic white men, who liked and respected Rogers and were aware of what had happened, raised a purse and bought him into freedom.

* * In 1852, Mrs. Mary Ann Israel-Ash of Sonoma County mortgaged her home and borrowed additional money to raise one thousand one hundred and one dollars demanded by a slave owner for the freedom of an entire family of slaves he was about to return to bondage in the South.

* * William Pollack and his wife came to California as slaves during the Gold Rush and settled in the Sierra town of Cold Springs with their owner from North Carolina. William washed clothes for the gold miners at night while his wife sold doughnuts to the fortune seekers day and night until they had the Carolinian's price for the freedom—one thousand dollars for him; eight hundred dollars for her. After buying their way out of slavery and obtaining Freedom Papers, the Pollacks moved to Hangtown (present-day Placerville) and founded the town's very first catering service.

★   ★   ★

Only a few months after California had become the thirty-first star on the U.S. flag, the new state flagged down prospects of freedom for the growing black population within its borders. The boisterous Legislature, reflecting its pro-slavery sentiment, enacted a law prohibiting the acceptance of African-American testimony in civil and criminal cases involving white persons. This statute was piled on top of previous anti-black legislation. One earlier law, for instance, limited militia membership to white males.

In addition to these laws, the black community had to worry through frequent legislative debates on the question of whether free blacks should be barred forever from entering the state. It was, however, the law excluding African-American witnesses from court proceedings that aroused and embittered black pioneers more than any other discriminatory act of the California Legislature. Its application had tragic consequences that spurred the San Francisco African-American community to organize the Franchise League and launch what turned out to be a lengthy campaign for the right to testify in courts of law.

## The Murder of a Black Barber

The murder of Gordon Chase in his Niantic Hotel barbershop at Bush and Sansome streets in San Francisco brought the right-to-testify issue to the fore. Chase, who had purchased his Freedom Papers with money he had earned working nights in a livery stable, was shot to death by a white man who had burst into the barbershop to demand an apology from the black barber's sister. The white man complained that Chase's sister had run after him on the street the night before, yelling, "Stop, thief! Stop, thief!" (This Chase's sister had actually done—after she had caught the white man robbing the cash box of her nearby millinery shop.)

The robber confronted Chase and demanded not only that he order his sister to take back calling him a thief, but that he be permitted to strip her and whip her with his belt. When Chase denied any knowledge of the affair the white man simply shot the barber to death as he stood next to a chair occupied by Robert Cowles, a citizen whose white skin belied his African ancestry.

The defense in the case contended that Cowles was an African descendant and demanded a medical examination to prove it—and thus prevent him from testifying against the white killer. After the examination, physicians testified that the texture of Robert Cowles' hair revealed him to be one-sixteenth African—and the murder case was thrown out of court. Six days later the non-tried white murderer, assisted by four unsavory gamblers, dragged Chase's sister from her millinery shop and tied her to a hitching post in front of the Niantic Hotel. Although she was stripped and whipped with a belt, the black girl steadfastly refused to recant her accusation.

The barbershop murder of Gordon Chase was perhaps the most flagrant of countless cases in which black people had been excluded as witnesses. Several black people, in fact, had been excluded as witnesses in defense of white defendants who wanted and needed their testimony. Finally, in the first concerted move by the first African-American rights organization in California, sixteen members of the newly formed Franchise League volunteered to go to Sacramento and lobby for repeal of the testimony law.

On May 22, 1852, members of the Franchise League finally persuaded a sympathetic legislator to present a petition from the San Francisco black community. The legislature, however, refused to consider it. By a vote of 47 to 1, it said: "Resolved, that the House, having heard the petition read, do decline to receive it or entertain any petition on such subject from such source."

The same plea to repeal the law was tried again the following year, and records maintained in the archives of state and local government reveal that the following happened:

At the legislature session of 1853, Mr. W. C. Meredith, a Democrat from Tuolumne, presented a memorial to the Assembly signed by Negroes, asking the repeal of the clause prohibiting Negro persons from testifying in the courts where white persons are concerned.

Instantly one member moved to throw the memorial out of the window; another did not want the Journal tarnished with such an infamous document.

The chair reluctantly ruled the motion out of order, and an appeal was taken finally in the greatest excitement. The petition was rejected and the clerk was instructed not to file it.

The Franchise League's black pioneers refused to give up. They continued to hold regular meetings, enlisted white support, and finally decided to hold a statewide meeting. A call urging representation at the First State Convention of the Colored Citizens of the State of California went out—via *The Elevator,* a militant newspaper owned and edited by African-Americans—to all black communities. Published under the motto, "Equality before the Law," *The Elevator,* which became the voice of the Colored Convention's executive committee, printed an article that read:

Your state and condition in California is one of social and political degradation; one that is unbecoming to a free and enlightened people.

In view of these wrongs, which are so unjustly imposed upon us, and the progress of the enlightened spirit of the age in which we live and the great duty that we owe to ourselves and the generations that are yet to come, we call upon you to lay aside your various avocations and assemble yourselves together on Tuesday, the 20th day of November, A.D. 1855, in the city of Sacramento, at 10 A.M., for the purpose of devising the most judicious and effectual ways and means to obtain our inalienable rights and privileges in California.

Black communities in ten California counties financed and sent forty-nine delegates to the three-day convention, which was held in Sacramento's Colored Methodist Church. William H. Yates, who had migrated to San Francisco as a free black in 1849, was the Committee's first chairman.

The delegates, among whom were such notables as James P. Beckwourth, George Washington Dennis, and Mary Chase, sister of the murdered Gordon Chase, adhered to their single purpose: They adopted a resolution asking the Legislature to authorize black people to give testimony under oath in California courts. The resolution branded the law as unjust, oppressive to every class of people, and as one "intended to protect white persons from a class whose intellectual and social condition was supposed to be so low as to justify the depriving them of their testimony." Delegate J. H. Townsend, a black man whose oratory eloquence matched that of any man's, addressing himself to the people of California, delivered the main address. Townsend pointed to substantial black casualties suffered in the War for Independence and in the War of 1812. He said the African-American soldiers had fought in those wars with every reason to suppose they were taking part in "the good fight for liberty."

In conclusion, Townsend had this to say:

"You have enacted a law excluding our testimony in the courts of justice of this state, in cases or proceedings wherein white persons are parties; thus openly encouraging and countenancing the vicious and dishonest to take advantage of us; a law which, while it does not take advantage of you, is a great wrong to us.

"At the same time you freely admit evidence of (foreign-born) men in your midst who are ignorant of the first principles of your government—who know not even the alphabet.

"Many colored men who have been educated in your first colleges are not allowed to testify, and why? (Because) our Divine Father has created us with a darker complexion.

"People of California, we entreat you to repeal that unjust law. We ask it in the name of humanity, in the enlightened age in which we live, because of the odium it reflects upon you as a free and powerful people."

The resolution and Townsend's impassioned plea fell once again on deaf ears. But, as the white society would soon learn, *quit* was not part of the African-American's vocabulary.

CHAPTER VI

# The Mother of Civil Rights in California

BEGINNING IN 1856, CALIFORNIA'S AFRICAN-AMERICAN PIONEERS PETI-
tioned the Legislature repeatedly, asking for repeal of the law that
prohibited black people from testifying in civil or criminal cases.
The formal petitions, signed by both black and non-black citizens
of prominence, followed three years of futile lobbying for repeal by
members of the San Francisco Franchise League.

**The African-American whose wife or daughter was raped by
a white man, without "white" witnesses, had no recourse to
justice.**

After suffering an angry rebuff in Sacramento in 1856, the Franchise League set December 9th of that year for the Second Annual
Convention of the Colored Citizens of California, and again chose
the state capital as the site for the conclave. Some sixty-one delegates
from seventeen California counties responded.

**The African-American who was robbed in open daylight was
defenseless if no "white" witness would agree to testify in his
or her behalf.**

The pre-Christmas meeting, unlike the restrained 1855 convention, produced strong statements revolving around the question of loyalty to the United States as well as some telling blasts at the white population in general. Delegate Emory Waters of Nevada County, however, probably best expressed the convention's more pragmatic feelings during an argument over the use of the word *white* in a proposed plea for public support.

> It is essential to a good understanding of the matter that, in an address to the public generally, we should retain this word. We want to appeal to the whites especially, to let them know we mean something definite.
>
> They have the power. We know it, they know it. We appeal to them as whites to use that power beneficiently toward us. We must appeal to them as superiors.
>
> —Emory Waters

Water's view was sustained.

Records of the convention proceedings reflect both the mood and the high caliber of black men and women who were in the fight for a citizen's basic rights in pro-slavery California. Biddy Mason, for instance, who had only recently obtained her Freedom Papers, and who was one of three Los Angeles delegates, had this to say about the law invalidating the testimony of black people in courts of law:

> This deprivation subjects us to many outrages and aggressions by wicked and unprincipled white men. By it, prejudice is aroused against us that would not exist but for this statute.

The loyalty issue (to the country) arose over a proposed resolution saying, "Resolved, that we claim our rights in this country as any other class, not as citizens by adoption, but by right of birth; that we hail with delight its onward progress, sympathize with it in its adversity, and would freely cast our lot in fortunes of battle to protect her against foreign invasion."

Delegate William H. Newby of San Francisco objected to the statements hailing the Nation's progress and committing black people to rush to its defense against aggressors.

**Before the 1856 convention met, California had its first African-American newspaper, *Mirror of the Times,* which circulated through agents in thirty counties from the Mexican border**

**to the Oregon line. The newspaper was edited by William H. Newby.**

A leading black intellectual, Newby had this to say in response to the "hail with delight" resolution:

> No man can expect me to do this in a country whose prosperity and wealth have been built upon our sweat and blood.

> What is the history of the past in America but the history of wrongs and cruelties such as no other people upon the face of the earth have been forced to endure? The same institutions that bless the white man are made the curse of the colored man.

> Let the whites put away their prejudice and hatred against the colored man and do a just part by us. And when they do this, we shall feel we have a country—that patriotism is a virtue.

Delegate James Hubbard of Sacramento said he loved the land of his birth but hated "the laws which sustain her slave pens and prisons, her auction blocks and the selling of human beings, the branding of men and the scourging of women, the separation of man and wife, parents and children. *Fight for the protection of these, no!*"

Other delegates, however, argued successfully against altering the resolution. Thomas Dettner, a Sacramento County delegate, delivered perhaps the most effective argument for changing the testimony law. Shrewdly aiming his remarks at the white man, he said:

> The law relating to our testimony in the courts of California is but a shadow. It affords no protection to our families or property.

> I may see the assassin plunge his dagger to the vitals of my neighbor, yet in the eyes of the law I see it not. I may overhear the robber or incendiary plotting the injury or the utter ruin of my fellow citizen, and yet in the judgment of the law I hear it not.

> The robbery may follow, the conflagration may do its work, and the author of evil may go unpunished because only a colored man saw the act or heard the plot.

> Is it not evident that the white citizen is an equal sufferer with us? When will the people of this state learn that justice to the colored man is justice to themselves?

Despite the eloquent speeches and impassioned pleas, despite the many petitions presented to the California Legislature, the Golden State's ban on African-American testimony remained.

Disheartened, but not willing to quit, the Franchise League returned to San Francisco to prepare for future battle.

★   ★   ★

The need for testimony rights, because of the black man's need
to protect life and property, was a clear requirement for manhood
as well as for livelihood. At the heart of this issue was the African-
American's prosperity and ability to accumulate material goods in
spite of discrimination and oppression.

> There is evidence that African-American farmers in Califor-
> nia were ejected from lands they had cultivated because they
> could not testify to their ownership.

In all societies propertied classes have insisted on legal and political
protection commensurate with their wealth. The African-American
society in California was no exception.

The growth of California's African-American population, as well
as its prosperity, is illustrated by the activities of Darius Stokes, an
African-American pastor, who, by September of 1856, had founded
fourteen African-American churches in the Golden State. Pastor
Stokes proved that the assessed valuation of property owned by the
black population of San Francisco that year was $945,000; of Los
Angeles, more than one million dollars. He revealed, too, that in
excess of five hundred thousand dollars had been sent home to the
South by California's African-Americans to purchase freedom for
members of their families. Pastor Stokes remarked that "men had
paid as high as two thousand dollars each for their companions who
were enslaved, to gain their freedom, and bring them to this State."
Among the men to whom Stokes referred were mine owners
James Cousins, Abraham Holland, and Gabriel Simms and a former
slave who had become one of California's foremost mining engineers, Moses Rodger. One African-American, Edward Booth, is
said to have purchased eight of his relatives and paid nine thousand
dollars for them, having earned the money by washing clothes for
the gold miners. In Los Angeles, Biddy Mason would eventually
give some twenty-five thousand dollars to purchase "a score of Ne-

gro children." Not to be outdone, however, was San Francisco's Mary Ellen Pleasant.

## The Mother of Civil Rights in California

Much has been written of Mary Ellen (Mammy) Pleasant—with emphasis largely on her activities as a madam who operated several bordellos for the high and mighty of San Francisco's golden era. A Georgia-born slave who came to San Francisco from Boston as a free woman of thirty-seven in 1849, Mary Ellen Pleasant, who was certainly no "mammy," managed to achieve wealth and influence in San Francisco. She did, in fact, operate a hostelry considered notorious by some. It is a fact, too, however, that a great many historians today view Mary Ellen Pleasant as "The Mother of Civil Rights in California." These historians now focus not on her operation of brothels—common in that era—but rather on her connection with John Brown in the fanatical abolitionist's audacious though abortive raid on the Federal arsenal at Harper's Ferry. This connection was accented in an obituary printed in the *San Francisco Call* on January 4, 1904:

> The remains of Mammy Pleasant, who died early Monday morning at the home of Lyman Sherwood, on Filbert Street, will rest tonight under the soil of the little cemetery in the town of Napa, to which her body was taken this morning.
>
> One last request of Mammy Pleasant was that there be placed above her grave a tombstone bearing her name, age, nativity, and the words: "She was a friend of John Brown's."

And a friend she was indeed.

★ ★ ★

With the money she had inherited from her first husband (in Boston), Mary Ellen Pleasant journeyed to the Golden State and opened the first of what would be several houses of ill repute. Shrewd, cunning, illustrious and frugal, this proud and determined black woman amassed a fortune by catering to the needs of San Francisco's male population, which then outnumbered the female by a ratio of nearly twelve to one, and she had attained a position of influential

prominence when, in 1858, the first news of John Brown's efforts
to free the slaves of the South was conveyed to the citizens of the
city by the bay. Being in full sympathy with the John Brown movement, Mary Ellen conceived the idea of lending the abolitionist financial assistance for the undertaking—and April 5, 1858, found her
eastward bound with a $30,000 United States Treasury draft, which
had been procured for her through the aid of Robert Swain and John
W. Coleman.

Reaching Boston, Mary Ellen arranged for a meeting with John
Brown in Windsor, Canada, and before leaving Boston she had her
draft exchanged for Canadian paper, which she converted into coin
and eventually turned over to Brown. During their conference in
Canada, Mary Ellen and John Brown agreed that he should not
strike a blow for the freedom of black people until she had journeyed
to the South and had aroused the feelings of rebellion among the
slaves.

Disguised as a jockey—Mary Ellen Pleasant was petite and slen-
der—she proceeded to the South, and she was engaged in her part
of the dangerous plot when she was startled by the news that Brown
had already made his raid on Harper's Ferry—and had been captured. Not long thereafter she learned that law enforcement authorities were in pursuit of Brown's accomplice. Mary Ellen immediately
fled to New York, remained there in hiding for some time, then
assumed the name of "Mrs. Ellen Smith" and made her way back
to the Golden State.

At the time of John Brown's capture, authorities found on his
person a letter reading: "The ax is laid at the root of the tree. When
the first blow is struck, there will be more money to help."

The message was signed "W.E.P." For months on end authorities
vainly searched for the author of the message. In later years it was
learned that Mary Ellen Pleasant had written the letter confiscated
from John Brown, but in signing it she had made her first initial
look like a *W*.

Man can only speculate as to what might have happened had John
Brown delayed his raid until after Mary Ellen had incited the Southern slaves. It is an established fact, however, that Mary Ellen Pleasant
always blamed John Brown for hastening his attack at Harper's
Ferry, which she claimed cost her in all more than forty thousand
dollars.

When Mary Ellen arrived back in San Francisco in the early part
of 1860, she renewed old acquaintances, made new ones, and estab-

lished herself as the recognized leader of San Francisco's black community, openly fighting racism throughout the Bay area.

In 1866 she sued a San Francisco streetcar company for not allowing her to ride its streetcars. She sued the company again in January of 1868, claiming that one of its drivers had told her that "colored people would not be taken aboard." She won the law suit, receiving damages in the sum of $500. She was often courted by San Francisco's wealthiest gentlemen, black and white, but it was one bachelor, quicksilver (mercury) tycoon Thomas Bell, on whom she set her sights—not for herself (she was already married to John James Plaissance, who operated a refuge for runaway slaves in the East) but for her protegee, Teresa Percy.

Ten years later, in 1876, Mary Ellen built a mansion on Webster Street. It took her a few years of maneuvering, but she succeeded in marrying Bell off to Teresa and moving them, a few orphaned children and herself into the mansion, which came to be known as the House of Mystery.

> Mary Ellen Pleasant's House of Mystery was razed on October 9, 1964, to make way for the University of the Pacific's dental school.

Despite the unsavory rumors and truths about her—she is said to have learned many useful and mysterious things from the great voodoo queen Marie Laveau—Mary Ellen Pleasant was one of America's greatest African-American heroine freedom fighters. She was responsible for establishing most of the first black families in San Francisco and in the Bay area in general. From about 1862–1890 she was the most outstanding businesswoman, black or white, in Northern California.

Mary Ellen's support of John Brown both financially and as his personal agent in charge of mobilizing the slaves for his impending rebellion was greater than that of any other person. She was responsible for securing more jobs for former slaves in San Francisco than anyone else prior to 1900. Practically every employer in the city, at one time or another, had people working for him recommended by Mary Ellen Pleasant. Hardly a windjammer or a clipper ship sailed out of San Francisco Bay that did not have a cook, steward or navigator whom she had supplied. Hotel owners turned to her when they needed cooks, waiters, chambermaids, or bellboys. Women, struggling to introduce a few domestic refinements into their businesses, called on Mary Ellen Pleasant for a suitable maid or nurse. Business and industry turned to her for every imaginable kind of worker, and she supplied them.

In addition to placing over three hundred African-Americans in jobs throughout Northern California, Mary Ellen employed over sixty in her own business enterprises.

Mary Ellen Pleasant, unlike Biddy Mason and George Dennis, died poor. Her grave in the Tucolay Cemetery in Napa is visited annually by members of the San Francisco Historical and Cultural Society as well as by members of the general public. The headstone identifies Mary Ellen Pleasant as *"Mother of Civil Rights in California. Friend of John Brown."*

In hindsight, it must be said that Mary Ellen Pleasant's contribution to the civil rights movement was an *"it's-time-to-make-a-stance"* gesture just as significant as Rosa Parks' was when she refused to give up her seat to a white man nearly 90 years later.

Among America's leading civil rights activists, Mary Ellen Pleasant ranks with the greatest, black or white.

★   ★   ★

The Third Annual Convention of the Colored Citizens of California assembled shortly after the Dred Scott decision of the United States Supreme Court.

> In the Dred Scott decision the U.S. Supreme Court held that a slave did not become free when taken into a free state, Congress could not bar slavery from a territory, and blacks could not be citizens.
>
> March 6, 1857

Perhaps because they faced a policy that completely denied African-Americans their rights throughout the nation, the 1857 convention had a smaller enrollment and internal dissension disrupted the proceedings.

The subsequent months gave birth to another petition campaign. In spite of technical difficulties in assembling the petitions from some of the rural counties and the inadequate funds sent from those areas, a respectable showing was made. San Francisco, Sacramento and Los Angeles counties came through as usual. Eighteen hundred signatures were gathered in San Francisco alone. The *Daily Alta,* a San Francisco newspaper, noted that "the number of petitions favoring the repeal of the statute disqualifying Negroes and Mulattoes from giving evidence . . . causes them (state legislators) no little uneasiness." As before, however, the petitions were ignored. The California Legislature was evidently not impressed with the fact that support for a change in the testimony laws had even come from San Francisco's Grand Jury, or with the fact that nearly three hundred lawyers had also given support to reforming California's existing testimony laws.

Although no more African-American conventions would meet in the Golden State until the end of the slave era, the *Mirror of the Times* continued to publish its militant message to California's black communities.

### Advice to Black Californians

Let every Colored resident of the State . . . abandon such positions as bootblack, waiters, servants, and carriers, and other servile employment, and if they cannot engage in trading, mechanical pursuits or farming, let them pitch into mining from which they have not yet been debarred; although it perhaps remains for the notorious Taney to determine how soon that will be done. Money can be made if followed with industry, accompanied with strict economy. And money will purchase stock farms, and certainly our people are as well, if not better qualified for that calling as any on the face of the earth . . .

—*Mirror of the Times*, December 12, 1857

Beginning in the latter part of 1856, the topic of education loomed up as a competitor to the issue of testimony. African-American communities throughout the state were sufficiently stabilized to be concerned about the education of black children. This concern was epitomized in a letter received by and published in the *Mirror of the Times:*

The necessity of establishing schools for the education of our youth would seem too evident to need urging. And yet there is scarcely a village or town in California that possesses a common school for the education of Colored children . . .

Without schools for the education of those who are to compose the next generation of actors on this great stage, we cannot expect our condition to be permanently improved—for it is upon the present youth of the country that we must make impressions that will perfect what we can only hope to commence . . .

—Thomas Duff, Mariposa, December 8, 1857

The white school systems in California showed virtually no inter-est in African-American children, most of whom obtained their basic education through the volunteer work of churches.

Enter Jeremiah B. Sanderson.

★   ★   ★

In 1852, the question of whether or not to go to California became intertwined with another issue that had long absorbed the intellectual energies of the eastern black leadership. This was the debate over whether black people should migrate to Africa, the West Indies, or South America. While the preponderance of African-American opinion opposed such migration, at times of great stress or harass-ment the emigration sentiment showed a considerable rise. But emi-gration was generally regarded as an emergency measure only. The passage of the Fugitive Slave Law of 1850 intensified the debate about emigration from the United States. Although emigration talk gained a new intensity in this period, majority opinion remained un-changed. In 1854 a statewide meeting of Massachusetts African-Americans took up the much debated issue. This group supported the general opposition to emigration, but it also took the occasion to declare that emigration to California was a different matter and described such emigration as "healthy" and "enterprising." Within six months of this gathering of Massachusetts African-American leaders, one of the most prominent among them, Jeremiah B. Sanderson, was on his way to California.

Born and raised in New Beford, Massachusetts, Jeremiah B. Sanderson forsook the cultural atmosphere of his native home and went to California for the sole purpose of aiding in the education of African-American children. He had been an intellectual stalwart among the Abolitionists and Friends of Freedom in New Bedford, headquarters city for Frederick Douglass, Harriet Tubman and other spirited leaders in the underground railroad movement. It was these individuals, no doubt, who provided the inspiration for Sanderson to go where he was most needed.

Sanderson arrived in the Golden State in 1853. Here he found his work waiting for him since African-American children in the state were not receiving any formal education.

**In the 1850s and 1860s, African-American children were not permitted to attend public school with white children, nor were**

they allowed a school of their own—except through a limiting
provision.

Sanderson took full advantage of the limiting provisions and in
1854 began the arduous task of founding and promoting schools for
black youths in San Francisco, Oakland, Sacramento, San Jose and
Stockton. His work was monumental.

According to entries in the diary of Jeremiah B. Sanderson, the
first school for African-American children in San Francisco was
opened on May 22, 1854. Sanderson's diary contains the following
1854 report of the San Francisco Board of Education to the Common
Council:

A school for the colored population of our city has been established.
It is located at the corner of Jackson and Virginia Place in the basement
of the St. Cyprian Methodist Church.

The lower room, which is eleven feet high and fifty by twenty-five
feet surface, is well lighted, ventilated and has its walls hard-finished.
This we have leased for one year, with the privilege of two years, at
the monthly rental of fifty dollars, payable monthly in advance.

Sanderson worked alongside Biddy Mason in furthering black
education in the Golden State, and he often had to serve as a teacher
until another could be found and trained.

Surmounting great difficulties, not the least of which was prejudice and lack of funds, Sanderson managed to establish schools for
the neglected youngsters of African ancestry in the Golden State's
capital city.

Today I opened a school for colored children. The necessity for this
step is evident. There are 30 or more children in Sacramento of proper
age and no school provided for them by the Board of Education. They
must no longer be neglected, left to grow up in ignorance, exposed
to all manner of evil influences, with the danger of contracting idle
and vicious habits. A school they must have. I am induced to under-
take this enterprise by the advice of friends and the solicitation of
parents. I can do but little, but with God's blessing, I will do what I
can.

—J. B. Sanderson's Diary, April 20, 1855

By 1858, despite hard, bitter battles, Sanderson had managed to
establish schools for African-American children in San Jose, Oakland
and Stockton.

★  ★  ★

Many of California's bigoted assemblymen found new excuses to be antagonistic to the African-American in 1858—the year of the infamous Archy fugitive slave case.

While the fugitive slave issue was all but nonexistent in California by 1858, the Archy case occurred because of the dullwitted stupidity of Archy's owner in bringing him to the Golden State. It took on spectacular dimensions because of the supreme court's decision that legally Archy deserved his freedom. But out of kindness to his owner, the court also decided he must return to slavery. The press all over the state roared in ridicule, and the African-American community, especially in San Francisco, was thoroughly aroused—and its aggressive concern and involvement offended the biased and tender sensibilities of the Golden State's legislators. It is not clear whether the militancy of Bay Area African-Americans had much to do with the rejection by the legislature of the testimony petitions, but it did have some bearing on a legislative attempt to register all free black people in California and bar future African-American immigration into the Golden State. Referring to the Archy reaction in San Francisco, State Senator Merritt, who supported anti-black immigration legislation, stated that "he (African-American) becomes insolent and defiant, and, if in sufficient numbers, would become dangerous, as evidenced by recent occurrences in one of our cities."

This was not the first effort to prevent African-Americans from migrating to California. An attempt that failed had been made at the 1849 Constitutional Convention. Then, in 1852, Assemblyman Crabb announced that he would introduce a bill to prevent future African-American immigration into California. (In the year of Archy's freedom, Crabb was on his way to meet his own fate [death] in Sonora.) It was not until 1857 that an anti-black immigration bill nearly became a law. By a 30 to 32 vote the bill was defeated in the Legislature.

★  ★  ★

The Archy incident was the most famous fugitive slave case to reach the California Supreme Court. Justices Peter H. Burnett, who had been the first elected white governor, and David S. Terry recognized that the master was not legally entitled to possess Archy Lee as a slave. But, since this was the first case and would be a hardship to the owner, they were "not disposed to rigidly enforce the rule." As stated, they returned the black man to his so-called owner.

**In the Archy case, the California Supreme Court exhibited that twisted legalism that all-too-often has robbed African-Americans of their God-given right to simple justice.**

The owner promptly started for Mississippi. In San Francisco he was intercepted by a new court action which hinged on the fugitive slave issue, and by court order Archy Lee was set free. Perhaps as a carry-over of the condescension toward African-Americans, this case comes down in history not as *Lee vs. Stovall* but as *ex parte Archy.*

# CHAPTER VII

# California's Black Contribution to the Civil War

THE YEAR 1858 WAS PAINFULLY DRAMATIC FOR CALIFORNIA'S AFRICAN-Americans. There was another serious attempt to stop African-American immigration and to label the African-American a pro-scribed class.

> Everything around us indicates a change . . . in the public sentiment toward us. . . . Our relationship to the California government is changing daily.
>
> —William H. Newby

The anti-black immigration bill was introduced in the assembly in March of 1858. Its provisions were harsh on African-Americans who were in violation of the bill as well as on white men who hired black people who were subject to its exclusion provisions.

General William T. Sherman liked to tell about his California friend, Persifer Smith, a white man who would "take off his cap

and make a profound bow to every colored man whom he
met in San Francisco because, he said, they were the only
gentlemen who kept their promises."

To the dismay of California's African-American residents, the
anti-black immigration bill was passed overwhelmingly in the assembly and sent to the senate.

A San Francisco corrrespondent for a black New York paper,
*The Weekly Anglo-African,* talked of the need for black territory
"by conquest or purchase" so that black people could send
their leaders "to be recognized in our country as men and
women . . . respectfully asking or demanding an interview with
the governments of Mexico or the United States, or any other
Government that might have territory to dispose of.

Uneasiness about the anti-black immigration bill was more evident in the Senate. An attempt to postpone consideration indefinitely
was narrowly defeated. State Senator Bell attempted to introduce
safeguards for California black people temporarily out of the state
or members of their families on their way to California. He won a
temporary delay on this point, but the Judiciary Committee by a
three to two vote rejected his suggestion. Maneuvering came to an
end with the passage of the bill 21 to 8. The maneuvering, however,
did pay off. The Senate included some minor revisions that required
the bill's return to the assembly for approval. The very impatient
and all-too-often partially drunk assembly had, however, in the
meantime adjourned. The bill therefore died.

Had this bill passed, at least two influential newspapers, the Sacramento *Daily Union* and the San Francisco *Daily Evening Bulletin,*
thought that it would be unenforceable. As it worked its way
through the Legislature, these newspapers reported the proceedings
with undisguised distaste. In their view it was unnecessarily harsh
to the African-American. The *Daily Evening Bulletin* defended the
California African-Americans by making a case for them—with
white man logic—as the best of the free African-American groups
in the United States. It saw some merit in preventing future immigration of black people but pleaded for more kindness in treating
the resident population. At least one outstanding leader of the San
Francisco African-American community took a thanks-but-no-
thanks view of this kind of support. Mifflin Wistar Gibbs wrote to

the *Daily Evening Bulletin* defending free black men and women everywhere in the United States, saying, in part:

> I appeal with pride to the history of the free colored people for the last twenty years in every free state in the Union. . . . During all that time, notwithstanding they have been subjected to the most unjust enactments and coerced by rigorous laws, pursued by a prejudice as unrelenting as inhuman, disregarded by the Church, and persecuted by the State—they have made steady progress, upward and onward, in oral and intellectual attainments.
>
> I admit the right of a family or a nation to say who, from without, shall be a component part of its household or community; but the application of this principle should work no hardship to a colored man, for he was born in the great American family, and is your black brother—and is interested in its weal or woe, is taxed to support it, and having made up his mind to stay with the family, his right to the benefit of just government is as good as that of his pale face brother who clamors for his expatriation.
>
> April 1858

Even as Gibbs wrote this ringing statement he must have been having doubts about remaining in the country of his birth. In the days following publication of his letter, African-American men and women in San Francisco were conducting indignation meetings and talking about going to Canada. The anti-black immigration bill had not yet died, and there was excitement in the north due to the Frazier River Gold Rush.

As a result of the Frazier River fever, British officials in Victoria, Canada, found it necessary to expand governmental functions. This required a building program that called for a large group of laborers, and the California Gold Rush had created a severe labor shortage in Victoria. British sea captains who knew about the Golden State and the events in San Francisco were in touch with Victoria officials and things began to happen. At an African-American mass meeting in San Francisco (in April 1858) black men and women were informed that they would be welcome in Victoria and that there was employment and land.

The result was an exodus of several hundred California black men and women led by a number of leaders of the convention movement, including Mifflin Wistar Gibbs.

**Mifflin Wistar Gibbs came to California as a free black of twenty-two in 1850. In 1851 he published a series of resolu-**

tions denouncing the state's anti-black laws. In 1855 he founded California's first African-American newspaper, *Mirror of the Times,* which was edited by William H. Newby. Gibbs was an active crusader for African-American rights and equality and took a prominent part in the conventions to protest discriminatory laws. In 1873 he became the first black judge in United States history.

With the departure of California's black people to Victoria in 1858, the convention movement seemed to fall into spiritual and organizational doldrums. There was no convention that year, and frustration produced accentuated internal bickering. Defeat was in the air—notwithstanding the fact that the anti-black immigration legislation never became law. A laudable effort at independent African-American journalism expired in spite of great sacrifices by its editor. In November 1858, the executive committee of the convention movement issued a report in which it announced that after much thought it had decided not to call for another testimony petition until there was a change of political administration in California. (This, of course, could only mean that African-Americans in the Golden State felt that their fortunes lay with an eventual Republican victory.) In this mood of depression and despair California's African-American leadership turned faintly to recourses that would be suggested more forcefully nearly forty years later when America's black people would experience the bitter fruits of home rule in the South. Foreshadowing Booker T. Washington, the executive committee report advised that

> pecuniary prominence, in a country so diversified as this, takes precedence over intellectual, and it should be our highest aim to seek the end we have marked out, through that mode which has formed a superiority . . .

The report did not, however, in any way call for surrender. (If Anglo-Americans had learned nothing else, they had learned that the African-American does not quit.) The convention's executive committee agreed to conduct another petition campaign if African-American communities in the Golden State responded with sufficient vigor and funds. This does not seem to have been the case before 1860.

★   ★   ★

The stormy fifties, in California and elsewhere, had one final thunderbolt—the John Brown raid at Harper's Ferry late in 1859. Lacking a clear and definite plan of campaign, Brown's foray—funded in part by Mary Ellen Pleasant—was doomed.

**Brown and twenty-one of his followers, five of them African-American, attempted to seize a government arsenal at Harper's Ferry in northwestern Virginia.**

Brown was executed, mounting the scaffold to the hangman's noose with impressive dignity. "God's angry man" was, however, destined for a lasting fame; soon the soldiers in blue would be singing "John Brown's Body." Abolitionism had its martyr in Elijah P. Lovejoy; now the Union had its martyr in abolitionist John Brown. He was dead less than a year when Abraham Lincoln, candidate of the Republican Party, was elected to the presidency. Feeling their security imperiled, the Southern states began to leave the Union. The North-South crisis—in truth, the slavery crisis—had moved into its final phase, and African-Americans, from the Adirondack Mountains in New York to the goldfields in California, were more than ready to move with it.

## Human Liberty

In the Civil War the African-American was both a symbol and a participant. The nearly four million slaves who became free furnished a concrete expression of one of the great goals of the war—that of enlarging the compass of human liberty. And, despite popular belief to the contrary, the African-American was not merely an on-looker, standing idly by and weeping in humble gratitude. In truth, African-Americans—male and female—were active on the battle-fields, behind the lines, and on the home front.

Although the causes of America's Civil War were numerous, the system of slavery was unquestionably paramount. To a key figure like Abraham Lincoln, slavery was the overriding cause of the war. In his greatest debates with Stephen A. Douglas in the late summer of 1858, Lincoln said that this nation could not go on indefinitely half slave and half free. Four years later, on August 14, 1862, when a delegation of five African-Americans, which included California's Abner Francis, visited the White House, Lincoln told them that "without the institution of slavery, and the colored race as a basis, the war could not have an existence." In his Second Inaugural Address of March 4, 1865, Lincoln pointed out that on the eve of the war, one-eighth of the population was made up of slaves. "All know," he said, "that this interest was, somehow, the cause of the war."

Though Californians were spared actual warfare at home, the Golden State was not able to free itself entirely from Southern influences.

If the Civil War became a crusade for freedom, it did not start out that way. The clash between the North and the South was not a week old before African-Americans discovered that they had a private war on their hands—the war of their complexion. On April 15, 1861, President Lincoln issued a call for 75,000 men, upon learning that Fort Sumter in the Charleston harbor had been seized. The response was all that he could have hoped for—a wave of enthusiasm sweeping the North. The martial spirit took hold as recruits lined up at the enlistment centers.

Sharing fully in this great enthusiasm were the country's African-Americans, who reasoned that since slavery was the root of the conflict, freedom would be the result. On the day after Lincoln's call, a group of Los Angeles African-Americans, meeting in the African-American Methodist Church funded by Biddy Mason, pledged to the President their lives and their fortunes. In San Jose a group of black businessmen offered to march with the first regiment that left their home state of Rhode Island. African-Americans in Merced formed their own regiment, and in Sacramento the black community offered its services, with James Hubbard pointing out that as American citizens, black people in Sacramento were anxious "to assist in any honorable way or manner to sustain the present administration."

African-Americans in San Francisco, meeting at the home of Mary Ellen Pleasant, declared their allegiance to Lincoln's government and offered to supply money, prayers, and manpower to help win the war. William H. Newby, who had objected to the "hail with delight" resolution of 1856, asked the War Department for permission to raise "from 5,000 to 10,000 free black men." Among the last of the volunteering letters was one to Lincoln from the Reverend Jeremiah B. Sanderson, who wrote:

If I can be of any manner of service here, should your excellency ever think it best to employ my people, I am ready to work or preach or fight to put down this rebellion.

Nothing came of any of these proposals. Every city to which California's African-Americans offered their services adopted a thumbs-down attitude. When Jacob Dodson, a Senate attendant who had been a scout for John C. Fremont, offered the services of 300 California African-Americans for the defense of the nation's capital, he was officially informed that the War Department had no intention of using African-American soldiers.

These refusals to accept African-Americans for military service were grounded in traditional practices and beliefs. Since the close of the Revolutionary War, it had been the custom to bar black men from the armies of America. Opposition to the African-American as soldier was rooted in fears that black men lacked the qualities of fighting men, that arming them would be an admission that white soldiers had not been valiant enough to do the job, that putting a gun in their hands might lead to slave insurrections—and in the deep, although unspoken, fear that to make the African-American a soldier would bring about a change in his position in American life.

The intention to bypass the African-American, however, had to be abandoned. The war had not ended in ninety days, as some had expected. And as both North and South girded for a contest of indefinite duration, the government at Washington had to take a second look at its "hands-off-the-African-American" policy. Indeed, the white soldier had not been valiant enough to do the job.

Congress preceded Lincoln in making a reversal, declaring on August 6, 1861, that any property that was put to use in aid of the rebel cause would be confiscated; if such property consisted of slaves, they were to be set free.

Two important measures were passed in the spring of 1862. By an act of March 13 military commanders were forbidden to return fugitive slaves to their owners. A month later slavery was abolished in the District of Columbia, giving freedom to some 3,000 African-Americans.

In the summer of 1862, Congress outdid itself. Early in June it passed a measure authorizing the exchange of diplomatic representatives with Haiti and Liberia. Later that month Congress abolished slavery in the territories, and on July 17 two measures were passed. The first provided that all rebel-owned slaves coming under United

States control should be considered captives of war and made free, a measure which differed from the first confiscation act in that it was now not necessary for the rebel-owned slave to have been put to use by the enemy. The second enactment authorized the President to receive African-Americans into the service of the United States to perform "any labor of any war service" within their competence; the volunteer's mother, wife, and children were to be given their freedom if he were a slave.

Like Congress, the chief executive found it necessary to address himself to the African-American. His slowness on this score was rooted in his natural conservatism, an inclination to bide his time. Further, when Lincoln took office he was of the opinion that the President had no right to interfere with slavery—perhaps because his wife, Mary Tood, owned slaves.

Finally, impelled to take action, Lincoln issued a preliminary emancipation proclamation on September 22, 1862. In it he stated that as of January 1, 1863, all slaves would be free in those states which were then still in the rebellion. As was to be expected, the South did not consider Lincoln's edict as an extension of the olive branch, and they condemned it soundly. But when January 1 came, Lincoln carried through his ultimatum and signed the final Emancipation Proclamation. A lengthy document, its chief provision was a declaration freeing all persons held as slaves in those states, or parts of states, which had not laid down their arms.

★ ★ ★

In California, the choice of supporting North or South remained. The legislature passed loyal resolutions, while Governor John G. Downey repudiated Lincoln's policy. "I do not believe," he said, "that an aggressive war should be waged on any section of the Confederacy, nor do I believe that this Union can be preserved by a coercive policy." Loyalty demonstrations answered pro-South appeals and California citizens rallied to both sides. The plain truth was that California was a border state, fairly evenly divided between Union and secession sentiment.

Although a divided Democratic vote in 1860 had allowed the Republicans to carry the state for Lincoln, they had polled only three-eights of the vote. Loyalty was not absolutely proved, and the state election of 1861 was looked upon as a significant test. The "Secesh" faction redoubled its efforts; Union sympathizers were greatly assisted by the black community's role in the formation of the Home

Guards, a sort of new committee of safety, which conducted propaganda for the North, kept an eye out for secrecy, and battled a number of societies pledged to aid the Confederate cause, including the Knights of the Golden Circle, the Knights of the Columbian Star, and the Committee of Thirty. Aided by such African-American notables as George Washington Dennis, Darius Stokes and Jeremiah B. Sanderson, the Home Guards made a systematic effort to swing the state to Leland Stanford, the Republican candidate. Helped by the firing on Fort Sumter, the death of pro-slavery Stephen A. Douglas, and especially the oratory eloquence of the black community's Biddy Mason and William H. Yates, the Republican and Union ticket carried the election.

Far from being silenced the Secesh faction continued its protests in press and pulpit, poem and harangue. Sometimes the criticism was direct, with the Union Army assailed as "a whining running army, that has disgraced our flag, lowered our cause and dishonored Republican chivalry," or with President Lincoln called an "unprincipled demagogue," and "illiterate backwoods-man," and a "narrow-minded bigot." On Thanksgiving Day 1862, the *Visalia Equal Rights Expositor* prayed: "O Lord we thank thee for letting the rebels wallop us at the battle of Pittsburg Landing—for letting them smite us hip and thigh . . ."

In San Francisco, the Franchise League responded to the most vicious of these attacks by literally confiscating the papers from the mails. When, however, this and other forms of persuasion failed to moderate the editors of the *Expositor,* Mary Ellen Pleasant, Darius Stokes, D. W. Ruggles, and several other African-Americans decided to take matters into their own hands. Determined to eradicate any and all Southern sympathy, these prominent black people broke into the newspaper office, totally destroyed the press, and pitched type, paper, and ink into the street. Reverend William Scott had the temerity to insist before his San Francisco presbytery that Jefferson Davis was no more a traitor than George Washington had been. Berated by California's African-American press and threatened by a mob of black citizens, Scott was forced to resign his pulpit and flee the Golden State.

Southern sympathizers in California made one major effort to strike for the Confederacy. Under the pretext of a commercial venture to Manzanillo, they loaded a quantity of arms and ammunition on the schooner *Chapman,* intending to intercept a Pacific mail steamer, convert it into a privateer, and ravage Union shipping in the Pacific. Sacramento's African-American community got wind of the plot, combined forces with the *Home Guards* and San Francisco's Franchise League, and seized the *Chapman* before the ship sailed out of the harbor.

Since Confederate sentiment was so strong, the federal government hesitated to draw many loyal volunteers out of the Golden State. Of the 16,000 who were enlisted, however, more than a third were African-American or of African ancestry. A few did garrison duty along western trails but the majority remained in the state. The California Battalion and the California Hundred, the latter of which included twenty-eight African-Americans, had been recruited in the East. They were attached to the Second Massachusetts Cavalry and participated in more than fifty engagements.

> The African-American's response to calls to become a soldier during the Civil War was heroic. By the end of the war, some 180,000 black men had volunteered, comprising between nine and ten percent of the total Union enlistments. These black men in blue took part in 499 military engagements, thirty-nine of which were major battles. Their death toll was high, amounting to nearly 37,000, which comprised more than one-fifth of their total.

On the whole, the California African-American volunteer acquitted himself laudably. He knew that he faced a number of discriminations; his period of enlistment was longer than that of others, he had little chance of rising to the rank of commissioned officer, his pay was lower than that of whites, he did not receive the same hospital or medical care, he was furnished with inferior firearms, and if he were captured by the enemy, he ran the risk of being treated not as a prisoner of war but as a rebellious slave taken in arms. Despite such disadvantages, however, his morale was likely to be above par. Typically, the California African-American who volunteered proved himself a dependable and resolute soldier. He knew why he had donned the blue uniform. He was fighting for a new dignity and self-respect, for a future in which his children would have greater opportunities. He felt that the army had something to offer him— it gave him the opportunity to make his mark.

Proof of the high spirits of California's African-American soldier was furnished by his courageous conduct on the battlefield. In fact, Secretary of War Stanton, in a letter of February 8, 1864, to Lincoln, attested to the valor of the black men who had joined the California Hundred, and to other black soldiers: "At Milliken's Bend, at Port Hudson, Morris Island and other battlefields, they have proved themselves among the bravest of the brave, performing deeds of daring and shedding their blood with a heroism unsurpassed by soldiers of any other race."

Matching the African-American's services with the land forces was his role in the Union Navy. Throughout its history, the Navy had never barred free black men from enlisting, and in September 1861, it adopted the policy of enlisting former slaves. Suffering during the entire course of the war from a shortage of men, the Navy was anxious to attract African-American recruits and to have them re-enlist when their tours expired. Black men responded in large numbers to the naval recruiters, eventually comprising one-quarter of the men sailing the Union fleet. The Navy treated its 29,000 African-Americans fairly well, quartering and messing them with whites and offering them some opportunity for promotion.

Four of these African-American sailors won the Navy Medal of Honor. Perhaps the best known of these was Joachim Pease, loader of the number one gun on the *Kearsarge.* One of the fifteen African-Americans on board this warship when she met the most famous of the Confederate raiders, the *Alabama,* in a historic sea duel off the coast of France, Pease, who had left the relative safety of San Francisco to fight with the Navy, was cited by his superior officer as "having shown the utmost in courage and fortitude."

Another approach to active service by the California African-American came when the California Column under James P. Beckwourth and General James Carleton marched through Yuma and Tucson to the Rio Grande to repel the Confederate invasion of New Mexico. Some twelve black men from Los Angeles served with the California Column.

California's African-American civilians also made several noteworthy contributions to the war effort. Many of the state's black women headed to the North to work as nurses in hospitals or camps. Others, like Biddy Mason, Mary Ellen Pleasant, and Mary Chase, formed groups designed to raise money for the families of the men at the front, to purchase flags and banners for the regiments, or to buy delicacies for the sick and convalescent soldiers. A number of African-American women's organizations in the Golden State had as their primary goal the assistance of newly migrating black people, distributing food and clothing to them. Typical of these charitable groups was the Queen of Angels Relief Society made up of forty black women of Los Angeles who were unselfishly devoted to helping African-Americans who had found their way into California. Some women's organizations, such as the Ladies of Color in San Jose, sent money to assist former slaves still in the South. On her own, Mary Chase, who had been stripped and publicly whipped by white men, sent $500 for the suffering freedmen of Savannah.

Under the auspices of freedmen's aid societies, a few of California's African-American women volunteered to teach in those regions which had come under the Union flag. The best known of these was young Ellen Mason, the eldest daughter of Biddy Mason. In the fall of 1863 Miss Mason arrived at St. Helena's in the Sea Islands of South Carolina. Here she joined another black female, Charlotte Forten, who had been educated in Massachusetts, and enthusiastically entered upon her duties as a schoolmistress, sustained by the golden opportunity to carry out her life goal of doing all she could for "my oppressed and suffering fellow creatures."

If African-American women in California took the lead in sewing for the soldiers and in assisting newly arriving black people, the Golden State's African-American men were active in trying to influence and sway public opinion in support of the war effort. Black men sensed that the war would bring about an improvement in their economic and social position. They started to read the newspapers more closely and to take a keener interest in public affairs. African-American spokesmen, such as D. W. Ruggles and the Reverend Jeremiah B. Sanderson, prodded public officials in California and elsewhere to stand firmly behind the war effort, and they acted as a whip and spur to Lincoln, successfully urging him to permit African-Americans to join the Army, to declare the slaves free, and to support equal suffrage.

> The right to vote was the issue that particularly gripped the attention of the person of color during the last years of the war. California's black leaders held the opinion (and rightfully so) that freedom without suffrage was basically a sham, political equality being the basis upon which other equalities were built. The Golden State's black residents had repeatedly informed high-ranking government officials of their desire for the ballot. In one instance, a suffrage petition sent by a group of San

Jose African-Americans was addressed jointly to the California Governor and United States President, dated March 13, 1863, and bore 75 signatures.

The greatest wartime expression of this desire for the ballot was a national black convention held in Syracuse, New York, in early October 1864, and attended by 144 delegates from eighteen states, including twenty-six black representatives from California. After four days of deliberation, Delegate William Henry Hall of California drew up an "Address to the People of the United States," which claimed that African-Americans had fully earned the right to vote and raised some pointed questions: "Are we citizens when this nation is in peril, and aliens when the nation is in safety? May we shed our blood under the star-spangled banner on the battlefield, and yet be barred from marching under it at the ballot-box?"

African-Americans wanted the franchise, stated the "Address," because they were men and wanted to be as free in their native country as were other Americans.

Working side-by-side with such renowned white Calilfornians as Leland Stanford, Colonel E. D. Baker, the Reverend Myron C. Briggs, and Thomas Starr King, California's African-Americans established themselves as both a vocal and physical force against Southern influences. (Stanford, the war governor, had been recruited into an anti-slavery group within the state—founded by the Franchise League—and which included the likes of Mary Ellen Pleasant, George Washington Dennis, Mark Hopkins, Biddy Mason, and Darius Stokes.) A most popular figure was William Henry Hall, a great orator and one of the most prominent African-Americans in the state. Hall's impassioned speeches did much to strengthen the Republican cause in California and to bring about the election of Leland Stanford. Of all of California's black people, however, none was more vocal nor more physical than a former slave named Moses Rodger.

## Moses Rodger and the Red Cross

Born a slave in Missouri, Moses Rodger seized every opportunity he could to obtain an education, giving special attention to mathematics and engineering. He migrated to California in 1849, at the peak of the gold rush, and was highly successful in working a few claims. With this gold, he was able to purchase mines at Hornitos, Mariposa County, California; Rodger, as the superintendent, guaranteed that the mines would be worked on a paying basis.

> Moses Rodger was an expert in his line and his opinion was always sought by intending purchasers of mines. He was a man of honor and his word was as good as his bond.
>
> —*Merced Star*

To establish his family where his children could be educated, Rodger built an attractive two-story house in Stockton, where, boring for a gas well, he spent thousands of dollars until he finally reached and tapped the source. His greatest fame, however, rests upon his eloquent solicitation for the Sanitary Commission, the Civil War precursor of the Red Cross. Largely through his efforts, and the efforts of Thomas Starr King, California contributed a total of $1,233,831.31—more than one-fourth of the entire amount received by the Commission.

★ ★ ★

Overall, gold shipments—and shipments of wool, wheat, and other materials—rather than fighting men were the Golden State's greatest contribution to the Union cause—and again, the unselfish efforts of the state's African-American population cannot be ignored.

In 1850 wheat production was estimated at 17,000 bushels. It rose to 5.9 million bushels in 1863—with a substantial amount grown (by African-American farmers) for and shipped to the Union armies.

> **Perhaps some five hundred million dollars flowed from California's gold mines in the years immediately before and during the Civil War, and this almost exactly equals the total amount invested in new industrial capacity in the eastern states over the same span. From Brown's Valley, Fritz Vosburg funneled hundreds of thousands of dollars in gold to Boston and Washington.**

It is rather presumptuous to make a one-for-one relationship here, but California gold—which was mined by white and black alike—can be said to have played a substantial part in creating the industrial supremacy that was so vital to the Union's ultimate victory over the Confederacy.

★   ★   ★

One of the factors contributing to the morale of the Golden State's African-Americans, whether they were risking their lives on the battlefield or dedicating their services on the home front, was the collective African-American attitude toward Abraham Lincoln. The state's black leaders might have been disappointed in Lincoln because of his lukewarm attitude toward equal suffrage. They might also have been puzzled by the persistence with which he held to the fetish of colonization. (In mid-April 1863, nearly 500 black people had been sent to Cow Island, Haiti, but the venture proved a complete fiasco, and Lincoln had to send a transport to bring the emigrants back to the United States.) Black leaders did not, however, press any criticisms against the President, realizing that the African-American rank and file would not listen, particularly after the Emancipation Proclamation.

With few dissenters, California's African-Americans viewed Lincoln as a man who was personally well disposed toward them—toward the man of color. They had heard of his graciousness to black people who had put in an appearance at the White House, whether on public occasions, such as a New Year's Day reception, or on personal visits, such as that of the Reverend Jeremiah B. Sanderson, who presented him with a huge, ornamented Bible. African-Americans, in California and elsewhere across the nation, saw in Lincoln a humanitarian whose love for his fellows embraced all sorts and conditions of men. They sensed that he was a growing man—ever learning, particularly in his concepts and ideals of liberty.

Said William Henry Hall:

> Lincoln's growth was nowhere better illustrated than in his Gettysburg Address of November 19, 1863. In a short speech at the dedication of the battlefield as a national cemetery for the soldiers who fell there, he pointed out that the living should highly resolve that America should have "a new birth of freedom." Thus did President Lincoln reveal that he had fully grasped the great truth that the war had become not a war to restore the Union as it was, but a war to reconstitute the Union on a broadened base of human liberty.

Within a month after the Gettysburg Address, Congress began debating a constitutional amendment prohibiting slavery throughout the United States and its territories. Few men were more concerned about the adoption of this measure than Lincoln; he needed no one to tell him of the limitations of the Emancipation Proclamation. In the campaign of 1864 Lincoln placed his party on record as supporting the proposed Thirteenth Amendment. Upon his request, the Republicans, at their convention in Baltimore in June 1864, and which included delegates from California, wrote such a plank into their party platform.

At this convention the Republicans also nominated Abraham Lincoln for the presidency, a very popular choice with African-Americans coast-to-coast. Lincoln won re-election by a comfortable majority, a victory which he regarded as a mandate by the people that Congress pass the amendment abolishing slavery. This viewpoint gained support on Capitol Hill, and on January 31, 1865, the House, following the lead of the Senate, gave the necessary two-thirds majority vote to send to the states a constitutional amendment doing away with slavery. Lincoln and African-Americans across the nation would have concurred with the editorial appraisal appearing in *The Pacific Appeal,* a black newspaper in California edited by Peter Bell: "The adoption of this amendment is the most important step ever taken by the Congress of the United States."

During the month of April 1865, the two most important events to African-Americans, as to the country, were the collapse of the Confederacy and the assassination of Lincoln. The former took place on April 9 when, at Appomattox, Lee surrendered his army to Grant. The latter took place five days later when, at Ford's Theatre, John Wilkes Booth fired a fatal shot at Abraham Lincoln's head. As African-Americans had been elated over Lee's surrender, so were they stricken by Lincoln's death.

But as that fateful April drew to a close, black people felt that they stood on the threshold of a new era. Slavery was dead, and they had played a part in bringing this to pass. Taking inventory of the war's four years, California's African-Americans felt that now they had a stake in America, that their future was in America—not in Liberia, Haiti, or elsewhere. The Civil War had deepened the African-American's sense of identity with the land of his birth, giving him the feeling that he mattered, that he belonged.

It was good for the African-American that his faith in America had been strengthened, for there were trying times just ahead.

CHAPTER VIII

# Political, Economical, and Social Change

SIX MONTHS AFTER THE COLLAPSE OF THE CONFEDERACY, AFTER LEE HAD surrendered his fallen army to Grant, the fourth California State Convention of Colored Citizens met in Sacramento (October 25–28, 1865) to celebrate the extinction of slavery—and to focus their attention and weaponry at discriminatory legislation, including the law prohibiting black people from participating in elections (voting) or holding public office.

Although black Californians enjoyed greater opportunities than African-Americans in other states, anti-black laws did exist, and there were disturbing incidents of blatant racism. The majority Union party in Yuba County, for instance, bitterly protested the removal of any anti-black laws, insisting "we still believe this to be a white man's government and the extension of the natural rights to the negro is degrading, impolitic and unnatural."

There was also the continuing threat of anti-black emigration legislation, as well as the fact that California's African-Americans were denied the right to exercise their voice in the education of their children, and they were excluded from the state's Homestead Act, which entitled white settlers to 160 acres or more of public agricultural land after working it for five years.

> Until 1863, if a white settler wanted the public land that a black settler had cultivated, all he had to do was to claim it. The black settler had no recourse for he was denied the right to bring suit or to testify in court.

Economic hardship was not uncommon, although countless black families had managed to prosper in the Golden State, particularly in business and real estate holdings. Listing 156 adults in 1865, for example, the black citizens of Marysville estimated their wealth at $163,690, while San Francisco's 1,600 African-American adults represented a total wealth of one million dollars. Sacramento's African-American community not only reported nearly a quarter million dollars ($241,845) in property but also proudly declared that *no black in the county needed to be supported by either public assistance or the benevolent societies blacks had established for their race's poor.* Of Sacramento's 478 black adults, 375 could read and write. (Sacramento's white adults did not fair so well; nearly half were illiterate.)

State law required California's African-Americans to pay school taxes, but other state laws prevented them from enrolling their children in "white" schools—and no public funding was provided for separate schools.

> Race did not in any way play a part in the planning for California's first public school. This keystone institution was established in San Francisco in 1848, two years before Congress admitted California to the Union.
>
> On September 24, 1847, the San Francisco Town Council appointed a committee consisting of William Alexander Leidesdorff, William Clark and William Glover to take measures for the establishing of a public school.
>
> A school house was erected on Portsmouth Square, dignified by the name of Public Institute, and on April 3, 1848, the school house was opened by Thomas Douglass, a Yale graduate, who received a salary of one thousand dollars a year.
>
> From this beginning has grown, with some interruptions, the public school system of California.
>
> Thus, at the very inception of what is today a multi-billion dollar educational system in the Nation's most populous state,

an African-American—San Francisco's William Alexander Leidesdorff—played a leading and major role.

Among the 1865 Convention delegates were former slaves who understood and appreciated the value of an education. Knowledge had enabled many of them to buy their own freedom; others had taught themselves to read and write. David Ruggles, who urged black Californians to pledge one dollar each month for their schools (he himself was willing to give five dollars), was a former slave who had been taught by an Englishman visiting his owner. By doing so, the British sojourner had risked imprisonment under the laws of Louisiana. Besides David Ruggles, delegates included William H. Yates, Reverend John J. Moore, James R. Starkey and Theophilus B. Morton (who was to become the first black librarian of the U.S. Court of Appeals). Each of these delegates were ex-slaves who had actively participated in the Abolitionist movement in the East. Morton had founded the Afro-American League of California. Yates, born a slave in Virginia, helped runaway slaves escape after gaining his own freedom. Prior to emigrating to California, Yates had worked as a porter at the U.S. Supreme Court, a steward, the owner of a hackney stable and a restaurateur—yet he possessed a knowledge of Congressional affairs and legal proceedings that qualified him to become the president of the First Colored California Convention. He was succeeded by William Henry Hall, who presided over the next two conventions.

Born in 1823 in Washington, D.C., William Henry Hall was a third-generation free African-American, entirely self taught until he spent two years at Oberlin College in Ohio studying for the ministry. Few black congregations were able to support a minister's family so Hall, with eight children, needed a more lucrative profession. Earlier, Hall had returned from the California gold rush and thus had been able to afford a splendid wedding ("without a parallel in the history of coloured society in New York") when he married Sarah Lavinia Bailey. Returning to the Golden State, the Halls settled first in Oroville, where William became a delegate for Butte County and a member of the Executive Committee for the California Colored Convention. By 1860 he was the owner of a billiard saloon in San Francisco, with personal property valued at $600. (Owner of the building that had formerly housed the Athenaeum, an African-American literary club, Hall opened his saloon on the premises, much to the chagrin of the puritanical faction of San Francisco's black leadership.) A year later, in the *San Francisco City Directory,* Hall listed his occupation as "barber," and in the 1870 Census he is still listed as a barber—which was one of the most lucrative occupations for black people at the time; his personal property had risen to one thousand dollars, his real estate to six thousand dollars. Like William H. Yates, who wrote under the pseudonym "Amigo," Hall (using the pennames Pericles and Uncas) contributed articles and letters to California's African-American newspapers, including the *Pacific Appeal,* published in San Francisco between 1862 and 1879, and *The Elevator,* which was the official organ of the State Executive Committee of the Colored Citizens of California.

At the 1865 Convention, William Henry Hall delivered an eloquent plea for an amendment to the California Constitution—one that would give African-Americans the right to vote. His speech at this fourth and last California Convention expressed the pride of black people.

**More conventions fighting for African-American rights took place in California than in any other state, except New York and Ohio, until the end of the Civil War.**

California's African-Americans were making and recording their own history and literature, training their own school teachers, and "disseminating useful information where it was never tasted or known before." Hall's style and agenda reflected the African-American convention movement of the time.

As other states continued the civil rights struggle, many residents of the Golden State slacked off. California's comparatively small population of African-Americans were exhausted from the movement's strain on their time and their finances. Further, support for equal rights from white Californians all but died after the Civil War. Compounding the lack of white support was the fact that many black people in California were either optimistic or resigned to living in comparative peace and comfort with their conservative white neighbors, and contented themselves with contributing money to African-American benevolence societies, churches and schools. Also distracting were the seemingly unlimited opportunities to make money that appeared to be available whenever there wasn't an economic depression. Still further, dissension among African-American leaders contributed to the difficulties of agreeing on a civil rights platform. Nevertheless, the topics William Henry Hall addressed in the 1865 Convention (and continued to address until his death in 1880) never became obsolete. The issues of better education—

> Our public school system permits no mixture of the races. Whilst I will foster by all proper means the education of the races, I should deem it a death blow to our system to permit the mixture of the races in the same school.
> —California State School Superintendent Paul K. Hubbs,
> *Sacramento Daily Union,* January 30, 1855

—of access to land ownership and job opportunities and political power simmered on for another one hundred years—until the Caucasian-created volcano erupted in Watts in 1965.

Hall's impassioned and eloquent speech did indeed reflect the pride and spirit of California's African-Americans:

> Mr. President—I have refrained from intruding upon the time of the Convention until now, but the importance of the question presented here for consideration, brings us before the American people of California, today, to ask their decision upon the great subject of negro suffrage. . .

> Fifteen years ago, when the despotism of slavery was at the height and plentitude of its power, and every interest, social and political, subserved its ends, California, in drafting a Constitution as one of the sovereign States of the Union, decreed that no bondsman ever should be held by legal enactment or constitutional law within her limits. In laying down this broad principle of liberty and self-government, her citizens were not actuated by the spirit of '76; they did not desire to recognize the negro as a man, nor to elevate him as a brother, but they seemed to be guided by an axiom of the learned Blackstone, in his theory upon the origin of governments, where he asserts that "The only true and natural foundations of society are the wants and fears of its individuals." The men of New England birth and education who exercised a predominating influence, comprehending the magnitude of this dictum, and stimulated by the immense mineral and agricultural resources opened to industry, could not tolerate a system that enabled one man with his hundred poor, black, ignorant slaves, to compete with the brains, the energy and the toil of the same number of white freemen. They knew they owed fealty to compromises and expedient fugitive slave laws, but the greater law of self-preservation outweighed all supposed obligations and consecrated the virgin soil of the young State to freedom. Sir, we have lived and prospered under the experiment, through the devastations of floods and fires, and Heaven still continues to bless the land. The motives that prompted the adoption of a free constitution in 1850 were those of policy, and are equally paramount now upon the expediency of negro suffrage. California

did not actively participate in the conflict of the great rebellion; she has no sins to atone for to her disloyal element for the entombing of thousands of Southern chivalry; but when dread embarrassment nearly neutralized the efficiency of the Government, when gold and silver were like drops of precious blood oozing from a decaying body, her hardy sons drained her hills and valleys to retard the inflation of a paper currency; to restore confidence to the farmer, the mechanic and the merchant, and once more to unbar the closed doors of the manufacturer to employment. What she failed to give physically was imparted materially, and every thousand hard dollars sent at such a critical time, from these golden shores, was equal to a brilliant victory won by the fearless Hooker—towering in the clouds, or the gallant Porter, ploughing the majestic waters of the Mississippi. The vital question to be seriously pondered over by the Union men, who have been baptized in the grace of the Emancipation Proclamation is: If it was impolitic, at the adoption of the State Constitution, to confide its influence and power upon those inimical to free labor, what can be gained now by permitting the same lurking, ambitious spirits to exercise privileges over the loyal negro, under the beneficient government they have aimed to strike from the family of nations? . . . A thousand pardons from a lenient President, a million voices sounding the redeeming grace of God's eternal word, will never remove the damning prejudice against the negro, and unappeasable hatred nourished against Yankee enterprises, Yankee ingenuity and Yankee success. The opponents of a reconstructed Government and of a reunited people are not yet appeased to the humiliation of defeat; they are of a proud and revengeful spirit, educated in the opinion that they were born to rule, and dispense whatever immunities may accrue; they have not yet relinquished the purposes they sought to accomplish upon the field of battle; they are determined again to be in power, to curb the despised Yankees in all their isms, and grind deeper down in despair the unprotected negro. To perfect this unholy purpose, they may be seen merging with Short and Long Hairs, rallying under every deceptive banner, spreading their canvas to catch the popular breeze of the great People's Party, and in order to mislead, divide and scatter those great elements of Unionism, founded upon the patriotism of the immortal Lincoln, they are endeavoring upon false issues against the negro's undoubted claims to equality before the law. I am here, sir, though of humble social position, and without notoriety, to warn those who are conservators of the public peace, in whose places another generation, perhaps not so well experienced, are soon to stand, that the loyal heart and well directed vote of the negro should now be summoned to counteract the deep laid schemes of involving this nation in another revolution—not a revolution swayed by vast armies, complete navies, and military heroes, eclipsing the world in wonderful daring, but an insidious revolution of public sentiment, undermining the virtue and morality of the people, and drifting every noble impulse of the human heart down the vortex of corruption.

This assemblage, in behalf of the colored people throughout the State, and whose labors are indissolubly bound with all her interests, ask to become equals before the law, not from sympathy with their condition, but as they are made amenable to all her simple justice demands that they should have a voice in selecting the administration of its powers. They seek it upon the assumption that they are no longer an enslaved race, but full citizens according to the decision of the Attorney-General Bates, and the recognition and acceptance of a black man in all his rights in the highest tribunals of the land. If the people of free and progressive California can jeopardize their reputations for these great qualities of discerning expediency, by withholding so great a boon, when considering their attitude with the progress of liberal principles, they will stand disgraced and condemned before the world for pretending to be governed by that sublime emanation that declares "all men free and equal."

It is urged by Copperhead malice and stupidity, that the negro is too ignorant to vote. May I not remind the authors of this evasive and flimsy pretext, that the negro in America, like the Israelites among the ancient Egyptians, have watched superior character, assimilated with the same ideas, and imitated the same virtues, until out of a servitude of two hundred and fifty years, they have not only made a name which is a power of strength among civilized mankind, but they have reared a nationality which is coextensive with the fame and future of the American people. The poor negro has indeed been severely scourged. Meeting the contact so long denied his ancestry, but which was essential to their full development, it has made them a new born race looking through a long vista of departed years, and mourning over the past barbarism of the race. Thank God, sir, they are in America, and especially in our beloved California, no longer discordant in feeling . . . The false duties of superstition have ceased to encumber their understandings, and truer oracles in the persons of refined colored men are reflecting the living light of truth; black men are making and recording their own history; writing their own literature, coining their own poems, preparing their own school teachers, and disseminating useful information where it was never tasted or known before.

The press, that mighty pendulum of human liberty, is now partly wielded by Anglo-African genius. Refined by the great variety of learning that is open to all, it is effecting a mighty work and changing the tide of events; its columns are perused in the mansions of rulers, the halls of legislation, the sacred precincts of the judiciary, and the humble cabin of the miner; it is emancipating the minds of those in wisdom and power from error, while it teaches its less favored votaries the grand principles upon which governments are founded, and its salutary prerogatives over all its subjects. Our people, being accustomed to act as directed, are quietly but surely receiving the new light that is breaking in upon them, and in anticipation of a higher sphere of action, are mastering the difficulties of language, the intricacies of social and political law, and the breadth and scope of the Constitution. What class of citiziens are they who would smother the infant efforts of a struggling race, just emerging from the darkness of a long night into the bright beams of a dawning day? Can it be the noble born American who will refuse us the right to drop a ballot as well as to aim a bullet? They should recollect their hours of youth, their days of manhood, and their decline of years, have been tenderly watched by the negro's kindness since the Republic was rocked in infancy. Can it be the warm and generous-hearted Irishman, who first received here, in his adopted country, those gems of liberty that reverted his imagi- nation back to the heroic death and epitaph of Emmet, the gifted eloquence of Walton, and the patriotic lessons of the incomparable O'Connell, whose thrilling tones ever went to the hearts of men for liberty and equality to all races of men? Sir, do not tell me it is the honest and toiling German, whose fatherland has so long kept the undimmed fires of freedom and independence so brightly burning. Why is it the charmed land that cradled renowned Luther and moulded the transcendant genius of Schiller? When did these people prove rec- reant? For their love and struggles for liberty had illumed all Europe and the world, from the dread conflicts of past ages to the memorable revolution of 1848. Do I hear that it is the chivalric son of gigantic France, whose own great Lafayette dedicated life and fortune to the maintenance of the rights of man? Have they degenerated from the electric of the Marseillaise battle hymn of liberty, or will they attempt to wipe from memory the aspirations of their sincere but dreamy Lamartine? To all these people of different races, speaking different languages, and having diverse notions of the true policy of the Ameri- can Government, I know that plausible argument will be produced by our antagonists against the negro's right to equality before the law. But every righteous cause has always been assailed by subtle argument and almost convincing logic. It is little over the lifetime of temperate men when England's most astute statesmen endeavored to make Americans believe that George III had a divine right to impose upon the infant colonies "taxation without representation;" but Patrick Henry, in the House of Burgesses of Virginia, and black Cripsus At- tucks, in the streets of Boston, demurred, and the once humble de- pendencies are now a mighty and expanding nation. I need not cite the massacre of St. Bartholomew, where the poor but faithful Hugue- not bit the dust of persecution, the horrors of the Spanish inquisition, and the inhuman cruelties of the monster Philip the Second—all of which have been justified by as potent argument as that now produced in opposition to the negro's elevation. The negro's right to vote is indisputable, because wherever his mind has been educated he has given the same evidence of proficiency, because he has measured steps with the highest perfection of man's courage, by three times singly rescuing the country from the most impending dangers; because the wise man who lived about the time the National Government was framed, gave black men the right to vote in North Carolina, Virginia, Maryland, Deleware, and many other slave States, without detriment to the general weal . . . The word white, Mr. President, in the Constitution of California, is anti-republican—at variance with the good sense of magnanimity of her people, repugnant to many of her sister States, inconsistent with the present age, and unwise when considered in connection with the intercourse soon to be established with the copper-colored nations of China and Japan. We, as black men, concede the fact that a few years since, when our interest was mingled with slavery and degradation, and when the interest of this flourishing State was under the dominion of such satellites as W. M. Gwin, and P. T. Herbert, and J. B. Weller, that the black race had nothing to look for but cold indifference and contemptible hatred; but now that the country is reeling upon the brink of ruin, with a yawning abyss of destruction awaiting to receive its crumbling wreck, we ask, calmly but firmly, shall we not be allowed once more to prop its mighty superstructure, so that it may stand the ravages of time? Remember, men in power, the vast responsibilities resting upon your judgment. Other nations have passed through somewhat similar ordeals like yours before they became strong and consolidated; but none like yours have ever been seen trying to devise escapes from the strongest and most reliable element of their support. If you are inspired by that patriotism that sinks all consideration of prejudice to the greatness and glory of America's future, then all will be well. But if expediency and narrow contracted views govern your councils, and the unmistakable purpose of Divine authority be disregarded, then, like the perverse nations of old, grand and now beautiful America will be mingling with their mouldering decay.

As was the case with the oratory eloquence of Delegate J. H. Townsend at the First State Convention of the Colored Citizens of California, William Henry Hall's impassioned speech fell on deaf ears.

★  ★  ★

The suffrage issue became the major African-American demand immediately following the end of the Civil War, but public feeling against allowing black people to vote continued strong for several years—so strong that in 1867 San Francisco Democrats won an election largely on the issue of preventing African-Americans from voting.

Voters in other states eventually settled the issue for the entire country by approving a constitutional amendment granting African-Americans the right to vote in U.S. elections.

The right of citizens of the United States to vote shall not be denied or abridged by the United States or any State on account of race, color, or previous condition of servitude.

The Congress shall have the power to enforce this article by appropriate legislation.

—15th Amendment

The 15th Amendment, which was not ratified by California, became the law of the land after national adoption. (The amendment was proposed to the legislatures of the several states by the 40th Congress, February 26, 1869, and was declared to have been ratified in a proclamation by the Secretary of State, March 30, 1870.)

★   ★   ★

Where the final years of the 1850s had been painfully dramatic for California's African-American population, the first few years of the 1860s seemed to signal a rise in the fortunes of black people in the Golden State. The cause of the convention movement was assisted tremendously by national development as well as human factors. The very first year of the new decade saw the arrival in California of the Reverend Thomas Starr King, who gave African-American causes a great deal of support, and the return of Mary Ellen Pleasant. In the same year one of the major figures in African-American journalism—Peter Bell—came to California, and an African-American press was soon born again on the West Coast. Bell had been associated with the African-American press in the East since its beginnings in the 1830s. He was a sophisticated, talented, learned and worldly journalist—and a meaningful addition to the leadership group in the California convention movement.

While the exodus to Victoria had resulted in the loss of Gibbs and others, the leadership of the 1850s had at all times contained a gifted and courageous group of men and women. Gibbs had worked with Frederick Douglass in the anti-slavery movement in the East. William H. Yates, who was president of the first California Colored Convention and was associated with all the subsequent conventions, bought his own freedom in Washington, D.C., as a young man. Becoming a porter in the United States Supreme Court, he experienced an unusual intellectual exposure. When he moved to New York, he became a Mason and was actively involved in the anticolonization movement. He migrated to California in 1851 and became an employee of the California Steamship Navigation Company. As a chief steward he plied the waters of San Francisco Bay and was undoubtedly able to function as a unifying agent in the convention movement.

William Henry Hall, who was president of the Second Colored Convention, had an equally interesting career before moving to California. In Washington, D.C., he was the fund raiser for a monument for Benjamin Banneker. In New York he too became a Mason and was active in that state in the campaign for African-American suffrage in the 1840s. Thomas Dettner was a correspondent of Frederick Douglass as were others in the convention movement. William Newby had also been a western contributor to Douglass' paper. He was editor of California's first African-American newspaper, *Mirror of the Times.* Newby's ability was recognized by the French government, and he was asked in 1858 to be the private secretary to the French Consul General in Haiti. New Bedford-born Jeremiah B. Sanderson was on the same platform with Frederick Douglass when the latter was discovered by William Lloyd Garrison. Most, if not all, of the printed proceedings of the California Colored Conventions are in Sanderson's handwriting. His great competence made him the foremost teacher, black or white, in the Golden State. In Los Angeles, Biddy Mason became one of the most indefatigable workers in organizing schools for black children and, like Sanderson, gained begrudging financial support from various boards of education.

When victory had at last been gained in the matter of testimony— In 1863 the State Legislature of California revised the testimony laws, and the African-American was, at long last, relieved of this deadly disability—Peter Bell, then editor of the African-American newspaper, *The Pacific Appeal,* wrote:

> We should be more guarded than ever against committing any acts that might be construed by the enemies of our advancement, as a consequence of the repeal of those unjust laws. . . . We should be patient and conciliating. . . .

And then he added with a remarkable quality of objectivity:

> We must not always suppose that every offense that may be committed against us is altogether in consequence of our color.

Early in 1864, editor Bell felt optimistic and wrote:

> A new era has already dawned and it is with yourselves to decide as

to whether you or your children shall be made capable of assuming the responsible positions which already await you. The Federal Government and the good and intelligent among the American people, are endeavoring to help you.

Peter Bell had no way of knowing that many generations of white Americans were yet to come who would try to freeze the African-American in his subordinate position in American life by telling him that he was trying to move too fast.

★   ★   ★

For a decade after the end of the Civil War California's African-American residents were more alive to national issues and the problems of Reconstruction than to local politics. Most were optimistic, linking freedom to a deepening sense of patriotism.

We are part and parcel of the great American body politic; we love our country and her institutions and we are proud of her greatness.
—Thomas Dettner

Fortunately for the Southern African-American, not yet accustomed to freedom, a number of California's black people ventured into the South to assist in whatever way they could. Harriet Mason, the youngest daughter of Biddy Mason, worked with the Bureau of Refugees, Freedmen and Abandoned Lands—which was popularly known as the Freedmen's Bureau—which Congress had established in March 1865, in the War Department.

During six years of service with the Bureau, Harriet Mason played an active role in establishing hospitals, distributing food rations and clothing rations, and treating hundreds of thousands of cases of illness.

The Bureau also established over 4,000 schools, from the elementary grades through college, charging no fees and often furnishing free textbooks. Nearly a quarter of a million former slaves received varying amounts of education through such efforts.

**After six grueling years with the Freedmen's Bureau, Harriet Mason took up residence in her native Georgia—and spent the remaining years of her life teaching reading, writing, and arithmetic to black children.**

California's African-Americans were also actively involved in opposition to the so-called Black Codes—laws for the control of the African-American. These were the work of state legislatures which had come into existence under the Reconstruction policies of Lincoln and Johnson, who had assumed that the seceded states had not left the Union, that their restoration should be speedy, and that the executive arm of government should take the lead in bringing it to pass.

The Black Codes, passed in the fall and winter of 1865–66, were designed and intended to take the place of the defunct slave codes, and the two had many features in common. But, in enacting the Black Codes, the Southern legislatures made one fatal miscalculation: they had no idea of the storm of opposition such measures would arouse.

On December 4, 1865, the Thirty-Ninth Congress appointed a Joint Committee on Reconstruction. Charged with inquiring into conditions in the former Confederate states, the Joint Committee of Fifteen, as it was popularly known, included as advisors two prominent black Californians—Theophilus B. Morton and J. H. Townsend. Of stern visage, and with skin the color of true black, Morton was regarded by Southern whites as a diabolical fanatic—and he returned their hatred, matching epithet with epithet.

For four months the Joint Committee held hearings and took testimony; subcommittees were sent to investigate reports submitted by Morton and Townsend. Giving full publicity to its findings, which inevitably tended to support its own point of view, the Joint Committee slowly but surely began to influence political opinion. Reflecting something of its own temper, Congress in early April 1866 passed a Civil Rights Act, which extended citizenship to the former slaves and, because of the recommendation of California's Theophilus B. Morton, stipulated that discriminations against them were to be tried in federal courts.

★　★　★

If Reconstruction left its mark on white America, it also affected black America's political life and means of earning a living. Reconstruction made the African-American a Republican. In the words of Peter Bell, and echoed by Frederick Douglass, the Republican party was the deck, and all else was the sea. A large number of African-Americans became Democrats, but they had to bear the reproaches of their fellow African-Americans and sometimes even the contempt of whites of their own party.

Politically, too, the experiences of Reconstruction led the African-American to look to the national government rather than to the state for protection. To the African-American, "local self-government" meant a denial of his right to take part in politics. Inevitably, then, the African-American looked to the federal government to ensure his rights; he became, as he remains today, an ardent supporter of federal control of the extension of federal power.

In getting a job and making a living, the period after Reconstruction was particularly galling to African-Americans. A laboring class shorn of political power is largely at the mercy of fate. This was the lot of California's black people.

The relatively small percentage of African-Americans who worked as salaried agricultural workers in the Golden State received an average annual wage of sixty dollars. With that sum they had to clothe themselves and purchase necessary articles for subsistence.

Like their rural sisters and brothers, African-Americans in California towns had problems. White laborers brought strong pressure to drive the black worker out of the skilled jobs. In instances in which African-Americans were able to retain their skilled occupations, they were forced to accept lower wages: African-American carpenters in the 1800s averaged $.75 to $1.25 an hour, whereas white carpenters received $1.50 an hour and up.

In jobs traditionally held by black people, the picture was somewhat brighter. African-American janitors outnumbered whites nearly eight to one. Black draymen and teamsters outnumbered whites by three to one, and black stonemasons outnumbered whites by more than two to one. Barbering remained among the better jobs held predominantly by African-Americans; Jefferson Herndon, who opened a shop in Sacramento, became well-to-do, owning and renting fifty shops within fifteen years.

Lesser occupations, notably those in domestic service, were likewise monopolized by African-Americans. The pay, however, was low: domestic cooks averaged $5 a month as late as 1902.

The plight of the African-American living in the city, and who was in search of employment, was intensified by the deepening color line. The doctrine of white supremacy and black separation permeated the job market as it did other aspects of California life. Increasingly the African-American found himself driven out of the "clean" and better-paid occupations. (At the close of the Civil War five out of every six artisans were African-Americans, but by the turn of the century the skilled black workers probably numbered not more than five percent of the total.) In essence, the relationship between the races had become one of "boss and black."

Ignored by the first coast-to-coast labor federation—the National Labor Union—African-Americans formed two national unions of their own. Both the National Negro Labor Union and the National Labor Convention of Colored Men were established in Washington in 1869. Although the latter established a Bureau of Labor to encourage and support the formation of African-American locals, both organizations were dominated by public figures who were civil rights advocates rather than labor union officers, such as Frederick Douglass and California's David W. Ruggles.

The fact that the national African-American labor union movement became political in its leadership was one of the reasons for its short life (less than five years). Leaders like Ruggles tended to equate the Republican party with the workingman's party and to subordinate the latter to the former. But there was another reason for the failure of the movement: the white workers were not to be won over. In an address issued in January 1870, the National Negro Labor Union urged whites to "join us in our movement, and thus aid in the protection and conservation of their and our interests." The invitation was ignored. Thus, the national African-American unions remained fatally outside the mainstream of organized labor, and by 1874 the separate national black union movement was dead. *The Pacific Appeal* carried a lead editorial entitled: "The Folly, Tyranny and Wickedness of Labor Unions," portraying the disillusionment of the black bourgeoisie and, to some extent, the black worker.

Organized labor's lack of forthrightness on the color issue inevitably turned the African-American into a strikebreaker. Since black people were unable to get jobs through the union, they got them directly from the employer. When white workers struck for better living conditions, black workers were offered their jobs. Ironically, in much of the job market the only way black people could get employment was by scabbing, which—it hardly need be added—widened the rift between the African-American worker and his white counterpart.

# CHAPTER IX

# A White Man's Country

TO THEIR LOT IN THE CALIFORNIA THAT TOOK SHAPE IN THE POST-RECON-struction years, African-Americans brought a variety of responses. They might rail at the fates, but they did not permit themselves to become immobilized by them. Americans, they must bestir themselves—take steps, do something.

And something they indeed did do.

★　★　★

The ratification of the 15th Amendment, and California's revision of the testimony laws in 1863, had come too late for many of the Golden State's African-Americans. Denied the right to testify in courts of law, California's black people had not been able to combat challenges against their ownership of vast amounts of land. As a result, hundreds of thousands of acres of California land owned by African-Americans was literally stolen by the white government.

In California's Spanish period a couple of dozen land grants had been made to black, Spanish-black and Indian-black settlers. In the Mexican period many more grants were made, including lands formerly used by some of the missions and in the last years a few grants that were as compensation. These lands remained in black families for generations, each passing on the land to the other.

The military governors represented, and the Treaty of Guadalupe Hidalgo more explicitly guaranteed, that titles to property that would have held good under Mexico would be honored by the United States. It turned out that there were more than 250 such claims by black people, some for only a few acres but others—like that of J. H. Townsend, who had inherited the land (105,000 acres) from his grandfather—in excess of 100,000 acres. These claims covered much of the cultivated land in the state, vast expanses of land grazed by cattle and horses, plus additional land not visibly in use.

The earlier experiences of white Americans had not prepared them to understand the propriety of large landholdings so customary in California. For cattle raising as it had been conducted in the province and as it was later to be conducted on the Great Plains, holdings of up to 11 square leagues (50,000 acres) were not excessive. Land was abundant, several acres were required to graze a cow, and black people—as was the case with non-black people—could own many head of cattle and still not be rich. Few white Americans could comprehend. Furthermore, the white government claimed that most of the grants were vague as to boundaries or seemed irregular in other particulars. It was argued that they should be reduced to the American norm before confirmation. Another proposal was that the ratification of all these titles—held by men and women of color—would leave none of California for the Americans (meaning white people).

Before any decision was reached, the entire issue was complicated by the gold rush. The broad holdings of the Mexican grantees now appeared fabulously and inexcusably rich. The inrushing tide of white Americans increased the pressure upon California's land supply thus jeopardizing the older titles. Prejudice against all things Mexican, and especially against black people holding Mexican land grants, began to escalate. In the Sacramento squatter riots, for example, the mood was to eradicate all preconquest titles without any formalities. In other words, white people were intent upon forcing black people off the lands that were rightfully black.

In 1851 Congress reviewed the problem. It had the benefit of two reports, one by Captain H. W. Halleck and the other by William Carey Jones. Halleck saw imperfections in most of the titles held by black people which would give the United States an entering wedge for breaking them. Jones, whose name appears on a number of petitions seeking revision of the testimony laws, after a careful examination of the California archives and consultation with Mexican and American officials in the province, reported that most of the titles were valid and that the very few which were fraudulent could easily be detected.

California senators, however, were more in sympathy with the squatters than with the black people who held titles to the land. The senators suspected many of the grants to be fraudulent and most of them excessive in size and pictured every California rancho owned by African-Americans as a prospective gold mine.

It was a white man's country, and black people—who are the true native Californians—were about to lose their lands.

In accordance with an act passed by the California Senate (February 6, 1851) and California House of Representatives (March 3, 1851), a board of three commissioners—all white—was installed in San Francisco in January 1852. Every claimant of land was required to appear before it within two years to present proof of title. As was to be expected, it was no easy matter for black grant holders to marshall the necessary proof for presentation. Their expenses were much increased because the commission, except for a short session at Los Angeles in the fall of 1852, held all its meetings in San Francisco. The commission wasted no time in acting on the 189 claims presented by California's black people—and it confirmed not a single one.

The worst feature was one prescribed by the law—that California's African-Americans had the burden of proof. Their claims were presumed faulty or fraudulent until positive proof to the contrary was brought forward. Denied the right to testify, or to bring suit, California's black people had no legal recourse against the commission. As a result, the lands they had cultivated, the lands they had legally owned, were virtually stolen from them.

★   ★   ★

One of the greatest victories for black Californians was the admission of their testimony in the State's courts, achieved in 1863. Most Colored Convention delegates had been actively involved in the eight year battle—twice as long as the Civil War—to change California's law of 1850 prohibiting blacks, mulattos (initially "persons having one-sixteenth part or more of Negro blood," then amended a year later to "Negroes or persons having one-half or more Negro blood") from testifying, whether for or against whites.

The right to equal testimony had been a primary concern for the first State Convention of Colored Citizens in 1855, and it remained a key issue during the Convention's 1856 and 1857 meetings—and for good reason: In Auburn, California, in June of 1857, blacks were precluded from testifying against several white men in the lynching of a former slave known only as "Dick." As a result, the white murderers were set free.

Ultimately, vigorous canvassing and signature-gathering from sympathetic whites won for the African-American the right to testify in California courts.

As stated, however, the right to testify had come much too late for many of the golden State's black residents.

★ ★ ★

Virtually propertyless, cut off from political life, and not faring all that well in the world of employment and education, African-Americans in California turned increasingly to their traditional center of hope—the church. The fading of the great expectations of Reconstruction days led the African-American to look anew to the church as an agency of uplift and inspiration. If not "For God and Country," as others had cried, then "For God."

In California, as across the nation, the white man's bias and prejudice brought about a separation of white and African-American churches. The theories of race held by most white Californians, which had led them to establish Jim Crow practices in secular life, made it all but impossible for them to welcome men and women of color into their church congregations. And the relatively small percentage of whites who were not averse to retaining or welcoming African-American membership were willing to do so only on condition that such members would agree to segregated seating and would not expect to take part in the church's social and/or business affairs. California's black people were not about to accept such stipulations. As a result, California Protestantism divided into all-white and all-black denominations.

**The Spaniards had transformed California into a Christian land, and to them, of course, Christian meant Roman Catholic. Protestant services and churches date from the gold rush.**

In 1866 African-American Baptist congregations in San Jose, Stockton, Sacramento, and San Francisco organized—under the guidance of the Reverend Darius Stokes—an association of their own; this was followed a few months later by a State-wide convention of African-American Baptist churches held in Los Angeles. By 1867 black and white Baptists in California were going their separate ways.

Other denominations experienced similar separation. Late in 1870 the Colored Methodist Church in America was organized, an offshoot of the Methodist Episcopal Church, South. African-American Methodism in California was further strenghtened by the coming of the African Methodist Episcopal Church and the African Methodist Episcopal Zion Church, which up to the Civil War had confined their work largely to the North. Like the Methodists, African-American Presbyterians in California began to form their own churches, over two-thirds of them taking this step by 1870. It was not until 1898, however, that the General Assembly of the Presbyterian Church in the United States actually transferred its African-American units to a newly organized African-American Presbyterian Church.

The problem of church separation touched even the Episcopalians, whose African-American membership was small. After the Civil War, this denomination continued to hold special services, known as "colored Sunday School," for its African-American communicants. This practice did not win black converts. Indeed, in San Francisco, where the Episcopalians were relatively strong among many African-Americans, the "colored Sunday School" had disappeared by 1880, its former members having either joined the two local African-American Episcopalian congregations or become Methodists or Baptists.

> Notwithstanding some lapses, as at San Luis Rey, the massive architecture of the missions well suited the California landscape. The church buildings of the early American period, of all shapes and styles or of no style at all, disfigured the scene more often than adorned it.

White and African-American, the denominations which attracted large memberships in the Golden State were desperately lacking in funds. This meant, particularly among African-Americans, that the church congregations were too poor to pay the salaries of college-trained men. Fortunately, however, an applicant's lack of formal schooling was not often a barrier to a call to a pastorate. Indeed, among some congregations an educated clergyman was suspect.

"Oh, for a studying ministry," lamented H. Edward Bryant in 1875. Presiding Elder of the Los Angeles District of the African Methodist Episcopal Church, Bryant spoke from experience: "I have visited many preachers, and have seldom found one with a single work on systematic theology, a dictionary, commentary or work on ethics."

Without formal training in theology or the arts and sciences, many African-American ministers were, in the words of Darius Stokes, "all sound and no sense, depending upon stentorian lungs, and a long-drawn mourn, for their success." Under such pastors, church services tended to become intensely emotional, with trances and weird singing.

Of necessity, the role of California's African-American clergymen was not confined to pulpit preaching and spiritual leadership. The African-American clergyman was, in the words of Peter Bell, editor of *The Pacific Appeal:* "a walking encyclopedia, the counselor of the unwise, the friend of the unfortunate, the social welfare organizer, and the interpreter of the signs of the times."

The African-American clergyman was a natural leader because his support came from the mass of people; therefore, he was in a position to speak more frankly on their behalf than an African-American leader whose job required that he have the good will of the white community.

The role of the African-American church, like that of its pastor, did not stop with Sunday service. California's African-American church was a highly socialized one, performing many functions. The church served as a community center, where one could find relaxation and recreation. It was a welfare agency, dispensing help to the sicker and poorer members. It was a training school in self-government, in the handling of money, and in the management of business. The church was the African-American's very own, giving him the opportunity to make decisions for himself, which was seldom available elsewhere.

**As in nearly all else, San Francisco's African-American community took the lead in establishing churches.**

Refusing to remain idle, refusing to play dead, California's African-Americans turned their efforts toward problems of education and employment for black people. Their concerns, brought to public attention at the Fourth State Convention of Colored Citizens in Sacramento in October 1865, also embraced the oppressed elsewhere in the world.

A formal expression of the convention sympathized with the oppressed of all nations, offered to extend African-American aid to free them from bondage, and resolved:

> That the results of the late unfortunate and unsuccessful revolutions of Poland and Hungary to free those countries from the tyranny of Russia and Austria cause regret and commiseration to every friend of human liberty.

> That notwithstanding the opposition we receive from Irish immigrants in America, whose prejudices against us are excited by the misnamed Democratic Party, every effort to rid Ireland of English bondage and establish Irish independence meets our cordial approbation.

William H. Yates, the San Francisco delegate who had bought his freedom from slavery in Washington, D.C., told the convention:

> I would like to see forty regiments of Irishmen defended by forty regiments of blacks. I would gladly be one of those to go across the Atlantic and help give liberty to the oppressed of Ireland.

Yates, as mentioned, was employed as a chief steward by the California Steamship Navigation Company of San Francisco.

The convention leaders, recognizing lack of education as a major factor contributing to prejudice against African-American Californians, urged black parents to aim their children at "the same high order of education developed among the white race."

Why African-Americans generally had little or no education was poignantly illustrated in an address by delegate D. W. Ruggles (an ex-slave who had been sold five times on the auction block in Louisiana). While serving his fifth owner, Ruggles related, he was befriended by an Englishman who was in the process of teaching him the alphabet when his owner found out about the basic academic exercise. The owner reproved his English friend, telling the astonished visitor he was liable to imprisonment by the state for helping to educate a black man in bondage. D. W. Ruggles, therefore, taught himself to read and write by firelight.

In its final message to the Golden State's nearly 5,000 African-American adults, the convention emphasized:

To gain eminence in the new field of political equality, toward which our journey tends, we must prove ourselves equal in art, industry and labor, as well as in knowledge and piety, to all others. We must not be satisfied with mediocrity; we must endeavor to excel.

Doing so would not be easy. After all, the white man fights to accomplish his ends; the African-American, to end what he is obliged to fight.

## California's Little James Meredith Case

A remarkable harbinger of events in this century at the University of Mississippi, Little Rock and elsewhere in the South, had its beginning on September 24, 1872 in San Francisco.

On that day an African-American child named Mary Frances Ward tried to integrate the Broadway Grammar School, a public school dedicated to the education of white children only. On the same day the California State Supreme Court agreed to consider a petition filed on behalf of Mary Frances, whose determined father demanded that his daughter be admitted to the school, her blackness notwithstanding.

It was a test case challenging the constitutionality of California laws banning children of African descent from public schools. African-American parents throughout the Golden State financed the court action after a long and unsuccessful campaign to change the law.

In 1885, the school laws had ignored non-white children. One law simply required "50 heads of white families" to petition for establishment of a school if they wanted one. The state would then support it. In 1860, California's African-Americans were specifically excluded by law from public schools—and any school accepting them could have had its state support funds cut off by the State Superintendent of Public Instruction.

The law at that time regarded the children of non-white parents as "prohibited parties." It provided that separate schools should be set up for them in districts where parents of ten or more submitted applications in writing for such a school. State funds, however, would not be provided. In 1866, non-white children who lived "under the care of white people" could be admitted to public schools by a majority vote of local school boards.

> Mary Frances Ward's knock at the door of the Broadway
> Grammar School in San Francisco was a let-me-in gesture just
> as significant as James Meredith's was to be in his introduction
> of the African-American to Mississippi exactly 90 years later.

San Francisco Attorney J. W. Dwindelle, in his 1872 appearance before the California State Supreme Court on behalf of Mary Frances Ward, delivered nearly verbatim the arguments the United States Supreme Court was destined to hear and act favorably upon in 1954.

> These colored children of African descent who are citizens have the right to be admitted to all the public schools of the State and cannot be compelled to resort to separate schools for colored children.
>
> We are told that by a just exercise of the police power of the Legislature these distinctions of color may be lawfully made and enforced.
>
> The police power! Gracious heavens! This is the power always invoked in desperate cases. The police power—the last resort of the tyrant, the last weapon for the assassination of written constitutions and of free institutions.
>
> —J. W. Dwindelle

Dwindelle contended (rightfully so) that segregation of school children violated the Bill of Rights and the Fourteenth and Fifteenth Amendments to the United States Constitution. The three-member court ruled that non-white children could not be legally excluded from public schools by reason of race or color if there were no separate and equal schools for them.

Events preceding the victorious decision for Mary Frances Ward, indeed for black children throughout the state, had thoroughly aroused African-American communities across California. In Oakland, an African-American school had been closed when black parents who lived in the vicinity had to move out of the district to areas where they could find employment. The children had no school near their new homes. The few remaining African-American families in the district where the school was closed managed to get their children into white schools and some white parents immediately withdrew their children in protest.

The closing of an African-American school in San Francisco around the same time was investigated by Delilah Beasley, who authored "The Negro Trail Blazers of California" in 1919. Mrs. Beasley recounted the incident in these words:

The Board of Education closed the Broadway School, not because there were not enough colored children attending to keep it open, but because, as one member of the Board of Education said: "It was a nuisance."

When asked to explain his remark more fully, he said, "It was too close to a white school on the same street."

After months of campaigning by leaders of the Colored Convention Movement, the Oakland school board finally agreed to admit children of African descent to public schools in the fall of 1872. The board evidently had seen the handwriting on the wall. Two bills pending in the Legislature at the time provided that all children should be admitted to public schools, regardless of color, and African-American determination to take the issue to court was crystallizing. The irony, of course, is that black people had to fight to attain educational opportunities for their children in a school system that had been developed by African-Americans, such as Pio Pico and William Leidesdorff.

> The University of Santa Clara traces its origins back to the College of Santa Clara and to classes conducted by Jeremiah B. Sanderson in 1851. The University of the Pacific, through a college, traces back to 1851, and the University of California, through the College of California, which it later absorbed, goes back to 1855. Both had several classes conducted by "women of color."

Just as the impetus for publicly supported schools in the Golden State was a result of the state constitutions drafted by the Republican-African-American regimes, so the strengthening of these schools resulted from the example set by the African-American and his church groups.

> As a patron of schools, the organized African-American church performed one of its greatest services. Bent upon giving its young people a Christian education and upon the better training of future clergymen, African-American church groups markedly expanded their school-funding efforts. Every major African-American denomination was represented in the movement, and individuals like Biddy Mason, Fritz Vosburg, Thomas Duff, and Moses Rodger contributed substantial amounts of money.

The poorer whites began to acquire some of the black man's faith in education, and to gradually overcome the opposition of economy-minded legislators and the banker groups they represented. White Californians, because of the esteemed efforts of African-Americans, had become school-minded.

In building schools with public monies, it was not possible to completely ignore the African-American—but less could be spent on African-Americans than on whites, on the grounds that there was little point in giving black people any training beyond the basic elements of reading and writing. Guided by this racist point of view, California's white school boards and prejudiced superintendents established separate schools which never were (nor have they ever been) equal. The length of the school year differed for white and black, as did the salaries for teachers. A school building for African-American children often turned out to be a hired hall, church basement, or vacant store.

California offered virtually no support to college-level work of African-Americans residing in the Golden State. The Morrill Act of 1862, which provided for the founding and maintenance of agricultural and mechanical colleges across the nation, was silent about dividing federal funds on a racial basis.

African-American parents, determined to provide educational opportunities for their children, supplemented the school monies that the state begrudgingly provided. Many went into their own pockets, giving what they could. Others raised money by holding rummage sales, giving suppers, and selling raffle tickets.

Such sacrificial giving, although meager compared to the total need, had its influence in enlisting substantial contributions from the great educational foundations then being established. Many of these philanthropic agencies showed either an exclusive or special interest in African-Americans.

**Thomas Duff and William H. Newby, both of whom remained active in the Colored Convention movements, were directly involved in successfully soliciting a $1,000,000 contribution to African-American education from the John F. Slater Fund.**

In addition to gifts from foundations, California's African-American schools received support from individual philanthropists. One of the earliest and most generous of such benefactions was Kate Douglas Wiggins' grant of $25,000 for the "uplifting of the colored population of California, and their posterity, by conferring upon them the blessings of Christian education." Wiggins took this step out of her admiration for Jeremiah B. Sanderson.

> To me he (Sanderson) seems one of the foremost of living men because his work is unique.
>
> —Kate Douglas Wiggins

Like a growing number of other people, black and white alike, Wiggins liked Sanderson's ideas about the best kind of training for African-American youth.

Sanderson believed in vocational education, the mastering of trades with the aim of becoming a skilled wage earner. His philosophy, in later years, was echoed by another African-American educator—Booker T. Washington, founder and principal of Tuskegee Institute. In schools established by Sanderson, young black women became proficient at cooking, sewing, and nursing, and young black men learned how to become better farmers or were taught the trades of carpenters, blacksmiths, plumbers, and painters.

Aware that many African-Americans resented industrial education, connecting it with slavery, Jeremiah B. Sanderson advocated education that developed character as well as mechanical skills. Though by no means the originator of vocational education, in his day Jeremiah B. Sanderson was its greatest exponent in the Golden State. Moreover, his influence outstripped that of anyone else. Before making gifts to African-American schools, prospective white donors sought Sanderson's assurance that their monies would be earmarked for his kind of education.

Sanderson's influence on education, like that of another man of African ancestry—William Alexander Leidesdorff—extended beyond the African-American world. An appreciation of schooling became increasingly evident among whites, and they proceeded to follow the pattern molded by Sanderson-founded schools. Years later, Booker T. Washington was not boasting when, in 1908, he pointed out that "it was the Negro schools in large measure that pointed the way to the value of education."

Similar words can be spoken about the African-American's impact on transportation, theater, and journalism.

★   ★   ★

The theater was a culture form that could respond buoyantly to the stimulation of gold. Although there had been amateur performances, the first professional to take a turn apparently was Gates Jefferson, a former slave who escaped to California at the beginning of the gold rush. In June 1849, he put on a one-man show in San Francisco near the Silver Street kindergarten in Tar Flat—a slum as tough as the Barbary Coast. In a rich baritone he sang several of his own compositions; in falsetto he mimicked an operatic diva. Next came a series of monologues in Yankee dialect, climaxed by a seven-voice rendition of a New England town meeting. Jefferson was followed by a minstrel show at the Bella Union, its run cut short when one of the "bones" was killed. Later in 1849, in a large tent at Clay and Kearny, Joseph Rowe presided over a circus featuring nine black acrobats and equestrians and a posing horse.

At Sacramento the Eagle Theater, featuring three "women of color," opened with *The Bandit Chief; or, The Forest Spectre*. Plays such as *The Wife, Dead Shot, Othello, Batchelor Buttons, William Tell, Rent Day,* and *Charles II* were also in the repertoire. In January 1850, this company, which now included eight African-American actors and actresses, brought legitimate theater to San Francisco. Although the manager of the troupe lost the first week's receipt at the gambling tables, the popular response encouraged other impresarios to provide similar entertainment.

The African-American paragon of the gold rush theater was a former slave named Buela Baines. Her debut was at a tiny log theater in Rabbit Creek—the same theater in which the white actress Lotta Crabtree made her debut.

In long-tailed green coat, knee breeches, and tall hat, Buela bounced on stage and danced a vigorous Irish jig and reel. After encores she appeared again—this time wearing a white dress with round neck and puffed sleeves and sang a plaintive ballad. The hardened miners went wild, showering the stage with coins, gold nuggets, and a 50-dollar slug. Brown-eyed, black-haired Buela, all of twelve years old but looking no more than ten, was their darling. (Crabtree started her career at the age of eight.)

Tutored by her ambitious mother and other willing helpers, Buela Baines made a rapid tour of the mining camps. She learned new songs and steps. A black minstrel named Williams Davis taught her to do a soft-shoe breakdown. Lola Montez introduced her to Spanish dancing and Jake Wallace taught her how to make a banjo ring. From others she picked up buck-and-wing and new bits of pantomime. Thus equipped she could put on a whole show in the style of Gates Jefferson. With barrel-top numbers at auctions, variety billings in the mines and in San Francisco, the city which gave her its heart, bits in the regular plays, and specialties between acts, Buela Baines had a busy childhood. In one little vibrant bundle of beautiful black energy she represented the things the Californians of this generation most prized: humor and pathos, high skill and lower buffoonery, mastery of the traditional forms and indulgence in pyrotechnics.

> The ebullience of the audience often made playing the San Francisco stage an exciting experience for African-American troupes. Making the circuit of the mining camps was even more of a test. Traveling by stagecoach or on horseback, putting up at primitive hotels, living on rough fare, and performing in makeshift theaters, the black troupers had to rise above circumstances. A play, often sharply curtailed, was the feature of each performance. To it the African-American artists added solos, dances, readings, impersonations, and skits—a combination of legitimate theater and vaudeville.

Performances, of course, were reviewed in such African-American publications as *Mirror of the Times* and *The Pacific Appeal*.

California writing began long before the golden era, and is distinguished for content more than for style. Palou's and Font's writings (*Life of Serra* and *Complete Diary,* respectively) were works of Christian duty. Other, lesser known writers, such as James Beckwourth and Jacob Dodson, were inspired by a conviction that the existing California experiences of which they had direct knowledge were eminently worth recording and would be read with interest in Mexico and Spain or in the United States. The same is true for the many African-American trail journals, ocean logs, and miners' diaries, such as that of Vosburg, Simms, and Holland.

The outset of the American period was marked by an increased African-American demand for reading matter—a demand that was met after a fashion by the shin-plaster journals started by Emory Waters in Nevada County and by Ellen Mason in Los Angeles. The demand continued to multiply. *Mirror of the Times,* edited by William H. Newby, was followed by Peter Bell's *The Pacific Appeal*. In Los Angeles, J. J. Neimore, who had escaped slavery in Missouri, founded and began to publish still another African-American newspaper, the *California Eagle*.

Quantitatively, California's African-American journalism scaled heights that without the gold rush would not have been attained for decades. For many years the state's black people could boast a per capita circulation exceeding even that of New York's black press. As for quality, praise must be more parsimonious. The presses, type, and paper available were uniformly inferior, composition and press-work were indifferent, and proofreading was an undeveloped art. Most of the sheets were partisan and reflected the malodorous state of California's local racist politics. One hopeful sign was a tendency to escape some of the inhibitions of eastern journalists.

**African-American journalists aimed to be fearless champions of the common people and to the best of their ability they adhered to that policy.**

Most African-American newspapers founded early in California contained a few literary pieces, which were received with enough favor to suggest in 1852 the issuance of a weekly paper largely devoted to such materials. This journal, *California's Golden Black,* which was founded by James Hubbard, included ordinary news but its distinction lies in its emphasis on literature. It flourished for nine years and was read more widely than any of its competitors, black or white.

**One major white contributor to California's Golden Black was Ina Coolbrith who, as a little girl, was carried across the Humbolt Sink by an African-American named James P. Beckwourth.**

**Coolbrith was one of hundreds of white people who owed their lives to African-Americans. Unlike the vast majority of the others, Coolbrith readily admitted it.**

To single out names such as Delano, Derby, Twain, Bret Harte, and Miller—as is the case in most books of California history—obscures the picture of the broader ranks of California writers. That there were many is an elementary fact; that they produced an astonishing quantity of credible literature is also admitted; that many of these writers were black is all-too-often overlooked or ignored. These early African-American Californians had a high estimate of their own importance—and rightfully so. They were the pioneers who had reached continent's end; almost overnight they were erecting a magnificent state; their gold was a decisive factor in preserving the union. California's African-American writers, from Peter Bell to William Newby to James Hubbard, steeped in this feeling, were sure they had something important to write about.

And they did.

CHAPTER X

# Steamboats, Stages, and Railroads

IN THE DROWSY CALM OF THE PASTORAL ERA CALIFORNIA HAD MADE NO transportation demands which could not be met by a saddled horse, an ox-drawn carreta, or the irregular sailings of the trading vessels. The incoming Americans wanted more modern means of getting about, for which they were willing to pay. The result was a revolution in communications within the state and a speedy provision of land and sea connections with other parts of the world, particularly the eastern states. And, as with virtually every other aspect of California life and history, the African-American played a significant role.

★   ★   ★

Commissioned by fellow miners, Alexander Todd came down to the San Francisco post office to carry up their mail at an ounce a letter. James Beckwourth cut the price to half an ounce and carried a thimble as measuring cup. With only 34 post offices in the state by June 1851, private mail carrying expanded and soon merged with a reverse flow of gold delivery. Adams and Company opened a San Francisco office in 1849 and Wells, Fargo in 1852. Their express

145

carrying was supplemented throughout the interior by many smaller outfits.

Carrying passengers was another opportunity. The first artery was the river line to Sacramento, plied by a miscellany of small craft propelled by sail or oar. A few round-the-Horn ships were worked up to Sacramento. By the late summer of 1849 side-wheelers were in commission, soon joined by the 400-ton *McKim* and the *Senator,* said to have netted her owners $60,000 a month. Within a year— and as predicted by William Alexander Leidesdorff—fifty steamers large and small were operating on the bay and the inland waterways. The *New World,* built for excursion duty on the Hudson, was boarded up and sent around the Horn. On the San Francisco-Sacramento run, along the same route first traveled by a black man, the *New World* cut the *Senator's* time from ten to six hours.

**Navigator for the *New World* was Lester D. Trivett, a black man whose knowledge of tides and currents made him invaluable to the *New World's* owners.**

Competitive rate wars, lowering the Sacramento fare from $25 to $30 to one dollar, led to organization of the California Steam Navigation Company in 1854, capitalized at $2,500,000—in which the president of the first Colored Convention of California, William H. Yates, played a prominent role.

Disasters were common. The waters were not thoroughly charted, many vessels were faulty, steamship inspections were lax, and the passion for racing led to boiler explosions. The first half dozen years saw a score of such accidents with up to 50 people killed. The Californians delighted in impromptu races and the more steam carried the better they liked it.

**It is interesting to note that not one African-American navigator was involved in any of the many steamboat accidents.**

At an early date steamships became the chief connection of San Diego, Los Angeles, Santa Barbara, San Luis Obispo, and Santa Cruz to the San Francisco metropolis. At these towns steamer day became a major feature on the calendar, and for several decades these ships provided the most favored transportation. Schooners and steamships, with more than a few African-American captains and navigators, were soon plying the wilder coast north of San Francisco, accepting passengers and general cargo, but chiefly loading lumber and other wood-related supplies at Eureka and less sheltered ports.

★　★　★

From San Pedro stages ran to Los Angeles. They were the way to reach Yosemite and many other points in the state. Wagon freighting also became a very active business, to and from the ports, ranchos, mines, forts, and Indian reservations, from Los Angeles to San Bernardino and back, and all the way to Salt Lake.

By the sixties a number of shortline railroads had been built where proven traffic already was available. The Los Angeles-San Pedro route, realizing Phineas Banning's scheme (and funded, in part, by George Washington Dennis), was ready for service in 1869. Six years later the Los Angeles and Independence Railroad, which looked across Cajon Pass to mines of the Nevada border, laid tracks to the Santa Monica waterfront and gave Los Angeles a second access to shipping.

★　★　★

In the autumn of 1849 John Whistman, with an old French omnibus and a mixed team of mustangs and mules, offered a ride from San Francisco to San Jose; the fare, two ounces (of gold). A competing line appeared. In the autumn of 1850 two experienced stage operators, Warren F. Hall and Jared B. Crandall, bought out Whistman and extended service to Monterey.

By the mid-fifties the California lines boasted newer and better equipment than anywhere else. On a conventional running gear with a pair of C-shaped springs anchored to each axle, thoroughbraces (manifold leather straps) were stretched to cradle the egg-shaped body of the newest coach—the Concord. Nine or ten passengers could be squeezed into the Concord, and about as many on top. Boots at front and back carried mail and baggage. The Concord weighed less than most coaches. Although driven at great speed— 10, 12, or even 15 miles per hour over unconscionably rough roads— they seldom needed repairs.

The driver was one of the heroic figures of the West. His wizardry in piloting a stage on a night run or careening down a mountain road and his exploits in foiling hold-ups and Indian attacks made him a legend. And indeed, to manipulate whip and brake and play upon the six reins so that each horse was individually controlled called for a virtuoso.

Of all California stage drivers, perhaps the greatest, most respected and most admired, was an African-American who drove a stage daily between Wawona and Yosemite Valley.

Yosemite Valley was first viewed in 1849, explored in 1851, and publicized in words soon read around the world in 1855.

William H. Newby, the editor of *Mirror of the Times,* published the very first printed description of Yosemite Valley in the *Times* of June 1855. The first white description was published a month later, on July 12, 1855, in the *Mariposa Gazette.*

Until 1874, all Yosemite visitors entered on foot or by horse or mule back. After that, they traveled in stagecoaches over the three pioneer roads into the Valley to see for themselves the reported wonders of half-mile-high waterfalls, sheer cliffs, and domes of solid granite. Celebrations and clouds of dust attended the openings of the African-American built Coulterville Road in June 1874, the Big Oak Flat Road a month later, and the Wawona Road the following year. All three were toll roads and two exist, in paved, realigned fashion, today. Only the Coulterville road has been bypassed by progress and modernization.

Today, well over two million people visit Yosemite Valley annually. This surge of sightseers, traveling comfortably on scenic highways and staying in fine motels or campgrounds equipped with modern conveniences, presents tremendous contrast to those hardy souls who rode in stagecoaches through rugged wilderness, placing their safety (if not their very lives) in the hands of the men who drove them.

## At the Reins

The stage driver was not an ordinary man. He held a high place in the West and was known to travelers as "Jehu," "Whip," "Knight," or by a variety of nicknames relating to his individual personality. He had to be skilled, strong, and at the same time accommodating to his passengers. Many of the stage drivers came to be well known, and descriptions of them were recorded by numerous wayfarers. They were a colorful set of individualists and decidedly rugged. Not one of them, however, was as colorful or as well-known as George "Alfred" Monroe, an African-American who had been born of a union between an Ashanti merchant-seaman and a white seamstress in San Francisco.

Author Ben C. Truman, writing for *The Overland Monthly* in March of 1898, had this to say of Alfred:

> Probably no man, colored or white, living or dead, has ever driven so many illustrious people. Grant, Garfield, Hayes, Blaine, Schurz, Sherman, Senator Stewart, Senator Morgan of Alabama, and hundreds of other Senators and Congressmen; Governors of many of the states; Bull Run Russell, George Alfred Townsend, Charlie Nordhoff, John Russell Young, and scores of other prominent journalists; Albert Bierstadt, Thomas Moran, Tom Hill, C.D. Robinson, and other famous artists; Mrs. Langtry, Lady Franklin, the Princess Louise, and many hundreds of other persons of consequence, have been taken into the great Yosemite by Alfred. He never had an accident, always made time, either way, to a minute; knew every peak and tree and rock and canyon and clearing and hut and streamlet by the wayside.

Hardy and inured to physical injury, Alfred was no less than the very personification of the California stage driver. He was ruggedly independent, and he faced his adversaries accordingly. He had pronounced opinions on politics and theology—"Can one cast eyes upon the scenic wonders and curiosity of Yo Semite and not believe in God?" he often asked his passengers—and he could converse rationally on all ordinary subjects.

Alfred had, too, a sense of justice—like Beckwourth's, of the very direct and immediate variety. He was quick to defend himself against any attack—from bandits, from hostile Indians, from the environment. Though nobody was more ready to befriend one in need, nobody was more swift to take action against the perpetrator of an action that he considered dishonest or threatening.

His passengers described him as "gentlemanly and accommodating," and he was a favorite with the ladies who lived along his route—the Wawona Road.

> Our driver and guide into the valley, a colored man of medium stature who goes by the name of Alfred, was shy and modest, yet outspoken and militant when anything threatened Yo Semite good.
> —Emily A. Hutchings, 1894

The Wawona Road was opened on July 22, 1876, and it followed old Indian trails into Yosemite Valley. The toll was collected at White and Hatch's, approximately twelve miles from Mariposa. At Clark's Station (modern-day Wawona), the road detached itself from the Indian route and ascended Adler Creek to its headwaters. Here it crossed to the Bridalveil Creek drainage and passed through several fine meadows, gradually ascending to the highest point on the route above Old Inspiration Point on the south rim of Yosemite Valley. From this point the road dropped sharply to the floor of the valley, and Alfred, the reins clutched tightly in his competent black hands, time and time again negotiated the stony defile downward; at places over loose sand and gravel, at others around the points of shelving rock, where one false maneuver would send horses, stagecoach and passengers a mangled mass two thousand feet below.

Sitting inside a stage driven by Alfred, George McNugget, publisher of the *Overland Express*, described the ride:

> Every nerve is tense; the muscles involuntarily make ready for a spring, and even the bravest lean timorously toward the mountain side and away from the cliff. The thought is in vain; should Alfred lose control of the coach, should the coach go, the passengers would infallibly go with it.

Sections of Alfred's Wawona-Yosemite Valley route passed over high terrain where deep snow persisted well into the spring. Early fall snow storms in these vicinities sometimes contributed to the hazards of travel, but this African-American "Whip" never had an accident, and always made time, either way, to a minute.

No person ever gave Alfred a small coin, as one would give a porter or a waiter; but a nice slouch hat, a pair of fine boots, a pair of gloves, silk handkerchiefs, or good cigars were always accepted with hearty gratitude.

Alfred's clothes were of the best cloth, made to order. His boots and gauntlets were fine fitting and of good pattern, and his hats were a cream-white, half stiff and half slouch. His orders were obeyed with the greatest celerity, and he was always the first to be saluted by the wayfarer, the passenger, the hosteler, the postmaster, and the man at the door of the wayside inn.

From its opening in 1875, until his death in 1886, Alfred guided his stagecoach over the Wawona Road, his reputation such that his passengers, knowing themselves to be in safe hands, became completely involved with the beauty, glaciers, and magnitudes of the mountains.

Alfred himself described Yosemite Valley:

Haze hung over the valley—light as grossamer—and clouds partially dimmed the higher cliffs and mountains. This obscured my vision but increased the awe with which I beheld it, and as I looked, a peculiar exalted sensation seemed to fill my whole being, and I found my eyes in tears with emotion.

Alfred was also quoted as saying he had never permitted but one man to take the reins from him in his life, and that man was President Ulysses S. Grant, whom Alfred referred to as "General."

**George "Alfred" Monroe, in 1879, was chosen over nine white drivers to drive President Ulysses S. Grant along the treacherous S-curves of the Wawona Road into Yosemite Valley. Alfred's fame as a driver led to Monroe Meadows in Yosemite being named after him.**

Grant's trip, as described in the words of the African-American who guided him:

The General drove nearly all the way to Inspiration Point, and lighted at least four cigars. He took in everything along the road, and made all the turns as perfectly as an old driver.

I had a fine crowd that day—the General and Mrs. Grant and Ulysses, Jr.—Mr. Young, who has since been Minister to China and is now Librarian of Congress; and there was Miss Jennie Flood, the only daughter of the wealthy bonanza man, who was jilted by young Grant; Miss Dora Miller, the only daughter of Senator Miller, who is now the wife of Commander Clover, United States Navy, and Miss Flora Sharon, who afterwards married Sir Thomas Hesketh of England. Miss Sharon was the prettiest girl I ever carried into the valley, and Mrs. Langtry the most beautiful and agreeable woman.

I have received presents from all members of the Grant family. The General himself gave me a silver-mounted cigar case containing eight cigars, and the girls sent me gloves and boots.

★　★　★

Despite the magnificence of the clippers and the industriousness of the splashing steamships, Californians—black and non-black—thought their state was entitled to an overland connection. Orators, such as James Hubbard and Peter Bell, insisted that the federal government had the manifest duty to forge a transcontinental link, which meant a railroad. Eastern blacks joined in, though on different grounds: national defense, national solidarity, and opportunity in the Pacific.

To throw tracks across 2,000 miles or more of unoccupied plains and mountains to the Pacific was beyond the resources of any magnates then in the business, and, with the small prospect for traffic, it was not a proposition attractive to private enterprise. The advocates of a Pacific railroad ignored the economic realities, just as they underestimated the difficulties of actual construction.

★   ★   ★

The first to rescue the Pacific railroad from the limbo of hazy generalities and to discuss it in terms that would impress engineers and bankers was a young construction engineer, Theodore D. Judah, and an African-American who had established an unparalleled standard as a mining engineer—Moses Rodger.

Judah and Rodger, white and black, without much fanfare, built the Sacramento Valley Railroad—which covered a distance of about twenty-two miles. Rails were laid expeditiously to Folsom, at a cost only slightly in excess of original estimates. Since a day was cut from the time required for freighting to the mines, the railroad was immediately profitable.

This railroad was California's earliest—and its construction was due, in large part, to the efforts of a black man. On a handcar over its first 400 feet of track, which had been laid by Chinese and African-American workers, Rodger and Judah enjoyed the first railroad ride in the Golden State. Logically, other sections of track might have been added, but at this point Rodger became disturbed by the company's heavy interest charges. He severed his connections and track laying came to a sudden halt.

In 1859 the California legislature was finally persuaded to call a Pacific Railroad Convention, which met at San Francisco on September 20, with a hundred delegates in attendance, including several members of the Colored Conventions. From this and other railroad conventions emerged what would eventually be ticketed The Big Four.

## Blacks and the Central Pacific Railroad

The four men whose sway over the Central Pacific Company was completed in the early 1860s are among the most famous in

California's history. They—Mark Hopkins, Leland Stanford, Collis P. Huntington, and Charles Crocker—had much in common. Each came to California in the gold rush. Each turned quickly from gold mining to the more profitable and less speculative avenues of trade. All were conspicious by their abundance of energy and their capacity for sustained effort.

Stanford became the titular head, the public relations officer in California, and the spokesman of the company in seeking subventions from the state and from the counties. Huntington became the contact man with the national government and became the purchasing agent and the chief money raiser in the East. Hopkins' role as office man was the least conspicuous, but as the balance wheel he restrained his rasher partners from steps that would have jeopardized the company. Crocker superintended construction and could complacently assert that, whatever the others had accomplished, he had built the road. (Like many other white men, Crocker's assertion is founded on fantasy, not fact. Crocker superintended construction; the railroad itself, however, was built on the sweat and blood of African-Americans, Chinese, and other non-whites.)

For the labor needed Crocker first attempted to rely on California's non-black population—Irish, Americans, Germans, and those of other nationalities. The wage scale had to be high and, worse yet, a majority of the recruits seemed to look upon railroad work as merely a convenient dodge for getting a free ride toward the Nevada mines. In spite of all that could be done the labor turnover was excessive. In desperation the Big Four considered heroic cures. One proposal was to bring up several thousand Mexicans, a solution of the labor problem to which southwestern railroads later turned for maintenance work and southern California agriculturists for crop harvesting. But Mexicans did not build the Central Pacific Railroad, nor did the 5,000 captured Confederate soldiers whom the federal government was requested to provide. The solution was found nearer at hand.

Crocker, on the advice of Mary Ellen Pleasant and Moses Rodger, decided to elicit the efforts of the Chinese and the Golden State's most illustrious peoples—the African-Americans. In the mines and in the northern towns the work of California's black people was already familiar. Because of the prevailing aura of white supremacy and black separation, most of Crocker's associates were skeptical that African-Americans possessed the skill and dependability required, but the initial "experiment" with 50 men of color proved that African-American skill and stamina was more than adequate, and even exceeded that of the less industrious white Californians. Thereafter, the African-American contingent was steadily increased. California supplied 500 in April 1865; by the end of the season the number had reached 1,000. Unlike the non-blacks before them, African-Americans never threatened to strike. They were tireless. Pick, shovel, and wheelbarrow were no mystery to them, and they soon proved themselves adept with drill, blasting powder, and the other equipment with which the line across the Sierra was to be carved.

By June 1868, the road was finally completed to the state line. Ahead lay the plums for which the Big Four had been straining, the open floor of the intermountain basin, across which tracks could be laid for half the amount of the promised federal subsidy, and the traffic of the Mormons at Salt Lake. Authorized in 1866 to build beyond the state line, the Central Pacific girded itself for a final sprint.

Answering the demands for speed, African-American foremen whipped their construction crews into highly expert machines. Using the factory method of division of labor, they perfected their techniques so that the rails went down at the rate of three, four, and five miles a day. In a final inspired burst of super-efficiency African-Americans laid ten miles in a single day.

As the two lines approached each other (the Union Pacific was rapidly advancing its tracks across Nebraska), the nation suddenly realized that they might not meet. Why should they? As the law stood, each road might continue on across the continent with uninterrupted enjoyment of land grants and federal subsidies. An alarmed United States Congress intervened at the eleventh hour to designate Promontory, Utah, as the place where the rails should meet.

The completion of construction afforded an irresistable temptation for dramatics. The stage was set early in May. By Saturday, the eighth, Stanford had arrived by special train ready for his histrionic role, but Vice-President Durant of the Union Pacific was delayed by washouts and by a strike occasioned by lack of money with which to pay his white workmen. The celebration had to be postponed until Monday.

The people of Sacramento, with Judge Nathaniel Bennet of Sacramento as the orator of the day, went ahead with their celebration on May 8. Judge Bennett congratulated his fellow Californians that they were "composed of the right materials, derived from the proper origins. . . In the veins of our people (Bennett declared) flows the commingled blood of the four greatest nationalities of modern days. The impetuous daring and dash of the French, the philosophical and sturdy spirit of the German, the unflinching solidity of the English, and the light-hearted impetuosity of the Irish, have all contributed each its appropriate share."

With never a thought to the contribution of California's African-Americans or the Chinese, Judge Bennett moved along to his peroration: "A people deducing its origins from such races, and condensing their best traits into its national life, is capable of any achievement."

**Judge Bennett would have been more accurate had he said, "In the veins of white people flows the commingled blood of the two nationalities which have had the greatest impact on American history—the Spanish and the African.**

The building of the Pacific railroad is often belittled. Parts of it needed early replacement and by business standards it was premature. But the railroad was built for reasons of state and public opinion, for the Union, and the development of the country. It was a national achievement and heralded a transformation of California and of the West—and its tracks rest on a foundation of Chinese and African-American sweat and blood.

★  ★  ★

California's initial enthusiasm for the Pacific railroad soon gave way to distrust and dislike. The change was an echo of the national conviction that railroads were responsible for most of the country's economic ills, including the panic of 1873. White Californians shared that opinion and had reasons of their own for holding the railroad to blame. Shopkeepers found their business thrown into confusion by the stocks of new goods brought in by the "iron horse." Western publishers had to compete with a deluge of printed matter flowing in from the East, and Sacramento, though it had led in the building of the Central Pacific, found itself declining to a way station. The railroad became a monster, the octopus. It became a target for criticisms for all those made discontented and bitter by the hard times of the seventies.

The Big Four quickly saw that their further success hinged on establishing a monopoly of California rails, particularly with regard to San Francisco Bay. They moved rapidly—aided by San Francisco's black community. The Western Pacific Railroad Company, the Big

Four under another name, was chartered to build from Sacramento to San Jose, and a branch from Niles to Oakland gave virtual monopoly of the Oakland waterfront. To control another approach they absorbed the California Pacific which had a Sacramento-Vallejo franchise. Its tracks were carried to Benicia, a ferry crossed to Port Costa, and rails continued to Oakland, completing the stranglehold on the East Bay.

> As had been the case with the Pacific railroad, the Western Pacific tracks were laid by black and Chinese workers. Crew foreman for the Niles-Oakland line was David W. Dennis, whose father, George Washington Dennis, played a major role in the building of San Francisco.

Through grants from the state legislature the Big Four next sought control of San Francisco's waterfront, but because of strong protests from *The Pacific Appeal, Daily Union, Daily Evening Bulletin* and others, this grant was reduced to a mere sixty acres.

> As editor of *The Pacific Appeal,* Peter Bell foiled the Big Four's attempt to get Congress to donate Goat Island, which under its more limpid name, Yerba Buena, is now the stepping-stone for the Bay Bridge.

Undaunted by Bell and other journalists, the Big Four purchased the San Francisco and San Jose, acquired two lesser lines circling the southern arm of the bay, and effectively bottled up peninsular traffic.

The railroad magnates also sought to dominate the rest of the Golden State. As early as 1865 they had chartered the Southern Pacific, ostensibly as a competitor, to build down the coast to San Diego. They also gobbled up an assortment of lines in the San Joaquin Valley, constructed occasional links, and extended through service to Goshen in Tulare County. Within twenty years, the Big Four had made the monopoly of California rails all but complete.

## African-American Resentment

Big business today is multiple; in modern California it is represented by banks, oil companies, utilities, industries, and manufacturers, chain stores, large department stores, metropolitan newspapers, and the like. In the late nineteenth century all other enterprises were so overshadowed by the railroad as to be reduced to the stature of small business. The railroad was the biggest landowner and the biggest employer; its owners were the richest men in the state; its influence on government was supreme. By arbitrary manipulation of freight rates it could make or break almost any merchant, industrialist, or agriculturist in the state. In part because of its very magnitude, the railroad supplanted Joaquin Murieta as public enemy number one and was blamed for everything that went wrong.

It was a period, furthermore, when many things seemed to be going wrong—particularly for California's African-Americans. California state government, never a glorious achievement of probity and efficiency, sank in the seventies to the nadir of disrepute. San Francisco's white officials had reverted to the roguery of the early fifties, while in Sacramento the manifestations of corruption were equally prominent. No branch of government seemed to be exempt—not the courts, the tax assessors, or the executive officers; yet it was the legislature that seemed to be guilty of the most flagrant abuses.

Among other economic abuses, one concerned land monopoly, long to continue a burning issue to the black people from whom the property had been taken. Many a black writer, from Newby to Bell to Neimore, had railed against the vast feudal estates of hundreds of thousands of acres held off the market and out of production for a speculative profit. African-Ameircan farmers in the 1870s, as in the twentieth century, found that much of the best land was withheld, and it was the railroad's millions of acres that stood out most prominently. Water for irrigation was controlled to an even greater extent by the monopolists, thereby contributing to the building up of still larger holdings.

Added to these factors were numerous instances when the railroads played fast and loose with prospective black purchasers, raising the price after the African-American family had put in excessive improvements or proceeding with summary evictions. The dramatic climax came in the Mussel Slough tragedy in Tulare County in 1880, where an attempted eviction led to the killing of twelve African-Americans (this had followed the killing of seven white settlers). The railroad, in both instances, had the law on its side, and four African-American farmers were sentenced to prison; but public opinion persisted that the railroad was in the wrong.

In the California wonderland of the 1870s, the law and state government was regulated by the railroad.

With these conditions, it is natural that a popular hue and cry should have arisen for curbing the railroad. But, with their characteristic faculty for obscuring the real issue, the reform leaders gave first attention to what they perceived to be a problem—the African-American.

# CHAPTER XI

# Cow Counties in Transition

THROUGHOUT THE FIRST AMERICAN DECADES SOUTHERN CALIFORNIA lagged behind by almost every index—population, mining, crop production, transportation, business activity, and urban growth. While central and northern California's African-American population mushroomed, the African-American population in southern counties rose slowly.

Most newcomers were white. They substantially exceeded the Spanish and Mexican older residents, and the original founders of Los Angeles—Africans. Although newcomer standards prevailed over most of the habits of the old regime, older elements persisted. Adobes gave way only gradually to bricks and boards, towns and plantings were served by zanjas, vineyards and winemaking went on, and cattle raising carried over methods, equipment, and vocabulary from the pastoral era. Coastal shipping, wagon freighting, and somewhat more incidentally the stage and local railroads had become important. The rise of newspapers, such as the *California Eagle,* schools, and churches symbolized and assisted the transition from Mexican to American and African-American. Southern California, because of the efforts of Biddy Mason, J. J. Neimore, and other

black people, outgrew vigilante justice, filibustering, fanatical parti-
sanship on Civil War issues, and the distresses of uncertainty of land
titles.

When at last the African-American laid tracks of the Southern
Pacific came down the San Joaquin Valley pointed toward a gateway
at Yuma or Needles, a civil issue arose on how to persuade the Big
Four to bring the rails through Los Angeles instead of veering off
from Tehachapi Pass to Antelope Valley. The price was set by the
railroad—a depot site, the Los Angeles and San Pedro Railroad, and
a donation in the amount of five percent of the assessed valuation of
the county, $602,000.

Two prominent white men, Benjamin F. Peel and former governor John G. Downey, headed a vociferous opposition, but Harvey
K. S. O'Melveny, backed by Biddy Mason, argued persuasively that
Los Angeles had to have the railroad. A torchlight procession and
more oratory persuaded the voters, and the agreement was approved
by nearly a three to one margin. In 1876 when the Tehachapi was
surmounted and the San Fernando tunnel holed through, Los Angeles could celebrate the true arrival of the "iron horse."

## Healthy Climate

The excellence of the southern California climate had been recognized as far back as Pedro Prat. Then, early in the Mexican period,
a governor moved south for his health. The gold rush brought a
sprinkling of persons more intent on regaining their health than on
getting rich. Other health seekers came from time to time, a few by
overland stage, more by ship or covered wagon. As early as the
forties, travel by prairie schooner had been recommended as a sort
of fresh air cure. In some instances it did cure; in others it proved
too heroic a remedy.

For a while southern California was too remote and too rough a
frontier to have much appeal as a health resort. By the seventies,
however, it was less beset by hostile Indians, bandits, and despera-
does—and it was outfitted with some improvements in transportation and accommodations.

**As had been the case with African-American railroad work-
ers, black people in Los Angeles effectually settled the too
frequent incursions of hostile Indians.**

Southern California black people also had developed a number of new pursuits in which invalids or their relatives might find employment. At the same time the medical profession was entering a phase in which change of climate was a favorable prescription. This combination of circumstances touched off a rush of health seekers which proved to be a chief dynamic for southern California development in the seventies, eighties, and nineties.

**Eula Mason, the middle daughter of Biddy Mason, opened a bordinghouse for "the handicapped and ailing of any race or color."**

The housing shortage was remedied by the building of hotels and houses in the old towns and by starting new towns in which such facilities might be made available. Old towns were enlarged, particularly Los Angeles, and a dozen or more new towns took shape, including Pasadena, Riverside, Sierra Madre, Santa Monica, Altadena, Palm Springs, Ojai, and Nordhoff—nearly all of which included construction efforts supplanted by African-Americans.

The migration of thousands and then tens of thousands of invalids to southern California was accompanied by a migration of doctors. Through their coming and through the experience gained in local practice with this bonanza of patients, a medical advance took place. It was evidenced in part by the opening of rest homes, convalescent homes, hotel-hospitals, and eventually sanitaria and hospitals specializing in tuberculosis and other maladies.

**By 1880 Biddy and Eula Mason owned and operated fourteen nursing homes, ranging from Riverside to Santa Monica.**

The influx of so many Americans, their enthusiasm about Southern California as a place in which to live, farm, and do business, led to a sudden awareness of glorious prospects. Astute real estate promoters, such as Biddy Mason, capitalized on this spirit of optimism. Others followed suit.

An enterprising promoter's first step was to acquire title to a tract on which his town could be laid out. It seemed to matter little what sort of land was chosen. The site of Ballona was swamp land; Chicago Park nestled in the rocky wash of the San Gabriel; Carlton perched precariously on a steep hillside east of Anaheim; Border

City and Manchester were stranded on the far slope of the Sierra Madre, their only real asset a noble view of the Mojave Desert.

The magnitude of the boom, particularly as it affected African-Americans, is indicated by several sorts of testimony. Real estate transfers involving black people recorded in the county in 1887 totaled $44,084,162 and, since many sales were on time contracts and many of the contracts were reconveyed at a substantial advance, it is a conservative estimate that the year's African-American sales surpassed $100 million. There are statistics for the amount of subdividing that went on. From January 1887 to July 1889, the records indicate 60 new towns plotted, with a total acreage of 79,350. Oldtimers who before the boom had known everyone in town suddenly found Los Angeles filled with new black faces.

## California Oranges

In 1860 the Golden State had only 4,000 bearing orange trees. Practically all were in southern California, with the largest concentration in William Wolfskill's Los Angeles grove.

**A former trapper and mountain man, William Wolfskill planted his orange trees with the aid of one of his closest friends—James P. Beckwourth.**

In the seventies and eighties orange growing forged to the front. Several innovations share the credit—not the least of which was the discovery of the agricultural possibilities of the uplands, such as those at Riverside.

Because of its multiplicity of environments and of subclimates California could have an almost unlimited crop list. It also could have diversity of agricultural methods: vineyards and orchards with irrigation, and other vineyards and other plantings for which irrigation was a necessity. One California specialty—sun-dried apricots, peaches, prunes, and raisins—capitalized on dry and unclouded inland summers. By the same token much of California agriculture—oranges, for instance—depended on irrigation.

Governor Felipe de Neve had been the first to recognize the water imperative. It was, however, a mulatto, Canadian-born George Chaffey, who came to California 103 years later who made the greatest contributions.

When Chaffey arrived in southern California in 1880, the transforming power of irrigation—which had been developed by Africans—was most strikingly apparent at Riverside. Brief residence in the area convinced Chaffey of the practicability of further development through irrigation. Late in 1881 he persuaded his brother and an African-American named Phillip de Fleurville to join him in acquiring a tract of land, bringing water to it, and selling it as farms and home sites.

On Thanksgiving Day of that year, as attested by county records, de Fleurville and the Chaffey brothers contracted for 1,000 acres of land in Rancho Cucamonga with an accompanying water right in the adjacent mountains. Subsequently the trio added another 1,500 acres. The colony was named Etiwanda after a half-black famous Indian chief of Michigan and Ontario. Construction of concrete pipelines to deliver water to the upper corner of each ten-acre tract began at once, and before the end of 1882 some 1,400 acres had been sold.

From Etiwanda, de Fleurville and the Chaffeys went on to a larger project on the gently sloping plain at the mouth of San Antonio Canyon. The site for this colony, later named Ontario, was acquired by purchase of railroad and government lands. To the skeptical it seemed that San Antonio Canyon could not furnish enough water to supply so large a tract, especially since the town of Pomona had valid claim to half the surface flow in the canyon. The trio, however, acting upon the Spanish-black adage that "the rivers of California run bottom upward," drove a tunnel into the canyon bed. Penetrating 2,850 feet, they struck a strong subterranean flow, which was conducted through a cement-lined ditch to a junction with the diverted surface water. To demonstrate the abundance of water the trio built a fountain near the Southern Pacific depot, which was turned on to spout high in the air whenever a train came through.

Ontario and Pomona engaged in more or less good-natured rivalry throughout these early years—and both communities flourished.

Ontario was chosen in 1903 as the model irrigation colony and was played up as such at the St. Louis World's Fair in 1904. The tribute was not only to the efficient use of water in crop production but also to the high achievement in town planning, educational provisions, home beautification, and social

benefits, much of which the trio of African descendants had
planned.

In addition to the Imperial Valley, de Fleurville and the Chaffey
brothers developed artesian water for another flourishing colony at
Whittier and had laid plans for extending irrigation in Owens Valley
in conjunction with hydroelectric development and an electric rail-
way to Los Angeles. In their last project they were foiled by Los
Angeles' own water and power designs, and their principal monuments remain Etiwanda, Ontario, Whittier, Imperial Valley, and,
less ponderable but equally significant, the methods which they de-
vised for California's material and social advancement.

> The Golden State's agricultural pattern was developed in
> large part by the work of generations of African descendants
> who introduced and refined methods of artificial irrigation. To-
> day, as a direct result of African-American endeavors, the Im-
> perial Valley is sometimes called the "American Nile."

Many historians now concede that the African-American's remarkable energy and expertise in establishing irrigation and water
facilities was perhaps the most critical factor contributing to the
relatively rapid founding of California towns, particularly those in
the southern part of the state.

★   ★   ★

Despite numerous incidents in which California's African-Americans were driven out of "clean" and better-paid occupations (a result
of the fact that the South's doctrine of white supremacy and black
separation had permeated and taken root in the California job market), several African-American entrepreneurs managed to acquire
wealth and fame in the Golden State. As a result of his affiliation
with the Chaffey brothers, for instance, Phillip de Fleurville, whose
parents had been slaves in Virginia, amassed property in excess of
$80,000; James Torfen, who had twice been sold on the auction block
in New Orleans before escaping to the West, achieved a monopoly
on catering and barbering in central California, and maintained
$56,000 in bank deposits in San Francisco; Stephen Smith and Wil-
liam Whipper were successful wheat farmers in the lower San Joaquin Valley; and Henry Lloyd of San Diego, who had witnessed the
lynching of his father (for "eyeing" a white woman), owned a bed-

stead factory with some twenty white employees. Biddy Mason, of course, amassed a fortune in real estate through hard work and clever investments, and the overwhelming success of the *California Eagle* brought its founder and editor, J. J. Neimore, wealth and fame.

As more and more African-Americans migrated to California, job opportunities for men and women of color decreased substantially. In July of 1893, when California's African-American population numbered 30,000, the African-American League of San Francisco (founded in 1890) called the first state-wide congress of African-American Leagues to deal once again with education and employment problems besetting black people.

The congress convened July 30, 1893, at California Hall, then located at 620 Bush Street, San Francisco, with delegates from numerous counties attending.

**Eula Mason attended the first state-wide congress of African-American Leagues to represent Los Angeles and her mother, who had died two years earlier.**

That prejudice based solely on skin color still blocked the African-American's economic and social advancement at that time was clearly demonstrated by many advertisements in the convention program and local newspapers. One advertisement inserted by a fabric firm proclaimed: "The color line is not recognized by our house."

The convention emphasized needs for racial unity, self-improvement, a generally higher level of jobs for California's African-Americans, and took pride in the local league's three year old employment program. A report to the convention, which had been prepared by J. J. Neimore, and which had been presented by Eula Mason, revealed that San Francisco's chapter of the African-American League had obtained the following jobs for members out of work: One U.S. mail carrier; one U.S. gauger; two U.S. mail clerks; 13 porters; one railroad clerk; three messengers; three clerks in departments of the municipal government of San Francisco; 60 deputy U.S. marshals as election officers; one painter and one gardener in the school department; 11 laborers in Golden Gate Park and one lady attendant at the park playground. (Total hired by the city: 17.)

A great number of delegates deplored the "prevailing desire" of African-Americans to be employed in menial jobs and made it clear that they believed this should be corrected by a healthier desire to launch businesses of their own. Accordingly, the convention urged

African-American men and women to establish business enterprises on a cooperative basis and in competition with white-owned firms where they were denied jobs as clerks or sales people.

All the delegates pledged themselves to do everything in their power to "inspire the youths of our race to qualify for employment in the store, the factory, the counting house, the different trades and all the other industries of life."

Speakers at this convention included San Francisco Mayor Adolph Sutro, *California Eagle* editor J. J. Neimore, and Mrs. Sarah B. Cooper, a prominent white woman who was associated with Mrs. Leland Stanford, Mrs. Phoebe Apperson Hearst, and Mrs. Miranda Lux in educational projects for children. Mrs. Cooper delivered an address entitled, "The Home—The True Foundation of the State."

A resolution adopted unanimously at the close of the convention called for annual New Year's Day celebrations of Emancipation Day by local African-American Leagues. Theophilus B. Morton of San Francisco, who was elected president of the federated African-American Leagues, presented the resolution.

**At the time he was elected president of the federated African-American Leagues, Theophilus B. Morton was a messenger for the U.S. Court of Appeal. He later became the first African-American librarian of the court.**

In the same year that the first state-wide congress of African-American Leagues met in San Francisco, a number of the Golden State's African-Americans ventured into Sacramento to help eradicate a perennial flood hazard—the uncontrolled Sacramento River.

In its lower course the Sacramento ran through a wide alluvial plain of deep, rich soil. The river had greeted the forty-niners with floods that drove them to the roofs. The hydraulic miners aggravated the problem by sending down huge quantities of debris that buried good farmland and raised the riverbed many feet.

As early as 1868 farmers along the west bank of the Feather River built a 17-mile levee to protect their lands. Their neighbors to the east objected that the embankment would merely shunt floodwaters onto their lands. The levee had that effect but it did not hold against recurrent floods. Piecemeal attempts to restrain the river by privately built levees were supplemented by a state program under the Drainage Act of 1880, which had been based on a report written by Moses Rodger. The Act, however, was declared unconstitutional in 1881.

Valley residents showed much more enthusiasm for a ban on hydraulic mining and were rewarded in 1884 with an injunction.

In 1883 the Caminetti Act, underwritten by Phillip de Fleurville, opened a new era. It authorized revival of hydraulic mining provided debris was controlled. More important, it set up a state agency, the California Debris Commission, in essence an authority for flood control. Under the commission's auspices Marsden Manson and C. E. Grunsky brought in an engineering report based on providing bypasses or stand-by auxiliary riverbeds. The mechanics proposed, and which had been outlined by de Fleurville, were to make the Sacramento and its tributaries run full for maximum scour but to use the bypasses to carry off quickly any excess floodwaters.

**The mechanics developed for controlling the Sacramento River were, in essence, all but identical to those used by Bantu tribes in Africa to control the Nile.**

Levee construction proceeded—more than twenty African-American men were hired for the project—but without shutting off the bypasses and with some levees along these auxiliary channels. The state and the federal government invested in dredging, jettying, and removing snags to give better depth and tidal scour at the mouth of the Sacramento. Much of the responsibility was still left to private leveeing, and subsequent floods demonstrated the inadequacy of the state and federal efforts.

Not all African-Americans were willing to work with water. In Los Angeles, San Jose, and Placerville, for instance, food service was all but a black monopoly, and most California towns had well-to-do African-American caterers and restaurateurs. In fact, the best schools of cooking were owned and operated by black people, including Harriet Foster's Southern Delights in Sacramento.

Additionally, as depicted in countless photographs, the African-American also was directly involved in helping to build houses, pave streets, construct wharfs for visiting steamers, and in erecting hotels for dusty overland travelers; in essence, in the very building of the Golden State. Never is this more evident than in the City by the Bay.

★ ★ ★

San Francisco—historically and culturally—deserves to be called California's first city. In the twenty years between 1848 and 1868,

San Francisco exchanged its flapping canvas tents, lean-tos, and rickety frame shacks to become a city; it exchanged, too, its cultural primitiveness for a cosmopolitan diversity of taste and ideas. This transformation of a makeshift pueblo and polyglot trading post into a confident metropolis was, relatively speaking, a rapid occurrence and was due, in large part, to the efforts of shrewd, forward-thinking African-Americans—many of whom had escaped bondage and servitude in the South. The German traveler Friedrich Gerstacker, who returned to a new *citified* San Francisco after only a year's absence in the mines, wrote:

> I really did not know where I was, did not recognize a single street, and was perfectly at a loss to think of such an entire change. Where I had left a crowded mass of low wooden huts and tents, men such as George Dennis had created a city in a great part built of brick, houses, pretty stores.

Like the City of Los Angeles in southern California, the City of San Francisco cannot ignore the fact that appreciable amounts of black blood flowed into its very foundation.

★　★　★

As the nineteenth century drew to a close, the general outlook for the African-American in California was not bright. A realist always, the African-American was not given to blinking the hard facts of life. As an American, however, he was of an optimistic turn of mind. A new century was dawning, and with it perhaps a better day. "After all," wrote J. J. Neimore, "even the most lonesome of roads must have its turning."

CHAPTER XII

# African-Americans and the New Century

FOR MOST CALIFORNIANS, THE DAWN OF THE TWENTIETH CENTURY GAVE birth to high hopes and great expectations for one hundred years of prosperity for their own generation and for the generations still to come. These hopes and expectations were not, however, shared by the Golden State's African-American residents.

Black Californians, having been driven out of the "clean" and better-paid occupations, had little opportunity to better themselves economically. Other than servant, janitor or boot-black, employment prospects for California's African-Americans were practically non-existent—just as they were almost everywhere else in the nation. Nevertheless, many thousands of African-Americans continued to emigrate from the South and take up residence in the Golden State.

The turn-of-the-century African-American took many paths in seeking to improve his position. But, as in education, all of the paths seemed to lead to an admirer of the late Jeremiah B. Sanderson— Booker T. Washington.

Sanderson died in 1875. He was struck by a train as he attempted to cross railroad tracks at an intersection in Sacramento.

As Washington put his stamp on African-American schools, so he put it on other aspects of black life, including economic activity, political preferment—appointment to offices—and the persuasive presentation of a philosophy of getting along with the white man.

One of the areas in which Booker T. Washington wielded influence was business enterprise. As might be expected from one who preached self-reliance and self-help, Washington shared the belief that the African-American's entry into the business world would furnish a road to racial advancement on all fronts. It would make for a well-to-do merchant class which would create jobs for ambitious youngsters whose color kept them out of the white-color occupations.

Believing that one way to stimulate African-American business was to bring its practitioners together, Washington founded the National Negro Business League in 1900. This organization became the black man's Chamber of Commerce, whose members might receive encouragement and inspiration from one another. One of the League's objectives was the formation of state and local branches, of which some 600 were in existence by 1915. The California branch was founded—in San Francisco, of course—in 1902.

The League's efforts to make the African-American a force in the Golden State's business world could hardly be called a success, for the African-American's achievements in the field of trade and commerce were relatively meager. There were, however, numerous individual success stories, and there were even a few instances of African-American businesses hiring whites. In Los Angeles, Niemore's *California Eagle* began employing white compositors, for example, and the African-American-owned Dry Dock Company, located in San Francisco, employed white carpenters.

On the whole, however, California's racist atmosphere prevented the African-American from becoming a successful entrepreneur. Generally, the only large-scale black businesses that managed to survive were those in fields in which there was no white competition. African-Americans had met with some success in the insurance business, basically because most white-owned companies refused to "write up" black people, whom they considered bad risks. Similarly, in the field of banking African-Americans were able to make a good start because white banks tended to discourage (or blatantly refuse) the deposit business of black people, feeling that it would cost too much to handle accounts which were likely to be both small and subject to frequent withdrawals.

African-Americans were likely to do well in the service fields which catered to a black clientele. African-Americans who operated undertaking establishments, such as that of Allan Mooreston in San Jose, were likely to survive and hardly less likely to prosper. Even more profitable was the beauty culture business. From the manufacture of products to improve the hair and skin, "Madame" C. J. Walker and Mrs. A. E. Malone each amassed over one million dollars.

But, outside the personal service and those fields which specialized in "race products," African-American businesses were generally small-scale, lacking in capital and in trained and experienced managers. Like Biddy Mason, George Washington Dennis, Mary Ellen Pleasant, J. J. Neimore, Delilah Beasley, and others, many African-American businessmen were motivated by a sense of race pride. But the fate of black business was more likely to be determined by the economics of buying and selling, of credit and debt, than by the exhortations of African-American leaders.

As a result of these circumstances, and a growing belief that prejudice was inevitable in a biracial society, many African-Americans decided that a separate state might be the answer. Such a quasi-independent all-black state was proposed in 1890 by the Texas Farmers' Colored Association. A similar impulse was behind the visit to the White House made by a delegation of twenty African-Americans, three of whom represented southern California black people, who urged President Harrison to appoint an African-American as secretary of the Oklahoma Territory.

To suggest making Oklahoma an African-American state was bound to arouse great resistance by whites and Indians. But since land was cheap and plentiful, the whites were not adverse to the formation of small, all-black towns. Beginning with Langston in 1891, a number of such Oklahoma towns came into existence. The largest of these was Boley, founded in 1904, whose inhabitants for five years voted in the Okfuskee County elections; when it was discovered that these African-Americans held the balance of power between the Republicans and the Democrats, however, the alarmed whites disfranchised them.

Oklahoma's all-black towns were destined to live on—and other all-black towns were destined to be born, such as one in Tulare County, California.

## Allensworth: California's All-Black Community

Though a small, dusty town where residents constantly battled heat and drought may seem an unlikely setting for a heroic effort at colony building and racial self-determination, this community of "race pioneers," with its commitment to limiting the parameters of prejudice, served as a beacon of hope to African-Americans in the Golden State and across the nation. The community, Allensworth, belied the notion of African-American inferiority and, in doing so, generated excitement, hope and confidence that

> *as soon as our race gets property in the form of real estate, of intelligence, of high Christian character, it will find that it is going to receive the recognition which it has not thus far received.*

This town and its founder, Colonel Allen Allensworth, deserve a kinder fate than relegation to a footnote or anecdote.

★   ★   ★

For African-Americans in California, the twentieth century's initial years were a nadir: the United States Supreme Court anointed racism's handmaiden segregation as the law of the land, a form of economic bondage known as share-cropping re-enslaved the mass of Southern blacks as well as poor whites and the black community's leadership was splintered by the acrimony between W. E. B. DuBois and Booker T. Washington. It was this atmosphere of uncertainty and discrimination that encouraged five "gentlemanly looking Negro men" (so recorded the Delano *Holograph* on June 13, 1908) to work toward the creation of a "race colony" in California.

Guiding this venture were the fervor and dreams of Allen Allensworth. Though born into slavery in Louisville, Kentucky, in April 1842, Allensworth refused to submit to that degrading institution. During his youth, despite laws forbidding the education of slaves, Allensworth mastered reading and writing, whetting his life-long appetite for learning. After two unsuccessful escape attempts, he finally succeeded during the initial years of the Civil War. Recognizing the importance of this struggle, Allensworth wanted to participate. He at first worked as a civilian aide to the 44th Illinois Volunteer Infantry for several months in 1862. But this service did not satisfy Allensworth. On April 3, 1863, he became a seaman, first class, of the United States Navy. During the remaining years of the war between the states, Allensworth saw duty on gunboats such as the *Queen City* and the *Pittsburg* before leaving the Navy in April 1865, with the rank of first class petty officer.

During Reconstruction, Allensworth underwent a religious conversion and decided to study theology at Roger Williams University in Nashville, Tennessee. While at the University he met and later married Josephine Leavell. After completing his studies, Allensworth maintained several pulpits in and around his native Louisville. His success as a minister propelled him into politics; he was one of Kentucky's delegates to the Republican National Convention in 1880 and 1884.

In 1882, a black soldier came to Allensworth for help, complaining about the lack of black chaplains in the all-black military units. He urged Allensworth to help recruit African-Americans to fill those positions. Allensworth did more than recruit: he decided to become a chaplain himself. He hoped that as a chaplain he could improve the lot of the average black soldier, help the race in its battle to win support and, at the same time, provide a secure future for his family. Thus motivated, Allensworth launched a concerted effort to gain appointment to the 24th Infantry (Colored) in 1884.

> **Allen Allensworth believed that to advance the African-American race and discredit the malicious eugenics fallacy of genetic inferiority, blacks had to work diligently and fulfill their potential—to "do for themselves" instead of relying on rhetoric and white philanthropy.**

First, Allensworth solicited testimonials and letters of support from a myriad of major and minor Southern politicians, both Democrats and Republicans. Then he drafted letters to President Grover Cleveland and to the Office of the Adjutant General. In these notes, Allensworth crafted a persuasive argument. He reasoned to Cleveland that by appointing a black chaplain, the President could "strengthed (his) administration among the colored people, particularly in the South." He also stated that he could "be of service in securing good discipline and gentlemanly conduct among the soldiers."

Finally, Allensworth, ever the pragmatist and fully aware of the reservation about social interaction between black and white officers, wrote, "I know where the official ends and where the social life begins and therefore (guard) against social intrusion." Allensworth's considered exertions were rewarded: in April 1886, he was appointed chaplain of the 24th Infantry with the rank of captain.

For twenty years, Allensworth ministered to the needs of his African-American flock as the 24th moved from Fort Apache in Arizona to Camp Reynolds in California to Fort Missoula in Montana. During those years, the captain not only saw to the troops' spiritual needs but also worked to raise their overall educational level. Throughout, he carried himself as an officer and a gentleman. And all in all, he was quite successful.

When he retired in 1906, Lieutenant-Colonel Allensworth and his family relocated to Los Angeles. But an ordinary retirement was unthinkable for this man so involved with the struggle to improve the position of African-Americans. Not least among the motives of Colonel Allen Allensworth was his desire to change white attitudes toward African-Americans.

Rather than spending his golden years in the California sunshine, Colonel Allensworth continued to promote the African-American race and promulgate the teachings of another individual who had come "up from slavery"—Booker T. Washington. The colonel, an ardent supporter of the Tuskegean, believed that if the African-American race was to rise, blacks had to be willing "to do for themselves," to rely on black self-help efforts rather than on white philanthropy. Allensworth was particularly fond of one admonishments published in the *California Eagle* by J. J. Neimore:

> Eschew cheap jewelry. Quit taking five dollar buggy rides on six dollars a week. *Don't put a five dollar hat on a five cent head. Get a bank account. Get a home of your own. Get some property. . . . Don't be satisfied with the shadows of civilization; get some for the substance for yourself.*[1]

To spread these and other ideas, Allensworth embarked on a speaking tour to inspire and educate African-Americans. Presenting lectures entitled "The Five Manly Virtues Exemplified," "The Battle of Life and How to Fight It" and "Character and How to Read It," the colonel sought to encourage thrift, instill the value of education and plot a strategy whereby the whole race might uplift itself. Allensworth's ideas, however, were restricted to theoretical discussion on the lecture circuit until he met William Payne, a gifted teacher and university graduate living in Pasadena.

Although different in age and temperment, Payne and Allen Allensworth were kindred souls in the struggle to improve their race. Payne, a graduate of Dennison University and a West Virginia native, had spent his youth in Corning, Ohio. Before settling in

---

[1]This statement is also credited to Booker T. Washington.

Pasadena in 1906, he had been an assistant principal at the Rendsville School and a professor at the West Virginia Colored Institute. Arriving in California, however, Payne soon discovered that if African-American teachers were rare, jobs for them were even rarer.

Recognizing the need for unusual measures, Payne and Allensworth plotted the creation of an all-black community—a colony of orderly and industrious African-Americans who could control their own destiny. The two men believed that in such a community, free of the debilitating effects and limits of racism, African-Americans could demonstrate that they were capable of organizing and managing their own affairs. The colony would prove to all Americans that black people were worthy of their rights and responsibilities as citizens. The soldier and the scholar envisioned a black community that would make opportunities for African-Americans—opportunities being central to the philosophies of both men. They believed that the disappointing status of the race nearly half a century after emancipation was due to circumstance rather than color. Yet most of the country, then embued with the "wisdom of Eugenics" (the science of selective genetics), believed that African-Americans were intrinsically inferior and therefore incapable of contributing to the American nation on its road to greatness. White Californians, of course, held this same belief. Payne and Allensworth believed that given the opportunity, African-Americans could live up to their potential and, in the process, destroy that malicious fallacy. Their colony, they believed, would provide that very opportunity.

**The very incarnation of J. B. Sanderson's and Booker T. Washington's racial self-help philosophy, Allensworth, California, belied the myth of African-American genetic inferiority by providing the opportunity for hardworking, orderly black Californians to control their own destiny.**

Another function of the colony that would eventually become Allensworth was to provide a home for the soldiers of America's four all-black regiments. Obviously this meant much to the colonel. In his promotional newsletter *The Sentiment Maker* (May 1912), the needs and desires of the soldier were stressed throughout. Headlines regarding "Home, Sweet Home" called out strongly to the wander-weary military men and their families.

To my comrades in arms, (May 1912) somewhere, sometime your

dream has been to have a home, classic, beautiful, with perfect congenial environment.

In Allensworth, it was promised: for a "small outlay of your present pay, you may become independent, yes even a richer soldier gentleman surrounded by people of your own kind, your own sort." As a final inducement, it was promised that the community would eventually possess a home for soldiers' families. Here, soldiers could leave their families "in a beautiful balmy California climate, surrounded by the very best environment," while overseas on hazardous duty. In short, life in this colony, for the soldier, would be a reward for a job well done.

As the mechanism to transform their ideas into reality, on June 30, 1908, Allensworth and Payne created the California Colony and Home Promoting Association with offices in the San Fernando building on Main Street and in downtown Los Angeles. Although Allensworth and Payne were the chief officers of the Association, several others also played significant roles in the colony's founding: John W. Palmer, a miner; William H. Peck, a minister; and Harry A. Mitchell, a real estate agent.

The association soon ran into difficulties, however, in the problems and expenses of acquiring choice land for a black settlement, and it seemed that the venture might flounder until, as one contemporary put it, "the Pacific Farming Company came to the rescue." This white-owned rural land development firm offered the Association prime land in Solito (or Solita, as it was spelled on Santa Fe Railroad schedules)—a rural area in Tulare County thirty miles north of Bakersfield. Solito/Solita, quickly renamed Allensworth in honor of the colonel, was a good site for the colony: it was a depot station on the main Santa Fe Railroad line from Los Angeles to San Francisco, the soil was fertile, the water seemingly abundant and the acreage not only plentiful but also reasonably priced.

Initially, many of the colony residents, including Colonel Allensworth, were surprised but gratified that a white company had come to their aid. Yet within five years the Pacific Farming Company would become the colony's adversary in a water controversy. Its corporation papers state that the Pacific Farming Company was organized in 1908 to develop rural land into town and village sites. This money-making venture, led by William Loftus of Fullerton and Los Angelenos J. R. Treat and W. H. Bryson, was headquartered in the Security Building at 508–510 Spring Street in the heart of the

Los Angeles business district (on land at one time owned by Biddy Mason).

Once the deal was consummated, the association began to market the colony as a haven for conscientious African-Americans who desired fertile land and a community where their "exertions (would be) appreciated." Within a year, the *Tulare County Times* reported that thirty-five families were residing in Allensworth. Although obtaining accurate figures concerning the early settlement is difficult, the colony generated enough excitement to attract pioneers from throughout the nation.

> The colony's population was greater than figures listed in government records because of Allensworth's floating population of people who would come and stay three or four months and go and the county registrar would know nothing about it.
> —Henry Singleton, former Allensworth resident

Population figures are also blurred by the fact that many individuals purchased lots but lived in other areas, intending to eventually make Allensworth their home. By 1912, however, Allensworth's official population of 100 had celebrated the birth of Alwortha Hall, the first baby born in the town, and enjoyed two general stores, a post office, many comfortable homes such as the one Allen and Josephine Allensworth built in 1910, and a newly completed school—the pride of the community—that also served as the center for the town's social and political activities.

The 1912–1915 period marked the apex of Allensworth as a thriving community. African-American newspapers throughout the nation noticed the tiny hamlet: *The New York Age* chronicled its growth, the *Washington Bee* congratulated all involved with the enterprise and the *California Eagle* gleefully exclaimed that "there is not a single white person having anything to do with the affairs of the colony."

Even the *Los Angeles Times* took note, labeling Allensworth "an ideal Negro settlement."

All the attention from African-American papers throughout the nation was not surprising; the national African-American community was starved for race victories. Newspaper editors, political leaders, businessmen and educators all were pleading for African-Americans to prove themselves to be more than a dark blot on the national character (as a Southern senator had once labeled them). In a sense, these individuals endorsed (though many did so unknow-

ingly) the belief of W. E. B. DuBois that a "talented tenth" must
lead the race to new heights. Positive actions such as those taken by
Allensworth residents were one way to portray African-Americans
in a more favorable light.

Also during this period, Allensworth's 200 affected the surrounding area's economic and political structure.

> Sources such as the Oakland *Sunshine* (a leading San Fran-
> cisco Bay area black newspaper) claim that in 1913 the citizens
> of Allensworth generated nearly $5,000 monthly in their busi-
> ness ventures.

Furthermore, voting registration records of 1915 listed an impressive array of occupations of colonists, including farmers, store-
keepers, carpenters, nurses and more, all suggesting that the colony's
business and industrial output was prodigious.

Allensworth's grain warehouses, cattle pens and storage bins
served the needs of the local farmers and the railroad. Business enterprises developed by the colonists included the large poultry farms
of Oscar Overr, a ten-room, seventy-five cents per night hotel run
by John Morris that also served as a restaurant, a large general store
owned by the Hindsmon family, a cement manufacturing enterprise,
plaster and carpentry shops and sugar beet agriculture. All this industry was geared to prove to the white man beyond a shadow of
a doubt that the black man was capable of self-respect and self-
control. Politically, Allensworth became a member of the county
school district, the regional library system and a voting precinct,
electing Oscar Overr as the first African-American justice of the
peace in post-Mexican California. In 1914, the *California Eagle* reported that Allensworth was comprised of 900 acres of deeded land
worth more than $112,500. In a strictly economic sense, this was an
auspicious beginning.

> It always seemed home to me. The grass was green, and wildflowers
> grew all over. I thought Allensworth was one of the most beautiful
> places I ever saw.
> —Gemelia Herring, former Allensworth resident

Along with this burgeoning sense of political and economic influence came a true sense of community. Allensworth became a town,
not just a colony. This is evident in the number of social and educa-

tional organizations that existed during Allensworth's golden age. The Owl Club, the Campfire Girls, the Girls' Glee Club and the Children's Saving Association met the needs of the young, while adults participated in the Sewing Circle, the Whist Club, the Debating Society and the Theater Club. The Children's Glee Club, modeled after the internationally known Jubilee Singers of Fisk University, was the community's pride and joy. Organized by Professor Payne with musical accompaniment provided by the able teacher Margaret Prince, the choir traveled "all over the various little white towns to sing." Though primarily a form of entertainment, the glee club was also a tool used to win support for the colony.

Along with the school, the library was the focus of many community activities. From the colony's inception, many had recognized the benefits of a public library system and on February 2, 1912, residents petitioned the Board of Trustees of the Visalia Free Library "to establish a depot station at Allensworth." Although the request was approved, the space designated for the reading room was inadequate, so in 1913 Mrs. Josephine Allensworth, as a memorial to her mother, donated land and money to build a library that "would do credit to even a larger community." This "coal box" style edifice, begun in May and completed in July 1913, at a cost of $500, had a "book capacity of 1,000." When the Mary Dickinson Library was dedicated on the Fourth of July, Colonel Allensworth immediately donated his private library to the enterprise. As word of the library spread, the community received books from Visalia, San Francisco and North Dakota. Tulare County supported the venture by paying the costs of a custodian for the facility, local Allensworth resident Ethel Hall.

The library became a hub of activity as Allensworth residents, reflecting the founders' concern with self-education, relentlessly explored its holdings. In 1919, a local periodical noticed the community's preoccupation with learning. The Visalia *Delta,* in an article headlined "Allensworth Folks Great Readers," delineated the varied interests of the colony in books about "questions of political economy, the warring nations in Europe and those dealing with the problems and interests of the colored race in America and elsewhere."

As in many other African-American communities in the Golden State, Allensworth's black churches were a major factor in the development of community spirit and mutual respect. The First Baptist Church held regular services in a "neat church edifice," while the first A.M.E. Zion membership worshiped in the school, and in 1916 plans were made to erect a structure "in the near future" for the Methodist congregation.

Another element in Allensworth's development of the sense of communal responsibility was the struggle to establish a state-supported industrial school. Early in 1914, Colonel Allensworth lobbied for an educational institute to be based on the model pioneered by Booker T. Washington in Alabama. Allensworth envisioned a "Tuskegee of the West" that would provide practical training in such technical fields as agriculture, carpentry and masonry to African-American youth in California and the Southwest. The colonel hoped that the establishment of such an institute would provide a strong economic base for the community by bringing both jobs and much-needed vocational training. William Payne, Oscar Overr and Allen Allensworth crisscrossed the state to elicit support for the proposal. Lecturing in San Diego, Los Angeles, Oakland and San Francisco, Overr eloquently conveyed the colony's desire to pattern the school after the land grant institution at San Luis Obispo. The *New Age* quoted Overr "voicing the sentiment of agricultural sections of the state for centers that will teach subjects fitting the boys and girls for the work they will find about them." This emphasis on "practical education" eventually sparked a controversy, but in early 1915 many saw the campaign as another positive, pioneering effort by the town. When a bill to create the school was introduced in the California State Legislature, the colony of Allensworth anticipated an exciting and prosperous future. It seemed that Allensworth would, as claimed by Delilah Beasley, "become one of the greatest Negro cities in the United States."

But that was not to be. Colonel Allensworth and Payne had been duped by the Pacific Farming Company.

Almost immediately, Allensworth faced several crises that led to its eventual decline. In 1914 the Santa Fe Railroad—never a supporter of "this colored town"—built a spur line to neighboring Alpaugh, thus allowing most rail traffic to bypass Allensworth and depriving the town of the lucrative carrying trade. The Santa Fe's decision was the culmination of a series of conflicts between Allensworth and that railroad—and racial prejudice. Initially, the trainline refused to change the name of the depot from Solito/Solita to Allensworth. In an article in the *Tulare County Times* in July of 1909, officials argued that the new name was too long to fit on signs or in the book of schedules. It was several years before the company relented and changed its policy. A more serious problem was the Santa Fe's employment practices. The corporation refused to hire African-Americans as the manager or ticket agents of the station located in the colony and, despite repeated letters and recriminations, the railroad continued to restrict black people to menial labor.

Further, the dream of having the "Tuskegee of the West" ended when the bill to create the school failed to pass the Legislature. It went down in May of 1915, partly because of strong opposition from the African-Americans in Los Angeles and San Francisco, who believed that a Tuskegee-like institution would implicitly sanction and thereby reinforce educational and residential segregation. It was these concerns that sparked what Payne called "the veiled threatenings and polite scathings" against Allensworth and the proposed polytechnic school. Payne and Overr responded to the almost overwhelming criticism in the African-American newspapers by writing articles and attending community forums. They argued that one school, such as the one under discussion, could not possibly open the floodgates of educational segregation. In fact, the colony sought nothing more than what was available to African-American communities in most states, wrote Payne in the *California Eagle*. He cited the benefits generated by alumni of other African-American institutions such as Hampton Institute, Tuskegee and the State Normal and Industrial School at Wilberforce University. These arguments notwithstanding, the battle was lost.

While these struggles raged, the community continued to reel under the long-standing water problem. As part of the initial purchase, the Pacific Farming Company had agreed to supply sufficient water for irrigation, regardless of how large the town grew, but as early as 1910 the Pacific Farming Company was failing to honor its commitment. Eventually the community sought and gained legal redress: the control of Allensworth Water Company passed to the town. But it was a Pyrrhic victory at best: the town now owned an outdated water system and had the unexpected burden of massive, unpaid taxes. Not until 1918 was the community able to rid itself of the tax burden and begin to upgrade the pumping machinery, and by then the water table had dropped too low and the equipment was ineffective.

But the single most critical factor in the community's decline was the death of Allen Allensworth in 1914. On September 13, Allensworth was in the foothill city of Monrovia to speak at a church. Shortly after he left the train station, crossing the street, he was struck by a speeding motorcycle and died the next morning. Riding the motorcycle were two white youths, E. S. White and W. F. Ray, who claimed that an "excited" Allensworth was responsible for the accident. But after the colonel's family filed a legal complaint, the two were arrested in late September. After funeral services at the Second Baptist Church of Los Angeles, with a military honor guard "of both races," Colonel Allensworth was interred at the Rosedale Cemetery on September 18, 1914.

> E. S. White and W. F. Ray never faced trial in the death of Allen Allensworth. In controversies between African-Americans and whites, then and now, it is almost if not quite impossible for a black man to obtain justice.

The Allensworth community was devastated. Although Payne and Overr assumed the leadership of the colony, no one could replace the colonel. Without Allensworth's spiritual guidance and leadership, the community began to disintegrate. By 1920 the two leading figures, William Payne and Josephine Allensworth, had left the area. Payne accepted a teaching job at El Centro, while Mrs. Allensworth returned to Los Angeles to live with her daughter Nella. The exodus continued during the years of the Great Depression and World War II. Henry Singleton painted a bleak and disappointing picture of the community's decline during this period:

> Any Negro that wanted to work in plowing, in potatoes or the grapes grown in Delano could just move into Allensworth, move into one of the empty homes. They could stay, no rent, no nothing, nobody owned it. Some of the houses were good, others were falling down. It was sort of a camping ground.

The lure of jobs in Oakland and in other war industry sites further decimated the town's population and in 1966, arsenic was found in its water supply. This seemed to sound the death knell for Allensworth. Yet the colonel's dream would not die. Beginning in 1969, various community organizations, led by Ed Pope and Eugene and Ruth Lasartemay, expressed interest and support in creating a state historic site at Allensworth. By 1973, the state had acquired the land and the advisory committee, under the direction of Dr. Kenneth Goode, began its work. In May 1976, the State Department of Parks and Recreation approved the plans to develop the park and on October 6, 1976, the park was dedicated. So the colonel's dream, if not his colony, endures.

★  ★  ★

When the Department of Parks and Recreation was collecting oral histories during the 1970s as a prelude to restoring the park, several former residents interviewed wondered why anyone was interested in Allensworth. After all, hadn't the colony failed? Why commemorate an unsuccessful venture?

While the colony existed as a symbol of hope for less than twenty years, it assumes greater significance in the context of the political and racial currents of pre-World War I America. From that era of segregation, characterized by vitriolic racism and the extralegal atrocities of "Judge Lynch," arose the ambiguous leadership of Booker T. Washington. His policies of accommodation to white racism mixed with his exhortations for black self-help and virtuous living were clarion calls for much of the African-American community. Certainly many early Allensworth residents agreed with Washington when he said:

> One farm bought, one house built, one home sweetly and intelligently kept, one man who is the largest taxpayer or who has the largest banking account, one school or church maintained, one factory running successfully, one garden profitably cultivated, one patient cured by a Negeo doctor, one sermon well preached, one life clearly lived, will tell more in our favor than all the abstract eloquence that can be summoned to plead our cause.

The community of Allensworth was an indirect result of Washington's philosophy of racial self-help. Here, African-American men and women who controlled their land and destiny could prove to white America that, left to their own devices, they could create businesses, churches, and communities that would contribute to America's rise to greatness. This concept is worth commemorating.

Also worth commemorating is Allensworth's role in the historical continuum of all-black towns. While most African-Americans have always believed that hard work, perseverance, education and the basic fairness of the American people would eventually lead to the triumph of justice and racial equality, if not for them then for future generations, other African-Americans have been less optimistic. These African-Americans doubted that a nation that had spawned the Ku Klux Klan and limited its black citizens' opportunities by

legislative and de facto discrimination would ever embrace the African-Americans as an equal. To some, the only hope lay in distancing
themselves from whites. For example, individuals such as Paul Cuffe
(eighteenth century) and Bishop Henry Turner (nineteenth century),
urged African-Americans to return to Africa, where one could develop one's talents to the fullest as well as reaffirm ties to the African
heritage. But such African repatriation plans met with limited success for the simple yet powerful reason that most black people
viewed America, not Africa, as their homeland and so greeted attempts to create African-American towns within the continental
United States with much more enthusiasm.

Black settlements have appeared on the American landscape since
the colonial era, an example of which is the community of Parting
Ways in Massachusetts. Like Allensworth, Parting Ways and countless other all-black communities, were a response to overt racism
. . . were heralded by the black press as "a positive step forward"
. . . were greeted with distrust and, at times, hostility by the neighboring towns . . . were begun with enthusiasm and pride but little
capital . . . and almost all have been forgotten.

Allensworth, California, differed from other all-black towns in its
sense of mission and use of those modern promotional tools previously described. Payne and Allensworth had hoped that by giving
their town the widest possible national circulation, their thriving
"city on a hill" would eventually change the attitudes of white
America. Thus the community tempered individual gain with the
need to help uplift the African-American race. And that is surely
worth commemorating.

One might just as well wonder why Americans commemorate
the failed defense of the Alamo, for the fact that Allensworth ultimately failed is not the most important fact about the venture. What
mattered then is that the attempt was made. And what matters now
is that white Americans finally discover the depths of character and
vision of those who, through their attempt to build a colony, tried
to provide an opportunity for men and women to transcend race-
based limits and thus control their own destinies.

# CHAPTER XIII

# Catastrophe, Corruption, and Conflict

AT A QUARTER PAST FIVE ON THE MORNING OF WEDNESDAY, APRIL 18, 1906, the big one rocked the city of San Francisco. A few minutes later the flames were leaping upward. In a dozen different quarters south of Market Street, in the working-class ghetto, and in the factories, fires started. There was no opposing the flames. There was no organization. There was no communication. There was, however, a number of people, black and white, who performed daring deeds to rescue the trapped and helpless—to rescue the town itself.

In Union Square, at the great St. Francis Hotel, stunned passers-by watched in petrified awe as a 34-year-old black woman named Agnes Grady raced into and out of the hotel's lobby, half-carrying, half-dragging the injured guests. All the while, the St. Francis, ignited from top and sides, was flaming heavenward. In the business district, two African-American students, Wilson Treemore and Ashton Wallace, volunteered to assist federal troops in preventing looting.

All the cunning adjustments of a twentieth-century city had been smashed by the earthquake. The streets were humped into ridges and depressions and piled with debris of fallen walls—through which Grady, Treemore, Wallace, and count-less other African-Americans carried the injured and dying.

Predictions were hazarded that San Francisco would not be rebuilt and certainly that Market Street would not flourish again, but, al-most before the ruins ceased smouldering, the rebuilding work began.

The richest thing in the city was not shattered by the earthquake. Neither did it shrivel in the fire. Nor did its potential diminish. It is above par. The spirit of the Negro in San Francisco today is the grand-est asset which the metropolis ever has possessed.
—Oakland *Sunshine,* April 21, 1906

San Franciscans, black and white, built their city anew, finding in the adversity a determination and a sense of civic pride which many had not known existed.

★   ★   ★

On the centennial of the birth of Abraham Lincoln, February 12, 1909, the grandson of William Lloyd Garrison, Oswald Garrison Villard, wrote a call urging all believers in democracy to join in a national conference for "the renewal of the struggle for civil rights and political liberty." Among the fifty-three signers were J. J. Nei-more, editor of the *California Eagle,* and Theophilus B. Morton, president of the federated African-American Leagues. In response to the call, two meetings were held in New York. Out of them emerged the National Association for the Advancement of Colored People.

The basic aim of the new organization was to wipe out discrimina-tion in American public life, or, in its own words,

to make 11,000,000 Americans physically free from peonage, mentally free from ignorance, politically free from disfranchisement, and so-cially free from insult.

Like other reform agencies, the N.A.A.C.P. was designed to oper-ate through state and local branches. In California, branches sprang up in San Francisco and Los Angeles almost immediately.

In protest against state and federal "Jim Crow," the Los Angeles and San Francisco branches dispatched representatives to New York to help with national efforts. In addition to sponsoring mass meetings in various cities across the nation, the N.A.A.C.P. also voiced its protest through petitions, collecting signatures of whites and African-Americans to be sent to the White House. The largest of the petitions was one bearing 20,000 names, of which 4,000 were Californians, and which was delivered to President Woodrow Wilson in person on November 6, 1913, by a delegation of six African-Americans headed by William Monroe Trotter and J. J. Neimore.

In opposing federal discrimination, the N.A.A.C.P. reflected a widespread sentiment among African-Americans. With rare unanimity they condemned the Wilson Administration. At its convention in 1913 the National Negro Press Association, representing 126 newspapers, sent a strong protest to the President. No occupant of the White House ever received so many private letters of protest from African-Americans. This full-scale attack on segregation in government jobs was not without its effect. Early in 1914 the Treasury Department began to abandon its discriminatory policies, almost as quietly as it had initiated them. Other federal departments were slower to root out prejudices, but the advocates of segregationalist practices—because of the efforts of such notable black Californians as Neimore and Morton—no longer dominated the thinking of the Wilson Administration.

To African-Americans in California the fight against "Jim Crow" in the federal government brought with it an increased sense of racial solidarity and a keener interest in national affairs, sentiments that would be deepened by America's entry into World War I in April 1917.

★   ★   ★

During the fifty years following the Civil War, America's attention had been riveted on domestic problems. Foreign affairs had been a major concern only during the brief interlude of less than four months in 1898 when the United States went to war with Spain. Although this conflict stirred America less deeply than any other foreign war, it spelled a farewell to her traditional policy of isolation and brought new peoples, many of them African-American, under her flag.

When the war broke out, there were four African-American units in the regular army—the Twenty-Fourth and Twenty-Fifth Infantry and the Ninth and Tenth Cavalry. Retained after the Civil War, when other African-American regiments had been disbanded, these four units had seen action against the Indian tribes in the West—and these "black regulars" formed a portion of the expeditionary force of 15,000 that landed in Cuba late in June 1898.

The Spanish-American War was a popular one in the United States, and the Army had no problem in securing volunteers. But African-American civilians who wished to enlist had a problem: since they were not members of the National Guard, they were not eligible for summons to the Army. To satisfy the clamor of the African-Americans, Congress passed an act authorizing the formation of ten colored regiments. Only four such units were organized, however, because African-Americans resented the War Department stipulation that officers above the grade of second lieutenant be white. Rather than join these national regiments, many African-Americans enlisted in the troops recruited by the states, in which there was no ban on African-American officers (except in Alabama).

Only the four African-American regiments in the regular Army saw battle service. These four units took part in much of the heavy fighting of the short war, particularly at the outposts to Santiago. They performed well in the celebrated charge up San Juan Hill. In the confusion and disorder of the charge, a white man named Frank Knox had become separated from his regiment, but, as he later wrote,

> I joined a troop of the Tenth Cavalry, colored, and for a time fought with them shoulder to shoulder, and in justice to the colored race I must say I never saw braver men anywhere. Some of those who rushed up the hill will live in my memory forever.

A sergeant in the Tenth Cavalry, Elijah Rolling, felt that the storming of San Juan Hill had forged a deeper bond of unity between the victors. A native of San Francisco, Rolling said that "white and Negro regiments showed that they were unmindful of race or color in the dedication to their common duty as Americans."

The naval service also had an African-American component. When the battleship *Maine* was sunk in Havana harbor—an event which helped spark the war—twenty-two African-American sailors lost their lives in the explosion. Some 2,000 black men, nearly ten percent of the total forces, were enlisted in the wartime Navy. As a rule, however, they served in menial capacities, with few opportunities to win individual notice. Charles Percy was an exception: a Stockton clergyman who enlisted as a cabin cook on the torpedo boat *Winslow,* he left the galley and came on deck to take a more direct part in the action and was killed shortly thereafter by a bursting shell.

If California's African-Americans did not expect the war to improve their lot, they certainly did not think it would be to their disadvantage. But in one sense it was, for it brought under American control hundreds of thousands of nonwhites, notably those in the Philippines. The United States found it necessary, at the outset at least, to govern these peoples without their consent. As a justification for this denial of the democratic principle, some influential Americans—newspaper editors, congressmen, and high-ranking military officers—put the theories of racial inferiority to a new use, applying them to the overseas peoples who had recently come under the "Stars and Stripes." The United States had entered the war in order to free Spain's colonies, and this—with the aid of the African-American—had been accomplished. But another of the war's fruits was America's increased devotion to the fetish of racialism—that peoples are inherently separated into greater and lesser breeds.

★   ★   ★

When the United States declared war on Germany in April 1917, some 20,000 African-American fighting men were available. Half of these were members of the Regular Army; the other half were the African-American regiments of the national guards of the several states. These two groups were quickly brought to combat strength, and then the War Department faced a problem: What should be done with the young African-Americans who were pouring into the recruitment centers?

As might be expected, California's African-American population had shared fully in the general burst of patriotism brought on by the declaration of war. California black people took particular pride in the fact that the District of Columbia National Guard, under the command of an African-American previously employed by J. J. Neimore's *California Eagle,* Major James E. Walker, had been mustered in to protect the nation's capital city. A former Los Angeles resident, Walker took over the assignment on March 25, 1917, twelve days before the war.

African-Americans of military service age quickly rushed to the colors after the declaration of war, the lure of the uniform exercising its customary potency. Black students left their California classrooms to answer the call, and Sacramento's American Negro Loyal Legion sent word to Washington that it could raise 3,000 volunteers on short notice. Army officials were not quite prepared for such an African-American eagerness to enlist, and, after a few weeks of uncertainty, the War Department issued an order to halt the recruitment of "colored volunteers."

> It looked as if the Negro, like a burglar, would have to break into this war (WW I) as he did the others.
> —George Myers, White House barber

Myers was right: the African-American was not to be by-passed for long, for if the volunteer service were closed to the black man, the draft system proved to be an effective equalizer. The Selective Service Act of May 1917, which required all men between the ages of 21 and 30 to register for the draft, was not discriminatory in itself, but its administration was in the hands of local draft boards, on which African-Americans did not serve. Boards in California, as in most other states, invariably tended to call up a higher proportion of African-Americans than of whites. (Of all the African-Americans registered in the draft, 31.74 percent were called to arms, whereas only 26.84 percent whites were.)

**Of the hundreds of African-Americans summoned to military service from California, a great number of them would have been placed in the exempted or deferred classes had it not been for the color of their skin.**

If most white people favored the drafting of the African-American, they were opposed to his receiving basic training in their communities. Many feared that training camps for African-Americans might lead to trouble, and, indeed, there were many appalling incidents. In Monterey, California, an African-American corporal was refused admission to a theater. The strong protests of his African-American regimental mates and those of the Golden State's black press forced the theater owner to apologize. Army officials, however, then issued a strong order to the African-American troops directing them to refrain from any act that would cause "the Color Question" to be raised. African-American soldiers were ordered to "attend quietly and faithfully your duties, and don't go where your presence is not desired." A more serious incident took place at San Diego, when Noble Crane was roughly handled for not removing his hat when he went into a hotel lobby to buy a newspaper. Crane's enraged army mates, black and white, were prevented from striking back by a hastily determined directive from the War Department, ordering the African-American unit to break camp and sail for France.

In San Francisco, an unsuccessful attempt by a group of black soldiers to board a street car "reserved" for whites led to a fight in which two civilians were killed. Severe punishments were given to the soldiers, with one of them being sentenced to death and two being sentenced to life imprisonment.

★ ★ ★

After their basic training camp the majority of African-Americans were placed in noncombat units—labor battalions and service regiments. Army officials believed that the black man was peculiarly fitted for manual work because of his familiarity with it and because of his "happy-go-lucky" disposition. The Navy followed a similar practice of assigning its 5,300 African-Americans to jobs that required more brawn than skill—messmen, water tenders, gunner's mates, and coal passers. African-Americans who could not read or write were hardly in a position to complain about being assigned to service and menial occupations, but such assignments were particularly galling to the many California blacks who left classrooms in order to enlist.

African-Americans with an education beyond that of high school felt that they should be trained as officers. Army officials, however, were not enthusiastic about commissioning "colored men." Indeed, at the outbreak of the war there was only one African-American graduate of West Point, Sacramento's Charles Young, and he was only the third black man to have finished the courses at the Academy.

At the outbreak of the war, Congress authorized the establishment of fourteen training camps for white officers, and *none* for African-American. California blacks protested this exclusion, forming—with other states—a Central Committee of Negro College Men, which held conferences with Army officials and paid visits to members of Congress. The effort to make officer training available to African-Americans received the strong support of the black press, particularly the Oakland *Sunshine* and the *California Eagle,* as well as that of Rodger Horn, an officer of the San Francisco chapter of the N.A.A.C.P., who broached the subject to the Army's General Leonard Wood and received his backing.

Finally the War Department authorized on May 19, 1917, a reserve officers' training camp for colored men. The camp was established at Fort Des Moines, Iowa, and on June 15 the candidates began their training. Four months later to the day, 639 African-Americans became officers in the United States Army.

The first graduates of the "reserve officers' training camp for colored men" included native Californians Lester Billings, David Gibson, Elijah Trotter, and Henry Dennis, grandson of George Washington Dennis.

The Fort Des Moines trainees comprised about one-half of the total number of African-Americans commissioned during the war. The quota of black officers was kept small. For example, despite a great shortage of physicians, the medical corps had only 100 African-Americans at the close of the war. Many black physicians were drafted as privates, a practice which drew a sharp criticism from the National Medical Association, an African-American group with a membership of 5,000, at its annual meeting in Los Angeles in August 1918.

One disappointed African-American seeker of a commission based his plea less on his qualifications than on his family. Oakland *Sunshine* reporter Ralph W. Tyler, in a letter to the Special Assistant to the Secretary of War, dated October 8, 1917, pointed out that in every one of America's wars, his family had been represented—his brother in the Spanish-American War, his father in the Civil War, his grandfather in the Mexican War, his great-grandfather in the War of 1812, and his great-great-grandfather in the Revolutionary War. "All served as privates," wrote Tyler. "The family, I think, has earned a commission by this time."

African-Americans who received commissions were, on the whole, men of intelligence and ability. They were often called upon to demonstrate a special kind of fortitude. White privates and lower-ranking officers did not always salute them. The attitude of some white superior officers was lukewarm; they honestly believed that African-American officer training was an experiment bound to fail.

Some superior officers were supercilious. J. J. Neimore, in the *California Eagle,* wrote of a colonel who met an African-American captain whose face seemed familiar:

"Haven't I seen you somewhere?" the colonel asked.

"Yes, sir," replied the man, "I was with you on the border; Captain French is my name, sir."

"Oh, I do remember," said the colonel, "you are Sergeant French."

"No, sir, I am Captain French."

"Well," said the colonel as he walked away, "if I forget and call you Sergeant, don't mind."

Did the African-American officer and combat soldier maintain high morale despite the many evidences of color discrimination? Such a question admits no ready answer. Undoubtedly thousands of black soldiers were bitter about their treatment, and hundreds sent complaining letters to Secretary of War Newton D. Baker and, after October 5, 1917, to Emmett J. Scott, who had been appointed as his special assistant "in matters affecting Negroes."

> To catalogue or specify all of the Negro complaints that have come to the War Department would be an almost endless task.
> —Emmett J. Scott

To grumble, however, was part of the ritual of the boys in khaki— black or white. Moreover, to the African-American soldier discrimination was nothing out of the ordinary, for he had been an African-American prior to becoming a soldier.

In the infrequent instances in which African-Americans performed poorly in combat, a number of special factors could be held responsible. African-American troops were not always placed under competent men; poor performance by high-ranking officers was tolerated in African-American troops as it would not have been elsewhere. Many white commanders simply assumed that African-American officers and soldiers would be failures even before they had been tested. One white general, Robert L. Bullard, for example, was convinced that African-Americans, being "slothful and superstitious," were emotionally unfit for war. Some commanders issued orders forbidding black soldiers from mingling with the French people at social affairs, often subtly spreading the word that *the African-American was vicious and depraved.* Such attitudes would certainly not tend to raise the military efficiency of the African-American troops in his command.

The two African-American combat divisions were organized in ways that hardly made for *espirit de corps.* The Ninety-Second Division was late getting to France because, unlike any other division that went overseas, it had no cantonment of its own. The fact that its various units had been trained in seven different camps is a valid explanation for the small difficulties it encountered during the early weeks of fighting. What was to have been the other African-American division—the Ninety-Third—never really materialized. One of its regiments arrived in France in December 1917, and the other three landed in April 1918, but all four were brigaded with the French troops.

Whatever their degree of discontent or resentment, the African-American troops did their job. The Ninety-Second Division arrived in France in June 1917, and seven weeks later moved to the front, where they remained until the end of the war, under enemy fire most of the time. The Division's artillery brigade, which included black Californians Davis Holder and Mitchell Stephens, became notable for its accuracy, and its engineer regiment, led by Charles Rodger, grandson of California's great black mining engineer, Moses Rodger, did front-line work in the Meuse-Argonne offensive.

The Ninety-Third Division likewise made a good record, winning high praise from French commanders. The 371st Infantry was cited by Marshal Petain as "exhibiting the best qualities of bravery and audacity." The 370th Infantry, led by Lester Billings, won twenty-one American Distinguished Service Crosses and sixty-eight French War Crosses. The entire 369th Infantry, first of the African-American troops to see action, won the Croix de Guerre for gallantry in battle; under continuous fire for a record-breaking period of 191 days, this regiment was given the honor of leading the Allied armies to the Rhine a week after the signing of the Armistice. The 369th could boast two soldiers, Henry Johnson of Stockton and Needham Roberts of San Francisco, who performed one of the most sensational exploits of the war.

> While on sentry duty at a small outpost on May 14, 1918, California's Private Henry Johnson and Private Needham Roberts were attacked by a patrol of from twelve to twenty Germans. Fighting back, although badly wounded, the two African-American soldiers routed their attackers. For this feat Johnson and Needham were awarded the Croix de Guerre.

Headline fame was most unlikely to come to over two-thirds of the African-American troops because they were in the service of supply rather than combat units. But even though their jobs were backbreaking and humdrum, the labor battalions were indispensable. Someone had to get the fighting men to the front and then to furnish them with food, supplies, and ammunition. Black worker-soldiers generally discharged their assignments in good spirits, and the morale of the stevedore units seemed to be particularly high. Visitors at their camps were impressed by the rapidity with which they worked. One of these admiring visitors, Ella Wheeler Wilcox, who had observed the work of California's Richmond Stone, wrote a poem in their honor, containing these lines:

> We are the Army of Stevedores, and work as we must and may,
> The Cross of Honor will never be ours to proudly wear away.
> But the men at the front could not be there
> And the battles could not be won,
> If the Stevedores stopped in their dull routine,
> And left their work undone.

Possibly one of the reasons for the relatively good morale among African-American troops was the attitude of black people on the home front, particularly in the Golden State. Almost in spite of their strong sense of realism, African-Americans were impressed by the wartime slogans calling for the self-determination of all peoples in a world made safe for democracy. African-Americans believed, as had their forefathers, that by taking part in the war they would have additional grounds for demanding better treatment after it was over.

Spurred by such hopes, African-American leaders and opinion makers gave full support to the war effort. In Los Angeles, J. J. Neimore wrote that African-Americans were fighting "in order that innate racial superiority as championed by the Germans and as practiced by other races and groups may die a deserving death."

The influential Oakland *Sunshine* urged California African-Americans to forget their special grievances and close ranks, shoulder to shoulder, with their white fellow citizens.

In support of the war, California's African-Americans formed circles for the relief of soldiers and their families. Various cities had their thrift clubs; the entire membership of the San Francisco Thrift Club reported itself as having bought as many war bonds and saving stamps as possible. An all-black bank, Mutual Savings of Tulare, was awarded first place among the banks of the country in the Third Liberty Loan Drive, having oversubscribed its quota nineteen times. Many individual black women held important positions on the California home front: Agnes Grady, who had received widespread praise for her heroic efforts during the San Francisco earthquake in 1906, was a field representative of the Women's Committee of the

Council of National Defense, and Charlotte Boucher, one of the editors of the Oakland *Sunshine,* served as a member of the California Council of National Defense, a sort of war cabinet to the governor.

African-Americans who had borne arms for the country, who had bled and died for the "Stars and Stripes," returned from Europe upon war's end with hopes for a better America. During the initial days of their return, it seemed as if their hopes were sound. They received a tumultuous welcome. When the 369th marched through the streets of San Francisco, the dense crowds cheered and waved flags, and high-ranking state and city officials were present on the reviewing stands. Offices and stores were closed for the day. In full war equipment the regiment paraded down California Street, bells and whistles sounding.

Some of the more quiet admirers of the African-Americans in khaki expressed their sentiments in verse, among them Charles S. Jones:

> Back from their days of danger daring,
> Over the leagues of foam,
> Back from the scenes of their far wayfaring
> Our dusky boys come home.

Among the spectators who lined California streets for the homecoming parade of the Golden State's 369th Infantry was the editor of the *California Eagle,* J. J. Neimore. The sight of the marching African-Americans put him in a reflective mood:

> The services which these representatives of their race have rendered in the war to make the world safe for democracy ought to make forever secure for the race in this their native land their right to life, liberty, and the pursuit of happiness.

Certainly this was the way California's African-Americans saw it, too.

★   ★   ★

As the war came to an end in Europe, African-Americans in California were forced to resume their war against race prejudice and corruption in the state's government.

CHAPTER XIV

# Harding, Roosevelt, and Black Californians

IN THE FIRST PRESIDENTIAL ELECTION HELD AFTER WORLD WAR I, THE Republican candidate, Warren G. Harding, campaigned on a platform calling for a return to "normalcy," a word he had coined. Harding meant that the country needed a rest from international involvements and from domestic reforms—a return to the "good old days." The decisive victory won at the polls by Republican office seekers seemed to prove that Harding had correctly appraised the mood of the voters.

In the election of 1920 the vote of the African-American went almost solidly to the Republicans. This did not mean, however, that black people had any desire to return to normalcy in their status. They wanted to play a new role in the America that emerged from the war, not return to the old one. But this would not prove easy.

Postwar America tended to swing to the right. The wartime emotions of group loyalty and hatred found an outlet in the persecution of those persons or parties held to be un-American. The spirit of intolerance took hold of many, particularly those who were frightened, or rural-minded, or who feared a changing America. The strong dislike for socialists frequently spilled over to include those who espoused the cause of the African-American.

Of all the expressions of postwar intolerance, the one that affected the African-American most was the rebirth of the Ku Klux Klan. The new Klan had been organized late in November 1915, near Atlanta, Georgia, by William J. Simmons. Until the end of the war, its membership was small, but it then grew rapidly, until it had 100,000 members by the end of 1919. The new Klan, unlike the old, did not confine its cowardly activities to the South but operated from Maine to California.

An African-American who incurred the hostility of the Klan would wake up one night to find a fiery cross burning on his lawn, and a day or so later he would receive a warning to leave the community. If such measures failed, sterner ones were employed (including, in many cases, lynching). The officers of the Klan usually denied that the organization resorted to terror, but its secrecy and its use of masks and disguises in dress were open invitations to lawlessness.

For a few years in the mid-twenties, the Klan was powerful. Its revenues, coming primarily from the initiation fees and dues of more than 4,000,000 members, made it an extremely wealthy organization—and one to be reckoned with in both state and national elections. In 1925, with the government's permission, the Klan paraded in the nation's capital, marching down Pennsylvania Avenue and past the White House. But its decline was soon hastened by the uncovering of extensive fraud by high-ranking officials. The Klan left its impress, however; its spirit and methods underlaid the racial violence that erupted in several California cities immediately after the war.

> In Long Beach, an incident that touched off a race riot was the sexual assault of a fourteen-year-old black girl. Walking home from school, she was attacked by four white men, one of whom raped her. No arrests were made, and a Long Beach police officer was overheard saying, "What's the big fuss? It was only a colored girl."

The causes of the race riots were many, among them the competition of whites and African-Americans for jobs and the moving of black people into formerly "lily-white" neighborhoods. In California the African-American's quest for employment and housing had become acute because the black population had increased. (The West had over 470,000 more African-Americans in 1920 than it had in 1910, the migration resulting mainly from the economic dislocations of World War I.)

Since the war brought a halt to foreign immigration, the pool of unskilled laborers and domestic servants that had been coming from Europe by the boatloads shrunk. The war also took out of the factories and put into khaki hundreds of thousands of skilled and semi-skilled workers, though the booming war industries demanded more workers than ever. Desperately in need of laborers, manufacturing companies turned to African-Americans. They sent labor agents into the South, where black people readily responded to offers of a good job and free transportation. Soon there was a wholesale migration of African-American workers spilling into the Golden State, and they were followed by their clergymen and physicians.

To the African-American migrants, however, California life was far from easy. After the intoxication of being out of the South wore off, the newcomers found that the sprawling, impersonal cities of the Golden State were not quite the land of promise they had expected. Though they no longer saw "White" and "Colored" signs every-where—California did, however, have more than its share of such signs—they quickly became aware of segregation in churches and social clubs.

> In California, the color line took visual form in the existence of a "black belt," a section of various cities—such as Los Angeles and Long Beach—characterized by rat-infested houses, poor health and sanitation facilities, high incidence of crime and juvenile delinquency, and cops too quick with their night-sticks and guns.

Adding to the plight of California's black newcomer was the worsening condition of the state's labor market. During the years following the war, employment dwindled rapidly. As government purchases of supplies came to an end, war contracts, and the jobs that went with them, were concluded. The demobilization of hundreds of thousands of soldiers further glutted the labor supply. Many African-Americans were laid off or fired. Those who remained on the payrolls were generally in such traditional occupations as road building, stockyard and longshore work, and railroad mainte-nance—"hot and heavy operations in the hot and heavy industries."

In domestic service the postwar outlook was not hopeful. The

need for servants was lessened by the construction of modern apart-
ments equipped with labor-saving devices. The service jobs that
remained were now sought by whites who had been displaced by
the new machines. Jobs that were once an African-American monopoly were passing into other hands.

The African-Americans who had left the South were not disposed
to return. But faced with unemployment, job ceilings, and ghetto-
like living conditions, they must sometimes have wondered whether
the California cities to which they had come were less a frontier of
escape than a new imprisonment.

★   ★   ★

Immediately after World War I Californians entered a period of
particular hysteria. The tensions of the war were partly responsible.
Resorting to dynamite as a means of persuasion toward unionism
was another factor, as was the I.W.W.'s (Industrial Workers of the
World) practice of sabotage, and by easy extension all Socialists were
assumed to be anarchists and nihilists.

**In the Golden State, a socialist was anyone who espoused
the cause of black people.**

With the Russian Revolution of 1917 engineered by men presumed
to be of the same stripe, social conflict in America acquired an international overtone which suggested that world upheaval was the
menace to be feared. The infamous Palmer raids and the unseating
of the Socialist members of the New York legislature are two well-
known consequences. The Golden State fell in with the hysteria with
its accustomed vigor and, as might have been predicted in terms of
prior episodes of social conflict, aimed retaliation primarily against
unionism.

As *modus operandi,* the state legislature in 1919 enacted a criminal
syndicalism law similar to the one with which Idaho had led the way
two years earlier. The act defined criminal syndicalism in dragnet
fashion as "any doctrine or precept advocating, teaching or aiding
and abetting the commission of crime, sabotage . . . or unlawful
acts of force or violence or unlawful methods of terrorism as a means
of accomplishing a change in industrial ownership or control, or
effecting any political change."

In terms of the act, guilt attached equally to doing the deed, advocating it, or belonging to an organization that advocated it. Penalty

was set at imprisonment for one to fourteen years. The California act bore general resemblance to those legislated by 21 other states, mostly Western, and by Alaska and Hawaii. Elsewhere the acts soon became dead letters but in California there was rigorous enforcement. In the first five years 531 persons were arrested, of whom nearly 400 were black. Of those arrested, black and non-black, 264 were brought to trial, and 185 were convicted.

The most widely noted criminal syndicalism prosecution was of a respected philanthropist Anita Whitney, who, despite repeated threats by the Ku Klux Klan, had routinely espoused the cause of California's black people, including doing volunteer work with the N.A.A.C.P. In 1919, at a state convention of Socialists and Communists, Whitney attended and took a strong stand against revolutionary unionism and in favor of working for reform through the ballot. The convention, however, voted a preference for the radical method. It also gave *pro forma* approval to the national convention's program, which in passing included endorsement of the I.W.W. Three weeks later Whitney was arrested for violation of the criminal syndicalism law.

In the protracted trial the bulk of the evidence adduced concerned alleged atrocities committed by African-Americans on behalf of the I.W.W. Ultimately, Whitney was convicted of the felony of association with a group which advocated, taught, or aided and abetted criminal syndicalism.

Appeals ran until 1927 when the United States Supreme Court by a split decision upheld the conviction. Foiled on that front, Attorney John Francis Neylan urged California Governor C. C. Young to issue a pardon. Impressed by this appeal and by the dissenting opinion of Justice Louis Brandeis and convinced that Anita Whitney, "lifelong friend of the unfortunate Negro," was "not in any true sense a criminal," the governor decided that "to condemn her to a felon's cell" was "absolutely unthinkable." He issued the pardon.

Resentment against the I.W.W. continued, in fact, mounted. In March 1924, the Ku Klux Klan demonstrated against it, because "they befriend the nigger." Other incidents followed, including a vigilante assault on a N.A.A.C.P. benefit in which I.W.W. members and their families were in attendance, and in which a number of African-American children were beaten and tortured.

★　★　★

In 1910 Mrs. Ruth Standish Baldwin, a wealthy white woman, called a conference of the various groups working in the interests of the African-American in the city of New York. Out of this conference came the National League on Urban Conditions among Negroes, later shortened to the National Urban League.

The National Urban League was designed with the city African-American in mind. But the League was America-centered in program and interracial in personnel. Although its aim was that of improving the living and working conditions of black people in cities, it did not consider itself narrowly racial.

> Let us work not as colored people nor as white people for the narrow benefit of any group alone, but together, as American citizens, for the common good of our common city, our common country.
> —Ruth Standish Baldwin

In California, local branches of the League tailored their programs to meet the specific needs of their own communities. But all branches sought to assist new residents by finding them suitable homes and jobs. At meetings held in the evenings in schoolhouse buildings across the state, branch workers urged African-American workers to make good on the job, to be efficient. In San Jose, branch workers urged local employers to hire African-Americans in new capacities and young black people to train themselves so that when the doors of opportunity swung open they would be ready to walk through. Branches in Los Angeles, San Francisco, Long Beach, and San Diego sought to prevent crime and delinquency by establishing departments for meaningful recreation.

Working with Los Angeles' branch of the National Urban League, Ed Cornelius Pope, a former Allensworth resident, published a monthly newsletter, *Golden Opportunity,* and conducted surveys and investigations concerning the state's African-American residents. To help keep unemployment down, Pope issued monthly bulletins listing the California cities in which jobs were available and those in which they were not.

**While striving to create interracial good will, California branches of the National Urban League called attention to the African-American's needs in education, health, public welfare, police protection, and equal justice.**

The postwar restlessness of California's African-Americans also found expression in the so-called Negro Renaissance—a creative out-pouring in literature, art, and music. Though like so much else in African-American life, this phase was part of a more general trend in American letters; the Negro Renaissance in the Golden State was distinctive in two major respects: as an effort to articulate the discontent of the African-American, it was also *an evidence of a renewed race-spirit that consciously and proudly set itself apart.* The state's black writers and artists, such as Delilah Beasley, made a deliberate effort to cease imitating others and to produce work that might be racial in theme but that would also be universal in depth and appeal. They sought to be writers, not African-American writers. Although their themes were African-American, they were fashioned with high technical skill and designed for an audience that was not exclusively black. There was not, however, any catering to whites.

All California writers of the Negro Renaissance agreed on one canon: the use of dialect was taboo. Their objection was not so much to the dialect tradition as to the literary and topical limitations it imposed. In the Golden State, African-American writers decided it was time to bury a school of black expression which abounded in stock characters who were full of grins and grimaces and whose English was quaint and mirth-provoking. The black dialect school was not without literary respectability, having included such well-known whites as Joel Chandler Harris of Uncle Remus fame and Thomas Nelson Page. Masters at blending humor with pathos, these dialect writers were able craftsmen and at the turn of the century had been widely read. But they generally put a comic expression, a comic mask, on the African-American, and what emerged from their pages was a caricature rather than a person.

Disdaining economic considerations and unconcerned about the approval of whites, the African-American writer of the twenties was concerned above all with expressing his own feelings in his own way.

If California's African-American writers had no ready-made audience, the same could hardly be said of the black musician. Those who were interested in serious music might face an uphill battle—

> Negroes don't understand good singing, and white folks don't want to hear it from them.
>
> —Roland Hayes

—but in popular music all avenues were open. This was not surprising, since the African–American had been (and continues to be) a prime contributor to American popular music. During the post-Civil War decades, California black people had contributed chanteys, folk ballads, and chain–gang, railroad, and hammer songs.

In the dance, as in music, the influence of the California African–American was unmistakable, with the Long Beach black community credited with creating a dance called the Black Bottom.

> The influence which the Negro has exercised on the art of dancing in this state, in the entire country, has been absolute.
> —Jack London

The "race-spirit" which infused the creative work of black writers and musicians in California resulted in part from their awareness of the historic role African descendants played in the Golden State.

In 1865, in a speech at the Convention of Colored Citizens in Sacramento, William Henry Hall referred to California's "golden shores." Not long thereafter, Peter Bell, writing in *The Pacific Appeal,* coined the phrase "the golden state." African-Americans have given much to California—not the least of which is its nickname.

In the early 1900s, as never before, California's African-Americans began to realize that their roots in the Golden State sink as deep, if not deeper, than those of any other race, except for the Indian. They began to realize, too, that men and women of color had contributed significantly to California history and culture.

★   ★   ★

Following their role in the taming of the Sacramento River, California's African-Americans focused their attention on Los Angeles, which faced a crisis in its water supply. The Los Angeles River, with its capacious natural subterranean reservoir under San Fernando Valley, had provided enough water along with what could be had from ground sources, but for continued growth more was needed. Between 1905 and 1913 the city, aided by the expertise of such African-Americans as Pomona's Winston Roberts and Wilmington's Morrow Davis, achieved its first "final" solution to the problem of water supply.

A dry winter in 1904 put the city managers into a receptive mood to listen to a proposition to bring in more water. An engineer and former mayor, Fred Eaton, assisted by Roberts and Davis, had located a large supply of water in Owens Valley and an ancient riverbed that would greatly simplify the problem of diverting this water to the parched city some 250 miles distant.

With the necessary options in hand, Eaton, Roberts, and Davis broached the matter to City Engineer William Mulholland, who endorsed it wholeheartedly to the city water board. That body acted at once to acquire the site, approved a plan for a $25 million aqueduct, and broke the news by asking the voters of the city to authorize the necessary bond issue. As an engineering venture the aqueduct was a most creditable performance. With a significant number of African-American laborers, the project was completed within time estimates, and below budget, and Los Angeles benefited not only by the 400/second-feet of water delivered but also by the provision of electric power at a very moderate cost.

> By tapping the Owens River, Negro laborers have helped do the greatest good for the greatest number.
> —*California Eagle*

In San Francisco, the African-American community involved itself in "political housecleaning," with the Reverend Francis J. Grimke launching a frontal assault on municipal corruption, particularly the political machine of Abe Ruef, which was in cozy intimacy with established vice and corrupt practices. Ruef's machine exacted extortion from saloons, gambling houses, bordellos, prize fights, and the like, but its more ambitious levies were upon French restaurants, telephone, gas, water, and streetcar companies.

Pressured by Reverend Grimke and other prominent African-Americans the San Francisco Grand Jury brought in five indictments against Ruef for practicing extortion against the French restaurants. Trial should have proceeded at once, but Ruef's lawyers, availing themselves of every possible loophole, were able to delay it for a few months. During the delay the prosecution, aided by Reverend Grimke's black task force, found proof that Ruef's regime had taken bribes from several public service corporations—and the grand jury subsequently returned 65 more indictments against him. Ultimately, Abe Ruef was sentenced to 14 years in San Quentin.

**With the discovery of what the African-American had con-**

**tributed to California life and history, old shames and embar-
rassments were displaced by new prides.**

In oil, as in water, California's African-Americans made a substantial contribution. Phineas T. Banning, founder of Wilmington, because of funds contributed by George Washington Dennis, managed
to establish wells in his city.

In the 80s new fields opened in the Puente Hills, at Whittier and
Summerland, and by 1888 production reached 690,000 barrels. E. L.
Doheny entered the oil business in 1893, bringing in a shallow well
in the West Second Street field in Los Angeles (a tract of land formerly owned by Biddy Mason). Other important finds were at
Coalinga, McKittrick, Midway-Sunset, and Kern River—not far
from Allensworth. State production increased to 4 billion barrels
in 1900. Technology advanced, in part by methods developed in
California by African-American riggers and laborers.

Even more noteworthy were new uses. One, discovered by Delbert Jefferson, a black man residing in Redondo Beach who had been
educated at Oberlin College, was to mix the nonvolatile residue with
sand to make asphalt paving blocks, foreshadowing large-scale use
in highway construction. Jefferson, who ultimately helped organize
the Julian Petroleum Company with Courtney Julian, also persuaded
Doheny to experiment with crude oil as fuel for locomotives. It
proved to be a cheaper, hotter, cleaner, and more convenient fuel—
and oil-burning locomotives soon became standard equpiment
throughout the Southwest. Widespread industrial use followed.

In the formative years of California's oil industry, though many
of the investments offered were highly speculative, the industry's
contributions to the state were substantial. Among them were a new
money crop worth increasing millions annually, a steadily expanding
payroll, and large capital investments in wells, refineries, tank farms,
and pipelines.

For the first time, and in part because of the efforts of California's
African-American citizenship, the Golden State had adequate power
for the machinery of transportation and industry.

★   ★   ★

Partly out of the San Francisco example and partly by independent
origin, an African-American movement for reform in municipal
government cropped up in other parts of the state. In Los Angeles
the spearhead was William Jefferson, brother of the man who played

such an active role in the founding of the Julian Petroleum Company. In association with Dr. John R. Haynes, William Jefferson saw to it that Los Angeles' new city charter, adopted in 1902, incorporated provision for the initiative, referendum, and recall. (The first use of the recall was to remove a councilman who had voted to award the city's legal advertising to the *Los Angeles Times* even though there was another bid $15,000 lower.)

Other cities indulged in lesser reforms. Sacramento voted itself a new charter and employed the initiative to grant a franchise to the Western Pacific Railroad (whose tracks followed the route through the Sierra charted by James P. Beckwourth). Santa Barbara and Palo Alto adopted new charters. San Francisco adopted the recall in 1907, and in several other municipalities the trilogy of initiative, referendum, and recall was made available.

> African-American leaders in California were most astute politicians, and the nation's black people (and more than a few whites) gave them an attention not completely distracted by the fiasco of Rooseveltian progressivism or by the First World War. The efforts of these black people stand as a high-water mark in California's record of political achievement.

If the postwar years brought forth a new African-American in California culture, this period was also marked by a new African-American independence in political party affiliation. In 1920 California's African-Americans had supported the Republicans, as had their forefathers, but within a span of ten years they were ready to move in a new political direction. This direction was not to the extreme left, despite the wooings of the socialists and the communists. Typically American, the black man was (and is) individualistic, not likely to submerge his personality in conformity to a party line from which there could be no deviation. The basic conservatism of the African-American in accepting new theories of government did not, however, extend to political party affiliation—for in the decade following World War I African-Americans made a major shift in party loyalty. Though in the presidential election of 1924, the African-American newspapers—such as the *Oakland Sunshine* and *California Eagle*—and voters again supported the Republican party, a change had been setting in, engineered in part by enterprising Democratic political bosses and machines in various cities. Democratic politicians had taken careful note of the large black migration from the South and, knowing that these newcomes were Republican-minded, had busied themselves in seeking them out and urging them to register and vote. They gave black people small political jobs, such as watchers at the polls, and provided small favors, such as baskets of food or tickets to an entertainment.

Although California black people remained Republican, the national African-American swung toward the Democrats. The newly elected Republican president, Herbert Hoover, did little to retain his party's slipping hold on the African-American. He gave few federal appointments to black people. When his Administration arranged to send Gold Star Mothers to France to visit the graves of their sons, African-American mothers were segregated and given inferior accommodations. Hoover remained silent concerning the more than fifty lynchings of African-Americans that took place during his Administration. In 1930 he nominated for the Supreme Court Judge John J. Parker of North Carolina, who ten years earlier had said that the participation of black people in politics was "a source of evil and danger to both races." The N.A.A.C.P. chapters in Los Angeles and San Francisco vigorously fought the nomination, holding mass meetings and sending petitions to congressmen, and California African-Americans were overjoyed when the Senate withheld confirmation of Parker.

In the presidential election of 1932 California's African-Americans overwhelmingly supported the *Democratic* standard bearer, Franklin D. Roosevelt, helping to make Hoover a one-term president. The vote of the California African-American in 1932 meant one thing: he had become an independent in politics. One observer, journalist Arthur Krock, hailed the African-American's behavior as a "splendid revolt" which indicated that when the black voters went to the polls they put out of their minds Abraham Lincoln and Jefferson Davis, "who were not running in 1932."

★　★　★

The main reason for the success of the Democrats in the presidential election of 1932 was the failure of the Hoover Administration to cope successfully with the great depression. Following the collapse of the stock market in October 1929, some eight months after Hoover had been inaugurated, the Golden State, and the nation in toto, went through three years of hard times unprecedented in its history. As the roster of unemployed mounted higher and higher, the African-American was particularly affected. White people were only too willing to become street cleaners, bellhops, and redcaps, ousting African-Americans from such jobs. The unemployed, black and non-black, tended to vote for Roosevelt in 1932 because in the election campaign he voiced deep concern for the "forgotten man" and pledged a "new deal" for the people.

Once in office Roosevelt took on the role of guardian of the national welfare, greatly expanding the activities of the federal government. Many of the New Deal programs were designed to assist the working classes and the poor, and African-Americans bulked large in both categories. Roosevelt did not design his program with the African-American in mind (the New Deal actually had no fixed policy toward black people), but he was opposed to any racial discrimination implementing it. Many of the decentralized New Deal programs placed great power in the hands of local officials, however, who did not deem it wise or expedient to practice equality, regardless of the policy line formulated in Washington.

It was clear, however, that the African-American would stand to gain by each of the objectives of the New Deal—relief, recovery, and reform. In California, African-Americans made up seventeen percent of persons on relief in May 1935. In direct relief—the giving of food allowances, clothing, and commodity surpluses—California's African-Americans faced little discrimination, but in work relief, black people received few skilled-labor or white-collar jobs. The Public Works Administration stipulated that in slum-clearance projects a quota of skilled African-Americans should be used. The low-cost housing activities of the P.W.A. greatly reduced the congested living conditions of black families in over twenty-five cities, including Los Angeles, Oakland, San Francisco, and Long Beach.

Two aspects of the recovery program—the industrial and the agricultural—were of major concern to California's black people. The National Recovery Act authorized the setting up of codes for various industries, codes which determined such matters as minimum wages and the length of the work week. In the early days of the agency the matter of establishing a low wage for African-Americans was seriously considered. Supporters of this viewpoint claimed that most California blacks were able to hold jobs only because they would accept a lower wage than whites, and that the wiping out of the pay differential would lead to the replacement of African-Americans by Anglo-Americans.

African-American leaders in the Golden State, influenced by the Urban League, expressed solid opposition to the special low-wage theory, holding that black people should contend for equal wages even at the risk of being fired. This point of view became the official policy of the N.R.A., and more than a few black people in California did lose their jobs.

As in industry, the most important of the New Deal measures in agriculture had some disadvantage to the African-American. The Agricultural Adjustment Act of 1939 authorized a reduction in the acreage of basic crops, including cotton.

> In California, early experiments in cotton production were disappointing. In 1910 a new attempt was made by David Benjamin, a black man who introduced a new variety, the Acala. Results were more encouraging and, when World War I boomed the market, plantings were greatly increased in Imperial Valley, Riverside County, and the southern part of the San Joaquin Valley.

Farmers who agreed to restrict crops were to receive payment from the government. In practice, however, the A.A.A. tended to dispose of agricultural workers, for many planters did not hesitate to evict tenants and fire field hands as they reduced their acreages. Even where tenants were not evicted, they did not always receive the checks which planters were supposed to pass on to them.

To African-Americans, as to the country at large, perhaps the most significant of the New Deal reform measures was the Social Security Act, passed in 1935. This provided both old-age insurance for workers and unemployment insurance for workers, the latter to be administered in cooperation with the states. The Act granted federal monies to the states for public welfare services, including aid to the blind and crippled, dependent mothers, and children and old people who were destitute.

The fact that farm workers and domestic servants were not included in the old-age insurance program was a particular blow to African-Americans. But the impact of the entire Social Security Act, with its point of view that the government had a responsibility to the less fortunate, was of inestimable value to a citizenship which was at a disadvantage in the world of work and in which the incidence of poverty was much higher than the national average.

One of the most significant New Deal measures affecting African-Americans in California was the Wagner Labor Relations Act of 1935. By guaranteeing the right of collective bargaining and by outlawing company unions, this Act greatly strengthened organized labor. It gave particular approval to the militant wing of the labor movement, which had not felt certain that it had government backing in its drive to organize the great mass-production industries, where many of the workers were not unionized. These industries— steel, iron, automobiles, mining, longshoring, shipping, rubber and garment manufacture—were the very ones in which large numbers of African-Americans were employed.

Unskilled workers, long excluded from the crafts-dominated American Federation of Labor, turned eagerly to the Committee for Industrial Organization, founded in 1935 on the premise that unions should be organized along industrial labor rather than craft lines.

**In 1938 the Committee for Industrial Organization took the name Congress of Industrial Organizations.**

From its beginnings in California, the C.I.O. followed a policy of equality for all workers, black and non-black. It may be pointed out that it was easier to incorporate black people into a new union than established ones, where racial discriminations had often become fixed. Many of the C.I.O. unions in the Golden State kept no records concerning members' race or color, and some insisted that the contracts they signed must contain clauses barring discrimination against members because of race or religion.

★　★　★

Though the African-American gave the lion's share of the credit for his economic gains in the 1930s to Roosevelt, in truth the President himself did not come to the foreground in racial matters. From black people he received the gratitude that more directly belonged to subordinates like Harold Ickes, who set a pattern for other cabinet officers by appointing qualified black men, such as William H. Hastie and California's Robert C. Weaver to responsible positions in the Department of the Interior.

In both 1936 and 1940 Roosevelt won overwhelming victories at the polls. However, his success in the latter campaign was not so much an approval of his New Deal measures as it was a vote of confidence in his foreign policies. In 1939 war had broken out in Europe, with France and England arrayed against Hitler's Germany. Roosevelt made little attempt to conceal his sympathies, which became more evident when France capitulated in June 1940. As Roose-

velt drew closer to England, it became only a matter of time before
the United States would be drawn into the conflict. When Germany's
ally, Japan, attacked the American naval base at Pearl Harbor on
December 7, 1941, it marked the beginning of a global war.

America's entry into World War II brought her face to face with
a number of new realities, not the least of which was the wartime
role of California's African-Americans.

CHAPTER XV

# Fighting for Peace

AMERICA'S ENTRY INTO WORLD WAR II PRESENTED CALIFORNIA'S AFRICAN-American citizenship with no problems of divided loyalty or emotional adjustment. Black people had no historical identification with Germany, Italy, or Japan, and even before Pearl Harbor had been anti-Hitler, having a natural distaste for the "master race" theories of the Nazis. Black people in the Golden State remembered that when the 1936 Olympic games were held in Berlin, Hitler had left his seat every time an African-American athlete won an event, thus avoiding the necessity of meeting him.

When the United States entered the war, there was a distinct note of "wait and see" in the writings of some black journalists in California who remained cold sober as America put out more flags, and African-American leadership in general took the stand that unless black people received better treatment they could not wholeheartedly and unreservedly support the war effort. Thinking only of the many indignities they had suffered, the rank and file of African-Americans may not have carefully weighed the California way of life, with all its imperfections, against the freedomless system of totalitarian powers.

> California was given by God to a *white* people, and with God's strength we want to keep it as He gave it to us.
> —William P. Canbu, Grand President,
> Native Sons of the Golden West, 1920

213

African-Americans of a reflective turn of mind supported the war in the belief that if America lost, men and women of color stood to be the greatest losers. In California, African-Americans high and low sensed that if they wanted to get something out of the war, they had to put something into it.

In the fall of 1940, when the national defense program got started, 90 percent of the holders of defense contracts used no African-Americans at all or confined them to nonskilled or custodial jobs. The National Defense Advisory Commission recommended to contractors that they adopt equal employment practices, but the new war industries evoked an old standby: the hiring of black people was "against company policy." Vast, sprawling plants took shape at Burbank, Inglewood, Santa Monica, Long Beach, El Segundo, and San Diego. The contracts poured in to Douglas, Lockheed, North American, Hughes, and a host of subsidiary parts suppliers. By June 1945, they totaled some $2,136,119,000 in San Diego County and $7,093,837,000 in Los Angeles County.

From considerably fewer than 20,000 employees in 1939 the work force rose to a peak of 243,000 in August 1943. "The hiring of black people was 'against company policy'. . . ." White workers were imported to industrial centers where qualified men and women of color were looking for jobs. Shipbuilding, like aircraft production, also increased. From a mere 4,000 workers in 1939 there was an upsurge to a peak of 282,000 in August 1943. Contracts amounted to $5,155,516,000. Nearly two-thirds of it went to the yards at Richmond, Sausalito, South San Francisco, and elsewhere in the Bay region. As was the case with the aircraft industry, African-American workers were often bypassed in favor of white employees.

῾ Job discrimination in the defense industry called forth strong protests by California's African-American press and welfare groups. Liberal whites joined in, as did many white newspapers. In many California cities, such as Long Beach and Richmond, African-Americans resorted to picket lines. But the most effective step was that taken by A. Philip Randolph, president of the Brotherhood of Sleeping Car Porters. Unable by conference-table methods to induce the Roosevelt Administration to take action against employment bias, Randolph proposed nothing less than a national African-American March on Washington, a direct action by 100,000 black people, more than 8,000 of whom traveled from California to participate. In the spring of 1941 Randolph organized the movement and set the date for July first. It was an all-black effort:

We shall not call upon our white friends to march with us. There are
some things Negroes must do alone.

—A. Philip Randolph

The Roosevelt Administration was puzzled by the threat of this
march, which was indeed something quite new in the African-
American protest activities. The President attempted to have the
march called off, finally summoning its leaders to the White House.
At this conference Randolph stated that the march would go on
unless the President issued an executive order prohibiting discrimination in defense industries. Faced with the very real possibility of
an embarrassing large-scale demonstration in the nation's capital,
Roosevelt yielded, issuing on June 25 Executive Order 8802, which
officially reaffirmed the government's policy of nondiscrimination
in employment.

With Roosevelt's Executive Order the color bar in employment
began to fade. The order directed that the vocational training program be conducted without reference to race, and it stipulated that all
future defense contracts should include non–discrimination clauses.
More importantly, it established a Committee on Fair Employment
Practice to investigate violations of the order. Through its field staff,
the Committee processed complaints and held public hearings. In
California, the Committee was instrumental in opening new job
opportunities for men and women of color, particularly in aircraft
plants and firms manufacturing airplane equipment, such as Lock-
heed-Vega and Douglas.

By the summer of 1944 there were about 100,000 Negroes in aircraft,
and they were about six percent of the total.

—Robert C. Weaver

The Committee was even more gratified by the results of the
training program; by October 1944, thousands of California's African-Americans had received pre-employment and supplementary
defense training. The acquisition of new industrial skills would inevitably lead to higher-level jobs.

President Roosevelt had been quick to extend the authority of the
committee to cover employment by federal bureaus and departments. In this sphere the results were gratifying almost beyond expectations. African-Americans, particularly women, were brought
into government service in mounting numbers.

Thanks to the Executive Order and an increasingly tight labor market, the African-American worker's outlook brightened with each passing month—a development which led many African-American civilians to become more and more enthusiastic about the war.

★   ★   ★

Notoriously wars are fought without sparing cost. Except for a strong effort to curb inflation, the United States made no pretense of economizing on World War II. There were times, however, when factors quite extraneous led to provident decisions. One was the selection of California as a major area for troop training. Continuing the process started before American involvement as a belligerent, the Army developed huge training camps near Monterey, Paso Robles, San Luis Obispo, and Santa Maria. The Marines opened a west coast Quantico near Oceanside; the Navy built up its facilities at San Diego; and the Air Force added major training fields near Victorville, Merced, and Santa Ana. These training centers amounted to more than 10 percent of the national total.

**As the war went on, the status of the African-American on the fighting fronts underwent a change.**

In October 1940, the War Department announced its two guiding principles concerning black people; the proportion to be enlisted would correspond to their proportion in the population, and black and non-black soldiers would not be intermingled. The Army thus reaffirmed its traditional policy of a separate regimental organization of African-American troops. The day after Pearl Harbor a group of African-American editors, headed by Los Angeles' Claude A. Barnett, director of the Associated Negro Press, met with War Department officials and urged them to create a mixed volunteer division—one open to all men irrespective of race, creed, color, or national origin. Perhaps the Army officials gave the proposal careful thought; at any rate they did not formally reject it until September 1943.

Although the Army retained its segregated pattern, it made changes in its draft procedures and officer procurement policies. In the operation of the selective service, there was little discrimination. Lieutenant Colonel Campbell C. Johnson, an African-American who had been born in Tulare County, California, was made an executive assistant to Selective Service Administrator Lewis B. Hershey, and African-American citizens held white-collar jobs in the selective service offices.

★ ★ ★

In breaking from tradition concerning the African-American, the Navy went much further than its sister service. When the war broke out, the Navy followed a "messmen only" policy for men of color, confining them to the Steward's Branch. There were no black officers. Ignoring criticism, Navy Secretary Frank Knox, in October 1941, reaffirmed the official policy: Negroes, he said, would be recruited only in the messman's branch.

Six months later Knox was forced to yield, announcing on April 17, 1942, that African-American volunteers would henceforth be accepted for general services as well as for mess attendants. Two incidents led to this reversal: first, continuous picketing by African-Americans at naval facilities in San Diego and San Francisco; second, the conduct of former San Jose resident Dorie Miller, messman third class on the *Arizona,* on the morning of the Japanese attack on Pearl Harbor. When the general alarm sounded, this courageous black man went on deck, helped remove the dying captain, and then manned one of the machine guns. The native Californian brought down at least four of the enemy planes before the sinking *Arizona* had to be abandoned. Miller was subsequently awarded a Navy Cross, pinned on him by Admiral C. W. Nimitz, and was the recipient posthumously of a Congressional Medal of Honor.

Knox's statement that African-Americans would be used for general service turned out to be somewhat less meaningful than it sounded, however. The Navy announced that beginning June 1, 1942, African-Americans could enlist for service other than as messmen, but they would not be placed on seagoing combat ships; instead, they would be limited to shore installations and harbor craft. Further, African-Americans were to be placed in separate units. Led by Claude Barnett, the black press and clergy sent up a chorus of protest over the "Jim Crow" aspect of the policy. But in June 1942, African-Americans began to receive basic training courses at the Great Lakes Naval Training Station, their compound taking the name of the African-American naval hero of the Civil War, Robert Smalls. By the fall of 1943 black sailors had been trained in more than fifty different job categories. Haltingly, but unmistakably, the Navy had begun to chart a new course.

The movement toward integration in the Navy stemmed from

two sources, the unenthusiastic behavior of the African-American seamen and the influence of naval officers like Christopher Smith Sargent. In addition to being segregated, African-American sailors found that they were assigned to the jobs of handling ammunition and loading ships. Their resentful attitude was evidenced by many widely separated incidents, including hunger strikes, demonstrations, and refusal to obey orders.

At Port Chicago in San Francisco Bay, 250 African-American sailors refused to load an ammunition ship after an explosion had killed 300 of their fellow servicemen. The mutineers were sentenced to long terms, but eventually the convictions were set aside and the men were restored to duty.

The African-American sailor's attitude toward unfair treatment speeded a better day for him.

The Navy also moved ahead in two other branches of its service. In May 1942, it accepted African-Americans into the Coast Guard in capacities other than messmen. One month later the Marine Corps began to admit African-American volunteers, for the first time in 167 years.

In the enlistment of African-American women the Navy lagged far behind its sister service. Though the women's reserve of the Navy (the Waves) was organized in the summer of 1942, it was not until late in 1944 that women of color were permitted to join, and then only after continuous pressure, led by a Sacramento-based African-American sorority council.

Unlike the Army or Navy, the Merchant Marine was integrated from the outset, keeping no files of seamen or officers by color or race. Fourteen of its government-built Liberty ships were named after outstanding African-Americans, four after black seamen who had lost their lives, and four after African-American colleges. Among the Liberty ship captains were four African-Americans, of whom the best known was California's Captain Hugh Mulzac, who by May 1944, had taken the S.S. *Booker T. Washington* across the submarine-infested Atlantic seven times.

By virtue of our valor, courage, and patriotism, things will be better for us.
—African-American Soldier, WW II

African-American soldiers undoubtedly did what they were called upon to do. Since most of them were in the service branches, they could be found everywhere in the Army's far-flung operations—building the Alaska-Canada Highway, constructing the Ledo Road linking China to India, cutting a path through the Burmese jungle, building airports in Liberia, unloading ships in half a hundred harbors scattered over three continents, and moving crucial supplies of ammunition to the front lines at the beaches of Normandy.

## An Experiment in Integration

Badly needing infantry replacements in Europe early in 1945, the Army decided to accept African-American volunteers to be organized as platoons for service as units in white regiments. Some 2,500 African-Americans placed in the infantry division of the First Army performed ably in the hard fighting on the east bank of the Rhine. When, subsequently, the white officers who commanded them were asked the question, "How did the black soldiers in this company perform in combat?" 84 percent replied, "Very well," and 16 percent, "Fairly well." Not a single officer checked any of the other categories in the questionnaire: *"Not so well," "Not well at all," or "Undecided."*

The mixed-units experiment had its effect on the Army. Late in 1945 the War Department appointed a board of generals to make recommendations about the use of African-Americans in the future. Among the thirteen proposals made by the board were those calling for the grouping together of black and non-black units, the assignment of African-American trainees to communities that would be favorably disposed toward them, and the expansion of opportunities for African-Americans as officers. The report did not, however, abolish segregation in the United States Army, which prompted an editorial in the *California Eagle* to conclude "A Negro American soldier is still first a Negro and then a soldier."

On the home front the war brought something old and something new to the African-American. If the old was painful, the new was hopeful and forward looking. A familiar sense of indignation grew out of a combination of factors, the foremost being the African-American policy of the Army. "No injustice embitters Negroes more than continued segregation and discrimination in the armed forces," ran a statement released on June 17, 1944, by the San Francisco chapter of the National Association for the Advancement of Colored People. African-Americans in the Golden State were also outraged by the mistreatment of black troops in communities where camps were located. California's African-American press carried innumerable stories describing the hostile behavior of white civilians and policemen toward black soldiers and WACS.

Some hostility toward men and women of color was no less than inevitable. In an America at war, the familiar patterns of black-white relations were upset, and one of the results was an increase of tensions, fears, and aggressions. In California, where the war transferred more than 700,000 people into the armed services, many white people found it convenient to blame someone for the new challenges in race relations, and they decided upon Eleanor Roosevelt. Viewing her as a symbol of outside interference, white Californians claimed that she was the inspiration behind the Eleanor Clubs formed by African-American domestics across the state.

*A white woman in every kitchen.*

—Eleanor Club motto

The "Eleanor Club" allegation was scarcely more credible than the rumor that African-Americans were buying up all the icepicks and would, during some convenient blackout, start an attack on the whites. The contagion of rumors spreading through the Golden State during the war years was a sobering indication of the extent to which white Californians were misinformed about the African-American and unaware of his real attitudes, not to speak of his considerable strides in education.

Tense race relations led to several racial outbreaks—one in Harlem, two in Detroit, and one in Los Angeles. These riots had a profound effect throughout the nation. They shocked the American white people into a realization that the status of the African-American had undergone a significant change that could not be ignored. As a result, cities and states throughout the country began to take a new interest in black-white relations. Public officials read the signs: by the end of the war seventeen governors and sixteen mayors had appointed commissions to formulate immediate and long-range proposals for the improvement of race relations.

One of the reasons for the changed status of the African-American was his greater economic security. In 1944, one million more black workers were to be found in civilian jobs than in 1940.

Between 1940 and 1944 the number of African-Americans employed in government service had jumped from 60,000 to 300,000. In California, the employment of African-American women in industry quadrupled during the war years.

World War II, like its predecessor, brought about a shift in the African-American population. About 333,000 men and women of color left the South, and some two-thirds of them went to the Pacific Coast. The African-American population of San Francisco in 1945 was five times greater than that of 1940; in Los Angeles 76,000 African-American newcomers arrived between April 1944 and April 1945.

Both the home-front African-Americans and the African-American soldier were hopeful that war's end would result in a better America for them. This feeling had been expressed by a conference of African-American leaders at Los Angeles in October 1942:

> We have the courage and faith to believe that it is possible to evolve in California a way of life, consistent with the principle for which we as a Nation are fighting throughout the world, that will free us all, white and Negro alike, from want, and from throttling fears.

It was in this spirit that California's African-Americans faced the postwar world.

★ ★ ★

World War II shook the United States from its isolationist moorings, convincing the large majority of Americans that a new world order was necessary. Man had shrunk the universe while at the same time multiplying the capacity for self-destruction. Such a perilous equilibrium seemed to require a new dedication to international cooperation.

**The United Nations Organization, established in San Francisco in June 1945 represented a worldwide response to a compelling urge to ensure peace.**

African-Americans had taken a keen interest in the founding of the United Nations, every major African-American newspaper sending a correspondent to San Francisco. Along with other selected organizations, the N.A.A.C.P. had been invited to send official observers, and they had chosen Walter White, executive secretary of the organization, W. E. B. DuBois, and Mary McLeod Bethune. The most prominent participant, however, was California's own Ralph J. Bunche, an African-American who was the State Department's acting chief of the Division of Dependent Territories. African-Americans in California, as well as across the country, liked the charter provision of the United Nations in which the member states pledged themselves to promote "respect for human rights and fundamental freedoms for all without distinction as to race, sex, language or religion." Black people also gave wholehearted approval to the statement (written by Ralph Bunche) subsequently issued by the United Nations Organization, "The Universal Declaration of Human Rights," whose first article opened with the line "All human beings are born free and equal in dignity and rights."

African-Americans were among the strongest supporters of the United Nations. They felt that it might play a role in bringing an end to the system of colonialism.

> In 1944, at a meeting in San Francisco, the representatives of twenty-five African-American organizations had stated that political and economic democracy must displace the prevailing system of exploitation in Africa, the West Indies, India, and other colonial areas. The war brought to black Americans a realization that the subjugation of dark-skinned peoples in distant lands tended to strengthen color prejudice everywhere, including their own country.

African-Americans welcomed the United Nations because it would sensitize the world to the problems of race and color and provide an international sounding board for yellow, brown, and black peoples to press their case.

The purposes of the United Nations Organization are many: to maintain international peace and security; to develop friendly relations among nations; to achieve international cooperation in solving economic, social, cultural, and humanitarian problems and in promoting respect for human rights and fundamental freedoms; to be a center for harmonizing the actions of nations in attaining these common ends.
—Ralph J. Bunche

Black people in America could use the United Nations to air their grievances—as indeed they did in 1947, when the San Francisco chapter of the N.A.A.C.P. presented to the United Nations' Office of Social Affairs a 155-page document with the lengthy title "A Statement on the Denial of Human Rights to Minorities in the Case of Citizens of Negro Descent in the United States of America and an Appeal to the United Nations for Redress." The African-American press in California knew that membership in the United Nations would make America more aware of its own unfinished business. The country's position as leader of the free world would certainly be questioned if it were unfair in its treatment of a particular group of its own citizens.

The African-American's attitude toward the United Nations went beyond an interest in black people, however, and even beyond an interest in the cause of the colonialist peoples. Like their countrymen, the African-American was acquiring a broadening view of the world. Men and women of color are among the most resilient of Americans, among those least likely to be chained to fixed assumptions. If the world moved toward new unities, the African-American would move, too. This widening horizon of interest and of service—this world view—was well exemplified by the grandson of a former slave, California's Ralph J. Bunche, who in 1946 became chief of the United Nations' Division of Trusteeship, who a year later became the secretary of the Palestine Commission, and who in 1948 succeeded in settling the thorny Arab-Israeli dispute, for which, in December 1950 he was awarded the Nobel Peace Prize.

CHAPTER XVI

# Challenging California's Racial Inequality

ON THE DOMESTIC FRONT THE MOST PRESSING PROBLEM FACED BY CALIfornia's postwar African-American was equality of job opportunity, though, fortunately, a few men and women of color were able to retain some of their wartime gains. With the cutback in war-related industries, however, African-Americans tended to lose jobs more rapidly than whites: in the two years following World War II African-American membership in the Marine and Shipbuilding Works of America dropped by more than 80 percent. But during these years the Golden State experienced an unprecedented peacetime boom, bringing relatively full employment. With labor in demand, industry had no problem absorbing black people, discharged servicemen as well as laborers. As late as January 1948, the percentage of unemployed black males did not compare unfavorably with that of whites—5.2 percent as opposed to 3.8 percent.

The national government contributed importantly to African-American employment after the war. The wartime Committee on Fair Employment Practice (F.E.P.C.), established by President

Roosevelt went out of existence in June 1946, but subsequent chief executives have issued orders proclaiming equality of opportunity in federally controlled employment and established committees to effectuate them.

> President Truman created a Committee on Government Contract Compliance; President Eisenhower created a Committee on Government Contracts (for contractual employment) and a Committee on Government Employment Policy (for federal employment). In April 1961, President John Fitzgerald Kennedy created a Committee on Equal Employment Opportunity, charging it with a two-fold task of bringing about equality of job opportunity in government contracts and in the federal government itself.

To the Golden State's African-Americans seeking employment opportunities and careers in postwar California the military branch of the federal establishment had much to offer. For the first time in history, black people were invited to join the Army when the country was at peace. Adopting a recommendation from a 1945 report, the War Department decided that the African-American should be given a continuing role in the Army, with his numbers corresponding to the ratio of black people in the total population. This new policy immediately attracted many African-Americans, particularly those in California—where military procurement continued. In fact, during the six months after V-J Day, over 17% of California's volunteer enlistees were African-Americans.

African-Americans joining the peacetime army found a serious, if familiar, drawback—they were assigned to segregated units. In San Diego, an African-American civilian group formed, on October 10, 1947, a Committee Against Jim Crow in Military Service and Training, headed by former army chaplain Grant Reynolds. Eight months later President Truman issued an order calling for equality of opportunity for all servicemen, at the same time creating a Committee on Equality of Treatment and Opportunity in the Armed Services to advise him about implementing the new order. In May 1950, the committee recommended that every vestige of segregation be removed in the Army, Navy, and Air Force.

The conflict in Korea hastened integration in the armed services. Racially mixed units fought side by side in the see-saw war in the Korean hills, with no apparent sacrifice of military efficiency.

White units showed little reaction when Negroes were sprinkled among their ranks. Some officers even reported heightened morale among their all-white units after Negroes were added.
—Lee Nichols
*Breakthrough on the Color Front,* 1954

A progress report from the Office of the Assistant Secretary of Defense, dated January 1, 1955, and titled "Integration in the Armed Services," bore out the conclusion of the United Press newsman Nichols. "Thorough evaluation of the battle-tested results to date indicates a marked increase in the overall combat effectiveness through integration." Two African-American soldiers in Korea— Private William Thomas and Sergeant Cornelius H. Charlton, a former San Jose resident—were awarded the Congressional Medal of Honor.

★   ★   ★

In bringing about a significant change in the status of the African-American since World War II, the role of the federal courts has been second to none. As no other branch of the national government, the courts had wrestled with the important question: Now, in the middle decades of the twentieth century, what is the meaning of equality in the concrete life of the American people? Free from the party politics a president must play and from the pressures of jockeying and bargaining that Congress must live with, the federal judiciary, particularly the Supreme Court, can grapple more singlemindedly with the meaning of freedom and equality.

In the early 30s the Supreme Court began to show an increased concern about civil rights and individual liberties. It began to go behind the formal law as stated in order to discover whether it was being fairly applied. It began to look beyond the laws enforcing segregation to see whether the separate facilities provided for African-Americans were in fact equal to those for whites. With such new considerations in mind, the Supreme Court in the 1940s made a number of significant rulings concerning discrimination in voting, in transportation, and in housing. In 1944 the Court decreed that in primary elections a political party could not exclude a voter because of race *(Smith vs. Allright)*; in 1946 it ruled that an African-American passenger in interstate commerce was entitled to make his journey without conforming to the segregation laws of the states through which the carrier might pass *(Morgan vs. Virginia)*; and in 1948 it ruled that restrictive covenants—private agreements to exclude persons of a designated race or color from the ownership or occupation of real property—were not enforceable by the judiciary *(Shelley vs. Kraemer)*.

With this increased concern about civil rights and individual liberties, a number of California African-Americans launched frontal assaults against discriminatory practices. In San Francisco, for instance, the African-American community, led by David Wilson, picketed construction sites until various firms hired black people to help in the mass production of housing. The construction industry, dominant during the war, set new records. As had been the case in many California cities, from San Diego to San Bernardino to Santa Barbara and from San Jose to Santa Rosa and Sacramento, African-American crews were brought in to pave streets and put in utility lines—and their role increased as house after house was built. In the tract housing at Daly City, African-Americans were part of the crews that poured concrete, raised the precut frames, shingled the roofs, plastered, hung doors and windows, painted, and cleaned up.

In the southern part of the state, Chrystalee Maxwell, an African-American staff nurse at Los Angeles General Hospital, forced the American Medical Association to drop the designation "colored" after the names of African-American physicians listed in its American Medical Dictionary.

> Prior to the verbal assault and concerted efforts of Chrystalee Maxwell, granddaughter of former slaves, the American Medical Association placed an asterisk behind the name of every African-American doctor listed in its dictionary of physicians.

After successfully forcing the American Medical Association to desegregate its American Medical Dictionary, Chrystalee Maxwell, who was to Los Angeles General Hospital what Florence Nightingale was to nursing, gave up civilian life to become a lieutenant in the Army Nurse Corps.

★   ★   ★

Beyond all other fields it was on public tax-supported education that the Supreme Court rulings had their most profound impact. In a series of cases from 1938 to 1950 the court, still operating under the "separate but equal" theory of the Plessy decision, sought to make the states meet the test of equality, much as Mary Francis

Ward had done in the nineteenth century in San Francisco. In *Gaines vs. Missouri* (1938) the Court ordered that an African-American applicant be admitted to the law school of the University of Missouri since there was no other acceptable way for him to get a legal training within the state. Ten years later the court ordered Oklahoma to provide Ada Louise Spiuel with a legal education, and to "provide it as soon as it does for any other group." (Spiuel had left Santa Barbara after failing to find a legal education opportunity in the Golden State.) Two years later the court ordered Oklahoma to desist from segregating G. W. McLaurin requiring that he sit at a designated desk in an anteroom adjoining the classroom, apart from other students, to sit at a designated desk in the library, and to eat in the school cafeteria at a special time. In the Sweatt case, decided on the same June day in 1950, the court ruled that an African-American applicant be admitted to the University of Texas Law School inasmuch as it was far superior to a hastily organized law school just set up at Texas State University for black people.

In all of these cases California chapters of the N.A.A.C.P. had sponsored the litigation, hoping thereby to undermine segregation. California chapters, as well as the national organization itself, believed that the South would abandon its dual system of education because of the large sums of money that would be required if African-American schools were made equal to those for whites. But this hope of attacking segregation by a flank movement proved to be fanciful, for the Southern states began to appropriate additional funds for African-American schools. The N.A.A.C.P. realized that by providing African-American schools and colleges with better buildings, better equipment, and better salaries for teachers and by changing the title "college" to that of "university," the South was in effect strengthening "Jim Crow" by establishing "gilded citadels of segregation" manned by African-American administrators and teachers who would have a vested interest in maintaining the status quo in racial education.

Realizing that its victories in the "separate but equal" cases were failures concealed in success, the N.A.A.C.P., on the urging of California's C. L. Dellums, decided to change directions.

★   ★   ★

C. L. Dellums migrated to San Francisco from Texas in 1925, planning to work his way through the University of California law school. It would not be that easy.

Dellums turned to the Pullman Company for a job soon after he discovered he could not find employment in the Bay area. The results of his job-seeking efforts illustrate the situation in which California's African-Americans found themselves during the roaring 20s.

> I applied for a waiter's job at the leading hotels. I was well qualified, having worked as a waiter in the finest hotels in Texas, but in San Francisco they were shocked to have a Negro ask for a job other than boot-black. There were no jobs for Negroes at San Francisco hotels, much less a room for one.
>
> —C. L. Dellums

Dellums, who founded the Western Regional Headquarters of the National Association for the Advancement of Colored People, joined the ranks of the Brotherhood of Sleeping Car Porters and was ultimately elected to the post of international vice president, with headquarters in Oakland. Remembering his frustrating job hunt in San Francisco, Dellums became an effective disciple of A. Philip Randolph, international president of the union and a civil rights leader. Randolph and Dellums wanted equal employment opportunities for African-Americans.

The determined African-American leaders, supported by a few white citizens in labor, the church and Jewish organizations, launched an attack against discrimination. Not long thereafter, Dellums led 8,000 black Californians to Washington to participate in Randolph's threatened march in the summer of 1941.

**Four Kaiser shipyards in Richmond employed 10,000 African-Americans after C. L. Dellums convinced the Kaiser interests a vast pool of qualified workers was being overlooked and ignored.**

Following Dellums' lead, the N.A.A.C.P. launched a direct, frontal attack on segregation in the public schools. Such an assault required careful preparation, but by 1950 the N.A.A.C.P. was ready. On May 16 of that year its legal counsel filed a suit in the federal court in Charleston, South Carolina, on behalf of sixty-seven African-American children asking that they be admitted to the public schools of Clarendon County without regard to race. This case, along with four similar ones, eventually reached the Supreme Court, all of them taking the name *Brown vs. Board of Education.*

The issue before the court was momentous. It had to decide whether a state or the District of Columbia had the constitutional power to operate segregated schools on the elementary and secondary levels. On May 17, 1954, the nine justices, three of them Southerners, rendered a unanimous decision: segregation of children in public schools solely on the basis of race is unconstitutional. Completely reversing the Plessy decision of 1896, the court declared that separate educational facilities were inherently unequal and hence deprived the segregated person of the equal protection of the laws guaranteed by the Fourteenth Amendment.

The Brown decision was immediately recognized as a revolutionary step in American race relations. The decision itself applied only to schools below the college level, but it had unmistakable implications for public institutions of higher education. And it had similar implications for any publicly operated facility—library, museum, beach, park, zoo, or golf course. Indeed, the Brown decision could be extended to any field in which segregation was imposed by state law. It did not apply to private groups or organizations, but it would undoubtedly cause many of them to re-examine their racial policies.

Simply stated, the Brown decision meant that America would have to look anew at its African-American citizens.

The abiding subconsciousness of the Negro turned overnight into an acute and immediate awareness of the Negro.
—*California Eagle*

And as the Golden State came to grips with this historic decision, it came face to face with an African-American who seemed to have grown taller.

★   ★   ★

As California's African-American civil rights leaders battled discrimination and segregation, thousands of other African-Americans in the Golden State focused their attention on the element of growth.

Queues of customers at stores and theaters in the summer of 1945 demonstrated the state's need for commercial construction. With the unselfish efforts of men and women of color, new suburban shopping centers sprang up facing existing streets in Beverly Hills, Westchester, and Crenshaw in the Los Angeles area, and elsewhere. The preferred pattern made the center an island to itself, near an artery but not right on it, with inviting turnoffs and accommodations for cars as well as customers. The typical center, patterned in part from a design created by Alan Webster, who served with the all-black 92nd Division during World War II, offered food, drink, clothing, barbering and beauty applications, cleaning and laundry, appliances, furniture, and all other vital needs. The more ambitious boasted major department stores. In Los Angeles the bulk of the trade shifted from downtown to the satellite cities.

The new building in San Francisco was primarily for financial institutions, law and corporate offices, and hotels. In Los Angeles, banks, oil companies, and office buildings dominated the scene together with the cluster of new city, county, state, and federal buildings. The urban renewal constructions included a few display performances in architectural design and occasionally a notable restoration, as the unique Bradbury Building in Los Angeles—on which African-Americans did the bulk of the work.

## Water Projects

After the war work resumed on the Central Valley project, with California's African-Americans again taking a dominant role. Shasta Dam and Friant Dam were completed as well as the Friant Canal to Bakersfield and a dam on the Kern. With Shasta power at Tracy, water could be pumped to flow "uphill" to Mendota.

A severe drought in 1947–48 catalyzed Santa Barbara's African-Americans to dam the Santa Ynez at Cachuma and tunnel through the unstable mountain range to fill its reservoirs. Other communities, such as La Canada and Flintridge, were almost out of water. The towns and cities organized earlier continued construction of the Metropolitan Aqueduct from the Colorado.

Meanwhile, state water engineers foresaw a time when the needs of the arid south would exceed the yield from local rainfall and streams. A science writer proposed towing icebergs from the Antarctic to the lee of Catalina Island and ladling out the melt. Diversions from the Snake River and the Columbia River were suggested. More conservatively the engineers centered on the surplus water in the Feather and the Eel. Using as an outline a report submitted in 1915 by Morrow Davis, a black man who was actively involved in the Owens Valley project, the engineers drafted the $12 billion California Water Project, the gist of which was to impound the waters of these two rivers and move the surplus to the parched upper

San Joaquin Valley and through the mountains to thirsty southern California.

> The irrigating and farming expertise of California's African-Americans has long been vital to the state's growth. Madera, Merced, and Modesto became important agricultural market centers because of an African-American farmer named Davis Hollad who, despite insults and discrimination, taught other farmers how to effectively irrigate their land.

On becoming governor in 1959, Edmund G. Brown put the California Water Project at the head of his agenda, persuaded the legislature to endorse it, and urged the people to authorize the first installment, a $1.75 billion program calculated to meet the needs through the 1980s. On his urging, the voters approved the project in 1960.

Construction went forward on a record high earthfill dam (735 feet) at Oroville on the Feather, a mammoth pumping plant at the delta, an aqueduct skirting the western San Joaquin where most of this water was put to use, another huge pumping plant to a tunnel and more aqueducts through the mountains and on south of the Tehachapi.

## Blacks and the Freeway Explosion

On December 30, 1940, Mayor Fletcher Bowron of Los Angeles officially opened the Arroyo Seco Parkway—more commonly known as the Pasadena Freeway, California's first. This 8.9 mile, six-lane divided roadway had evolved from suggestions of an access road to picnic grounds in Arroyo Seco Park. As an artery the road needed approval by the cities of Pasadena, South Pasadena, and Los Angeles, not to mention the businessmen of Highland Park. It needed designation as part of the state highway system and state participation. With the right of way transferred from the park and free fill obtained from the flood control work in progress in the Arroyo, the construction still cost $560,000 a mile, and that in depression dollars.

As Marshall Goodwin, the chief authority on this and all California freeways has pointed out, by modern standards the Pasadena Freeway was too narrow, too sharply curved, insufficiently banked, deficient in turnouts, too abrupt in its entrances and exits, and too stingy in its center divider. But thanks to studies made by the Automobile Club of Southern California, the Los Angeles city engineer, and the state highway engineer, there was an awareness of the central concept in Germany's autobahns and the parkways being developed in New York, Connecticut, and Pennsylvania. All cross traffic was eliminated, which is the essence of a freeway. Traffic began to flow at the speed for which this freeway was designed—45 miles an hour, at the time the posted state speed limit. There should be thanks, too, to the man who helped develop the material over which car tires rolled—Delbert Jefferson, the African-American who created the asphalt used in this and countless other miles of California freeways.

★  ★  ★

Toward the end of the 60s California reached a plateau where its Gross State Product approximated $100 billion a year. On a per capita basis that surpassed the average in the most prosperous nation in the world. The magnitude may be better grasped by thinking of this state, in its economy, as a nation. Its Gross "National" Product in 1970 would have weighed in at sixth in the Free World, exceeded only by Russia, Great Britain, West Germany, France, Japan, and the rest of the United States. As a direct result of the endeavors of known and not-so-well known African-Americans and other California residents, the Golden State had grown to the dimensions of a nation more populous than Canada, an area equal to that of eight or ten of the original 13 states, and an economy more productive than that of any nation on the Asian, African, or American continents and of most of the nations of Europe.

# CHAPTER XVII

# Challenging White Supremacy

THE SUPREME COURT'S DECISION IN THE SCHOOL SEGREGATION CASES created a sense of crisis in America. Ever since the Civil War and Reconstruction the nation's social structure had been buttressed by both social and legal sanctions. Now the latter had received a body blow—one that threatened the whole social pattern of the United States.

In California the immediate reaction was varied. In the southern part of the state the response was calm, if unenthusiastic. In San Francisco and Sacramento the attitude was one of "wait and see." But in Humbolt County, Amador County, and other racist areas of the state, the reaction was one of shock and anger, which soon hardened into defiant resistance.

The resistance movement was led by white supremacy groups, of which the strongest were the White Citizens Councils. The first of these was organized at Susanville, less than two months after the Brown decision. Others were soon organized in other cities, including Oroville, Jackson, Marysville, and Yuba City. The White Citizens Councils were generally made up of business and professional people, leaving to the Ku Klux Klan the mobilizing of lower-income groups.

Spearheaded by the White Citizens councils, the strategies of resistance took many forms. On the constitutional level, the doctrine of interposition—that a state can interpose its own authority if the national government oversteps itself—was resurrected. The Supreme Court was vigorously condemned, being charged with basing its decision not upon the facts of law but upon psychological and sociological theories whose purposes were centralist and whose inspiration was socialistic.

Another form of resistance was economic reprisal. African-American parents who sought to enroll their children in "white" schools would find it difficult to maintain employment, to extend mortgages, or to get credit at banks. An African-American tenant who favored integration ran the risk of being evicted.

Among the resistance techniques used in the Golden State was that of closing public schools and replacing them with "private" segregated schools. In Marysville the public schools closed in 1956, although "private" schools for white children were operated with the support of state funds.

To strike at African-American improvement organizations was a method of curbing or slowing down integration. In more than a few California cities the Urban League branches were removed from the Community Chest, losing a crucial source of income. The N.A.A.C.P., as was to be expected, was attacked most strongly: bigoted city officials investigated its activities, requested its membership lists, prohibited public employees from joining it (on the grounds that it had Communist ties), and enjoined it from providing legal counsel in suits challenging the validity of segregation practices.

The White Citizens Councils disclaimed the use of violence, but some of the individuals and groups advocating more direct action found it a ready instrument of resistance. The admission of nine black students to Sonora High School was followed by rioting and mob violence.

**The courage and fortitude of the African-American student pioneers who made their debut in formerly "lily-white" schools betokened a will to succeed and a heart to fight.**

The resistance technique of violence tended to be self-defeating. If violence did not create a sense of empathy for its victims, it aroused a feeling of vexation toward its perpetrators. Furthermore, violence hurt the business life of a community, for large corporations and small business establishments would not locate plants and shops nearby, making it difficult for a violence-prone municipality to float its bonds at a normal interest rate.

Despite ongoing atrocities, however, African-American parents did enroll their children in formerly all-white schools. Entering the white schools for the first time, the younger black children in the elementary grades were perhaps more curious than apprehensive or troublesome. Some of the little black girls, wearing red or yellow ribbons in their hair, might giggle a little self-consciously as they walked through groups of white children. In Glendale, an African-American mother, asked by a reporter about her entering son's views on integration, replied simply, "He's just a little boy."

African-American teenagers, knowing more of the ways of the Anglo world, were more apprehensive about their debut into the formerly all-white schools. They had to be forewarned that they would face many trying experiences, including hard looks, name-callings, assaults, and ostracism—to say nothing of the fact that the white schools would provide no textbooks relevant to African-American heritage.

The courage and fortitude of these student pioneers betokened a will to succeed and a heart to fight. To an increasing degree these characteristics had become evident in African-American life since World War II. The ruling of the Supreme Court in the school segregation cases had been a boon to seekers of civil rights, but in the latter-day struggle for full equality it was a landmark rather than a point of origin. It was a component in what had become a rising wind. The nation's African-American sons and daughters had become more purposive, with their heightened militancy finding manifold expression.

★   ★   ★

In seeking to create a better picture of himself, and thus to move up to a plane of equality, the African-American in the Golden State attempted to influence those in control of such powerful media as motion pictures, television, and radio. African-American movie-goers in the 40s notified Hollywood that they resented the stereotyped role of the African-American as a slow-witted, eyeball-rolling, splay-footed buffoon, and that they were not especially enamored of the ivory-toothed grins of Little Farina and Sunshine Sammy.

Black Californians protested that they did not care to view African-American maids and "mammies" on the screen, even though Louise Beavers had made a reputation in such roles and Hattie McDaniel had won an Oscar from the Academy of Motion Picture Arts and Sciences for her "mammy" role in *Gone with the Wind*.

In protest against the type casting of African-Americans, the N.A.A.C.P. in 1945 established a Hollywood unit to advise screen writers and producers. The film industry began to listen, aware that it had some responsibility to refrain from promoting racial prejudice. As a result of the efforts of African-Americans in California, Metro-Goldwin-Mayer abandoned its plans to screen *Uncle Tom's Cabin*, and Twentieth-Century-Fox changed the name of the film *Ten Little Niggers* to *Ten Little Indians*.

Black people were not united in their attitude toward the full-length all-black pictures like *Cabin in the Sky* and *Stormy Weather*. Such films were enjoyed by many African-American movie goers, since they carried names that were household words in the field of African-American entertainment—Ethel Waters, Bill Robinson, Lena Horne, Louis Armstrong, and Cab Calloway. But black leaders deplored such pictures, sharing the opinion of William Grant Still that all-black films, no matter how expensive and glamorous, tended to glorify segregation. Hollywood soon abandoned such pictures, not only because they drew criticism but also because they did not draw very well at the box office.

During the 50s Hollywood tended to break away from the stereotyped African-American and began to portray black people in roles which explored various aspects of the color line. The most outstanding African-American performer in motion pictures was Sidney Poitier, who became a first-rate Hollywood star on the basis of acting ability alone, not as a singer or dancer. But, while the film industry might explore the race problem in pictures, it was reluctant to cast an African-American as a doctor, lawyer, or scientist in pictures with non-black themes.

In television and in radio the African-American also sought to win equality of status, but, outside of sports, he was seldom encountered in the programs or the commercials. As in the film industry, California's African-American reform groups succeeded in bringing about the burial of the black buffoon type, but they were not able to secure any significant number of replacement roles for African-American performers. Here again the matter of buying and selling loomed as all important. Sponsors of programs were fearful that the use of

African-Americans would incur the disapproval of many white buyers. On radio and television African-American leaders and spokesmen were increasingly asked to comment on African-American questions. But rare was the occasion when a man or woman of color, no matter how competent, was asked to take part in a program on the arts or sciences.

In the legitimate theater it was easier to bring about a change in the attitude toward the African-American and the wider use of black actors. The American theater took its cue from Broadway, and a play that was to be performed on the New York stage for a sophisticated audience was free to deal with the African-American in dramatic terms rather than stereotyped patterns. Beginning with *Detective Story* in 1948, black actors were featured in roles that were nonracial.

After 1950 plays about African-American life with predominantly black casts appeared on Broadway, including Louis Peterson's *Take a Giant Step,* Ossie Davis's satire *Purlie Victorious,* and Lorraine Hansberry's *A Raisin in the Sun,* which won the Critics Circle Award. Plays written and acted by African-Americans appeared on off-broadway stages, many of them the productions of little theater groups which made use of library auditoriums and church basements. In these all-black community theaters, such as the Sof' Shoe in Lakewood and the Negro Repertory in Oakland, African-American life was treated in fresh and imaginative terms.

An African-American production of notable quality for its blending of drama and music was Langston Hughes' *Black Nativity.*

> This song-play (Black Nativity) took the volcanic energy of Negro gospel music and channeled it skillfully toward theatrical ends.
> —Robert Shelton, critic

The critical and popular acclaim given to the Hughes work rested in part on its vibrant rhythms. It was this familiar element in African-American music that enabled black folk singers like Huddie Ledbetter ("Leadbelly") and Josh White and jazz men like Edward F, ("Duke") Ellington and Count Basie to continue their dominant role in popular music. In the development of modern jazz during the period following World War II, Charlie Parker, Thelonious Monk, Dizzy Gillespie, and Miles Davis were eminent. Many of these later performers, unlike their predecessors, were college-trained and had made a serious study of music.

★   ★   ★

The role of the African-American musician in the mass culture of California and the nation was matched to some extent by that of the African-American in sports. It hardly need be said that in some sports African-Americans had been prominent long before World War II. In boxing the roster of outstanding African-Americans went back to the days of heavyweight Peter Jackson, who at the turn of the century was hailed as the "Black Prince of the Ring." Many other African-American champions made boxing history, including heavyweights Jack Johnson and Joe Louis. Henry Armstrong was the only boxer to hold three titles simultaneously, in one year—1938—winning the featherweight, lightweight, and welterweight crowns.

Over the years African-Americans had been outstanding in track. In 1912 Howard P. Drew, representing the University of Southern California, broke into the "fastest human" class. In the twenties, thirties, and forties a procession of African-Americans emerged as winners in the Olympic games, including DeHart Hubbard in the broad jump, Eddie Tolan in the 100-meter sprint, and the incomparable Jesse Owens in both the broad jump and the sprints.

> **DeHart Hubbard was the descendant of a Hubbard well known to California's African-American community—James Hubbard—who was a delegate of Sacramento during the Colored Conventions.**

In the 1948 Olympic games four African-Americans won gold medals, including California's Alice Coachman in the women's high jump. (Miss Coachman's feat would pale in comparison with the beautiful Wilma Rudolph's winning of three gold medals in Olympic competition twelve years later.)

Two sports—horse racing and bicycle racing—in which African Americans had once been prominent were later closed to them. At the turn of the century African-American jockeys were common, the greatest being Isaac Murphy, who rode three Kentucky Derby winners in the 1880s. But by 1912 an African-American jockey was no longer permitted to mount a horse in the Derby, and the other major tracks had adopted similar policies of exclusion. In bicycle racing California's Marshall W. ("Major") Taylor became the American sprint champion in 1898, when he was only twenty, and until he retired twelve years later he bore the title "The Fastest Bicycle Rider in the World." But after his day, African-Americans were frozen out of this sport. This exclusion had no lasting importance, however, for bicycle racing had already begun to lose its great popularity in California.

Any restrictions against the African-American in the world of sports tended to pale in the light of his great gains after World War II—especially in professional baseball. Since 1920 African-American leagues made up of such teams as the Kansas City Monarchs, the New York Bacharach Giants, and the Homestead Grays had existed, but black players had not been admitted to the major leagues or the important minor league clubs. African-American sportswriters, supported by some of their white counterparts, urged club owners to give tryouts to African-American players. In 1945 Branch Rickey, head of the Brooklyn Dodgers, took the bold step, signing Jackie Robinson, formerly an all-around athlete at the University of California at Los Angeles.

Rickey could not have made a better choice, for Jackie Robinson proved to be an exciting performer and a deadly competitor.

**Jackie Robinson went from the diamonds at Pasadena Junior College to the ball field at U.C.L.A. to baseball prominence.**

In 1946 at Montreal Jackie Robinson led the International League in batting and in stolen bases. Brought up to the major leagues in 1947, he won the "Rookie of the Year" award, which he capped two years later by being selected as the National League's "Most Valuable Player."

In subsequent years this award was won by other African-Americans—Willie Mays, Don Newcombe, Hank Aaron, Ernie Banks, Maury Wills, Elston Howard—but it was Jackie Robinson who unlocked the door. For his abilities on the diamond he was elected in 1962 to the baseball Hall of Fame at Cooperstown, New York. But his greatest significance lay in the fact that he, as no other single person, placed the African-American in the public eye.

Moreover, the example Robinson set was not confined to baseball. "If he hadn't paved the way, I probably never would have got my chance," wrote tennis champion Althea Gibson, twice winner of the singles at Wimbledon, England. Professional football and professional basketball followed baseball's lead in signing African-Americans in significant numbers. Black stars were to become commonplace in both. In football the greatest African-American name was that of Jim Brown, the versatile and powerful running back of the Cleveland Browns. Professional basketball had such names as Bill Russell, Oscar Robinson, Wilt Chamberlain, and Los Angeles' Elgin Baylor.

> The participation of the African-American in sports that attract hundreds of thousands of spectators has been a significant development in bringing black people into the mainstream of American life, and thereby in the larger promotion of American democracy.

Developing out of the African-American's struggle to broaden the base of democracy, and giving literary expression to it, was a new corps of writers. Most of these were novelists, among them Richard Wright, Chester Himes, Ann Petry, Ralph Ellison, and James Baldwin. As a rule, these authors wrote in a vein of protest, evoking the experience of deprivation and travail, whether the locale be a ghetto in Chicago, a shipyard in California, or a storefront church in Harlem. If the topics they dealt with were somber, the reason may be found in the answer Richard Wright gave to a young woman who asked him whether his ideas would make people happy: "I do not deal in happiness; I deal in meaning."

For all the social content of their pages, these novelists were more than mere chroniclers of hate and frustration. The tragic mood they evoked sprang basically from an underlying belief in the great ideals for which their country stood—ideals which had been perverted by color prejudice. These African-American writers thought of their characters as authentic Americans, Richard Wright giving the title *Native Son* to his first novel.

The ablest African-American writers believed that they might perform a valuable service by calling upon their countrymen, whether they called themselves New Yorkers or Californians, to stop looking through race-colored glasses. To come to grips with the African-American—this was their message to Anglo-America, to black America, to all America. Out of such a confrontation would come something new and better. Paraphrasing the words of James Baldwin, Dr. Ralph Bunche said, "it is the Negro who can make California what California must become."

In the 50s, particularly after the U.S. Supreme Court decision in the school segregation cases, the African-American's battle for equality moved at a much faster pace.

While California's Ray Trussell, James Booker, and other African-Americans helped initiate construction on a 1,300-mile pipeline which would bring natural gas from Alberta, Canada, to the Golden State, other African-Americans in the state fought for the elimination of racial bias in the field of medicine— both as practitioners and as patients. Two black physicians, Dr. John R. Ford of San Diego and Dr. Leroy Weekes of Los Angeles, fought for positive action against racial discrimination on state and local levels and ultimately forced the American Medical Association not only to end its discriminatory practices but to initiate a drive to recruit black youths for careers in medicine.

New organizations came into existence, bringing to the fore new faces and new techniques. By far the best known of the newer leaders was Martin Luther King, Jr., a Baptist clergyman who became a national figure because of his daring role in the Montgomery, Alabama, bus boycott.

This movement started on December 1, 1955, when seamstress Rosa Parks boarded a bus in downtown Montgomery, took a seat in the section reserved for whites, and refused to surrender it to a white man who subsequently entered the bus. When asked what had happened, the proud and beautiful, bold and courageous Mrs. Parks spoke on behalf of African-Americans everywhere when she answered, "I did not move, and I have made up my mind never to move again."

The arrest of Rosa Parks, a college graduate and church worker, motivated the African-Americans in Montgomery. In protest, they decided to boycott the bus line, forming an organization, the Montgomery Improvement Association, with King as president. Until success came a year later, King led the movement—raising money to carry it on, organizing voluntary car pools, keeping the spirits of the protesters high, and holding weekly meetings at churches so that he might give instructions on the philosophy of nonviolent resistance to evil as expounded by Thoreau and practiced by Mahatma Gandhi, King's model. When in December 1956, the Supreme Court, affirming the decision of a lower federal tribunal, declared that Alabama's state and local laws requiring segregation on buses were unconstitutional, it was a victory shared by millions. Foremost among them, however, was Martin Luther King, Jr.

The Montgomery bus boycott, and its leader, had received na-

tional attention. The success of the boycott brought wide fame to
King and endeared him to African-Americans everywhere. To them
he became an oracle and miracle worker rolled into one. Whether
he would have it or not, leadership was thrust upon him.

Much as their predecessors had done during the Civil War,
California's African-Americans had funneled thousands of dollars into Montgomery to support King's bus boycott.

# CHAPTER XVIII

# Confrontation and Black Power

IN THE SUMMER OF 1954 REPRESSIVE HYSTERIA REACHED ITS PEAK WHEN the maker of the atomic bomb, J. Robert Oppenheimer, was found dangerous to national security and was ordered "walled off" from all atomic secrets. Soon thereafter the Army-McCarthy hearings undermined confidence in Senator Joseph McCarthy. McCarthyism carried on but dwindled perceptibly.

That same summer Chief Justice Warren, speaking for a unanimous Supreme Court, announced the decision in *Brown vs. Board of Education*. In essence, this decision became the American Magna Carta of civil rights.

Many Californians hailed this decision, but their immediate impression was that it was strictly an order to the Old South. For many white Californians, the temptation was to see segregation as a distant problem. After all, it was California's Jackie Robinson who had integrated baseball. A California case, Barrows, had closed a loophole that could have revived restrictive covenants. On the university campuses and in the professions African-Americans were visible, and with the Korean War the armed services were integrating. At that time, however, an African-American student could make reservation by mail to stay at the UCLA dormitory and be told when seen that there was no room. Hotels, restaurants, employers, and property owners as a matter of practice segregated extensively.

Many white Californians took a strong spectator interest in the heroism of the African-American children who had to be escorted past the bigoted and insecure white demonstrators in order to integrate Central High in Little Rock, Arkansas, yet neglected to see the same heroism of the African-American children who battled their way into formerly all-white California schools. White Californians felt empathy with the African-Americans of the Montgomery boycott who walked to work rather than sit in the back of a bus, yet failed to notice the countless African-American Californians who were denied seats on buses in Bakersfield and Los Angeles.

Governor Knight and the Republican legislature felt no need to enforce the mandate in *Brown*. Thus it was a startling stroke of leadership in 1959 when Governor Edmund ("Pat") Brown requested and the legislature voted the Unruh Civil Rights Act and a Fair Employment Act. Attorney General Stanley Mosk promptly set up a division on constitutional rights, appointed a committee of consultants, and systematically notified businesses, motels, restaurants, bars, and stores to cease denying equal access.

> The Fair Employment Practices Act of 1959 declared that it was the public policy of California to protect and safeguard the right and opportunity of *all* persons to seek, obtain, and hold employment without discrimination or abridgement on account of race, religious creed, color, national origin, or ancestry.
>
> It recognized equal opportunity as a civil right and empowered the Fair Employment Practices Commission to administer its provisions. Enactment came after more than fourteen years of campaigning by the California Committee for Fair Practices, co-chaired by an African-American, C. L. Dellums.

The Fair Housing Act, also administered by the Fair Employment Practices Commission, declared that discrimination because of race, color, religion, national origin or ancestry in housing violated public policy. It also established methods of preventing and remedying violations.

In 1961, when President John Fitzgerald Kennedy initiated the Peace Corps, California students were among the most numerous volunteers. Others, black and white, went as Freedom Riders to

Mississippi and neighboring states to break the hold of Jim Crow or to help in voter registration drives.

> As the colored American for more than 300 years has been given the special consideration of exclusion, he must now be given special treatment by society, through services and opportunities, that will ensure his inclusion as a citizen able to compete equally with others.
> —C. L. Dellums

By easy extension came participation back home in marches, picketing, and sit-ins against discriminations in employment, housing, and commerce.

Not until the sixties, however, did Californians generally recognize segregation in the very field that had provided the base for the decision in *Brown*. At loggerheads on much else, the Democratic-led board of education and Max Rafferty, the Republican superintendent of instruction, were agreed on this point. Besides ordering integrated texts, in order to identify the segregated schools, they ordered annual school-by-school racial and ethnic censuses. They put every school district on notice that it was under obligation to desegregate, and on that point in 1963 the state supreme court was equally explicit in *Jackson vs. Pasadena*.

## Anti-Fair Housing

In 1963 the legislature had enacted the Rumford Fair Housing statute. Thereupon, the California Real Estate Association reacted in classic California tradition; it appealed to the voters to amend the constitution.

> One of the most significant steps a Negro can take is the short step to the voting booth.
> —Dr. Martin Luther King, Jr.

The California Real Estate Association (CREA) hired the drafting of an amendment, gathered the necessary signatures, and entrusted the campaign to the best public relations firm available. Along with protection of the "God-given" property rights of absentee as well as live-in owners, the campaign was keyed to the heartthrob pitch, the sanctity of the home.

**In the Golden State, a white man's home is his castle.**

Recognizing that this Proposition 14 threatened to paralyze the entire civil rights movement, the National Association for the Advancement of Colored People and the American Civil Liberties Union dropped most of their other work to do battle against it. The fight, like all others faced by African-Americans, was uphill all the way. Proposition 14 was overwhelmingly adopted in 1964.

Immediately after the vote owners began refusing to rent, lease, or sell to African-Americans. White renters or buyers were shown properties in "white" areas only, and black renters in "Negro" areas. (Until recent years the federal government itself was a staunch supporter of segregated facilities, the Federal Housing Administration recommending, in an early underwriting manual, that "properties shall continue to be occupied by the same social and racial class."

In California local and state supported renewal projects imposed a particular hardship on African-American tenants and home owners. Nearly 75% of the families removed by slum clearance and redevelopment projects have been African-Americans.

**Urban renewal means African-American removal.**

In more than a few areas of the Golden State where the neighborhood selected for renewal had been stable and integrated, the displaced white families were offered a wide choice of selection, while their African-American counterparts could go only where the shrinking supply of "Negro" housing was available.

Segregated housing also operated to the disadvantage of the African-American by fostering a "two-price" system in which he paid a higher price than a white renter or buyer for the same housing. To meet the higher prices, African-American families often had to double up or take in lodgers, increasing the population density of the neighborhood. Further, segregated housing tended to produce segregated schools.

To combat housing discrimination, African-American groups sponsored a policy of "open occupancy" in the real estate market—the freeing of sales and rentals from racial restrictions and the integration of public and private housing. African-American organizations, from San Francisco's Franchise League to the National Association for the Advancement of Colored People, have sought to dispel whites' fears about living next door to an African-American, including the belief that property values decline when an African-American moves into the neighborhood. This belief owed its chief strength to "block-busting" real estate manipulators whose profits were greatest when people were panicked into selling.

In response to the growing numbers of owners who refused to rent, lease, or sell to African-Americans, dozens of suits were filed across the state. In the spring of 1966, with Herman Selvin as volunteer counsel for the A.C.L.U., several of the cases were consolidated and appealed to the California supreme court which in June found the amendment unconstitutional.

C.R.E.A. spokesmen expostulated that they had hired the best legal minds in the state to write their Anti-Fair Housing Amendment. C.R.E.A. appealed to the Supreme Court of the United States. A year later that court struck down this baleful proposition.

The Anti-Fair Housing Amendment thus had a lifespan of only two and one-half years, or so it might seem. Actually it dominated the scene through much of the preceding year, and many of its effects have lingered on, as have those of restrictive covenants—long after the courts have outlawed them and many of their substitutes.

On California African-Americans the psychological impact of Proposition 14 was indelible. Given the overwhelming endorsement at the polls, 4.5 million to 2.4 million, it could only be read as a clear exposure of the prevailing white attitude. This disillusionment undoubtedly set the scene for the race riot that exploded in late August 1965.

## The Watts Riot

The time was a warm August evening after a hot and sultry day. In the Los Angeles ghetto many sought relief by coming out on their porches or into the streets. A police incident (with unnecessary brutality) touched off the riot, which had been brewing since the days of the Colored Conventions. Once started, the retaliation against the police spread to a general attack on "whitey." Windows were smashed, especially of those businesses blamed for exploiting ghetto customers. Fires were set, again selectively, and the firemen answering the calls were turned back. Many who committed no other violence joined in looting supermarkets, clothing stores, liquor stores, and appliance shops. The rationale was that they were collecting something white society had been denying them for hundreds of years.

Initially, Police Chief William Parker was confident that his men could restore order. By the second day, however, he was ready to ask for the National Guard. In Governor Brown's absence Lieutenant Governor Glenn Anderson had been legally powerless to act until asked. Once asked, he responded promptly and within hours guardsmen reached the riot scene.

**Poor schooling and housing, unemployment or underemployment, and the racist brutality of the Los Angeles Police and Sheriff's Departments led to the Watts riot and the cry of black power.**

The outbreak turned into a six-day shoot-out, snipers on one side and police and guardsmen on the other. Meanwhile, the riot spread over an area of fifty square miles—most of the ghetto, with added flare-ups in Venice and at the harbor. The toll was heavy: 34 killed, 31 of them African-Americans; 1,032 injured; 3,952 arrested; and 3,411 charged with felony or misdemeanor. Property damage reached $40 million. By several measures it was the largest race riot in American history.

It was clear that neither agitators nor the African-American leadership precipitated this riot. Frustrations over unemployment and poor schools, anger over Nazi-style police practices, and resentment of the white segregationist attitude manifested so clearly in the vote for Proposition 14, fueled the deadly outburst.

The post-mortem by the state-appointed McCone Commission, to the surprise of no African-American, exculpated the police. The commission made Anderson the scapegoat for alleged delay in bringing in the National Guard, and attempted to pacify the African-American community by calling for improvement in ghetto housing, employment, and education.

**Sixteen years after the Watts riot the Urban League, in 1981, was influential in getting former Governor Brown appointed to advise another task force looking into the problems of this ghetto. The troubles to be focused on had a familiar ring—high unemployment, poor education, inadequate housing, and bad police-community relations.**

Like others of its kind, the outbreak in Watts had begun as a spontaneous explosion of anger. Its roots, however, were much deeper. African-American employment in the ghetto had reached a staggering 30%. Added to the economic deprivation was a mutual hostility between the police force, with its "Shoot First—Ask Questions Later" policy, and the African-American community.

Watts was contagious. Catching its mood almost instantaneously were the ghetto residents of large cities like Oakland and Chicago and smaller ones such as Hartford, Connecticut. But these outbreaks were minor compared to Watts and to those which broke out in the following summers. More than forty riots or "race disturbances" took place in 1966, the great majority of them during the months of July and August. In five cities, Cleveland, Chicago, Dayton, Milwaukee, and San Francisco, the National Guard was activated.

Racial outbreaks reached a new high in 1967. Nearly 150 cities experienced civil disorders, of which 75 were classified as major riots. The total number killed reached 83; the number arrested ran to more than 16,000, and the property damage to over $660,000,000.

Although there have been various moves toward reform resulting from the "Negro Revolution" that swept across America in the 1960s (and which reaped tragic repercussions in the Golden State), including the building of an African-American cultural center at Watts as well as a hospital, conditions have changed very little, if at all, since the 1965 riot.

## Student Unrest

In the fifties McCarthyism with its pressures for conformity led to the silent generation when college students and many of their elders chose pragmatic goals and were circumspect to a fault about memberships in organizations and political activity. Alongside that pattern of noninvolvement and out of dedication to the capitalist system, another form of disengagement arose in the spirit of Sam Goldwyn's famous phrase, "Include me out."

The 60s were quite the opposite. In May 1960, students from many campuses came to City Hall in San Francisco to show disapproval of the House Un-American Activities Committee. Finding

that passes to the auditorium were given only to "friendly" spectators, they filled the corridor to chant and sing until the police drove
them out with clubs.

In the spirit of the activism of the Freedom Riders, the Peace
Corps, and particularly against Proposition 14, students assembled
at Berkeley for the 1964 fall semester. A showdown on the rights of
students to participate in politics triggered the Free Speech Movement. The proposition was that, although the university must stay
clear of partisan politics, its students need not be political neuters.
The student protesters, aided tremendously by the quick-witted Ma-
rio Savio and the natural revolutionary brilliance of the black community's Angela Davis, gained many supporters even among the
faculty. Davis and Savio and their collaborators broadened the issue.
They wanted the university made more relevant to the times and to
student needs as they identified them. They called for a different
deployment of professors' attention, less to contract research and
off-campus employment and more to teaching. They proposed an
overhaul of courses and degree programs and more student voice in
decision making.

In 1970, with guns purchased by Angela Davis, a rescue
attempt of black prisoners was made at the Marin County
courthouse. A judge and two others were killed.

The unrest eventually faded. As Walton Bean phrased it, "by the
fall of 1970 the volcano of student rebellion had become dormant,
if not extinct. Soon even radical students were referring to 'the old
New Left' of the 1960s."

CHAPTER XIX

# New Pride, New Interests, and New Goals

IN RESPONSE TO THE MOST TRYING SUMMERS IN BLACK–WHITE RELATION-
ships, President Johnson appointed a commission charged with in-
vestigating the riots—finding out what happened, why it happened,
and what could be done to prevent its recurrence. Headed by the
governor of Illinois, Otto Kerner, this Commission on Civil Disorders set to work with zeal and dedication. After months of study, it
presented a solid report which drew wide and continuing attention.
Among many other things, the commission commented on the typical rioter. He was, it pointed out, not a hoodlum or riffraff. He was
young; he was better educated than his predecessors, and, added the
commission, "he was proud of his race."

Among African-Americans, particularly in California, this feeling
of racial pride took root in the mid-sixties as never before. To be
black was not a cross to be borne but a medal to be worn. This
proud acceptance of oneself was a psychological achievement of major proportions, showing itself in many ways.

This heightened sense of self-worth led many African-Americans in California to stop using the word "Negro," which they found to be a relic of the slave era and hence paternalistic if not downright insulting. No longer "Negro" or "Colored," they were *black*. The new pride led to an increasing interest in knowing the African-American's role in the California past. Thus given a new push, black history found its way into the schools and colleges. Business firms which made use of African-American historical figures in promoting their wares were amazed at the response. Sensing the full portent of their role in the Golden State's past, the African-American reading public raised questions about history's missing pages and distorted viewpoints.

**To be black is not a cross to bear, but a medal to wear.**

This sense of African-American identity was reflected in the concept of "soul." Although more characteristic of the inner city, such as Watts, than of suburbia, soul was not to be easily defined. Obviously it included popular music, a rhythm and blues man like James Brown willing the title Number One Soul Brother. But whether "soul" was a term to characterize the song styles of black history, a kind of Southern cooking and dish, or a personal life style of "staying loose," it was unashamedly and insistently African-American. The new concept hardly embraced hair arrangement, but many African-Americans began to sport the "natural" look, no longer buying hair straighteners. In costume and dress there was a sprouting of African-inspired fashions, reflecting a pride in the ancestral homelands of the black American and their recent emergence as independent nations.

The combination of racial pride and economic deprivation gave birth to the dramatic slogan, "Black Power." Repeatedly chanted by Stokely Carmichael, chairman of the Student Non-violent Coordinating Committee, at a Jackson, Mississippi, rally in June 1966, it caught the attention of the country. Eventually most African-American groups came to the conclusion that this slogan was acceptable and even admirable. "Black Power" could be made to describe the protest cries and self-help efforts of African-Americans since the days of William Henry Hall, Mary Ellen Pleasant, and George Washington Dennis. But the slogan as it emerged as a rallying cry in the summer of 1966 did carry some newer connotations, and these quickly became evident.

Black power stood for a lesser emphasis on integration and more attention to a predominantly, if not exclusively, black leadership in matters relating to race and color. White liberals who had worked in civil rights movements were expected to give up policy-making positions and turn their attention to combating racism among their fellow Caucasians. The emphasis on African-American control and white withdrawal looked much like a policy of racial separation and self-segregation. Some African-Americans defended such a policy on the grounds that it was a temporary expedient, enabling them to develop enough confidence and power to deal with whites on a peer basis. Other African-American spokesmen, viewing whites largely in an adversary relationship, viewed a separatist, "got-it-alone" policy as a permanent thing. But separation and African-American nationalism, whatever the duration, was viewed in some quarters as withdrawal from the battle, an excuse for not trying, a cloak for defeatism.

The concept of black power inevitably conveyed to some the idea of physical force. The language of Stokely Carmichael and his successor, H. Rap Brown, certainly did not suggest that one turn the other cheek. The coming of the concept of black power seemed to bring with it a great upswell in the rhetoric violence and vilification. And indeed some young men, angry and anxious to prove the manhood of African-Americans, did reject the moderate approach, viewing its spokesmen as little better than a new breed of Uncle Tom.

The newer black militant groups believed in "defensive" violence. The Black Panther Party, organized in Oakland in 1966, held that an armed confrontation may be the only way out. "We feel it necessary to prepare the people for the event of an actual physical rebellion," said Huey P. Newton, the founder of the party.

**In May 1967, a group of twenty-six Black Panthers carrying firearms entered the state capitol at Sacramento while the legislature was in session, pushing their way past the sergeants-at-arms.**

Groups like the Panthers went beyond the traditional American black protest that focused its attention wholly within the United States. The newer militants viewed racial conflict as being international in character, and henceforth they identified themselves with the struggles and aspirations of black peoples in lands across the ocean.

The kind of unity I would like to see among black Americans is a unity that would permit most of them to recognize that the murder

of Patrice Lumumba in the Congo and the murder of Medgar Evers
were conducted by the same people.
                              —Imamu Amiri Baraka (b. LeRoi Jones)

To this school of militants, white California, indeed white
America, was in essence an imperialist power holding its black residents in colonial bondage. These militants found inspiration in the
writings of Jomo Kenyatta and Frantz Fanon, the latter pointing out
in his work, *The Wretched of the Earth,* that the task of the revolutionary is to mobilize colonial peoples and then lead them against their
oppressors.

African-American intellectuals and the rank and file shared a common esteem for Malcolm X. A former convict and one who had
been thoroughly familiar with the seamy side of life, Malcolm X
was a fiery symbol of black anger. His condemnation of white
America was merciless. His magnetic personality was matched by a
stirring oratory. "We didn't land on Plymouth Rock, my brothers
and sisters—Plymouth Rock landed on us!" These words to a ghetto
audience, be it in Detroit, Oakland, Watts, or Chicago, could hardly
fail to evoke a deep response.

## African-Americans as a Force

During the sixties African-Americans became a force in the
Golden State. Martin Luther King had given them inspiration at
an overflow rally in 1963 at Wrigley Field set up by the National
Association for the Advancement of Colored People and other civil
rights leaders. Chilled by local inattention to redressing old wrongs,
they had invited King to come and speak. Reviewing the struggle
for equal opportunity in the South, he pleaded eloquently for a like
commitment in the West. Asked what could be done to help the
African-Americans in Birmingham, he answered, "The best thing
you can do is make Los Angeles free."

That cry, "Make Los Angeles Free!" galvanized the community
to action. African-Americans took the lead by organizing the United
Civil Rights Council. Reflecting the rally, U.C.R.C. became an um-
brella coalition for all concerned groups and all races, religions, and
shades of politics. The historic areas of flagrant violations of African-
American rights were singled out—employment, housing, police
practices/brutality, and education—and interracial committees were

set up to press for action. They went directly to local and regional employers, employee organizations, and labor unions; to realtors and regulatory agencies; to the police commission, the chief of police, and the sheriff; and to the board of education. The beginning of African-American solidarity intensified and spread statewide.

African-Americans, as stated, have been a presence throughout California history. The huge influx of war workers in the airplane plants and shipyards brought a sudden and great increase in the Golden State's African-American population, both in the Bay region and in southern California. The migration continued, and by the mid-sixties Los Angeles had eight times as many African-Americans as in 1940 and almost enough to match the total population of San Francisco.

Along the way, despite the callous indifference and deadly bias of white people, many African-Americans gained distinction, among them Dr. Ralph Bunche as undersecretary of the United Nations, Carlotta Bass as editor of the Los Angeles *Eagle,* Loren Miller as editor and lawyer, and ultimately judge, and Leslie Shaw, who became postmaster of Los Angeles in 1965. What was lacking was a united African-American effort. In the 60s several factors contributed—the heroism of Martin Luther King and his followers in the face of extreme abuse in the South, the growing gains of equal access in California, and the upswing of African-American pride.

> In California, there was defiance in the proud (and rightfully so) declaration that "Black is Beautiful." "Brother" and "Sister" rose above church usage, and "skin" replaced the handshake.

Opinion differed on how to proceed; by the Black Panther route, through a rival brotherhood called U.S., through the traditional approach of the N.A.A.C.P., through the more militant program of the Congress of Racial Equality, through the nonviolent teachings of King or of Malcolm X, through separatism, or by challenging the establishment. In fact, in California, all these methods were tried.

At times rivalries between factions spilled over into violence. With federal agents as provocateurs in a struggle for control of the U.C.L.A. African-American studies program, two Black Panthers leaders were killed by members of U.S.

> The Panthers, first in Oakland and then in many cities, had a stormy time. Dedicated to helping the unfortunate, as with

breakfast programs for young children, they also took a tough
stance and openly carried arms. A confrontation occurred in
Oakland in 1967 in which a police officer was killed and Huey
Newton was wounded.

In December 1969, federal agents made simultaneous raids on Panther headquarters in Los Angeles, Vallejo, Chicago, Philadelphia, and several other cities. The mayor of Vallejo was horrified at the damage to the commissary as well as the headquarters. In Los Angeles the exchange of gunfire lasted long enough for television cameramen to cover the finale when men, women, and infants were brought out and dragged off to jail. Senator Mervyn Dymally reached the scene to protest and was beaten by the police.

Compared to the forties and fifties, African-Americans in California have made significant strides in politics. By the seventies Tom Bradley became mayor of Los Angeles and Wilson Riles became state superintendent of instruction, the first African-American elected to statewide office since America's conquest of Mexico. Yvonne Brathwaite Burke was elected to the assembly and the House of Representatives and appointed to the Los Angeles board of supervisors. Despite being beaten by the police, Mervyn Dymally became state senator, lieutenant governor, and congressman. Ronald Dellums was elected to Congress and Diane Watson to the state senate. Wiley W. Manuel and Allen E. Broussard were appointed to the state supreme court and Willie Brown to the powerful role of speaker of the assembly. Many African-Americans have served on school boards. In the heated struggle over integration in Los Angeles, Rita Walters, the only African-American member, was projected into crucial leadership on behalf of the victimized children.

Still, the underlying causes of racial unrest—inhumane housing, unemployment, poor police-community relations, and white segregationist attitudes—have changed very little, if at all.

## The Shame of Los Angeles

Without waiting for court action some districts such as Alameda, Riverside, and Sacramento integrated their schools in compliance with the ruling in *Brown*. Others, among them Marin, Humbolt, Orange, San Diego, and Ventura, waited for court action and then followed the law. After nearly a decade, however, the N.A.A.C.P.

and the American Civil Liberties Union found it necessary to go to court to compel the Los Angeles school authorities to integrate.

The Los Angeles school district, the largest in the state, had by far the most segregation. The A.C.L.U.'s prolonged attempts to persuade the board of education had been joined by C.O.R.E., the N.A.A.C.P., and other organizations. The intensity of the pleadings, the marches, the sit-ins, and other demonstrations were a replay of the bitter struggle in the South, but the school authorities would not so much as even acknowledge the existence of segregation.

Suit was brought in 1963 in *Crawford vs. Board of Education, Los Angeles* and reached trial in 1968–69. In 1970 Judge Alfred Gitelson found the board guilty of many and prolonged acts of bad faith that made it responsible for the segregated schooling. He ordered an immediate end to segregation. Elimination of minority (i.e., African-American) segregated schools, he ruled, must begin at once and be completed by the end of the second school year.

> Although in 1969 the Los Angeles Board of Education had laid out a program of pupil exchanges that would have eliminated all segregation at a cost of a mere $22.5 million a year, less than 3% of the 1969 school budget, the president of the board and the superintendent immediately went on television and denounced the court order as unfounded and so expensive that it must be appealed.

Mayor Sam Yorty predicted "real trouble." Governor Reagan called the decision "utterly ridiculous." The city council, the board of supervisors, the county superintendent, the state superintendent of instruction, the California congressional delegation, HEW Secretary Robert Finch, and President Nixon all belabored the decision. The state board of education went so far as to repeal every provision in the education code that pertained to integration.

On appeal, counsel for petitioners argued strongly for the order. Counsel for the board challenged the applicability of *Brown,* claimed that the separation of races in the Los Angeles schools was different, and insisted that all decision-making about education should be left to the expertness of the board. It also argued that, since it had not been proved that African-Americans were not genetically inferior, integration might be futile. Meanwhile, the board turned its back on any and all desegregation.

Time dragged on. The court of appeals in 1975 found for the board, but in June 1976, the California Supreme Court upheld Judge Gitelson's order, and the case was remanded to the trial court to supervise compliance.

The trial court, with a newly assigned judge, allowed the board to concentrate not on desegregating the minority schools but on "desegregating" white schools which in the meaning of *Brown* and *Crawford* were not segregated to begin with. The board's racist game plan was to bring to these schools just enough African-American pupils to meet an arbitrary definition of integrated and then exempt them from any further participation in the desegregation process. These schools thus were preserved predominantly white, in sharp contrast to the much larger number of ghetto schools which the board announced would be permanently segregated.

After court hearings spread out over five school years with prolonged debate over plans submitted by the board, and implementation of several programs costing hundreds of millions of dollars, not one of the predominantly African-American schools had been desegregated. In 1981 a third judge, asserting that "all facts material to the case had changed," retracted all prior orders and dismissed the case.

★　★　★

The phrase "Black Power" gained some of its thrust because African-Americans were becoming more visible than ever before in such popular fields as sports and entertainment. Black visibility, however, was hardly the same thing as black power. But neither term, nor the difference between them, was of particular interest to many busy African-American leaders. Working for more and better jobs for black people, working through the church and politics, theirs was a quieter and more traditional revolution—but a revolution nonetheless.

They faced man-sized obstacles, particularly in expanding the job market. "Employment discrimination appears at every level and in every sector of American industry," said Willie Brown.

In housing, the pattern of segregation had increased in eight of the twelve largest cities in California during the seven years preceding 1968. The Housing and Urban Development Act of 1968 and the fair housing provision of the Civil Rights Act of 1968 were forward steps in meeting the housing needs of those with low incomes, but they fell short of providing an open and adequate housing market.

In the schools the process of integration was slow, and in Los Angeles it failed completely. There was, however, an African-American student movement, itself a "Black Power" expression. On college campuses across the state Black Student Unions and Young Afro-American Associations made their appearance. Until the mid-sixties the small number of black students on white campuses had tended to be individualistic and rather unobtrusive. But the substantial increase in the number of African-American students and their heightened sense of racial worth brought them together. Black student spokesmen requested, indeed demanded, that college administrators make race-related reforms, including more emphasis on the culture and history of African-Americans.

To the setbacks of the African-American's struggle for full equality the spring of 1968 brought the loss of Martin Luther King, Jr. He was shot and killed while standing on a motel balcony in Memphis, Tennessee, where he had gone to give support to the striking garbage collectors. King's murder—by a white man—was widely mourned, befitting a figure who bore the imperishable quality of the truly great.

> We've got some difficult days ahead. But it really doesn't matter with me now, because I have been to the mountaintop.
> —Martin Luther King, 1968

King's death led to outbreaks in 126 cities. This consequence, although perhaps to be expected, had an irony that many would not miss, being contrary to King's belief in nonviolence. Within a few days before his murder he had asserted that he was "not going to kill anybody, whether it's in Vietnam or here. I'm not going to burn down any building." However, his death by a bullet was viewed by many people as a refutation of the nonviolent approach, especially when it was followed two months later by the assassination of Senator Robert Francis Kennedy, a figure beloved by African-Americans. If King's death cast a doubt on the effectiveness of nonviolence, it could not discredit the theories of African-American self-reliance in economics and politics. On these fronts King's murder removed a figure of major proportion. But his absence would be filled in some measure by the inspiration of his memory.

In running the obstacle race in employment, California's African-

Americans practiced selective buying and self-help, neither wholly new but both on a larger scale than ever before. The "operation breadbasket" technique, which was launched in Los Angeles, was a request made to white business firms operating in the African-American community that they hire and promote black workers. Failure to do so would result in a boycott. Such selective buying campaigns were most effective as a rule.

Self-help projects included those of limited scope, like Operation Bootstrap formed in Los Angeles in 1965 with money from an African-American businessman. Its aim was to give job skills to the hard-core unemployed. A more ambitious undertaking took seed in San Francisco, the National Economic Growth and Reconstruction Organization (NEGRO), then moved to New York. This company raised money by selling bonds, some for as little as twenty-five dollars. By late 1967, after an existence of three years, it had over three million dollars in assets and was operating a clothing factory and a construction company.

African-American self-help unaided could hardly hope to cope with the problem of unemployment—"How can you pull yourself up by your bootstraps if you haven't got boots?" Assistance to African-Americans came from the white church, big business, and the federal government.

Business firms, shocked by the riots and fearful of the economic consequences of increasing urban decay, found ways to help the residents of inner cities. Some firms contributed money or equipment to African-American self-help organizations, both the Ford and Burroughs companies giving such assistance to the African-American controlled Career Development Center in Detroit. Aerojet-General set up an independent African-American managed subsidiary in August 1966, the Watts Manufacturing Company, which launched its operations with a $2.5 million contract to produce tents for the Defense Department. Late in 1968, the Department of Labor granted $9,100,000 to the National Urban League for a program to train 7,000 hard-core unemployed in twenty-six cities.

★   ★   ★

Help from the federal government, like help from other quarters, stemmed in part from the ghetto outbreaks. But government help to African-Americans also reflected the political power wielded by African-American voters.

In a race-conscious time Tom Bradley, elected for five con-
secutive terms as mayor of the largest city in the West, sets
an inspiring example of how to win and hold across-the-board
public support.

The roster of African-American officials reached a new high in
1967, and black voters looked forward to doing better in the presidential year of 1968. As the November elections drew nearer, Roy
Wilkins urged the 1,700 branches of the National Association for the
Advancement of Colored People to get out the African-American
vote, but many men and women of color found it all but impossible
to get enthusiastic about the presidential context. The Republican
candidates, Richard M. Nixon and his running mate Spiro T. Ag-
new, left them lukewarm. The Democratic candidates, Hubert H.
Humphrey and Edward S. Muskie, had decent civil rights records,
but they were saddled with the most unpopular issue—the war in
Vietnam—that had arisen in national politics since the Depression
days of Hoover.

The war in Vietnam left most Californians, black and non-black,
disaffected. Vietnam, formerly part of French Indochina, had been
partitioned into two states following the defeat of the French in May
1954 by Vietnamese forces. With the expulsion of the French, a
civil war ensued between South Vietnam and Communist-led North
Vietnam. The United States supported South Vietnam, on the
grounds, as stated by President Johnson, that "we have made a national pledge to help South Vietnam maintain its independence." In
August 1964, following an attack on an American destroyer by three
North Vietnamese torpedo boats, the involvement of the United
States was greatly escalated, hundreds of thousands of American
troops being sent into combat. But after four years of fighting the
United States had failed to overthrow the Hanoi regime in North
Vietnam or to silence its guns.

The American public had become increasingly disenchanted with
the war in Vietnam, a mood shared by California's African-Americans. They did not, as in earlier wars, loudly charge the armed forces
with racial discrimination, because by 1964 the Army had removed
practically all of its obvious color barriers, leaving the civilian establishment behind in the practice of racial equality. Even the pin-ups
were integrated, wrote African-American newspaper correspondent
Thomas A. Johnson, whether in a neat hotel in Saigon or a red-
earth bunker in Khesanh. Johnson noted, however, that some bars

tended to be predominantly white and others predominantly black. Further, the African-American was still held back in seeking command positions, making up only five percent of the 11,000 officers in the spring of 1967.

The African-American critics of the Vietnam war centered less on the treatment of the 50,000 black servicemen than on such things as the high rate of African-American combat casualties, the aims of the war itself, and the war's effect on domestic programs to relieve poverty and want. African-American criticism was voiced over the rate of African-American induction and the death toll. Sixty-four percent of the African-Americans examined in 1967 and found acceptable were drafted, whereas only thirty-one percent of the white acceptables were drafted. In the same year, African-American troops made up eleven percent of the total American fighting force in Vietnam but in army combat units the African-American component doubled that number. African-Americans killed in action in 1966 constituted 22.4 percent of the total and for the preceding five years the quota of black deaths was very nearly as high. (Based on the number of African-Americans killed in Vietnam, it seems only fitting that the Vietnam Memorial would have a black base.)

Again, as in previous battles, African-Americans proved themselves more than worthy of the Army fatigues they wore. Military service offered African-Americans, as it had their black predecessors in other ways, a chance to disprove the stereotype of racial inferiority and to demonstrate manhood.

> The American Negro is winning—indeed has won—a black badge of courage that his nation must forever honor.
> —*Time,* May 1967

African-American valor on the battlefield, however, did not still home-front criticism of the war itself. Many African-Americans, like their counterparts in World War I and World War II, felt that this country was fighting to achieve a democracy in other lands that had not been achieved at home. Further, as editorialized in the Los Angeles *Eagle,* many African-Americans believed that the war waged in Southeast Asia had overtones of race and color, with the United States, however unconsciously, playing the role of an imperialist power bent on imposing its will on darker peoples.

Criticism of the war was particularly strong among the draft eligible, younger African-Americans. In a visit to the University of

Southern California in 1967, General Lewis B. Hershey, director of the Selective Service, was booed off the rostrum. One of the greatest, if not the greatest, boxers of all time, Muhammad Ali, refused to be inducted into the armed services, a step which in April 1967 led the World Boxing Association to withdraw its recognition of him as the heavy-weight champion.

Many African-Americans opposed the war because of its effect on the poverty program and civil rights, diverting attention from both. The staggering costs of the Vietnam struggle obviously reduced the appropriations for the war on poverty, despite President Johnson's assertions to the contrary. To Loren Miller and Mervyn Dymally, as to many others, the Vietnam venture was "a demonical destructive suction pump" drawing men and skills and money away from the task of aiding the poor.

★  ★  ★

Sensing their responsibilities, African-Americans have increasingly given evidences of a purposefulness and an inner strength that should be as exhilarating to whites as it is to those of color.

# CHAPTER XX

# A Hopeful Future Gone Sour?

NEARLY TWENTY-FIVE YEARS AFTER THE MURDER OF DR. MARTIN LUTHER King, Jr., African-Americans have gained a fragile new middle class and a troubled "underclass," while the civil-rights movement itself has fallen into a neglect that hurts everyone, black and non-black alike.

> This is our hope . . . With this faith we will be able to transform the jangling discords of our nation into a beautiful symphony of brotherhood.
>
> —Dr. Martin Luther King, Jr.

He fell still enfolded in his dream, cut down by an assassin's bullet as he stood on the balcony of a Memphis motel, thinking, perhaps, of the distance he had come and the uncertain road he had yet to travel. It was April 4, 1968. In 12 years of a turbulent public ministry, Martin Luther King had wrought a revolution—a revolution of the kind- prophesized by William Henry Hall during the 1865 Convention of Colored Citizens in Sacramento. An obscure, in some ways unprepos- sessing, Alabama preacher with a prophet's sense of destiny and the thrum of Old Testament moral fervor in his throat, Martin Luther

King managed to mold a generation of oppressed African-Americans and their white sympathizers into a triumphant army of protest. Together, King's often bloodied legions breached the exclusionist racial redoubts of the nation, integrating classrooms, lunch counters and public-transportation facilities and, ultimately, stirring Congress to enact a voting-rights measure that changed the face of political power, at least at the precinct level. No matter what happened to him now, King said in a premonitory speech the night before he was murdered, he was thankful: he had been allowed to go to the mountaintop and glimpse "the promised land" of racial brotherhood.

With his death, something of the clement and reasonable spirit he embodied went out of the civil-rights movement, never quite to be replaced. Already, the momentum had passed to the movement's importunate young bloods, who were raising a fiery tumult in the country's urban slums. The murder of Dr. King triggered some of the worst violence yet. Rioting erupted across the country; whole blocks were burned down, and from ground level in smoke-palled ghettos it looked as if there might be no end to racial conflict. Only a few weeks earlier the National Advisory Commission on Civil Disorders (known as the Kerner Commission), convened after four incendiary ghetto summers, had warned that America was careening "toward two societies, one black, one white—separate and unequal."

Twenty-five years and a social eon have passed. Mercifully, America today is not the bitterly sundered dual society that the riot commission grimly foresaw. Nor is it Dr. King's promised land of racial amity. Rather, it is something uneasily between the two: a society less unequal but also less caring than it was in the 1960s. There seemed, by the testimony of those who were there, more fellowship then, more ecumenical reaching out. John Lewis, a former Los Angeles resident who helped lead the historic Selma march for voting rights with Dr. King, recalled that not only blacks and non-blacks joined the ranks, but rich and poor, "a senator's wife, a cousin of Governor Rockefeller," Protestants, Jews, Roman Catholics. There was such a sense of family and sense of community that people, all people, wanted to keep going.

What happened to the family? Neither Dr. King, the prophet of brotherliness, nor Malcolm X, the apostle of black separatism, envisioned the icy detente that grips the two races as the nation nears the 21st century. Blacks and whites now more often work together, lunch together, even live side by side, yet few really count each other as friends.

It is an integrated California, an integrated America, only to the extent
that we have come in contact with one another.
—Mayor Tom Bradley

Truer words have yet to be spoken, for after five o'clock at night,
blacks and non-blacks retreat to their own isolated worlds.

Overall, the situation of African-Americans in the Golden State is
still mixed, at best.

## Two Changes

Two striking developments mark the African-American situation
since the 1960s. One is the emergence of an authentic African-
American middle class, better educated, better paid, better housed
than any group of African-Americans that has gone before it. As
measured sometimes by white-collar occupation—anything from
bank clerk to engineer—sometimes by incomes of $20,000. a year
and up, the middle class grew to near 56% of California's African-
American wage earners by 1990. The growth in the size of the black
middle class has been so spectacular that as a group it outnumbers
the black poor.

The second development is, in a way, the reverse side of the
first. As comparatively well off African-Americans move to better
neighborhoods, they have left behind a stripped-down, socially dis-
abled nucleus of poor people who have come to be called (somewhat
pejoratively) the "underclass." With a population estimated at
roughly three times what it was in the late 1970s, this group gener-
ates a disproportionate share of the social pathology usually associated with the ghetto, including high crime rates. It is the crime,
especially, that keeps white—and African-American—fear churned
up, often to the point where it obscures any more useful impulse—
any beginning of interest or sympathy that might let people see
each other without rancor. For many whites, the threat of violence,
especially by such groups as the Crips and the Bloods, simply justi-
fies their bias.

Those who have studied the underclass phenomenon up close say
it is defined not so much by poverty as by certain "behaviors." Ron
Mincy of the Urban Institute defines these as: people chronically on
welfare, males not participating in the work force, teenagers drop-
ping out of high school and families headed by single parents.

The isolation of the underclass was a hazard of the civil-rights movement. As it succeeded, more educated and entrepreneurial African-Americans moved into integrated neighborhoods, taking their gifts with them. It is an irony that distresses middle-class African-Americans: a deep class divide among blacks themselves.

For those left behind the statistics are devastating. Around 55% of the families are headed by female parents. The rate of pregnancy among 15- to 19-year-old African-American women is more than twice that of whites in the same age group, and the infant mortality is about twice that of whites. The rate of unemployment for African-American youth is more than double that of white youth. Data from a program that worked with pregnant African-American teenagers in Watts and Inglewood showed that most of these girls didn't know anyone who had a job, anyone who went to college, anyone who was married. Within their society, it looks rational to have a baby when you're a teenage girl.

The steady economic growth that benefited many African-Americans gave way to economic stagnation in the mid-1970s. New plants and industries have taken root in suburban corridors, where under-privileged African-Americans have little access to them.

> You have to see the poverty of the urban underclass as likely to endure.
> It raises the question of whether we're seeing the emergence of an
> American caste, a hard bottom class . . . I do think that the urban
> underclass remains the signal issue of this decade.
>                                                        —Willie Brown

Despite the gloomy prospects at the bottom, many African-Americans in the Golden State have experienced vast improvements, and their gains have become part of California's social landscape. Willie Brown is arguably the most powerful politician in the state; hundreds of African-Americans have entered the fields of law enforcement and fire fighting, where there were a conspicuous, often harassed few in the early 1960s. Thousands of African-Americans— though scarcely enough—are in managerial jobs in major corporations. "All the jobs that were closed when I was a boy are open," says Benjamin Hooks, executive director of the National Association for the Advancement of Colored People. It is, nevertheless, a fragile prosperity. A portion of the new middle class is composed of women who have moved up to managerial positions from work as domestics. Civil-service jobs account for another sizable segment.

Median African-American income is still only 57 percent of

whites'. The black poverty rate rose to 31% in 1990, nearly three times that of whites, reported the National Urban League, which also noted "a decade-long pattern of decline" in African-American college enrollments, partly due to rising college costs.

In spite of increased white acceptance of African-Americans, the races continue to live apart; indeed, housing is the single most segregated aspect of California life. The number of discrimination complaints received by the Department of Housing and Urban Development over the past 15 years has increased substantially. In 1990, 31% of African-Americans lived in neighborhoods that were 90% or more black, while 6 of 10 whites lived in neighborhoods that were in effect all white.

> In the Golden State, whites are still fleeing as African-Americans fan out among them. It's clearly the case that the number of African-Americans in a neighborhood, be it San Francisco or Santa Ana, matters to most white Californians.

In California, there continues to be a mixture of progress and resistance in white attitudes, more enthusiasm for "abstract principles" of integration than for putting them into practice. Californians on the whole no longer appear very concerned about the African-Americans among them, except as potential sources of crime. There is a feeling almost of impatience that African-Americans should still be wanting things. The African-American cause seems less appealing than it did in the 1960s. The old images of the police and National Guard clubbing and shooting African-Americans in Watts, and the cries of "Make Los Angeles Free!" could provoke outrage. But they have been replaced by the more ambiguous images of African-Americans today, staring reassuringly from television and movie screens or menacingly from police mug shots— toting briefcases, lunch pails or Uzi assault rifles.

The old civil-rights networks of academics, community-service workers, government officials and foundation people have fallen apart. Jack Boger, of the N.A.A.C.P. Legal Defense and Educational Fund, recalls that when teams of interviewers traveled around the Golden State in 1990 to ask various experts what they thought the Defense Fund should be focusing on, the typical greeting they got was, "Hey, what are you all doing, haven't had anyone come to talk to me in years." Many liberals believe that the "benign neglect" of civil-rights issues counseled by Daniel Patrick Moynihan when he was an adviser to President Nixon turned, under Reagan and Bush, into something less benign. In California, Reagan, as governor, did to the African-American what he did to them as president. Likewise, Deukmejian and, more recently, Pete Wilson.

Officially, the state government hews to its goal of a "color-blind society" in which, presumably, no one benefits because of race. In practical terms that means that the Justice Department, once a champion of affirmative action, has turned consistently adversarial toward African-Americans in court cases on that issue.

Surprisingly, some African-Americans seem to accept the idea of keeping a low profile on civil-rights consciousness. Like their white counterparts, middle-class African-Americans are too busy succeeding now, some old-line African-American leaders think, to contribute to the continuing civil-rights effort. Many, in fact, have come to scorn integration as a goal. Faring better economically, on the whole, they reject the notion that their well-being depends on living next door to whites. Even those who support integration seem to see it less as a moral imperative than a practical necessity.

> You have to be where the opportunity is. Wherever white people are, there is excellent opportunity. The system sees to that.
> —Los Angeles *Eagle*

The whole movement has taken on that pragmatic, down-to-cases character. The arena has long shifted to the courts, where civil-rights lawyers carry on the battle for school busing and affirmative-action hiring practices against an often shrill opposition from local citizens.

Meanwhile there are signs of a revival of interest in the unfinished civil-rights revolution. Television, newspapers and magazines are beginning to take a fresh look at the problems of African-Americans. And rightfully so. The neglect of the last 15 years has allowed the problems to fester and grow to where they have become visible again. Business is also taking a new interest.

**Projections indicate that the labor force in California will, in the 21st century, be increasingly drawn from minorities.**

Indeed, the entire country is nearing the day when its population will be half minorities. In some Western cities, not African-Americans but Hispanics have become the largest minority group. They bring with them their own profile of poverty. But it is the African-

Americans whose history has been so long and painfully intertwined with the white Californians'.

> No one in the world . . . knows Americans better or, odd as this may sound, loves them more than the American Negro. This is because he has had to watch you, outwit you, deal with you, and bear you, and sometimes even bleed and die with you, ever since . . . both of us, black and white, got here—and this is a wedding.
> —James Baldwin

In the 1960s the civil-rights struggle spun off some of the highest and lowest moments in that historic symbiosis—from the jeering and brutal assaults of white racists, to those buoyant and hopeful summer nights in Mississippi when blacks and non-blacks took pot-luck together after registering black voters through the long, sweltering day. Yvonne Brathwaite Burke, who became a vocal force in California politics, describes one of those nights:

> That was an experience, just to see white people coming around the pot and getting a bowl and putting some stuff in and sitting around talking on the floor . . . sitting there laughing. I guess they become very real and very human—we each to one another.

That kind of spirit led to revolutionary change. More than two decades later, however, despite the progress, it seems that African-Americans and whites have lost the sense of each other's common humanity.

## The Fiery Christening of the 1990s

In South-Central Mobile they're called klansmen. In South-Central Los Angeles they're called cops. In March 1991, an amateur photographer videotaped a mob of them beating an *unarmed, unresisting* black man. When the beating was over, Rodney King, 25, an unemployed construction worker, had suffered eleven fractures of his skull, a crushed cheekbone, a broken ankle, a burn on his chest, internal injuries and brain damage.

Inasmuch as the vicious Klan-like attack had been captured on film, Ira Reiner, LA's white district attorney, had no choice but to indict the cops, Stacey Koon, 40, Laurence Powell, 28, Timothy Wind, 30, and Theodore Brisen, 38, on charges of assault with a deadly weapon and excessive use of force "under color of authority." Evidence of guilt was overwhelming. Nevertheless, some thirteen months later, each cop was acquitted by a jury from which blacks had been excluded—and African-Americans took to heart the long-ago spoken words of Frederick Douglass: "At a time like this . . . it is not light that is needed, but fire; it is not the gentle shower, but thunder."

Unlike the Watts riot, which was a fight for economic survival, the "fire and thunder" of April 29, 1992, uprising in South-Central Los Angeles was retaliation against racial injustice. The toll: 58 dead, 2,400 injured, 11,700 arrested, and $717 million in damages. On a positive note, however, the "fire and thunder" led to the resignation of Police Chief Daryl Gates, ("Gates was to the LAPD what David Duke was to the KKK," say many South-Central residents) and to the nationwide amplification of the oratory eloquence of minority leaders such as Maxine Waters, Diane Watson and Patricia Moore, each of whom blasted the city (and country) for rigging justice against African-Americans.

★ ★ ★

The race dilemma is still California's toughest problem. Undoubtedly, a still awesome job in race relations looms ahead, for, as African-Americans know well, if others do not, some freedom is not full freedom. The task ahead, however, is not any one group's alone—it falls upon everyone, black and non-black. Anyone who takes a close look at the African-American will discover that he is in the grip of the same purpose as his fellow citizen. Indeed, the passionate rhetoric of the black militant and much of the riot behavior of the slum dweller alike found their motivation in a desire for equal justice and equal opportunity, these as golden as the Golden State itself.

African-Americans in California have come a long way since pioneer days when their children were confined to segregated schools, when they were denied the right to vote or hold public office, when they were denied the right to testify in state courts and the right to participate in the homesteading of public lands. Today, in housing, in employment, in education, no door can be locked to the African-American. If they find one locked, we—Californians—can open it for them—or kick it in.

It is time that the residents of the nation's 31st state come to grips with the fact that it has been the African-American who has helped make California what it is—and it is the African-American who can make California what California can and must become.

CHAPTER XXI

# The Overlooked Contributors to California Life

MEN AND WOMEN OF AFRICAN ANCESTRY MADE SIGNIFICANT CONTRIBU-
tions to the development of California. Among them are:

**William Alexander Leidesdorff** (1810–1848). Born in the West
Indies, Leidesdorff was a prosperous merchant captain in New York
and New Orleans. Moving to San Francisco in 1841, he began shipping between this small village and Honolulu. In 1844, Leidesdorff
became a naturalized citizen of Mexico and was granted 35,500 acres
of land along the American River. In 1845, he became American
Vice Consul, representing U.S. interests in Mexican-owned California. He was instrumental in founding San Francisco's first public
school and built the first hotel—the City Hotel at Kearny and Clay—
and a large waterfront warehouse, the forerunner of today's World
Trade Center in the Ferry Building.

**James P. Beckwourth** (1798–1864). A native of Virginia, Beckwourth began his trail-blazing career with the Rocky Mountain Fur
Company in the 1820s. During the Gold Rush, he guided many of

the wagon trains to California, and in 1851, discovered the safest pass through the Sierra Nevada. Beckwourth Pass became a key route into the Upper Sacramento Valley.

**William M. Robison** (1821–1899). A stagecoach driver for forty years, he carried Wells, Fargo & Company's Express on the run between Stockton and the gold mines. Born a slave in Gloucester County, Virginia, Robison gained his freedom while fighting the Seminole Indian War of 1836. He came to California during the Mexican War and settled in Stockton in 1850. Always active in community affairs, he served as a delegate to the 1856 State Convention of Colored Citizens in Sacramento.

**George A. Monroe** (1834–1886). For eighteen years, Monroe drove the stagecoach for the Yosemite Stage and Turnpike Company, and was called "the best stagecoach driver in California." One of the highlights of his career occurred when Ulysses S. Grant was his passenger. Other presidents who enjoyed traveling with him were Rutherford B. Hayes and James A. Garfield. Monroe Meadows in Yosemite National Park is named in his honor.

**Grafton Tyler Brown** (1841–1918). Born in Harrisburg, Pennsylvania, Brown moved to San Francisco in 1855. He became California's first black artist, specializing in illustration, printing and lithography. In 1865 he established his own business, remaining in the city until 1881, producing stock certificates, bill-heads, maps and portraits. Brown drew many of the scenes in the *Illustrated History of San Mateo County* (1878).

**Allen Allensworth.** Born into slavery in Louisville, Kentucky, in April 1842, Allensworth escaped to the North, and joined the Union infantry; became a preacher; was twice a delegate to the Republican National Convention; created Allensworth, an all-black "race colony" near Bakersfield.

**Moreno.** African slave; interpreter of Indian languages for Junipero Serra; transported the very first seeds of flowers and vegetables planted in California's soil.

**El Negro.** African descendant who guided Don Gaspar de Portola to the San Francisco Bay; first man to set eyes on the "great arm of the sea."

**Pedro Prat.** Ashanti descendant credited with saving the lives of countless conquistadors; surgeon on the *San Carlos*.

**Santiago Pico.** Accompanied Portola on the thousand-mile trail to San Francisco; called giant redwood Palo Alto; city today bears that same name.

**Maria Rita Valdez.** Black grandparents among founding members of Los Angeles; owned Rancho Rodeo de Las Aguas, today known as Beverly Hills.

**Pio Pico.** First elected governor, 1832, of California; established foundation for educational structure by creating schools at Santa Barbara, Los Angeles, Santa Clara, San Jose, San Luis Rey, and San Diego; established school of instruction to train teachers.

**Antonio Pico.** Member of Constitutional Convention of 1849; helped to determine that California would enter the Union as a free state.

**Oscar Overr.** Resident of Allensworth; first African-American justice of the peace in California.

**George Washington Dennis.** As a slave, helped establish the El Dorado Hotel in San Francisco; purchased his freedom; invested in real estate with marked success; built the first livery stable in San Francisco; opened the first wood and coal yard; purchasing agent for British government.

**Biddy Mason** (1818–1891). Former slave who became the most successful businesswoman in Los Angeles; leading figure in the black community; founded California's first nursing homes; donated land for the building of schools and churches.

**Peter Lester.** Successful San Francisco businessman; leader of the African-American community before migrating to British Columbia in 1858.

**Mifflin Wistar Gibbs** (1828–1903). Established California's first black newspaper, *Mirror of the Times;* leader of Colored Conventions in 1850s; became the first black judge in U.S. history; United States Consul to Madagascar.

**Peter Bell.** Editor of *The Pacific Appeal,* an African-American newspaper published in San Francisco; leader of the California convention movement.

**Reverend Jeremiah B. Sanderson** (died 1875). Educator and leader of California convention movement; founded schools in northern California for African-American children.

**William Payne.** Gifted teacher and university graduate; instrumental in the founding of Allensworth.

**Mary Ellen Pleasant** (1814–1903). "The Mother of Civil Rights in California"; leading businesswoman in San Francisco; funded raid at Harper's Ferry.

**William Pollack.** Bought his freedom while working gold mines in California; established very first catering service in Placerville.

**James H. Townsend.** Leader of the California Colored Conventions; spokesman for the black community.

**William H. Newby.** Leading African-American intellectual; editor of California's first black newspaper, *Mirror of the Times;* delegate to the California Colored Conventions; private secretary to the French Consul General in Haiti.

**Moses Rodger.** Mining engineer; owner of several gold mines in California; helped build railroads.

**Abner Francis.** Correspondent of Frederick Douglass; delegate to the Colored Conventions in California.

**William H. Yates.** President of the first California Colored Convention; employee of the California Steamship Navigation Company.

**Jacob Dodson.** Scout for John C. Fremont on his first trip into California.

**Fritz Vosburg, Abraham Holland, Gabriel Sims.** Owners of the Sweet Vengeance gold mine in Brown's Valley; operated profitably throughout mining period.

**Mary Frances Ward.** Her knock at the door of the Broadway Grammar School in San Francisco in September 1872 was a let-me-in gesture just as significant as James Meredith's was to be in his introduction of black people to Mississippi University exactly 90 years later.

**Darius Stokes.** Pastor; founder of the first African-American churches in the Golden State.

**Theophilus B. Morton.** Leader of the black community; first black librarian of the U.S. Court of Appeals.

**David W. Ruggles.** Delegate to California Colored Conventions; led battle against discrimination; fought for right to testify in courts of law.

**Thomas Ward.** Former slave; first African-American hired as a surveyor by the U.S. Government.

**Buela Baines.** Child actress; captured the heart of San Francisco during gold rush.

**J. J. Neimore.** Founder and editor of the *California Eagle,* the first African-American newspaper in Los Angeles.

**Stephen Smith** and **William Whipper.** Successful wheat farmers in the lower San Joaquin Valley.

**Delbert Jefferson.** Raised funds and helped organize the Julian Petroleum Company, one of the first such companies in the Golden State.

**Davis Hollad.** African–American farmer who helped turn Madera, Merced, and Modesto into important market centers.

**Hugh Mulzac.** Merchant Marine captain who by May 1944 had taken the S.S. *Booker T. Washington* across the submarine-infested Atlantic seven times.

**Henry Lloyd.** African–American entrepreneur; owner of a bedstead factory in San Diego with some twenty white employees.

**Chrystalee Maxwell.** African–American staff nurse at Los Angeles General Hospital; helped force the American Medical Association to drop the designation "colored" after the names of black physicians listed in its *American Medical Dictionary.*

**Louden Nelson** (1800–1860). Successful African–American entrepreneur; willed all his property to Santa Cruz School District.

**William Henry Hall** (born 1823). President of second Colored Convention in California; intellectual; leader of African-American community.

**Thomas Bradley.** Elected mayor of Los Angeles, 1973.

**Dr. Ralph Bunche.** First African-American to win the Nobel Peace Prize, 1950; undersecretary of the United Nations.

**Dorie Miller** (1919–1943). Navy hero of Pearl Harbor attack; awarded the Navy Cross and the Congressional Medal of Honor.

**Wilson C. Riles.** Elected California State Superintendent of Public Instruction, 1970.

**Dr. John R. Ford** and **Dr. Leroy Weekes.** Fought for positive action against racial discrimination on state and local levels; forced the American Medical Association to end its discriminatory practices and to initiate a drive to recruit black youths for careers in medicine.

**Huey P. Newton.** Founder of the Black Panther Party.

**Leslie Shaw.** Became postmaster of Los Angeles, 1965.

★  ★  ★

Thousands of African-Americans who were active in the development of California did not attain the prominence of the aforementioned but were of its flesh, blood, and bone. They, too, should be remembered.

# California's African-American Tourist Attractions

Following are brief descriptions of some of California's many African-American tourist attractions and interesting places to visit:

**Mount Gains Gold Mines** at Hornitos, Mariposa County; site of mines formerly owned by mining engineer Moses Rodger.

**Headquarters of Wells Fargo Bank,** San Francisco; located on the site of waterfront warehouse built by William Alexander Leidesdorff.

**Beckwourth Pass;** U.S. Highway 70 through the Sierra Nevada in Plumas County.

**Mount Zion Hospital,** San Francisco; located on land formerly owned by George Washington Dennis.

**Tombstone of Mary Ellen Pleasant,** "The Mother of Civil Rights in California"; Tucolay Cemetery in Napa, California.

**Colonel Allensworth State Historic Park;** located in Earlimart, California (about 35 miles north of Bakersfield).

**Leidesdorff Crypt Plate;** located in Old Mission Dolores, San Francisco.

**Mary Ellen Pleasant Community Park;** located on Octavia Street between Bush and Sutter, San Francisco.

**Monroe Meadows** in Yosemite National Park; named in honor of George A. Monroe, "the best stagecoach driver in California."

**Skyscraper hotel at corner of Kearny and Clay,** San Francisco; site of William Alexander Leidesdorff's City Hotel—the first hotel built in San Francsico.

**Allensworth: An Enduring Dream;** exhibit at the California Afro-American Museum, 600 State Street, Exposition Park, Los Angeles.

**La Punta de los Muertos,** "Dead Men's Point"; where many of

California's first black ancestors were laid to rest; about four blocks south of the Bazaar del Mundo, near Old Town Plaza, San Diego.

**Sonka's Apple Farm;** site of "rancho" worked by Abner Francis during gold rush; located on Cherokee Road in Tuolumne, California.

**Sweet Vengeance Gold Mine;** near Douglas Flat, California (east of Highway 4).

**Corner of Bush and Sansome Streets,** San Francisco; site of murder of Gordon Chase—incident that spurred the San Francisco African-American community to organize the Franchise League.

**St. Cyprian Methodist Church,** corner of Jackson and Virginia Place, San Francisco; site of first school in northern California for African-American children.

**Missions** built in California by Africans and Indians beginning in 1769 at San Diego.

# For Further Reading

Abajian, James de T. *Blacks in Selected Newspapers, Censuses and Other Sources* (Boston, G. K. Hall, 1977).

Alexander, Charles. *The Battles and Victories of Allen Allensworth* (1914).

Bancroft, Hubert Howe. *History of California.*

Beasley, Delilah. *The Negro Trail Blazers of California* (Los Angeles, 1919).

Bonner, T. D. *Life and Adventures of James P. Beckwourth, Mountaineer, Scout and Pioneer of the Crow Nation of Indians.*

Daniel, Douglas Henry. *Pioneer Urbanites* (1980).

Durham, Philip and Jones, Everett L. *Negro Cowboys* (New York, 1965).

Foner, Philip S. and Walker, George E. *Proceedings of the Black National and State Conventions* (Philadelphia: Temple University Press, 1980–86).

Gibbs, Mifflin W. *Shadow and Light, An Autobiography* (Washington, 1902).

Holdredge, Helen. *Mammy Pleasant* (New York, 1953).

Ramsey, Eleanor M. *Allensworth: A Study in Social Change* (Ph.D. dissertation, UC-Berkeley, 1972).

Robinson, Jini M. *Allensworth Town Is Born Again* (master's thesis, UC-Berkeley, 1975).

Weatherwax, John M. *The Founders of Los Angeles* (Los Angeles, 1954).

★ ★ ★

Diary: *Reminiscences of Alvin Coffey.* Society of California.

Monographs: *California History Series, Negro Historical and Cultural Society* (San Francisco, California).

Pamphlet: *The Amateur Tour Director's Handbook: People Who Shaped San Francisco* (Koit, 1985).

★ ★ ★

Most of the following newspapers are available on microfilm at the Bancroft Library, and provide interesting reading:

*Pacific Appeal*, published in San Francisco.
*Mirror of the Times*, published in San Francisco.
*California Eagle*, published in Los Angeles.
*Oakland Sunshine*, published in Oakland.

# Bibliography

Baldwin, James. *The Fire Next Time* (New York, 1963).

Berry, Mary F., and Blassingame, J. W. *Long Memory: The Black Experience in America.* Oxford, 1982.

Davis, Charles T. *Black Is the Color of the Cosmos: Essays on Afro-American Literature and Culture, 1942–1981.* Garland, 1982.

Duniway, Clyde A. *Slavery in California after 1848; Annual Report.* American Historical Association, 1906.

Foner, Philip S. *History of Black Americans.* 3 vols. Greenwood, 1975–1983.

Franklin, John Hope. *From Slavery to Freedom: A History of Negro Americans.* 5th ed. Knopf, 1980.

Gutman, Herbert G. *The Black Family in Slavery and Freedom, 1750–1925.* Pantheon, 1976.

Hornsby, Alton, Jr. *The Black Almanac.* 4th ed. Barron's Educational Series, 1977.

Hughes, Langston, and others. *A Pictorial History of Blackamericans.* 5th ed. Crown, 1983.

Jackson, Florence. *Blacks in America, 1954–1979.* Watts, 1980.

Kluger, Richard. *Simple Justice: The History of Brown v. Board of Education and Black America's Struggle for Equality.* Knopf, 1976.

Litwack, Leon F. *Been in the Storm So Long: The Aftermath of Slavery.* Knopf, 1979.

Meltzer, Milton, ed. *In Their Own Words: A History of the American Negro.* 3 vols. Harper, 1964–1967.

Peters, Margarte. *The Ebony Book of Black Achievement.* Rev. ed. Johnson Publishing Company, 1974.

Shuck, Oscar T. *History of the Bench and Bar of California.*

Sterling, Dorothy. *Tear Down the Walls! A History of the American Civil Rights Movement.* Doubleday, 1968.

Stevens, Leonard A. *Equal! The Case of Integration vs. Jim Crow.* Coward, 1976.

Young, A. S. *Negro Firsts in Sports.* Chicago, 1963.

# Index